Big City Pack

MARISA CHENERY

ELLORA'S CAVE
ROMANTICA
www.EllorasCave.com

THE CANUCK WEREWOLF

Rylee doesn't have high hopes for the Victoria Day weekend camping trip, seeing as she's been roped into taking her brother and his juvenile friends. But her mind is changed when she spots a gorgeous man on a hiking trail. She'd like to be zipped in a sleeping bag with him, no doubt about it.

Atticus came to Elora Gorge to get away from his father and his demands that his son find a mate. Like yesterday. Atticus needs time away from being groomed to be the pack leader and the endless stream of "suitable" mates thrown his way in hopes of stirring his mating urge. No luck yet. But then he spots a shy mortal who draws him like no other.

The tent heats up quickly, but before Atticus can tell Rylee what he is, he discovers a member of his pack has followed him with the intention of claiming him for her own. Not only does he have to convince Rylee she's his mate, he must also prove she can trust him.

A WEREWOLF AT THE FALLS

As a cocktail waitress at Fallsview Casino Resort, Jorja has been witness to some brow-raising moments. But she's never been part of one until a hot-as hell patron in her section pulls her into his lap and kisses her senseless. Talk about a generous tipper. Lady luck has smiled on her indeed.

What was supposed to be a weekend of harmless gambling takes a dramatic turn when Kian's wolf scents his would-be mate. Consuming her lips as if his life depends on it in the middle of a crowded casino is bad enough—but giving in to his mating urge and claiming her before she knows his true nature is nothing short of a disaster. And when a fellow pack member shows up and lets the wolf out of the bag, Kian is forced to admit not only who and *what* he is, but what he did. He may need more than luck to pull this one off.

WEREWOLF'S TREASURE

Treasure never dates clients. A rule that ensures repeat business in the real estate market. But when her sexy-as-all-get-out buyer hinges his offer of purchase on her willingness to have dinner with him, she wavers. If ever there was a reason to look the other way, this was it. The fact she can't wait to see what wicked things he'll do to her body is just an added bonus.

Soren hoped to secure a primo home when he arranged to view a penthouse. He didn't expect to be taken to his knees by the scent of his would-be mate. Being in close proximity has his wolf clawing to get to her. Or get on her. He's not picky. But it's tricky with these mortals. Soren must find a way to let her know about his furry side without sending her screaming into the outskirts of Toronto. His mating urge will push his control to the limits—especially when Treasure takes every opportunity to get him to go all the way.

WEREWOLF CLAIMED

As werewolves go, Draven isn't exactly a spring chicken. At fifteen hundred years old, he's beyond ready to find his mate and settle down. He's watched as his pack mates introduced their women one by one. But the fairer sex doesn't stir him. He craves the hard planes and strength of a man's body. He yearns for the day when destiny delivers the one chosen for him.

Wyatt has come to Buck Lake to spend his two-week vacation. It doesn't get off to the best start, however, when the bum motor of his fishing boat strands him in the water. Being rescued by a man who can only be described as a walking wet dream certainly improves his outlook. And when he finds himself in a heated embrace with his rescuer, his whole trip is made.

But Draven has a secret. And a former pack member hell bent on revenge would like nothing more than to destroy any chance the new couple has at a happily ever after.

LOVED BY A WEREWOLF

At her cousin's wedding, Sierra is stuck on drunk-brother patrol. When he slips out of the reception with a married woman, Sierra must go in pursuit. But her efforts are in vain and she finds herself on a hiking trail along the edge of the property. She's not alone, however. A wolf is staring her down as if she'll be his next meal. Damning her brother to the pits of hell won't get her out of this one.

Cale knew he'd found his mate the moment he caught Sierra's scent while in wolf form. Things don't start off well, however, when she throws a rock at him. Not to be deterred, Cale disappears into the forest, where he shifts to man. No rocks go flying when he approaches her this time, and soon the two of them can't keep their hands off each other. But Cale has a furry secret. One Sierra must accept—because living nine hundred years without her has been enough for this werewolf.

An Ellora's Cave Publication

www.ellorascave.com

Big City Pack

ISBN 9781419965852
ALL RIGHTS RESERVED.
The Canuck Werewolf Copyright © 2011 Marisa Chenery
A Werewolf at the Falls Copyright © 2011 Marisa Chenery
Werewolf's Treasure Copyright © 2011 Marisa Chenery
Werewolf Claimed Copyright © 2011 Marisa Chenery
Loved by a Werewolf Copyright © 2011 Marisa Chenery
Edited by Grace Bradley.
Design by Syneca.
Photography by curaphotography and sababa66@shutterstock.com

Trade paperback publication 2012

With the exception of quotes used in reviews, this book may not be reproduced or used in whole or in part by any means existing without written permission from the publisher, Ellora's Cave Publishing, Inc.® 1056 Home Avenue, Akron OH 44310-3502.

Warning: The unauthorized reproduction or distribution of this copyrighted work is illegal. Criminal copyright infringement, including infringement without monetary gain, is investigated by the FBI and is punishable by up to 5 years in federal prison and a fine of $250,000. (http://www.fbi.gov/ipr/)
This book is a work of fiction and any resemblance to persons, living or dead, or places, events or locales is purely coincidental. The characters are productions of the author's imagination and used fictitiously.
The publisher and author(s) acknowledge the trademark status and trademark ownership of all trademarks, service marks and word marks mentioned in this book.
The publisher does not have any control over and does not assume any responsibility for author or third-party Web sites or their content.

BIG CITY PACK
Marisa Chenery

THE CANUCK WEREWOLF
~11~

A WEREWOLF AT THE FALLS
~79~

WEREWOLF'S TREASURE
~139~

WEREWOLF CLAIMED
~209~

LOVED BY A WEREWOLF
~275~

THE CANUCK WEREWOLF
ઝ

Dedication

To my fellow Canadians.

Chapter One

Gritting her teeth for the umpteenth time since she'd started this trip, Rylee looked into the review mirror of the Dodge Caravan van she drove with her nineteen-year-old brother, Luc, and his two friends. They were in the seats behind her, seeing who could top each other for grossness. The teenage male, she sometimes thought, became retarded once puberty set in.

She breathed a sigh of relief when she saw the entrance to the Elora Gorge Conservation Area up ahead — their destination. It was the Victoria Day long weekend, the celebration of Queen Victoria's birthday. And given that it was the May twenty-fourth long weekend — or May two-four as it was called by teenagers, meaning a twenty-four case of beer — it was the time people in Ontario planted their gardens, opened their cottages up north for the summer or went camping. The latter was what she'd been roped into doing. It was also the first of two holidays Canadians were allowed to set off fireworks. July first, Canada Day, was the second.

Rylee drove to the gatehouse and told the woman who stepped out to greet them that she'd already reserved a serviced campsite. After giving directions on where to find their site, the woman waved them through.

It didn't take her long to find it. She parked the van not too far from the single picnic table for their use. Rylee got out and opened the sliding door on the driver's side as her brother and his friends piled out the other side. She pulled the bags that held two tents from the very back.

She'd just carried them over to the tent pad to be set up when she heard one of Luc's friends say he wanted to check out the gorge. The others quickly jumped onboard with that idea. Like hell were they going to stick her with all the work.

Rylee put two fingers in her mouth and let out a shrill whistle, bringing the three teenage boys up short. "You guys aren't going anywhere just yet. We have to set up the campsite."

"Come on, Rylee," Luc whined. "We were cooped up in the van for the drive. We'll take a quick look at the gorge and come right back. I promise."

She put her hands on her hips, and with a stern glare, shook her head. The drive from Kitchener, where they lived, to Elora was hardly a long enough trip to have had the boys feeling cooped up. No, it was a ploy to get out of having to actually work. Luc usually managed to worm his way out of doing things with their mother, but it wasn't going to work with her. Being twenty-four to his nineteen, she'd looked after him more than a few times while Luc had been younger and she knew all his tricks.

"Nice try," she said. "Considering it only took forty-six minutes to get here, it wasn't all that long a drive. Since it wasn't my idea to come with you on this camping trip, all of you are going to set up the tent you're going to sleep in. I'm not Mom. I'm not going to put up with your lazy-ass ways."

Luc made the annoying whining sound he always made when he didn't get things his way. "I don't know why Mom insisted you had to tag along."

"*I* do. First, she didn't feel comfortable letting you drive her van this distance, and second, she figured the three of you would get up to no good without adult supervision."

"I wish Mom would stop treating me like a baby. I'm nineteen, not nine," Luc grumbled as he and his friends joined her at the tent pad and got to work setting up their four-man tent.

"Maybe she would if you'd stop acting like one, Mr. Whiner. The quicker you get the job done the faster you can go do whatever you want. Since we couldn't check in until two, it's already creeping up to late afternoon. Setting up a tent in the dark is not fun."

Even though spring had arrived and the nights weren't quite as long as they were in the winter, the temperature could still drop with the chance of frost once it got dark. Rylee had made sure she brought an old quilt with her just in case her sleeping bag wasn't warm enough.

She left the boys to it as she moved a short distance away to set up her own two-man tent. It didn't take long for teenage laughter to be heard as her brother and his friends set to work.

After quickly putting her tent up, Rylee went back to the van to grab her air mattress and sleeping bag. She'd leave the quilt in the van until she knew she'd need it. With both rolled-up items in her hands, she turned around to find Luc's friend, Josh, standing behind her. He gave her a big smile as his gaze looked her up and down. She resisted the urge to roll her eyes. Just what she needed—a nineteen-year-old hitting on her.

"Was there something you wanted, Josh?"

"We have our tent almost set up and I thought I would come and see if I could give you a hand."

"That's nice of you, but I can manage on my own."

"Are you sure? I'd be happy to help you put your sleeping bag inside your tent."

She just bet he would. "No, really I'm fine. If you want to make yourself useful, why don't you grab the other sleeping bags and take them to your own tent? Where you will be sleeping while I sleep in mine—alone. Got it?"

Josh gave her a smile Rylee was sure melted many a teenage girl's heart. He was good looking, she'd give him that, but way too young for her. She liked her men, well, men.

He reached around her, deliberately brushing up against her, as he picked up one of the sleeping bags. "Well, you know where I'll be if you change your mind."

This time Rylee did roll her eyes before yelling over to her brother. "Luc? Come and help lover boy over here get the rest of the sleeping bags."

Once Luc and his other friend, Nick, joined them, her brother gave Josh a shove. "Stop hitting on my sister, perv. I told you she'd shoot you down."

Nice. Luc could have given her fair warning about Josh's interest in her. But of course her brother never thought that far ahead. Once the boys returned to their tent, Rylee went to hers. She unzipped the flap and ducked inside. Unrolling the air mattress, she realized she'd forgotten to bring the pump for it. Great, now she'd have to blow it up herself the hard way.

After what seemed an agonizingly long time, where Rylee had made herself a bit lightheaded, the air mattress was blown up with her sleeping bag unrolled on top of it. The joys of camping. At least having a serviced campsite—meaning there was running water and electricity available—meant she didn't have to totally rough it. Plus there was a washroom with showers that had hot and cold running water.

Hearing three male voices just outside her tent, Rylee poked her head out the flap. "You guys get finished?"

The boys stopped and turned in her direction. Luc answered for them. "Yes. We're going to check out the gorge."

"Just be careful. If you fall into it and kill yourself, Mom will kill *me*."

"We're not that stupid. We'll be back in a couple of hours."

Rylee watched them walk away. This was going to be a fun weekend. Not. It wasn't as if she liked having to be the only responsible adult on the camping trip. The gorge with its twenty-two-meter-high cliffs that the Grand River rushed through was a very real hazard. More than a few people had fallen to their deaths. Having camped here plenty of times with her family while growing up, she knew the conservation area had signs posted with warnings and barriers set up.

With nothing left to do at the moment with regard to setting up the campsite, Rylee decided she'd go for a walk and do her best to avoid meeting up with her brother and his friends. With three kilometers of hiking trails on the conservation area that offered views of the deep gorge, it wouldn't be too hard to do.

Taking a circuitous route to the hiking trail, she walked down the road that wound through the other campsites. She appeared to not be the only one who'd recently arrived at the conservation area. At one site Rylee caught the flash of blond hair in the sunlight. Slowing her steps, she turned her head to get a better look.

She sucked in a sharp breath. The blond man she saw literally took her breath away. Rylee walked even slower as his head suddenly jerked up from the tent he'd been setting up and he looked directly at her. She knew it was rude to stare, but in his case, she couldn't stop herself. He was everything she found attractive in a man. He had to be at least six foot five. She couldn't help running her gaze over his well-muscled body. It made her pussy clench at the sight of his broad shoulders, defined chest and muscular thighs showcased inside snug-fitting blue jeans and a semi-tight black t-shirt. His hair was long, touching the top of his shoulders and so blond it appeared almost white.

The way he stared at her had Rylee all of a sudden feeling shy, along with aroused. What chance did she have with a man who looked like him? Not much. And there was no way in hell she'd go over and talk to him just in case she made a fool of herself. Finally managing to pry her gaze off him, she ducked her head and continued on her way.

Once she reached the trails, she actually enjoyed the peace and quiet of it, though it did nothing to cool her heated thoughts about the blond man. Rylee stopped at the first spot that gave her an unobstructed view of the gorge. She went to the rail and looked down, way down. It was a breathtaking sight. Looking at the river going through it, she observed that the water level seemed a little on the high side. Considering the big dumping of rain they'd had a couple of days ago, she wasn't surprised. In the warmer months people could rent inner tubes and go tubing on the Grand. In May the water would still be too cold for that.

Her thoughts wandered. A pair of wide shoulders, a gorgeous face and blond hair kept swirling inside her head. Even though she was afraid to approach him, she hoped he'd still be outside at his campsite when she walked back to hers. She'd make a point of taking the same route. She could easily see herself spending a great deal of the weekend walking by that very spot hoping for a glimpse of him. Too bad she hadn't brought her digital camera and her cell phone didn't have one, either. Rylee wouldn't mind sneaking a couple shots of him to take back to Kitchener with her. God, she was pathetic if she'd resort to that, but it was better than having nothing but the memory of him.

She closed her eyes, lifted her face to the sun and took a deep breath. The heat felt good on her skin. After the long winter months where temperatures could drop to minus thirty degrees Celsius with the wind chill, Rylee looked forward to the hot summer days. She hated winter. She'd rather be sweating her ass off than freezing any day. And considering how sunny and warm it was today, it wasn't too hard to see summer wasn't all that far off.

At a noise that sounded between a groan and a moan, Rylee opened her eyes and turned in the direction it had come from. They widened when she took in the blond man who stood a short distance away. Glacial-blue eyes stared back at her. Seeing the look of hunger in them, Rylee found herself frozen in place, unable to pull her gaze away. Holy shit, the star of her future sexual fantasies had found her. Her libido shot into high gear at the sight of him. If he so much as approached and touched her, in any way, she was liable to fall on him and kiss him like there was no tomorrow.

* * * * *

Atticus had been more than ready to get out of Toronto, away from his family and pack for the long weekend. And especially from his father who was pack leader. Being the oldest son put Atticus next in line for whenever his father decided to step down, which wouldn't be for a very, very long time. But that didn't stop the pack leader from grooming his son, getting him ready for the position that would one day be his.

It was getting to be a bit too much, especially now that his father had decided Atticus needed to find his mate and set to work producing the next generation. He lost count of the number of times unmated females had been paraded in front of him in the hopes they would trigger his mating urge, something all male werewolves went through when they found their would-be mates. So far that hadn't happened. They'd all been supermodel pretty, as all of his kind were, but none of them had done anything for him.

Needing to get away, Atticus had picked Elora Gorge Conservation Area to spend the Victoria Day long weekend…by himself. It had enough wooded area so he could shift into his wolf form and go for a run. It was also a place his father would never come. Camping was beneath the pack leader. Atticus, on the other hand, loved to be outdoors away from the large city Toronto was. Here he could be what he was—a werewolf who wanted to smell the clean scents around him and enjoy the wind in his fur.

Planning on hitting one of the hiking trails to take in the smog-free air, Atticus wanted nothing more than to go wolf and take a long run. Since it was the middle of the afternoon with more than a few mortals around, he'd have to wait until the cover of darkness.

He hadn't been at his campsite for very long, had just started to set up his tent, when a scent came out of nowhere and slammed into him like a punch to the gut. His mating urge instantly came to life and his cock went rock-hard. Looking up, he found a woman slowly walking past his site. Drawing in great gulps of air, Atticus filtered out the many scents around him, concentrating on the one that had his body going haywire.

Hers.

The longer he stared, the harder his cock got. And when she stared back at him with marked interest, he wanted to throw back his head and howl. Before he could pull his thoughts together, she ducked her head and hurried on her way. But he wasn't prepared to let her go so easily. He finished setting up his campsite and went after her.

Following the scent trail, he walked at a brisk pace. He rounded a corner and saw her standing at a rail looking down at the gorge. Her long, light brown hair fell to the middle of her back. His gaze ran hungrily along her slim form as his cock jerked inside his jeans. This mortal was his would-be mate. Aroused, he wanted nothing more than to go to her, take her to the ground and bury his aching cock inside her. And his wolf wanted her as well.

As he slowly closed the distance between them, a small part of his brain that still functioned thought of what his father's reaction would be once he learned Atticus' mate was mortal. The pack leader wouldn't be at all pleased. He thought it was beneath a werewolf to mate with a lowly mortal. Atticus had no such feelings.

Coming within a few feet of the woman, he came to a standstill and drew in a deep breath, filling his lungs with her scent. It would now be permanently etched on his brain, never forgotten. He'd be able to find her anywhere just by following it. Another breath, and a groan close to a moan punched out of his chest before he could hold it back.

She turned, her gaze latching onto him. As she looked him up and down with the same stark interest as before showing in her dark brown eyes, he hungrily stared back, fighting the wolf's growl that threatened to break free. She was pretty in a girl-next-door kind of way. Her looks did more for him than any female werewolf's supermodel beauty ever would.

Her gaze stayed locked to his as he closed the remaining distance between them. It took everything in him not to reach out, pull her close and claim her lips. His mating urge rode him a little harder when he smelled the heady scent of her arousal in the air around them. It would continue to ride him until he claimed her as his mate the first time they made love. That would be when their souls joined, truly mating them.

"Hi," he said, his voice gruff with the pounding need throbbing through his body.

She gave him a shy smile. "Hi."

"Nice day for a walk."

"Yes, it is."

"Can I join you? This is my first time coming to the gorge."

She nodded and shifted a little farther down the rail. "Sure. Not that I could stop you since this is a public place."

He joined her at the rail and peered down the long drop to the river below. She shifted to stand beside him. Her nearness had him fighting to maintain control. If he wasn't careful, his eyes would mutedly glow, something they did whenever he became very aroused or angry.

To make small talk, he said, "Great scenery. Makes it worth the drive from Toronto." Out of the corner of his eye, Atticus saw her turn her head in his direction.

"Is that where you're from?" she asked.

Feeling as if he had himself tightly reined back, he turned away from the view to face her and nodded. "Yes. Do you live here in Elora?"

"No. I live in Kitchener."

"I've never been there, but I've heard about it."

"Let me guess," she replied with a grin, "you've heard about our Oktoberfest? Or, as I like to call it, the big drunk."

He grinned. "I do believe that came up during the conversation I had with one of my friends who has visited Kitchener."

She smiled. "I thought so. And I bet this friend of yours made his visit when Oktoberfest was on. He more than likely spent some of his time in the Concordia Club's big tent drinking beer and eating Oktoberfest sausage."

Atticus chuckled. "Yes, but he consumed more beer than sausage. By the pitcher full, to be exact."

"I don't call it the big drunk for nothing."

"Have you ever been?"

"No. It's not really my thing. Though, I once rented an apartment across the street from the Concordia Club for about a year. During Oktoberfest, the polka music they played was loud enough to be heard inside my apartment, even with all the windows closed. That's the closest I've come to going Oktoberfesting."

He stuck out his hand. "I'm Atticus, by the way."

She put hers in his and gave it a shake. "I'm Rylee."

Atticus continued to hold her hand, reluctant to give up even this small amount of contact. The feel of her touching him made him crave a taste of her. His gaze focused on her lush lips. It would be so easy to pull her closer using their joined hands, bend and kiss her. As if she'd sensed his thoughts, the tip of Rylee's tongue came out and licked her bottom lip as the scent of her arousal grew stronger.

That was enough to have him acting before he could rein himself back under the rigid control he'd been holding. With a moan that bordered on a wolf's growl, Atticus yanked her against his chest and buried his other hand in the hair at her nape. He took her lips in a heated claiming, sweeping his tongue along the crease until they parted to allow him entrance.

He twined his tongue with hers, stroking. The taste of her went straight to his head, making his libido go into overdrive.

A true growl of approval pushed out of him as he released her hand and she placed it on his chest. Dropping his hands to her hips, he pulled her even closer, grinding his aching cock against her. Rylee moaned, and kissing him deeper, sucked on his tongue.

The rest of the world seemed to fall away until Rylee became the center of his universe. Her scent, the taste of her on his tongue, the feel of her against him and the small sounds of pleasure she made had his mating urge demanding he take her right then and there.

The sound of a loud wolf whistle had Atticus unthinkingly lifting his head, his upper lip snarled as a low growl rumbled out of him. Seeing three teenage boys standing not too far away, he quickly closed his eyes and took a deep breath to calm himself. His eyes had to be glowing. He had to get himself back under control.

If Rylee had noticed what he'd done, she didn't show it when she pushed out of his arms and turned to glare at the boys. "I thought you guys would be off doing whatever."

One of the boys who had the same colored hair and eyes as Rylee said, "We're hungry and thought we'd look for something to snack on, and to see what time you would be cooking dinner. But I can see you're a little busy right now. And I have to say, seeing my sister making out, gross. I think Mom should have been more worried about what you would get up to on this camping trip than me."

Atticus now saw the family resemblance between brother and sister in their features and not just their shared coloring. He watched Rylee cross her arms over her chest and narrow her gaze at her brother.

"Don't push it, Luc," Rylee said. "And who said anything about me cooking you dinner? You know how to roast a hot dog over a fire just as well as I do. So do Josh and Nick. And if you find what I was doing gross, you can keep on walking."

Atticus bit back a smile. Rylee and Luc reminded him of what he and his twin sister used to be like while in their teenage years, which at nine hundred years old, had been a very, very long time ago. Once they'd matured, the sniping had stopped and they remained close to this day.

In an excuse to make sure he'd spend more time with Rylee, Atticus broke into the conversation. "I have something better than hot dogs. Why don't we all have dinner together? I'll bring steaks and the barbeque. I'll even cook them."

"I could go for some barbequed steak," said one of the boys.

One of the others replied, "I'm with you on that one, Josh."

"I guess that's settled then," he said. He caught Rylee's gaze. "If that is okay with you? You're the chaperone."

She nodded. "I'm fine with it."

"Good." Atticus turned to the boys. "Why don't you return to your campsite while Rylee and I go get the food and barbeque?"

The three boys nodded before heading down the trail, leaving Atticus alone once again with Rylee.

"Don't you think it would be easier just for us to come to your campsite instead?" she asked.

Yes, it would, but getting her to help him lug the barbeque back and forth—not that he really needed it—was more alone time he'd have with her. He assumed Rylee and the boys would only be here for the long weekend, same as he, which meant he didn't have much time to work on claiming her as his mate. Given the fact she was mortal with more than likely no knowledge of werewolf kind, made it that much harder.

And once he claimed her and their souls joined, they wouldn't be able to stand being apart for any length of time. A few hours away would seem as if they hadn't seen each other in a year. Their minds would play tricks on them, make them think something had happened to the other. And during that time, all they would be able to think about would be being together again. Once they did, they would end up having desperate, hot sex.

Atticus made sure some of the arousal still flowing inside him showed in his eyes when he gazed at Rylee. "It might be easier, but it gives me a chance to have you all to myself. The boys don't know where my campsite is. We can take as long as we want."

Rylee's chest rapidly rose and fell as she breathed faster. "Then let's go," she said softly.

Taking her hand, Atticus set them into motion. With each step he took toward his campsite, the hotter his blood became.

Chapter Two

Rylee felt her heart thudding against her ribs as it beat madly. She was so turned-on at the prospect of being alone with Atticus she could hardly think straight. The kiss they'd shared before Luc and his friends had interrupted had been bone-melting good. With Atticus' hard cock grinding against her, she was pretty sure he'd have had her coming while he kissed her socks off.

Normally Rylee didn't paw at a guy she found attractive without getting to know him a little better, but with Atticus it was different. For some unknown reason, she felt comfortable around him. She also wanted to screw his brains out. Badly. The instant their gazes had met, she'd wanted him. Even now, holding his hand as they walked to his campsite, all she thought about was ripping his clothes off to explore his hard, muscular body with her lips and tongue.

As if he knew what she thought, Atticus turned his head and gave her a gaze so hot an ache pounded between her legs. It wasn't too hard to figure out he wanted to continue where they'd left off once they reached their destination. She was all for it. Rylee had no idea where things would go with him, but she wasn't willing to let him slip between her fingers. Considering herself only okay in the looks department, having a man who looked like Atticus—a man that could have any woman he wanted with a crook of his finger—so obviously attracted to her could be a once-in-a-lifetime chance. Suddenly the dreaded camping trip with her brother had turned out to be the best of her life.

At Atticus' campsite—far enough away from hers so the boys wouldn't be able to find it easily—Rylee allowed him to walk her over to the two-man tent. He pulled her to a stop in front of it.

"Do you trust me, Rylee?" he asked quietly.

Surprisingly, she did. There was something in his eyes that made her feel protected, cherished, as if she'd already become special to him. It might just be wishful thinking, but it didn't stop her from feeling as if he was trustworthy.

She nodded. "I do." He graced her with a sexy smile that had her pussy clenching and wetness leaking into her panties.

"Good, because all I can think about is seeing if you taste as good as you smell." He put his arms around her and pulled her close enough for her to feel the hard ridge of his erection pressing against her belly. He bent and nibbled on her earlobe before he said in a husky voice right into her ear, "I've waited a long time to find you."

Rylee shivered, need heating her blood. She had no idea what Atticus meant about waiting to find her, but right about now, she didn't care. She just wanted him to kiss her, touch her, make her come.

He released her and unzipped the tent's flap. Knowing perfectly well what she would be getting herself into, Rylee ducked inside. Atticus followed her in, zipping the tent closed once again.

Being the large man that he was, Atticus seemed to make the tent feel very small, not that it mattered much once he took Rylee in his arms. She fell into his embrace as he sat on the sleeping bag and pulled her onto his lap so she straddled him. She moaned when their lips met and her jean-covered pussy made contact with the large bulge in his pants. She wrapped her arms around his neck and kissed him with a hunger that matched his.

Atticus' large hand came up and covered her breast. He brushed his thumb across her taut nipple, making it tighten even more. His tongue pushed its way inside her mouth to meet hers, mimicking how she wanted him to take her with his cock.

Rylee rubbed herself against his erection and it twitched between her legs. He felt thick and long, big enough to give her a good ride. Unwinding her arms from around his neck, she dropped her hands to his shoulders, then down to his waist. She took hold of the bottom of his t-shirt and lifted. Her knuckles grazed a smooth, hairless chest on the way up. Atticus pulled away, releasing her breast, and yanked his shirt off over his head.

She sucked in a breath, her gaze running over his well-defined chest and six-pack abs. He was a work of art. She'd never been with a man as muscular as Atticus, and she liked it.

He took her hands and placed them palm down on his pecs. "Touch me. I want to feel your hands running all over me."

At his husky words, Rylee did just that. She skimmed her hands up to his broad shoulders and down his arms before going back up again. At his chest, she used the tips of her fingers to circle each of his flat nipples. They beaded under her touch.

Rylee caressed her hands down his abs to the top of his jeans. Atticus stopped her before she could go any farther. She looked at him to find his eyes closed to mere slits. She could have sworn they seemed to mutedly glow for a split second before he blinked and it was gone.

"Not yet," Atticus said. "First, it's my turn to touch you."

Wanting nothing more than to feel his hands on her, she pulled her shirt off and dropped it to the bottom of the tent beside them. "Then touch me."

Lowering his head to the top of her chest, he reached around her and unhooked her bra as he made a wet trail with his lips and tongue across the tops of her breasts. He brushed the straps down her arms and off. Rylee moaned and pressed herself closer when his lips closed over one of her nipples, the tip of his tongue circling the tight bud. As he sucked, she felt a corresponding pull deep inside her pussy. She panted, sinking her fingers into his hair to hold him to her.

Atticus shifted to her other breast and gave it the same attention. Rylee couldn't stop herself from grinding against his hard cock, desperately wanting to have it buried inside her pussy. "I need more," she told him in a breathy voice.

He released her breast and slowly lowered her to her back on the sleeping bag. "I'll give you more."

Shifting to straddle her, he undid the button and zipper on her jeans. Bending to rain kisses across her stomach, Atticus pulled her pants past her hips and down her legs. Rylee kicked them off once they reached her ankles. The sound of her fast beating heart thundered in her ears as he hooked her panties with his fingers and dragged them down and off.

She forgot to breathe for a few seconds when Atticus shifted lower on her body, spreading her legs farther apart with his broad shoulders. At the first swipe of his tongue along her pussy, all the air left her lungs in a whoosh. He made a real-sounding animalistic growl as he licked her from bottom to top, circling her clit with the tip of his tongue.

He licked and sucked until she rocked against his mouth. One finger and then another pushed inside her slick opening, causing a loud moan to push past her lips. In and out he stroked, sucking on her clit at the same time. Her body coiled tighter, an orgasm edging ever nearer.

"Let go," he said against her. "Come for me, Rylee."

As if her body answered his commands, her climax took her over. Her inner walls clutched at the fingers inside her pussy as wave after wave of intense pleasure swept through her. She cried out, calling Atticus' name.

He slowly made his way back up her body, kissing her skin as he went. The rasp of his zipper being pulled down sounded loud in the tent. He took her lips in a heated claiming while he pushed his jeans down far enough for his cock to spring free. Rylee reached between their bodies and wrapped her hand around his hard length. She pumped it up and down, squeezing his shaft in a tight fist. Atticus flexed his hips, pushing tighter into her hand. The same animalistic growl he'd made before rumbled out of him again.

Her arousal increasing, Rylee shifted subtly under Atticus. She kissed him deeper, sucking on his tongue as she used her grip on his cock to lead it to her pussy. Pressing down, she only managed to get the very tip of him inside her before he placed a restraining hand on her hip.

He broke contact with her mouth and buried his face in the crook of her neck. "No," he said gruffly. "It's too soon."

She didn't think so, but Atticus didn't give her much choice. He pulled out of her and squeezed her hand around his cock harder. He pumped his hips, then with a strangled moan, he came on her stomach.

The sound of their heavy breathing filled the small confines of the tent. Slowly coming down from her sexual high, Rylee couldn't help but notice Atticus' cock was still hard in her hand. He'd come, the proof of it was on her skin, but he hadn't softened one bit.

Atticus pulled out of her grip and shifted to lie at her side. He lifted himself on one elbow and reached for his shirt. Using it, he cleaned up the mess he'd made on her stomach.

Once finished, he brushed a gentle kiss across her lips. "We should go to your campsite. The boys are waiting for us."

Rylee looked pointedly down at his erection before she met his gaze. "You're still hard."

He kissed the tip of her nose. "Don't worry about it."

"Don't you want to...you know, finish what we started?"

Atticus pushed himself into an upright position before helping her to sit up. "We will, just not now. I got my taste of you. That's enough to tide me over."

"Okay, but I'm going to be perfectly blunt here. Why? You're here for the weekend only, the same as I am. What about living for the moment?"

He wrapped his hand around her nape and bent his head slightly to stare into her eyes. "Is that what you want? A fling for the weekend and then go our separate ways? What if I don't want that? How would you feel if I told you I'm not willing to just let you walk away and out of my life forever?"

Rylee swallowed. Could Atticus be serious? "We just met. How can you already know you want to stay with me? Yes, we're good together when it comes to sex, what little we've done in that department, that is. But is it enough, though? Don't get me wrong, I'd love to see this go past the weekend, but look at you. With your looks, you could get a woman who is much prettier than I am."

Atticus closed the distance between their mouths and took her lips in a hard, demanding kiss. He didn't stop until he had her clutching his shoulders. He pulled away, his gaze filled with hunger and need.

"I don't want to ever hear you knock yourself like that again, understand? You're beautiful," he said, his serious tone telling her he meant every word he spoke. He took one of her hands and led it to the large bulge in his pants. "No other woman has made me as hard as you do. All I can think about doing is burying my cock inside your pussy, taking you until neither one of us can move. I want to claim you, make you mine, but it's too soon. You're not ready for that yet."

Rylee found herself speechless. No man had ever told her he wanted her that much. A part of her brain that seemed to still be functioning properly thought Atticus moved too fast. But the rest, the part that had thought she'd never end up with a man like him, wanted to hold on and never let go. She knew nothing about him except for his first name and that he lived in Toronto, but being around him just felt right.

"What's your last name?" she blurted.

He smiled. "It's Thorp. And yours?"

"Horst. What do you do for a living?"

His smile broadened. "You want to know if I'm a good financial catch?"

"No. This is my way of getting to know you a little better. If it will make you feel any better, I'll go first. I work as a cashier at The Real Canadian Superstore."

"All right. I guess you could say I'm in the family business. My father wants me to take over once he decides to step down."

"In other words, you and your family are rich."

"Well, I do drive a BMW and have a Learjet at my disposal."

"Yeah, you're rich."

Atticus chuckled. "Enough of the questions for now. We'd better get a move on before your brother and his friends come looking for us."

Rylee nodded, gathered up her clothes and dressed while Atticus took out another t-shirt from the bag that sat in the corner of the tent. Her gaze followed his movements. Sexy, gorgeous and rich, he almost seemed too good to be true. She had no idea what she'd done to end up finding him, but she could only hope her luck stayed true and he'd really want to stick around for a while.

*****

Atticus carried the portable propane gas barbeque grill while Rylee carried a plastic shopping bag with the steaks. Before they'd left his campsite, he'd seen her glance over at his black BMW X1 five-door coupe more than a few times. From the sound of things, his would-be mate didn't have as much as he did when it came to money, but once she was his, that would change.

As they walked, he kept sneaking looks at Rylee. God, how he wanted to drag her back to his tent and do all the things he wanted to her, but he wouldn't. He couldn't fully make love to her until he was ready to claim her. And he wasn't. Neither was she ready for him to do so. She needed to know what he was. Once the mating bond formed between them and their souls joined, there would be no going back. Ever. Rylee deserved to have the choice to accept him or not.

Which meant he looked forward to his mating urge riding harder, making him crazy. The hand-job Rylee had given him hadn't taken the edge off, if anything it made it worse. The only thing that would calm the urge was penetration. Everything else would just intensify it. And it wouldn't help that when he managed to sleep he'd have erotic dreams of her.

Reaching Rylee's campsite, Atticus saw the three boys sitting at the picnic table. They already had a fire going in the fire pit. From the items strewn over the top of the table, it looked as if they had been roasting marshmallows on the ends of some metal skewers.

"Hey," Rylee said as she placed the shopping bag on a clear space on the picnic table, "those were supposed to be for later tonight." She picked up the bag of marshmallows that was now a quarter full. "Thanks for leaving some for me," she said with sarcasm.

Luc shrugged. "I told you we were hungry, and you and your friend over there seemed to be taking an awful long time."

Atticus set the portable grill on the table next to where Rylee had put the steaks. "I'll get the meat cooking. My name is Atticus. And I'm not just your sister's friend, I'm her boyfriend."

"Holy shit, you work fast," Luc said with a shake of his head.

"I guess there goes my chances with Rylee," the boy named Josh said.

Atticus eyed the teenager. Even though he knew the boy wasn't any threat, his wolf didn't like the idea of another male showing interest in his would-be mate.

Rylee groaned. "Josh, you never had a glimmer of one even before I met Atticus. Sorry, but I like the men I go out with to be closer to my age, and not teenage boys."

Josh put his hand over his heart and pretended he'd been shot. "You got me. I don't think I'll ever recover."

"Until the next pretty girl you see, that is," Rylee said with a chuckle.

"She got you there," the boy named Nick said, laughing.

It didn't take Atticus long to get the steaks on the grill. Rylee cleared the mess off the picnic table and set out some paper plates. Once the boys' and her steaks were done, he pulled them off and put his on. Being a werewolf, he liked his the rarer the better.

After a few minutes, they all sat down, helping themselves to the potato salad Rylee had taken out of the electric cooler plugged into the campsite's outlet.

She eyed his steak as he cut into it. "You'd better make sure that thing isn't still mooing before you eat it."

He grinned. "It isn't. You want to try a piece?"

Rylee grimaced. "Ah, no. That's all right. I like my steak on the rare side, but that is too much like raw meat to me."

They ate the rest of their meal in silence, the teenage boys at the table practically inhaling theirs. After they'd all gotten rid of their plates in the garbage, they sat around the fire. Darkness had already started to set in.

After a while, Josh went into the four-man tent and came out carrying three five-hundred-milliliter bottles of cola. He gave one to Luc and Nick. When the boys opened them and took a swig, Atticus' sensitive nose picked up more than the scent of pop.

Leaning in to Rylee, he said in a low voice only she could hear, "You'd better check what they're drinking. I don't think it's exactly what it appears to be."

She narrowed her eyes. "Shit. That's just what I need."

Rylee stood and walked around the fire pit until she stood in front of the boys. She held her hand out to Luc. "All right, hand it over."

"This one is mine. Didn't you bring any pop of your own?"

"Yes, but I want to taste yours." When Luc didn't hand it over right away, Rylee snatched it from him and took a swig. She then started to cough. "Holy hell, how much rum is in here?"

"Enough," her brother replied. "Now give it back. We're all nineteen, so it's not as if we're underage."

"True, but alcohol is strictly forbidden in the conservation area. If we get caught with it they'll kick us out." Rylee looked at each of the boys. "Now hand it over, all of you."

With groans and comments of her wrecking their camping trip, the three boys gave her their bottles of cola. Rylee walked to the end of the campsite where the trees bordered it and dumped the contents of the bottles.

Grumbling, the teenagers left the fire pit and went into their tent. Rylee sat next to Atticus and sighed deeply. "This is going to be a fun weekend. I can already tell."

He laughed. "How about you grab the rest of your marshmallows and we'll cook them over a fire at my campsite. I'm sure Luc and his friends won't get into too much trouble for a few hours."

She turned her head and met his gaze, the look in her eyes showing she'd be more than interested in doing other things besides roasting marshmallows. "That sounds wonderful," Rylee said in a voice that had dropped a few octaves, the sound of it wrapping around his cock, making it strain against his zipper.

He stood the same time she did. "I'll get the grill, you get the marshmallows."

Another bout of heavy petting would have him feeling as if he'd lost his mind, but Atticus was more than willing to suffer.

Chapter Three
❦

Even though the paved road that connected all the campsites was lit, it wasn't well lighted. Being a werewolf, Atticus had no problem seeing into the darkest shadows as if it were day. With Rylee at his side, he guided her down the road in the direction they needed to go. He had to hold himself back from setting a faster pace. Rylee's legs weren't as long as his and if he wasn't careful he'd leave her behind. As it was, she seemed to be walking at a fast clip just to match his strides.

They were just about to step into his campsite when a wolf's howl sounded in the night. Atticus came to an instant standstill, stopping Rylee by standing protectively in front of her. He knew it was no regular wolf, but another of his kind. A werewolf's howl had a different tone than a wild wolf's.

Rylee looked at him. "Was that a wolf? As far as I know, Elora doesn't have any wild wolves, and definitely not around the conservation area."

He slowly got them moving again. "No, that wasn't a wolf. People are allowed to have dogs here. Maybe it was one of them."

She gave him a look that said she didn't believe him. Atticus had been grasping at straws, but he made no further comment. Senses on alert, he searched his campsite, paying particular attention to the trees surrounding the back and one side of it. The wind shifted, blowing into his face. He cursed out loud.

"What's the matter?" Rylee asked.

Atticus put the grill down on the picnic table, gaze trained to the line of trees to the side. Before he could answer her question, a slim blonde woman stepped into the site. As a

37

member of his pack, and sometime bed partner, he knew her quite well. Marla's presence wasn't a good thing.

Marla closed the distance between them, brushed Rylee out of the way and threw herself against him. Atticus put his arms around her to steady her or she would have knocked him off balance. She must have taken it as encouragement. She went up on tiptoe, sank her hands in his hair and kissed him. He tried to pull away, but that only caused Marla to yank harder on the strands between her fingers. With a low growl of warning, he bit her bottom lip, and with hands on her hips, pushed her away.

She smiled and licked her lips. "I always like it when you bite, especially when we're in bed."

Atticus heard Rylee take a sharp breath. He turned toward her and saw a hurt expression flicker across her face before it disappeared. "I think I'll go back to my campsite." She took a step back.

"Wait, Rylee," he said as he reached for her. She knocked his hand away. "Don't go. Marla is the one who is leaving."

The female werewolf gave a short, sexy laugh. "Come now, Atticus. I came all this way to see you. I'm not going anywhere." She put a hand on his chest and smoothed it back and forth. "I thought we'd enjoy the night in a way we've done more than a few times. It's never been in a tent before, though."

"I'm out of here," Rylee said in a strained voice. "I hope you…enjoy…the rest of your weekend, Atticus."

She spun on her heel and practically ran out of the campsite. Atticus tried to follow, but Marla pulled on his arm.

"Let her go," she said. "I'm here now, so you don't need to lower yourself to consorting with that mortal."

Atticus angrily rounded on Marla. "What the fuck are you doing here? I thought I made it perfectly clear the last time we were together I didn't want to see you anymore."

His anger didn't seem to faze her. "You were just upset. You've had time to cool down." She stepped closer to lean against his chest. "We're good together. Why would you possibly want to give that up?"

With another growl, he pushed Marla away. "I haven't changed my mind. You aren't my mate, and I'm not willing to pretend you are just because you've spread your legs for me a few times. You weren't that good of a lay."

She growled as her hand shot out to slap him, but Atticus caught her wrist before she connected. "Bastard. It's a perfect arrangement. Your father would stop trying to find you a mate and I get to be 'mated' to the pack's next leader."

He roughly shoved her hand away. "My being the son of the pack leader is the only reason why you've shown me any interest. Sorry to say, I don't need you anymore. It looks as if I already found my mate."

Marla's gaze shifted to where Rylee had disappeared before she looked back at him. "You can't be serious. That lowly mortal cannot be your mate. Your father won't stand for it."

"He's just going to have to get over it. Rylee *is* my mate. Even now my mating urge is riding me." He let thoughts of his would-be mate fill his head, knowing full well his eyes would be mutedly glowing in response.

"Don't be an idiot. There's a reason why we call them mortals. We might not be immortal, but we are extremely longed-lived. You're nine hundred years old with the potential of living to three thousand. You'd bind yourself to one of them, even though you'd be lucky if she lived to be a hundred?"

Atticus ground his teeth to stop the howl of frustration that threatened to break loose. "That's no concern of yours. Now get into your car, wherever you parked it, and go back to Toronto. You're not welcome here."

"My car is in the parking lot close to the gatehouse. I went wolf to track you and followed your scent to your site. And I'm not leaving. If anything, it should be quite entertaining to see you trying to woo your mortal. I'm sure she knows nothing about what you truly are." Marla gave him a condescending smile. "I'll be here to pick up the pieces after you've told her and she runs from you in fright."

She reached out to touch him again. Atticus backed out of range, snapped his teeth and growled deep in his chest. "Admit defeat. I hope you enjoy sleeping in the tent alone, because I have no intention of being anywhere near you for the rest of the night."

Giving her another snarl for good measure, he turned his back on Marla and walked away. She'd made a mess of things between him and Rylee. He just hoped he could fix it.

* * * * *

How could I be so stupid? Rylee didn't know whether to punch something or cry. She'd fallen for Atticus' promises of wanting to be with her for longer than the weekend. She'd believed him, and the longer she'd been around him, the more she'd let how she felt about him grow. She'd believed every bullshit line he'd given her. Hearing him tell Luc he was her boyfriend had turned her insides to mush.

But it figured it was too good to be true. And seeing the blonde with the supermodel good looks at his campsite, her throwing herself at him and him not doing a whole lot to avoid her kiss, Rylee had felt as if she'd been duped. What Atticus had gotten out of playing her, she didn't know. It wasn't as if she'd fucked him, thank god. Maybe he got his jollies from picking average women, stringing them along by holding out the ultimate prize, and after they gave him what he wanted, he tossed them aside. Well, she wouldn't be another notch on his bedpost. The way the blonde had spoken, it was obvious they were intimate, very intimate, longstanding friends.

So angry, mostly with herself, Rylee stomped along the road to her campsite, mentally calling Atticus every swearword she knew. If it weren't for Luc and his friends, and that they'd paid for the site for the entire long weekend, she would have packed everything up tonight and gone back to Kitchener. Right now, she wished she'd told her mother a big resounding no when she'd called her and asked her to go camping with her brother.

At the campsite, Rylee saw the three boys had come out of their tent and sat around the fire pit. She chucked the bag of marshmallows at Nick who happened to be closest. "Here, you guys can finish them."

"What happened to Atticus?" Luc asked.

"Don't mention his name again," she snapped.

"I thought he was your boyfriend."

"*Was* being the operative word. Let's just say back at his campsite, his other girlfriend was there waiting for him."

"Damn," Josh said. "Are you sure you don't want to come and cry on my shoulder?"

Not in the mood, Rylee flipped him off. "Shut up, Josh." She looked at each of the boys. "I'm going to be in my tent, reading. If any of you do anything to piss me off, be forewarned I'll string you up by your balls. Got it?"

Each one of them nodded. As she took a step toward her tent, Luc asked, "What if Atticus comes here looking for you? Do you want me to hurt him for you?"

Despite her foul mood, she chuckled at the absurdity of that. Her brother was only two inches taller than her five foot eight. And a bodybuilder he was not. Atticus could crush him with one hand behind his back.

"I don't think so," she said. "If he does show up, which I highly doubt since his real girlfriend looks like a supermodel, just tell him to get lost."

Inside her tent, Rylee switched on the battery-operated lantern and pulled out the book she'd brought along with her.

She'd figured she'd need it to keep herself entertained while Luc and his friends did their own thing.

While she read, she did her best to forget about Atticus, about the way he'd held her close, kissed her with a longing she'd thought wasn't an act. But time and time again those thoughts kept rising to the surface. She couldn't stop thinking about him. It was ridiculous. She'd only spent a few hours with him, but it felt as if they'd been together a lot longer than that.

Rylee had only been reading for fifteen minutes when she heard the sound of Atticus' voice outside her tent talking to the boys. She clearly heard him say he wouldn't leave until he'd talked to her after Luc told him to get lost. Pissed off that he would have had the gall to show up, she angrily unzipped her tent and went to confront him.

"I don't want to talk to you, Atticus," she said as she stomped toward him.

"Just give me a chance to explain."

Rylee stopped a short distance away from him. "Explain what? That you enjoy leading on women who are taken in by your good looks? Did you and your supermodel girlfriend have a good laugh over it?"

"Marla isn't my girlfriend. And I didn't lead you on."

"Right. It didn't look as if you were fighting her off too much when she kissed you. And what was it she said? Oh yes, she liked it that you bit while you sucked face with her."

Atticus had his jaw clenched so tight Rylee saw the muscle along it jump. "I bit her as a warning to show her she'd gone too far."

"So you haven't ever slept with her?"

He ran a hand through his hair. "I'm not going to lie to you. I have slept with her, but it was nothing serious. And the last time I was with her was over a month ago. I also made it clear I was done with her. She followed me here thinking she'd be able to change my mind."

"Why should I believe you?"

"Damn it, Rylee." Atticus looked at the three teenage boys who were avidly listening to their conversation. He closed some of the distance between them. "We need to finish this in private."

She shook her head. "No, we don't. As far as I'm concerned, this conversation is over." Rylee turned to walk back to her tent, but Atticus had her by the arm, turning her toward him after one step.

"Rylee, please," he said. "Don't do this. I meant it when I said I wanted us to last longer than the weekend. What can I do to get you to give me another chance?"

She yanked her arm out of his grasp and crossed her arms over her chest. "For starters, where is Marla now? If she means nothing to you like you said, you should have had no problem sending her on her way." At Atticus' silence, Rylee shook her head. "You didn't send her away."

"I did. She refused to go. I have no intention of going back to my campsite tonight. Tomorrow morning she'll be gone, even if I have to physically put her in her car."

With a laugh that held no humor, Rylee said, "Well, don't expect me to invite you to sleep in my tent." She slowly backed away. "Leave, Atticus, and don't bother coming back."

Finished all she had to say, Rylee turned and walked to her tent. She didn't look at Atticus as she crawled inside and zipped it closed.

* * * * *

After leaving Rylee's campsite, Atticus headed for the hiking trails and the thicker bush. He plunged into the trees and went deep enough to keep what he did from mortal eyes. Drawing on the spark of magic that lived inside him, he used it to bring on the change. He held out his hand and saw it gradually shimmer, blurring as he shapeshifted into his wolf form. His eyes would be glowing as well. Atticus willed his clothes away at the same time.

Once the change was complete, he took off in a loping run. Usually going wolf and running made any anxiety or stress he felt melt away. This time it didn't work. In this form, the mating urge was stronger. The need to go back to Rylee, claim her as his mate, was almost too much to resist. She was his, goddamn it. And it wasn't as if he could just ignore his mating urge and it would go away. It wouldn't, especially after his having had a taste of her.

Atticus ran a little faster, winding his way unerringly through the trees. Somehow he had to earn Rylee's trust again. He had to convince her Marla meant nothing to him, and never had. Rylee had willingly gone into his arms once, she'd do it again. He just had to show her a second time how good they were together. To do that, he had to get close to her, really close to her. And he knew the only way that would happen was if he didn't give her a chance to refuse him. Like sneak into her tent and wake her with his lips and tongue.

A course of action set in his mind, Atticus decided he needed to wait a little bit longer to make sure Rylee would be asleep when he arrived at her campsite. Making a wide loop back to where he'd started from, he heard the sound of a branch snapping in front of him. He stopped as the figure of another wolf moved out from behind a thick tree.

Keeping to her wolf from, Marla walked silently toward him. She'd purposely stepped on the branch to let him know she was there, since her scent was downwind of him. Like all their kind, she could move in the trees without making a sound. He snarled his upper lip when she drew even with him, rubbing her side against his. Her dark blonde fur contrasted with his white. He snapped his teeth at her, causing her to quickly jump away.

Marla circled around to his other side and attempted to brush up against him once again. Atticus knew what she tried to do. She wanted to entice his wolf, but he wanted nothing to do with her, same as the man. Rylee was now the only female for both of them.

A second attempt was more than Atticus could stand. He used his body to shove Marla away before he charged her. He clamped his jaws around her throat and took her to the ground on her back, holding on as he growled. She yelped, then whimpered, her tail coming down between her legs.

Even though Marla had submitted, he held her by the throat for a few more seconds before he released her. She jumped to her paws, her tail still tucked. After he growled and snapped his teeth once more, she spun away. To get her moving, Atticus gave her a none-too-gentle nip to her rump.

Satisfied she wouldn't try to approach him again at least for the rest of the night, he continued on his way to Rylee's campsite.

* * * * *

Marla only went as far as it would take to make Atticus think she'd left him. She stopped and hid herself behind a wide tree and cautiously peered around it. She watched the white wolf lope away. He might have thought his display of dominance was enough to have her running back to his campsite with her tail between her legs, but he was dead wrong. Just as he was dead wrong about being able to cut her out of his life so easily. Atticus wasn't her mate, but she wanted the prestige that came with being known as the mate to the next pack leader. Some mortals married for power or to better their social status, why couldn't she?

Once she figured Atticus had put enough distance between them, she moved out from behind the tree and followed, making sure she kept downwind of him. Her hackles rose in anger when she realized he took a long route to another campsite. Marla kept way back out of sight, but with her keen eyesight, she easily saw the two tents set up. Shifting her gaze to the white wolf who hadn't left the trees, she saw his body shimmer and blur as he took on his human form. He then silently made his way into the campsite, walking a direct path to the smaller of the two tents.

Furious he would seek out the mortal when he could have her, Marla silently eased deeper into the bush. It disgusted her that Atticus would actually want to claim the woman as his mate. The mortal needed to be taken out of the equation if Marla ever stood a chance of snagging Atticus as her own.

Chapter Four

On silent feet, Atticus stepped out of the trees at the back of Rylee's campsite and walked to the two-man tent. He kept his ears open for any sound coming from the other larger one, but didn't hear anything. It was late enough for Rylee and the three boys to be asleep.

He crouched in front of the small tent and slowly unzipped the flap. Atticus crept inside and did it back up again. The sound of Rylee's deep, even breaths in sleep met his ears when he turned toward her. She lay on her back, zipped up in a sleeping bag on top of an air mattress. He ran his gaze over her. Just the sight of her made him ache. Marla had been right about one thing—his father would be furious with him for binding himself to a mortal mate. Not that Atticus cared. He'd already started to fall for Rylee, hard, and he wasn't going to give her up for anyone. He just had to convince her of that first.

Atticus crawled over to Rylee. He froze in place when she shifted and quietly said his name on a breathy sigh. The smell of her arousal filled his nose, making his cock instantly rock hard. A smile played across his lips. She dreamed of him. Rylee wasn't a female werewolf, but she seemed to be affected by the mating process. Females didn't have a mating urge, but once they met their soon-to-be mates, they had erotic dreams about them just as the males did.

Taking it as a good sign, Atticus cautiously opened the sleeping bag. Rylee still wore her jeans and t-shirt. He stretched out beside her on his side, supporting himself on his bent arm. After a quick check to make sure she still slept, he used the tip of his index finger to circle a taut nipple that showed through her shirt. Rylee moaned, arching her back.

He plucked at her nipple as he bent his head and tongued the other, wetting the material of her t-shirt. Rylee moaned again, pushing her chest closer. The scent of her arousal increased in intensity. Dropping his hand as he tugged at the tight bud with his teeth, Atticus placed it on her mound. Using his fingers, he stroked her pussy through her jeans. In response, she lifted her hips.

"Atticus," she said on a whimpered moan.

He lifted his head and said loud enough to wake her, "I'm right here, Rylee."

She jerked and her eyes fluttered open. "Atticus?"

"It's me."

"What the hell do you th—"

He cut her off by turning her head his way and sealing her lips with his. They remained stiff, but eventually softened as he licked and sucked, not backing down. Angling his mouth for a tighter fit, he stroked his tongue along the seam of her lips. Much to his pleasure, Rylee opened, giving him access to fully taste her. Their tongues met, twining, tasting.

She groaned into his mouth as she kissed him back hungrily. With a hand on her hip, Atticus rolled her to her side and against him. He lifted her leg and put it over his hip as he ground his throbbing cock against her pussy. Rylee draped her arm around his shoulder, stroking his back as she matched his movements.

Releasing her mouth, he said huskily, "Give me another chance, Rylee. I meant every word I said about Marla being nothing to me. I only want you. It will always be you now that I've found you."

"I want to believe you, I really do. But how can you know that already? And you did kiss Marla."

"No, I didn't. She kissed *me*. I only held onto her to stop her from unbalancing me. And I *did* bite her to show her I thought she'd gone too far. She knew that. She only said what she said to piss you off."

"Well, it worked."

"Too well." Atticus rolled Rylee to her back and shifted so he lay half on her with a leg between hers. "Marla is just a spoiled bitch who doesn't like not getting what she wants. She's more interested in me because of what I'll be once my father steps down than me as a man."

Rylee reached up and ran her fingertips along the side of his jaw. "You don't have to worry about that with me, since I really don't know anything about what your father does, nor does it have any bearing on how I feel about you. I will say it hurt to see you with Marla. I have a hard enough time believing someone who looks like you would actually find me attractive."

He kissed her again, showing her she had nothing to worry about. Once he had her panting and clutching at his back, he lifted his head only far enough to say, "Why wouldn't I want you? You're beautiful, more so than Marla, because you're beautiful on the inside as well where she never will be. You're everything I could ask for in a mate."

"A mate?"

Atticus silently cursed himself for not watching what he said. "I meant girlfriend."

To stop Rylee from saying anything more about his slip-up, he took her mouth again. He closed his eyes to hide them from her as he kissed her the way his mating urge demanded. Carnal, hard and possessive, he fed from her lips, his tongue twining with hers.

His cock throbbing in time with his rapidly beating heart, Atticus lifted his leg to press against her pussy. Rylee moaned into his mouth while she rode his thigh. The heat of her soaked through his jeans and into the skin beneath. He needed to touch her, feel her skin pressed to his.

In two swift movements, Atticus had Rylee stripped of her shirt and bra. He took hold of the back of his t-shirt and yanked it over his head, tossing it against the side of the tent.

Settling back on top of her, he reveled in the feel of her taut nipples brushing against his chest.

He made a wet trail of kisses along the side of her jaw to her ear and swirled his tongue inside it before he gently took the lobe between his teeth and tugged. Continuing downward, Atticus licked a path to where Rylee's shoulder and neck met. He nipped her there. It was a spot where he wanted to feel her sink her teeth into him and leave a mark to show he was hers. A bite there was also one of the greatest turn-ons for a male werewolf.

Shifting lower on her body, Atticus lifted one of her breasts and swirled his tongue around the taut tip. Rylee arched her back, offering him more. He opened his mouth and sucked the nipple inside. Her husky moan made his cock jerk and pre-cum leak from the tip.

He continued to suck at her breast as he brought his fingers down to the top of her jeans. He undid them and shoved his hand down the front of her panties. His fingers encountered wetness when he caressed along her pussy. The feel of her so wet for him, he wanted nothing more than to bury his cock inside her and pound into her. She'd let him, he knew she would, but not yet. Marla had almost screwed things up between him and Rylee. He didn't need to mess it up himself by claiming her before she knew what she would be getting herself into.

Atticus switched to her other breast and pushed two fingers inside her pussy, stroking in and out. Rylee's inner muscles clamped around them, making him wish it was his cock they squeezed instead.

Plunging his fingers faster, he used his thumb to flick her clit. Rylee gasped, lifting her hips to match the pace he set. Letting go of her nipple, Atticus lifted his head to look at her. Seeing she had her eyes shut, he used the opportunity to observe her. She was even more beautiful with her lips swollen from his kisses and her cheeks flushed with desire. He wanted to watch her face while she came.

Moving his fingers in a determined pace, thrusting as deep as they could go, he worked her harder. Her soft moans filled the small tent. "Come for me, Rylee."

"So close," she panted. "Just a little bit more."

To push her over the edge, he added a third finger, his thumb rubbing her clit at the same time. As she came, her face formed a mask of pleasure. A loud, whimpered moan pushed out of her. To stop the boys in the other tent from hearing her, Atticus surged up and covered her mouth with his, swallowing the rest of her cries. He didn't release her lips until she'd settled beneath him.

Hiding his eyes, he closed them and rested his forehead against hers. She caressed his back. "You're not going to fully make love to me again, are you?"

"No."

"I can't understand why you're holding off when it's what both of us want, but I won't push, since what you're doing to me instead is pretty damn good." She pushed on his shoulder until he rolled onto his back. "I'm not selfish, so it's my turn to make you feel as good as you made me."

Rylee's fingers fell to the top of his jeans and she made short work of undoing them. With a few tugs, she had them worked past his hips and down his legs. Atticus kicked them the rest of the way off. Free of its tight confines, his cock jerked as she ran a finger down its length.

"Did I ever tell you I like that you're just as big here as the rest of you is?" she asked while trailing her fingers up and down his shaft.

"No," he said in a tight voice.

"Well, I do. If you're not going to put this big cock of yours inside my pussy, I'm going to have to put it inside something else."

A growl threatened to break free when Rylee straddled his legs, bent and dragged the flat of her tongue along the same path her fingers had taken. Keeping his eyes shut, Atticus focused on her every touch.

She wrapped her hand around his cock and pumped it up and down. Unable to hold still, he lifted his hips, helping her work him. It felt good, but he didn't want to come by her hand. After a few more pumps, Rylee's fingers circled him in a firm grasp as she licked the head of his shaft like she would an ice-cream cone. She was going to kill him.

"Rylee," he said with a groan.

She didn't answer. Instead, she took him inside her mouth. A low growl rumbled out of him. She sucked on his cock, taking him almost to the back of her throat. His shaft hardened even more. What she couldn't handle, she stroked with her fist.

Lifting his head, Atticus cracked his eyes open. The sight of Rylee's head bobbing up and down as she sucked him off was enough to have his balls drawing up close to his body. The point of no return raced up to meet him. Grinding his teeth to stop from howling, he climaxed, giving her everything he had.

Once she released him, he pulled her down on top of him with her head pillowed on his chest. He wrapped his arms around her, holding her tight. As blowjobs went, that one had been pleasurable to the extreme. Making love to Rylee would more than likely be nothing short of mind-blowing.

Their breathing back to normal, Rylee lifted her head. "You're still hard. This is the second time I've made you come and you were able to keep it up. Is this something you can do all the time, or only once in a while?"

Atticus chuckled. "What would you say if I told you I can stay hard for hours, even after I've come more than once?" And he could. All male werewolves could keep an erection for that length of time, coming several times before going soft.

"Then my reply would be I'm one lucky girl. So when do I get to try this nifty ability of yours? Other than just with oral sex?"

"Before the end of the weekend. I promise you." Atticus tucked some of Rylee's hair behind her ear. "I want you to get to know me better first."

"I thought that was what we were doing?"

"We are, but there are some things about me I'm not ready to tell you." He felt her stiffen against him. "I assure you it isn't anything bad, at least I hope you won't think it is."

"As long as it isn't another ex-girlfriend who will come to hunt you down and try to take you away from me, I guess it can't be all that bad."

He ran his hand up and down her back. "No, it isn't that."

She drew circles on his chest. "Whatever it is, Atticus, don't wait too long. Too much more of what we've been doing and it's going to frustrate the hell out of me."

"I promise I won't."

For one thing, his mating urge wouldn't allow it. Tomorrow he'd use the day wisely to try to slowly ease into the topic of him being a werewolf and her, his mate. If he did it right, she'd accept him for all that he was. If he didn't, there was the real possibility of her running from him in horror.

* * * * *

Rylee woke to the sensation of warm heat surrounding her. She opened her eyes to see it was no longer dark inside the tent. Looking over her shoulder, she smiled. Atticus lay on his side spooned against her back. He had his arm over her waist with his hand covering one of her breasts. A muscled leg was between hers. She lowered her head and snuggled deeper into his embrace. He didn't stir.

She smiled again. He'd woken her during the early morning hours with his fingers playing her like a fine-tuned instrument. One thing was sure—Atticus gave the best oral sex she'd ever had in her life. He knew exactly how to touch her, to lick and gently nip to arouse her until all she thought about was coming.

And true to his word, even after she'd made him come, his cock had stayed hard. Like he was now. She felt the length of him pressed against her backside. Rylee knew he wanted to wait for her to get to know him better first, but she wanted all of him. The thought of pushing him to his back, straddling his hips as she impaled herself on his thick shaft made her pussy weep with need.

Rylee pushed her bottom against his cock. It twitched in response. Atticus' hand tightened on her breast as he nuzzled her hair out of the way to kiss the back of her neck. "I have to say I like waking up with you in my arms," he said in a sleepy voice.

"And I think I could get used to having my own human furnace warming me." She rubbed against his erection again. "I could also get used to waking up to this every morning."

Atticus made a soft animalistic growl, something he'd done a few times during the night. Instead of finding it freaky sounding, Rylee found it sexy as hell. She liked the thought of driving him so wild he made noises like that.

With a hand on her hip, he pressed her tight enough against him she couldn't move. "I'd love more than anything than to indulge in what you're blatantly offering, but the boys are awake."

Rylee lifted her head and looked in the direction of the tent's entrance. "Are you sure? I don't hear anything."

As if on cue, she saw a shadow appear at the side of the tent and then move to the front. She groaned when she heard Luc call her name.

"Rylee? Are you awake? We're hungry and want some breakfast," he said in the whiny tone he used on their mother.

"I'll be out in a few minutes, but don't expect much."

"What's the hold-up? You slept in your clothes like we did. I'm coming in."

Before Luc could bend for the zippered flap, Atticus said in a loud voice, "You do, boy, and I'll throw you out by the scruff of your neck like the pup you are."

"Atticus?" Luc asked slowly.

"Yes. Go away. Your sister will come out when she's ready."

"Sorry. I didn't know you were in there with her."

Luc's shadow disappeared as he walked away. Rylee giggled. "That should keep him quiet for a while. I swear I don't know how my mother puts up with his whiny ways. Luc whines and she gives him whatever he wants. I'm glad I don't live at home anymore."

"He'll grow out of it."

"I doubt it. My mom spoils him rotten. I think she does it because she had a miscarriage between me and Luc." She rolled out of Atticus' arms and sat up. "I guess we'd better get out there. I'll whip up some bacon and eggs on the camp stove for all of us."

"I can help."

Rylee watched Atticus sit up. Her gaze ran over his hard body, landing on his erection. God, she could spend an entire twenty-fours in bed with him and would still want more.

"You're staring at me as if you'd like to have me for breakfast instead," Atticus said.

She dragged her gaze up to his. "For breakfast, lunch and dinner."

He cupped the back of her head and kissed her soundly. "After I make sure Marla has gone, we can sneak away to my campsite."

"I'm all for that."

Rylee pulled on her clothes from the day before. While Atticus went to take care of Marla, she'd hit the shower. Once he was dressed as well, she unzipped the tent's flap and ducked to step outside. Looking up at the sky, she saw dark cloud masses were moving in. It figured the weatherman had gotten the forecast wrong. But it wasn't all that surprising to see rainclouds. It wouldn't be the first time she'd gone camping on the Victoria Day long weekend and had it rain. If it didn't get too heavy she could stick it out.

She took the camp stove out of the van and brought it over to the picnic table. The three boys were already sitting there, watching her and Atticus, who had come up behind her. "I hope you guys like bacon and scrambled eggs, because that's all I'm making."

All three boys nodded, then Luc asked, "When did he show up? I thought you were done with him."

Atticus put his arm around her waist and pulled her back so she leaned against his chest. "Your sister and I worked things out late last night after you were asleep."

"So does that means you're her boyfriend again?"

"Yes. And it also means you'll be seeing more of me from here on out."

"Great," Luc said sarcastically.

After that, Rylee got the eggs and bacon from the electric cooler and started the breakfast. Once everyone had their fill, Atticus helped her wash the dishes in the small plastic tub she'd brought for just that job. Of course the three teenage boys didn't offer to help.

Before Atticus left to go to his campsite, he pulled her aside and kissed her. Pulling away, he cupped her face in his hands. "Hopefully I won't be too long."

"Just as long as you come back."

"I will. Since I want to take a shower and change my clothes as well, I shouldn't take more than an hour. If I go over, come to my campsite and wait for me."

She nodded. "All right."

"See you in a bit then."

Rylee watched Atticus walk away. She'd give him that hour and not a minute more. If she found Marla still at his campsite, she'd toss the bitch out on her ass. Atticus was hers and she wouldn't give him up without a fight.

Chapter Five

Atticus hoped when he arrived at his campsite he would find Marla had been long gone. He ended up not being so lucky. The thorn in his side sat at the picnic table drinking Tim Horton's coffee. A Timmy's bag was on the tabletop along with another cup of coffee.

He walked over to Marla and glared down at her. "I thought I told you to leave once it was morning."

Ignoring his statement, she said, "I drove into Elora and bought us breakfast."

"You should have just kept on driving until you reached Toronto. I told you I don't want you here."

"And I told you," she said as she stood, "I wasn't going to let you go. I know you spent the night with your stupid mortal—her scent is all over you—but you mustn't have claimed her as your mate yet, or you wouldn't be here by yourself. Having second thoughts?"

"None. And I already ate. Rylee made me breakfast. You can take your coffee and food and leave."

Marla's face flushed red with anger and she growled low in her throat. "I'll go straight to your father and tell him about your little mortal."

Atticus growled back, crowding close so she had to look up at him. "Go ahead. He can't stop me. Rylee is mine and I love her."

"How can you love someone who is so beneath you? Werewolves are the superior race. We always will be."

"It was easy to fall in love with Rylee. If that hadn't been a possibility, my mating urge never would have kicked in.

And that's why it never did with you. You're too bitchy for my taste." Marla's hand, fingers curled in a claw, went for his face. Atticus caught her wrist and squeezed until she whimpered. "Try that again and I'll make you pay. Now are you willing to leave under your own volition, or do I have to haul you over my shoulder and take you to your car?"

She wrenched her wrist free of his grasp. "I'll go, but I still think you're lowering your standards by taking a mortal as your mate. I wonder what your father will do when you bring her home. No one from our pack has ever bound themselves to one before."

"Then it's about time we brought in some new blood. Goodbye, Marla."

Atticus calmly stood by as Marla gathered up the rest of the breakfast she'd bought and flounced out of his campsite. Once she disappeared up the road out of sight, he waited a good ten minutes to make sure she wouldn't come back before he collected clean clothes and the things he'd need for a shower.

There wasn't any doubt in his mind Marla would go straight to his father as soon as she got back to Toronto. Atticus had no idea what his reaction would be. It wasn't as if he got to choose who his mate was. Not that he'd want anyone besides Rylee. And it was true, their pack did need some new blood in it. Once he became pack leader with Rylee at his side, the superiority complex most of his kind had when it came to mortals would end. They'd either accept her or they were more than welcome to go lone wolf.

* * * * *

Rylee managed to hit the women's washroom at just the right time. There wasn't anyone using the shower. She pounced on it before anyone else arrived. It didn't take her long to wash her hair and body. By the time she shut off the water, she heard voices on the other side of the stall door. She dried herself and dressed in the clean clothes she'd brought with her before she stepped out into the washroom area. A quick pit stop at the sinks to brush her teeth, then she was on her way back to her campsite.

The three boys were where she'd left them, sitting at the picnic table. From the looks of it, none of them had changed their clothes. She put the things she carried in her tent and came back out with her comb.

Using her fingers to help untangle the knots in her damp hair, she said, "Aren't you guys going to shower?"

Josh shook his head. "We're camping, Rylee. That means you don't shower and you wear the same clothes."

"We're going to be manly men," Nick added.

She shook her head. "No, what you will be by the end of the weekend are stinky teenage boys."

"A little man stink doesn't hurt anyone," Luc said.

"I beg to differ," she said in return. "I'm telling you right now, if you three smell too bad, I'll take you down to the Grand River and dunk each of you in the freezing cold water. I'm not making the trip back to Kitchener in the van while you stink me out."

"What if it was Atticus? Would you dunk his ass in the river as well?"

She smiled. "It won't come to that. Unlike you three, he's gone to take a shower right now. I guess he doesn't think it's manly to reek like a pig."

Finished combing out her hair, Rylee returned to her tent to put the comb back in her bag. While she did that, Luc ducked inside. She gave him a questioning look when she turned to look at him.

"Did you and Atticus really work things out last night?" he asked.

"Yeah, we did."

"What about his other girlfriend? Is she gone?"

"She really wasn't his girlfriend. More like a fling who didn't want to let go. Along with showering, Atticus went to make sure she left."

"Can you trust him? You just met him, Rylee. For all you know he could be a horn dog and is playing you both."

"I trust him."

"Are you absolutely certain you can? Some guys are like that, you know? They think with their dicks and not their brains."

Rylee chuckled. "I've met a few men like that. Atticus isn't one of them."

"If it were me, I'd want to make sure. I know you think I'm a major pain in the ass sometimes, but you're still my sister and I want to watch out for you."

She gave him a hug and a kiss on the cheek. "You might be, but I still love you anyway. I'm just waiting for the day you grow up and stop being that pain in the ass. And thanks for looking out for me."

"I just don't want to see you hurt." Luc hugged her back. "I guess I'll go back outside. I can't have Josh and Nick think I'm actually getting along with you or anything."

Rylee laughed. "God forbid."

After Luc left, what he'd said about trusting Atticus wouldn't leave her head. *Shit.* Now she was second-guessing herself. Luc was right, she really hadn't known Atticus long enough to judge whether he'd told the truth about booting Marla out of his campsite, or just feeding her a line of bullshit.

He'd said to give him an hour, but with the doubts she felt, Rylee wondered if it wouldn't be a good idea to surprise him, go to his campsite and see if all was as he'd said. If Atticus was there alone, she'd tell him she'd missed him and couldn't wait any longer to see him. And if he wasn't there, and in the shower like he'd said, she'd just wait until he returned.

Rylee left her tent, zipping it closed behind her, and told the boys she'd be back later as she headed for the road in front of their campsite. As she walked, she thought of what she'd do if she *did* find Atticus with Marla. She'd probably kick him in the balls first, then slap the haughty bitch who was with him.

She hoped that wouldn't be what she found when she arrived at Atticus' campsite. She really did. Her feelings for him had grown stronger during the night. She'd never fallen for a guy so fast, or so hard, which left her wide open for him to easily hurt her. The few other boyfriends she'd had were nice while they lasted, but when they parted ways, it was amicable. Rylee was actually still friends with one of them. But with Atticus, it would be totally different. Her feelings were already too invested. If she didn't know any better, she'd say she had started to fall in love with him. Having never been in love before, what she felt for him was too new to say for sure.

Rylee found Atticus' campsite empty. No Atticus, and most importantly, no Marla in sight. Some of the worry she'd felt drained away. At least she hadn't caught them in each other's arms. Walking farther into the site, she looked at the tent, but couldn't see any shadows or hear any sounds coming from it. He had to be showering.

Prepared to wait for him to return, Rylee headed for the picnic table to sit. Glancing at the line of trees that ringed one side of the campsite, she caught sight of someone standing inside them. Changing direction, she walked over to the edge of the site. She managed to see what looked to be the back of Marla as she ran deeper into the bush.

Not taking the time to think about what she was doing, Rylee went after the other woman. If Atticus had sent her on her way, Marla had no right to be hanging around spying on them. Working up into a good anger, Rylee pushed through the thick bush intent on finding the person who'd put her in such a foul mood.

Seeing brighter light up ahead, she worked her way there in as straight a line as the trees would permit. Rylee hadn't seen a glimpse of Marla again, but she bet that was where she'd gone.

Just before she reached her destination, she heard the sound of a wolf howling very close to where she was. She quickly spun around. Her eyes widened when her gaze landed on the wolf a short distance from her. Its fur was a dark blonde color. It stared at her and curled its upper lip in a snarl as it growled deep from its throat. Where the hell had the wolf come from?

Rylee swallowed when it took a step toward her. She backed up, trying to keep the same distance apart, but her movement only caused the wolf to break into a lope. Spinning, she took off at a run, heading for the brighter light up ahead. Branches slapped her in the face and pulled at her hair while she ran. She didn't stop for anything, and she didn't dare look behind her to see where the wolf was.

Breaking through the trees, Rylee just about slammed into the barrier that marked the edge of the gorge. Nowhere left to go but back into the bush, she turned only to be brought up short at the sight of the wolf almost directly behind her. She backed up with her hands behind her until she hit the barrier.

She couldn't hold back a shriek as the wolf bunched its back legs under it and lunged toward her.

* * * * *

Atticus returned to his campsite a little later than he'd thought he would. He'd had to wait for the shower. Luckily there had only been one other person ahead of him. He hadn't seen Rylee at the women's, but really hadn't expected to. There was another set of washrooms where his campsite was.

He walked into the site and took a deep breath to pick up the scents around him, mostly to make sure Marla's remained old. Atticus smiled when he detected Rylee's, which was fresh. Thinking maybe she was inside his tent, since he didn't see her anywhere else, he crossed to it and unzipped the flap. His smile fell away when it turned up empty. Where could she have gone? Her scent wasn't all that old. She had to be around somewhere.

Going back out, he went in search of her scent trail. His muscles clenched when he found it leading into the trees that bordered his campsite. What reason could Rylee have had to go into the bush? None he could think of.

Not liking this one bit, Atticus followed her scent trail. Some distance into the trees, he picked up another scent. If he'd been in his wolf form, his hackles would have been rising. Marla's scent had mixed with Rylee's.

The sound of a wolf's howl coming from somewhere in front of him had Atticus shifting to wolf form as he took off at a run. More agile on four paws than two feet, he ran at a fast clip, never wavering from Rylee's scent. Marla had gone way too far this time. And he knew it was her, he recognized her howl.

A shriek ripped through the trees. Atticus ran faster. He broke through the bush just in time to see Marla lunge at Rylee in her wolf form. To escape Marla's sharp claws and teeth, his mate climbed over the barrier at the edge of the gorge. His stomach twisted at the sight of Rylee so close to it. One misstep and she'd fall to her death.

Before she could make another lunge at Rylee, Atticus slammed into Marla, forcing her back. Unlike the night before, she didn't back down. If it was a fight she wanted, then it was a fight he'd give her. He'd also show her she didn't stand a chance against him.

Using teeth and claws, they went at each other. Their growls and howls filled the air. Not risking the chance of being distracted by Rylee, and his need to make sure she was safe, he focused entirely on Marla. He didn't hold anything back. He went for blood.

The fight didn't last very long. In a matter of minutes he'd raked his claws along her side, leaving a bloody trail through her fur. Atticus took her down with his jaws around the back of her neck and bit down hard enough to go through her thick fur and into her skin. Marla yelped and whimpered. He gave her a good shake to get the message across that he could have easily snapped her neck this way, then released her. With a growl and a snap of his teeth, he sent her on her way. This time Marla would go home. She took off into the trees at a fast run, her tail tucked.

The threat to Rylee now out of the way, Atticus turned in her direction. She still stood on the other side of the barrier clutching it with both hands. As he slowly approached, she let go and held her palms out as if to hold him off. His heart jumped into his throat when she took a step back, putting her even closer to the edge of the steep drop.

He smelled the acidic scent of her fear. This was not good. Her fear of him as a wolf could make her do something rash. That only left one option—he'd have to shift in front of her to talk her back over the barrier. He only hoped she wouldn't fear him more afterward.

Standing still, his gaze meeting hers and holding it, he called on the magic inside him and shifted. Her eyes widened and she breathed at too fast a rate, but her gaze never left his while he made the change from wolf to man, willing his clothes back on at the same time.

Atticus held out his hand. "Rylee, it's all right. Marla's gone. Come back over the barrier."

Her mouth opened and closed a few times before she managed to speak. "The other wolf was Marla? What the fuck are you?"

She still hadn't moved from the edge. "I'm a werewolf." He motioned her with his hand. "Come away from the gorge and I'll explain everything."

Rylee shook her head. "I don't think so. Stay away from me."

He saw her take another step back, her foot partly hanging over the edge. No longer able to stand there and do nothing, he jumped the barrier faster than any mortal could and pulled her into his arms. He spun and leapt over to the other side.

Rylee punched and slapped him. "Let go of me, freak!" she screamed.

Atticus grabbed her by the wrists and forced them behind her back. "Stop it, Rylee. I'm not going to hurt you." Once she settled, breathing heavily, fear a real thing in her eyes, he said, "I'm no different than I was before you knew what I am. Now that it's out in the open, I can finally tell you what you are to me."

She shook her head. "This changes everything. Let me go."

"No. Not until you hear me out. You're my mate, Rylee. I knew it the instant I smelled your scent and my mating urge kicked in. You're the woman who is meant for me. I've been alive for nine hundred years and have waited a long time to find you. I don't want to lose you."

"I don't want to be a mate to a fucking werewolf, especially an immortal one at that."

"I'm not immortal, just long-lived."

"No difference. I don't want it. I don't want you."

The last thing Rylee said had Atticus letting her go. It hurt to hear her say she didn't want him because of who he was. It was obvious he wasn't going to be able to get through to her. Her fear of him was too great.

"Can't you at least try to give us a chance?" he asked in a low voice.

"I can't," she said as she slowly sidestepped around him. "I just can't. What you are freaks me out too much. Marla was going to rip me to shreds. Who is to say you won't do the same to me one day."

"Forget about Marla. She only went after you because you're mortal and she wants me as her own. But you're my mate, the woman I want to have at my side, always. And being what you are to me, I could never hurt you. The mating bond that would form between us once I claimed you would never allow it. Our souls join, become one."

Rylee shook her head again. "You're asking too much of me. I can't." She took a step back from him. "I'm going to walk away now. Please don't come after me."

Atticus then did the hardest thing he'd ever done—he let his mate walk away and out of his life.

Chapter Six

It was Tuesday and Rylee was back to work. After Atticus had revealed what he was to her, she'd raced back to her campsite, bullied the three teenage boys into quickly taking down the tents and then had them on the road back to Kitchener in a matter of an hour. They hadn't been happy with her, but she'd ignored their protests.

After getting the boys home, and talking her way around why they'd returned so early when her parents had asked, she'd gone straight to her apartment. There she stayed for the rest of the weekend, not even bothering to join her family when they'd gone to the Centennial Stadium to watch the fireworks on Monday night.

She'd also spent much of that time thinking about Atticus. Now over her initial fear of him, she found herself coming to grips with what he was. If she hadn't seen him shift from wolf to man, she'd never have believed werewolves existed. When she really thought about it, he didn't appear all that scary in his wolf form. Marla had been the one who'd scared her more than anything. Atticus had defended her, fought Marla off.

Then there was the whole thing about her being his mate. Did she want to be the mate of a werewolf? She didn't know, mostly because she really didn't know all that much about his kind. Not that she'd stuck around long enough for him to teach her.

Even now she couldn't stop thinking about him. If she was honest with herself, she missed him, a lot. It almost felt as if there was a part of her missing. She felt on edge, unable to settle. And she didn't like it. If being with Atticus again was the cure, there really wasn't much she could do about it. Yeah, she knew he lived in Toronto, but she had no idea where. And in a moment of weakness, she'd tried to look him up on the internet and found nothing. Being rich, his phone number was more than likely unlisted.

At the end of her shift, she heard her name being paged over the loudspeakers, telling her to go to customer service. Wondering what was up, she logged out of her till while the girl who was to take over waited for her to leave.

Hoping it wasn't a pissed-off customer, Rylee headed for the customer service desk. What she saw there when she arrived had her coming to a standstill. Atticus stood there smiling at her. He'd found her.

He crossed the distance between them. "Hi, Rylee."

"What...what are you doing here? How did you find me?"

"Well, there is only one Real Canadian Superstore in Kitchener. I figured I would take the chance and see if you were working today."

"You came from Toronto to see me?"

"No, just from Elora. I stayed until today. When I found out you were working today, I waited until your shift ended to come." He gave her a pleading look and said in a quiet voice, "We need to talk, Rylee. Please don't push me away. I missed you. I can't stop thinking about you."

Rylee closed her eyes for a second and swallowed. Being around Atticus again stirred up all the memories of how good it had felt to be in his arms. How badly she'd wanted him to make love to her, and how she still wanted him. Right now, all she saw was the man she'd fallen for, and she had. And the way he looked at her, with love showing in his eyes, she found herself unable to refuse him.

She nodded. "All right, we can talk. My apartment isn't too far from here, just down on Highland Road. You'll have to drive since I decided to walk to work today."

"Thank you, Rylee."

Once they were outside in the parking lot, Atticus guided her to his BMW. The drive to her apartment only took all of two minutes. She directed him to the visitor parking and then she let them into the building. Taking the stairs to her second floor apartment, Atticus followed behind her.

Inside, she closed the door and locked it. She leaned against it and stared at Atticus. God, she'd missed him. He wore blue jeans and a dark gray t-shirt that molded his powerful upper body to perfection. She felt drawn to him, as if the edginess she'd been going through would disappear as soon as he held her once again.

She pushed away from the door and motioned for him to follow her into the living room. They sat on the couch facing each other. Rylee looked into his eyes and saw they mutedly glowed. "Your eyes are glowing. They did that just before you shifted from a wolf."

"I'm not going to shift. It's because I'm aroused. I can't help it. You're my mate, I want you. My mating urge has been riding me hard for days, and not being with you has made it worse."

"Don't you have any control over it?"

"No. All male werewolves go through this when they first meet their mates. And it won't go away until he has claimed her. Made her his so no other male can take her away from him."

"Until the mating bond forms. How does that happen exactly?"

"Making love, our souls will join. Once in place, we won't be able to stand to be apart. You'd be mine for the rest of our lives."

"You mean the rest of my life. I'm what you called a mortal, remember?"

Atticus shifted closer and wrapped his hand around her nape. "No, our lives. I don't think I could live another two thousand years without you."

"Are you saying what I think you're saying?" Rylee asked hesitantly. "You would give up the rest of your long life when I..."

"Yes. Life wouldn't be worth living without you in it."

"Oh god. I'm starting to feel a little bit freaked again."

"Just breathe, Rylee."

"This is all so much. You being a werewolf, living for so long. Us being mates." She let out a shaky sigh. "I want you, but I don't know if I can handle everything that comes with you."

Atticus lowered his head to meet her gaze. "This will work, Rylee. We will work. I need you to believe in that. Without you, I'll feel as if a part of me is missing, never to be whole again."

She closed her eyes for a second before opening them again. "Then help me to understand."

"Know this, once mated, I can never leave you, never cheat on you, will be there for you always."

Hearing him say those words made her heart pound in her chest. The prospect of having him forever was a temptation she couldn't ignore. To never have to worry he'd stray, that them being mates literally meant it was for life, wasn't something she could ever get out of another man. Only with Atticus would she get that kind of guarantee.

"What of your family? Will they be willing to accept me?"

He sighed. "I'm not going to lie to you. My father, who is leader of my pack, won't be thrilled with you being mortal. But I don't care. You're mine. If he won't accept you, I'll go lone wolf if I have to. Give up everything."

"Lone wolf?"

"That's what a werewolf is called when they are no longer a member of a pack. An outsider."

"You'd do that for me?"

"No question."

She gave him a tremulous smile. "Then how could I possibly refuse you if you'd do all that just to be with me?"

Before she said anything more, Atticus leaned in and kissed her. She sighed, feeling as if everything was right in her world once again. This was what she'd been missing, this was what she'd been longing for. Just him and her and the passion that flared to life between them.

Knowing she wanted him with every fiber in her being, Rylee kissed him with all the pent-up emotions that had ridden her when they'd been apart. She wanted him, wanted to be his mate. And being his would be the only thing that would make her feel whole again.

She put her hands up his shirt and ran them across his wide chest and down his defined abs. Landing on the top of his jeans, she undid them and shoved her hand inside to wrap around his hard cock.

Atticus jerked away, meeting her gaze. "Are you sure this is what you want? Once it's done there is no going back. That's why I didn't make love to you before. I wanted you to have the choice. You have to be able to accept what I am."

She squeezed his shaft, eliciting a groan from him. "I want this. I want you. In Elora, I was scared. I've had a few days to think about it, about what you are. Just take your time easing me into your world."

"I can do that." He claimed her lips again and kissed her until they were both panting with need. "I love you, Rylee, my mate."

"I love you too, Atticus. Make me yours."

Holding her close, he stood, and with his mouth sealed to hers, he carried her down the short hallway to her bedroom. He crawled onto her bed and slowly lowered her to the center of it. The feel of him coming down on top of her, his hips settling between her legs made her libido skyrocket. An ache built in her pussy as wetness pooled, her body readying itself to take his.

Rylee yanked at his shirt and said against his mouth, "Off. Take it off. Take it all off."

Clothes went flying as both of them undressed. Rylee sighed, arching against him as they came together skin-to-skin. Her heart thundering against her ribs, she buried her hands in his white-blond hair and kissed him with all the need and longing building up inside her. He growled, feasting from her mouth. The sound kicked her libido up another notch.

Atticus took her hand and led it to his cock. She wrapped her fingers around it and pumped up and down. He rocked his hips into her. Wetness leaked between her legs. She wanted him inside her, now. She was more than ready for him.

Holding him, she led him to her slick entrance, rubbing the head of his cock against her until he was bathed in her wetness. As she pressed down on him, taking the tip inside her pussy, he didn't stop her. With a loud groan, he seated himself to the hilt with one stroke.

Squeezing her inner muscles around him as he moved in and out, Rylee put her legs around his waist, taking him even deeper. Their moans filled the room as they strained against each other.

An orgasm built. Just before she fell over the edge, Rylee felt a part of Atticus reach out to her. A part of her reached for him in return. They both sucked in a breath as the two parts joined and became one. Atticus rode her harder, sending her flying into a climax. Whimpering his name, her inner walls clutching his shaft, she rode out the waves of pleasure that bombarded her.

After the last wave hit, Atticus lifted her head and led her mouth to where his shoulder and neck met. "Bite me, Rylee. Hard. Leave your mark on me."

He shuddered when she licked him there, his muscles tightening. Doing as he asked, she bit him. He moaned, thrust into her one last time, his cock pulsing deep inside her, filling her with his cum.

Atticus collapsed on top of her. Rylee held him close as she caught her breath. "I felt it," she said.

"So did I. The mate bond formed. You're mine now."

"And you're mine." Rylee shifted under him and felt his cock filling her up. "You're still hard."

He grinned and kissed the tip of her nose. "Something all male werewolves can do. It allows us to take our mates over and over again for hours."

She moaned. "You'll wear me out."

"One more time, my mate. The way my wolf wants you, then you can rest."

He pulled out of her and urged her onto her stomach. With hands on her hips, Atticus got her up on her hands and knees. He licked the indent of her spine up to her neck as he shifted to kneel between her spread thighs. The head of his cock brushed her clit when he nipped the top of her shoulder.

Aroused again, she pushed back against him, wanting him inside her pussy. With his hands on her hips to hold her in place, Atticus surged forward, giving her his full length. He took her in fast thrusts, his balls slapping against her as he rode her. Rylee pushed back to meet his strokes, feeling another orgasm quickly building.

Atticus thrust faster, his cock growing even harder. In and out he moved. Reaching around her, his fingers found her clit. All it took was a couple of strokes and she came. He howled, coming with her.

Out of breath and still buried deeply within her, he rolled them to their sides and held her close. Rylee closed her eyes. Happy to stay just where she was, she snuggled deeper into his embrace. Content as she hadn't been in days, she let herself drift off to sleep knowing her werewolf mate would always be there to hold her close.

* * * * *

Spending the rest of the day and night in bed, Atticus and she had managed to do a lot of talking in between bouts of lovemaking. She'd also agreed to return to Toronto with him to meet his father the next day. Now that they were mated, Rylee figured it was best to get it over and done with as soon as possible. Atticus had explained how Marla would have more than likely left Elora and gone straight to the pack leader. And the longer they waited to confront Atticus' father, the more lies Marla would have the chance to tell.

The over an hour drive it took to reach Toronto had Rylee's stomach twisting with nerves the closer they got. The sensation increased when Atticus drove them to York's King Township where the mansion he lived in with his parents was located.

Atticus reached across the seat and squeezed her leg. "Relax. You'll do fine."

"Right. As if I can relax when I know you're risking the ties with your family because of me."

"It's a risk I'm more than willing to take. You're my world now."

Nothing like putting a ton of pressure on her or anything. As Atticus slowed and turned into a long drive of a mansion, Rylee blew out a breath to calm her nerves. It didn't work. Once he parked his BMW, she got out and walked around the back of it to stand beside Atticus. He linked their hands together and guided her to the front door.

He opened it and allowed her to walk inside ahead of him. The foyer was a display in rich elegance with its gleaming hardwood floors and high cathedral ceiling. Atticus led her through and into a spacious living room. The two people in the room, a man and a woman who sat on the large, black leather couch, looked in their direction once they stepped inside.

Rylee easily recognized the man as Atticus' father. He was a very slight older version of his son. The woman, who she presumed was her mate's mother, didn't look much older than Atticus. Both were extremely good looking.

Atticus' father wore a scowl as they walked toward them. "So," he said, "Marla was right. You did take a mortal for your mate." He said the word "mortal" as if it left a bitter taste on his tongue.

"Yes, I did. This is Rylee, my mate."

"You know how I feel about mortals, and still you bound yourself to one. As the next pack leader, you need to be an example to the rest of the pack."

Rylee felt Atticus stiffen beside her. "I've made my choice, Father. If you think that makes me less of a man because I've chosen to follow my heart, then so be it. And if you find you can't accept Rylee for what she is to me, I have no qualms about going lone wolf."

"You'd give up your status in the pack for a mor—"

"Grant!" Atticus' mother shouted, cutting his father off. "I usually don't interfere with pack business, but this is our son. I for one am not willing to just let him walk out of our lives because you can't get over your uncalled for dislike of mortals."

"You can't exp—"

She cut him off again. "Yes, I do. Unlike you, I have no problem with my son taking a mortal mate. All that matters is his happiness." His mother stood and walked over to Rylee. She kissed her cheek. "Welcome to the family, dear. I'm Krystal."

"Thanks."

Krystal turned back to Grant. "I suggest you get a quick attitude adjustment, or I'll go visit my sister for a day—without you."

Rylee had to bite the inside of her cheek to keep from laughing as Grant's face paled. Atticus had explained what happened when mated couples were separated. It was a threat not to be taken lightly.

Obviously his father didn't want to go through any of it. He cleared his throat, stood and came to stand at his mate's side. "I welcome you to our family, Rylee. I look forward to getting to know you better."

Krystal linked her arm through his. "See, that wasn't so bad, after all." She looked at Atticus. "Why don't you show Rylee the rest of the house?"

Atticus kissed his mother on the cheek. "I'll do that."

Rylee allowed Atticus to pull her out of the room. He took her to the upper level and into what she presumed was his bedroom. Once safely behind the closed door, he yanked her into his arms and kissed her until her knees gave out on her.

He pulled away and smiled. "That went better than I thought it would."

"I think you have your mother to thank for that."

"She rarely stands up to my father, so when she does, she usually ends up winning." He wrapped her tighter in his embrace and walked her backward toward the king-sized bed. "It seems to me it has been far too long since I had you last."

Rylee smiled. "Then we should do something about it."

"Oh, we will."

As Atticus pushed her down on the bed, Rylee knew there wasn't anywhere else she wanted to be.

The End

A WEREWOLF AT THE FALLS

Chapter One

Jorja walked into the Fallsview Casino Resort ready to face another evening shift as a cocktail waitress. The casino was one of two at Niagara Falls, on the Canadian side of the border. She'd worked there for just over a year. She didn't mind the job, and especially didn't mind the tips she made.

Crossing through the casino, Jorja glanced over at one of the blackjack tables and had to do a double-take when her gaze landed on two extremely good-looking men sitting there. One had longish, black hair while the other wore his blond hair short. The dark-haired man snagged her attention more.

She noticed the men sat at one of the tables she'd be serving. A few butterflies fluttered inside her stomach. She'd be able to get a better look at the dark-haired man. Not that she thought she stood a chance with him. But Jorja could do all the looking she wanted. And look she would.

Since it was a little early for the start of her shift, Jorja headed to the bar where she saw Connie, who she would be taking over for. The woman gave her a smile when Jorja drew even with her.

"Hey, Jorja. How goes it?"

"Not bad, Connie. And you?"

"I can say the same." Connie nudged her with her elbow. "Did you see the two pieces of eye candy on your way in?"

Of course Jorja knew exactly who Connie referred to—the two hunks at the blackjack table. "How could I not? I'd have to be blind not to. Have they been here long?"

"All day, and have been drinking the entire time."

Jorja frowned. "I guess that means I'll have to cut them off soon."

Connie shook her head. "Not yet. Those two can hold their alcohol. They're just starting to feel good, if you know what I mean. I've never seen anyone able to drink like they have and not be passed out on the floor. And they have to be loaded cash-wise to afford all the drinks, and make some of the hefty bets I've seen them make."

"I'll keep an eye on them, though. They have to reach their limit at some point."

"Let's hope it isn't for a little while, for your sake. They tip really well," Connie said with a laugh. "You should go put your purse and coat away, because I'm out of here soon."

"I'll just be a few minutes."

Jorja left Connie and went to the room in back where the staff had lockers to store their belongings while working. She put her purse and coat inside hers. Before she left the room, she gave her skirt a couple tugs and smoothed the front of her blouse by running her hands down it.

After she returned to the bar, Jorja watched Connie walk toward her from the direction of the blackjack table where the two men sat. She then listened as the other woman placed an order with the bartender.

"They're still okay to serve?" Jorja asked.

"Yeah. I'll let you give them their drinks. The blond ordered the beer while the dark-haired one wants the vanilla vodka."

"Are you sure? What about the tip?"

"You have it. Like I said before, they've tipped really well. Since I'm now officially off the clock, I'm leaving. Have a good night, Jorja."

"You too."

Once Connie left, Jorja placed the two drinks the bartender had readied on her tray. With a deep breath, she headed over to the blackjack table. She felt those stupid butterflies in her stomach the closer she came. At age twenty-five, she would have thought she'd be way past the stage where she became nervous at being around a man she found attractive. That wasn't the case, though. She just hoped she wouldn't make a fool of herself by stumbling over her words when she served them. That tended to happen as well.

Jorja arrived at the table and stood in between the two chairs the men sat on. She reached to give the blond his beer first. She'd just placed the glass of vanilla vodka on the table in front of the dark-haired one when she found herself grabbed around the waist and pulled onto his lap. She let out a small gasp, which ended up muffled as his mouth landed on hers.

Jorja felt her body go up in instant flames as the man hungrily moved his lips over hers. His tongue delved inside her mouth, stroking and tasting. Her eyes closed as she kissed him back. She forgot where they were, that she sat on the lap of a strange man in the middle of a busy casino, kissing him back as if she needed him to survive.

His hand buried in her long hair and held her exactly where he wanted her. Jorja barely held back a moan when she felt the length of his erection pressing into her backside. Her pussy clenched. A throbbing ache between her legs matched the rapid beat of her heart.

Finally when one of the slot machines played the sounds it made when someone won, Jorja came to her senses. Her eyes flew open and she pushed at the man's chest. His response was to hold her tighter and make a surprisingly real-sounding animalistic growl.

Feeling desperate—knowing all of this would be recorded by the surveillance cameras in the ceiling—Jorja grabbed a fistful of his longish, black hair and pulled his head back until he was forced to break their kiss. Her gaze landed on his eyes, which she swore seemed to glow mutedly for a split second before they appeared to be a normal shade of light brown.

"Mine," he said in a husky voice that seemed to fan the embers of her desire to life once again.

"Aw shit," said his friend. "First Atticus and now you."

His friend's words seemed to distract him enough for Jorja to break out of his embrace and slip off his lap. Flustered, and still turned-on, she fled, not even bothering to collect the money the men owed for the drinks.

Kian found it more than a little difficult to get himself back under control. But it was understandable, considering the momentous thing that had just taken place. And being three sheets to the wind didn't exactly help matters, either. He'd found his mate. Seemingly out of nowhere her scent slammed into him, causing his mating urge to go into high gear.

His cock had gone instantly rock hard, and all he could think about was claiming the female who would be his. Realizing she stood at his side, and reacting on instinct alone, Kian pulled his would-be mate onto his lap and kissed her as the mating urge demanded.

Only her physically pulling his mouth off hers had stopped him from trying something more than just a kiss. The scent of her arousal had intoxicated his already drink-befuddled mind, making him completely forget where he was. His whole being had centered on the woman in his arms.

Now that she was gone, Kian found his brain worked marginally better, but not by much. He gave his head a shake, hoping to clear it more. All that managed to do was make the room spin. Now, of all times, he'd finally reached the point of being a little drunk. Being a werewolf, that was no small task. It literally took three times the amount of alcohol a mortal could handle—and one who had a high tolerance at that—to give him a buzz. His friend Soren and he had worked on their present condition all day.

"Damn it," Soren said, his voice sounding a bit slurred. "You would have to up and do this right now. Couldn't you have waited until after our gambling weekend was over?"

Kian scowled. "As if I have any control over it." He looked at the mortal blackjack dealer who watched them avidly. "You know what."

To his ears, his voice didn't sound any better than Soren's. He reached for his glass of vodka and took a big sip. Having ordered it straight up, it burned all the way down.

"Are you sure you should be drinking that?" Soren asked. "Considering what just happened to you, I would think you'd want to cool it on the alcohol."

"As you said, considering what happened to me, I need it. But I do think I'm done gambling for the night." Kian stood and collected his winning chips to cash in.

Soren did the same, then said, "Shit. Your woman took off so fast we didn't get a chance to pay for the drinks. If this were Vegas, we wouldn't have to worry about it, since they're all free. Too bad it's illegal in Canada for casinos to just give away drinks."

Kian smiled and shoved his chips at his friend. "Stop your griping. You take these and cash them in for me while I take care of our unpaid tab."

"And I suppose you won't be leaving the bar any time soon."

"Probably not."

"Fine. I'll return with your winnings, then I'm hitting the slot machines for a while."

Kian watched Soren head off before he walked toward the bar with his drink in hand. His gaze zeroed in on the woman who stood there with her back facing him. Her long, golden-brown hair fell in waves to the middle of her back. The black skirt she wore hugged her curvy hips just right. He followed it down her ass to her long, toned legs. She wore black high heels that accentuated them even more.

He was just about upon her when she turned with a tray full of drinks held in her hands. Spotting him, her cheeks turned a lovely shade of pink. Her gaze jumped everywhere, as if she didn't know where to look. When she finally looked him in the face, Kian noticed her eyes were blue-gray in color.

"Can...can I get you something else to drink?" she asked stiltedly.

Kian held up his half-empty glass. "Not yet, but soon." He took a step closer, but she lifted the tray of drinks higher, using it as a barrier between them. As if that would keep him away. He let it go for now. "But my friend and I forgot to pay for our drinks before you...left in a hurry."

Her cheeks pinkened even more. "Oh. All right. I have to serve these first. Or better yet, if you don't want to wait, you can pay the bartender."

"I'd rather wait for you. That way I'll know for sure you got your tip."

"O...okay. I'll be back then."

He smiled and turned to follow her with his gaze. His would-be mate was more than he could have asked for. She wasn't supermodel-pretty like female werewolves, but that didn't make her ugly by any means. She was pretty in a cute kind of way. And she totally appealed to him.

Kian chuckled to himself when he thought of how nervous she was around him. Just something else he found attractive about her. He was going to enjoy cozying up to her and getting her used to him. Taking a seat on one of the barstools to wait, he tossed back the rest of his drink. It looked as if he were going to have to work for his mate, and there was nothing wrong with that.

* * * * *

At the opposite end of the casino, Jorja made sure she took the circuitous route to the last table she had to serve drinks. She stalled for time. Her heart still thudded at a rapid

A Werewolf at the Falls

pace and she felt more than a little shook up. How the hell could she go back to the bar and not make a total ass of herself? Just the few words she'd had with the dark-haired man, who had practically kissed her senseless, had turned her into a stuttering fool. And it didn't help that his deep voice seemed to sink right into her and cause her body to go into overdrive.

Pull it together, Jorja. He was just a man. Just an utterly gorgeous, hunk of a man who she wanted to screw her brains out. And judging by the hot kiss he'd laid on her, he was more than a little interested in her. Maybe she stood a chance, after all. Yeah, as long as she didn't scare him off with her stupid nervousness and lack of ability to string words together.

Jorja served the last of the drinks she carried and took a deep breath as she headed back to the bar. She could do this. She was a mature woman who'd been around a bit. Her virginity had been lost several years ago. There was no reason why she couldn't carry on a perfectly normal conversation with a man who happened to look like an underwear model.

Her small pep talk seemed to work until she spotted the dark-haired man's friend sitting at one of the slot machines. He turned his head to look in her direction and gave her a knowing wink. That did her in again, making her think of the heated kiss she'd shared with his friend for all to see.

She hurriedly continued on her way. At the bar, Jorja felt another rush of heat zip through her body as she met the gaze of the man in question. There was no mistaking the look of hunger that lurked in his eyes. She swallowed, pulled herself up straighter and walked over to where he sat.

"W-Would you like to p-pay for those drinks now?" Oh god. Could the floor open up and just swallow her, please?

He gave her a sexy grin that made him even better looking. "Sure. But first, what's your name?"

"Jorja."

He held out a twenty-dollar bill. "Keep the rest as a tip, Jorja. By the way, I'm Kian."

Even his name sounded sexy. She took the proffered bill. "Thanks."

Jorja turned to the bartender and handed him the money. While she waited for him to give her the change, she felt Kian's gaze on her the whole time. She ended up being startled when he spoke again.

"Will you have a drink with me, Jorja?"

After pocketing her tip, she turned back to Kian. "I can't. It's not allowed while I'm w-working."

"Then how about after you're off?"

"I just started my shift."

"I guess I'll have to wait until you're done."

"That won't be for hours."

He took her hand and tugged her to stand between his spread legs. With the height of the barstool he sat on, it made it so they were almost equal in height. "I don't mind waiting. I'll sit here all night, watching you work."

Normally, after her shift ended, she was dead on her feet and only thought of going home to bed. If Kian did stick around for that long, Jorja would be more than happy to have one drink with him.

She jerked her head in a short nod. "All right." She looked around at her tables and saw a customer signal her over. "I have to go."

Kian released her hand and let her take a step back. "And like I said, I'll be right here, waiting."

Jorja said, thankfully without a stutter, "I'll see you then."

She walked away from the bar feeling as if lady luck had looked her way for once.

Chapter Two

As promised, Kian stayed at the bar for the rest of Jorja's shift. The later it got, the busier the casino became, which meant he didn't really have much time to talk to his would-be mate. But he watched her, his gaze rarely straying. Soren would come to the bar to sit with him for a while and then go off to try his hand at one of the gaming tables. One time he tried to convince Kian to go get something to eat at the buffet. Kian refused. Instead he slowly nursed drink after drink. By the end of Jorja's shift, Kian was pretty loaded, not that anyone would be able to tell. He hid it well.

He knocked back the last of his drink and waited for Jorja to finish up. Soren had long since returned to his hotel room. Kian was thankful they had each decided to get separate ones. Having a friend sawing it off in the other bed while he tried to get to know his soon-to-be mate better wouldn't be very conducive.

At Jorja's final return to the bar, carrying her purse and coat, he asked, "Will you still have a drink with me?"

She nodded shyly. "Just one."

Jorja went to sit on the barstool next to his, but Kian stopped her. "Not here. The bar is closing. I already bought a bottle of wine." He nodded toward the bottle sitting on the bar in front of him. "Come up to my hotel room."

She hesitated for a few seconds. "I don't know. I really can't stay for long. I have to get some sleep. I have another night shift tomorrow."

He put his hand over his chest. "I promise I won't hold you up too much."

"When I agreed to the drink I thought we'd have it down here, not in your room."

"I promise I'm not some deranged stalker or anything. I just want to get to know you better. Somewhere where there will be no interruptions."

Jorja appeared to think it over as she chewed on her bottom lip. "I'll go on one condition—I tell someone I work with your name and suite number. J-Just in case."

The last bit had come out with a blush. Kian understood where Jorja was coming from. She didn't exactly know him well enough to be accepting an invitation up to his room.

"Agreed," he said. "You go tell whoever you want while I wait here for you."

Jorja nodded and went farther down the bar to speak with the bartender. Kian watched the exchange and saw the man nod. His would-be mate returned after that.

"It's done," she said. "I-I just have to phone down to the bar and let him know what your suite number is."

"Then it looks as if we're all set."

Kian grabbed the wine bottle around the neck and picked it up before he slipped off the barstool. The room spun a bit for a few seconds, but he quickly got a handle on walking straight as he took hold of Jorja's hand with his free one.

They silently walked through the casino to the bank of elevators that would take them up to his Parlor suite room. A single, quiet ding announced the arrival of a car, and Jorja and he stepped inside. The doors closed with them being the only ones in the elevator.

Kian pushed the button for the correct floor, then stepped back to Jorja's side. Her scent wafted around him inside the small space. Now that he was around her, in close quarters, his mating urge rode him harder, digging its claws into him. His cock hardened. He leaned closer until their shoulders touched and he took a deep breath. He smelled the scent that was hers alone, but mixed into it was the scent of Jorja's arousal. It wasn't strong, but it was definitely there.

He had to close his eyes for a second to rein himself back under control. The pounding need that thrummed through his body demanded he take her, claim her as his. Kian couldn't let things get out of hand. With Jorja being his mate, he couldn't just sleep with her and be able to walk away if he wanted to. The first time mates made love their souls joined, became one, forming a mating bond. Once it was in place, one couldn't be away from the other for any real length of time without suffering. Each would think something had happened to the other. The need to be together would override almost everything else. And when the separated couple reunited, explosive sex happened soon after, reaffirming the mating bond.

The elevator dinged again once it reached their stop. Kian guided Jorja off the car and down the long hallway to his room. In front of the door, he let go of her hand and fished the keycard out of his jeans pocket. He fumbled it once before he managed to get it into the slot on the door correctly and unlocked it.

He shifted to the side to allow Jorja to step into the room first. After she used the phone to call down to the bar with his suite number, she put her coat and purse on the couch and crossed to stand in front of the back wall, which was completely filled with a row of windows.

"Even though I live here in Niagara Falls, I can never get enough of watching the Falls, especially when they are lit up at night," she said.

Kian joined her at the windows. His room gave a spectacular view of the Horseshoe Falls. The tumbling water had been lit with blues and reds. "Yeah, it is pretty awe-inspiring. But I prefer the view inside the room."

Jorja turned her head to look at him. Her cheeks were stained red. "I...I have to agree with you on that."

Seeing and hearing her nervousness return, Kian decided to distract her with the wine. He lifted it higher for Jorja to see. "I had the bartender open this, so I just need to pull out the cork. I forgot to ask for a couple of wineglasses. Hopefully you won't mind using the small tumblers from the hotel room."

She smiled. "As long as I don't have to drink it out of the bottle, I'm good."

He put the wine bottle on the small table in the conversation area, then went to the bathroom to collect the tumblers. Shortly after that, he had the wine poured and sat on the couch with Jorja.

"I hope you like red wine," he said.

Jorja nodded, then took a sip from her glass. "It's good."

Kian took a big gulp of his, even though it would only go straight to his head. In his present condition, his wolf had more of an influence over him than he normally allowed while in human form. And right now, his wolf wanted Jorja. Add the mating urge into the mix, and Kian felt his control slip as each second went by.

He waited until she'd had a few more sips from her glass before he took it from her and placed it on the table with his. Kian inched closer and reached out to stroke a finger along her soft cheek. Her lips parted and the tip of her tongue came out to wet her bottom lip. His gaze became glued to her lush mouth. It was too much. He had to have another taste of her.

Kian shifted his hand to cup her cheek and brought his mouth down onto Jorja's. A wolf's growl of satisfaction punched out of him before he could stop it. She stiffened at the sound, but soon pressed herself closer when he deepened the kiss, pushing his tongue between her lips.

The taste of her cranked his arousal and need for this woman up another notch. His head, already swimming from the alcohol he'd consumed, swam even more. And more of his wolf instincts took over. He wrapped his other arm around her waist and pulled her chest tightly to his. Knowing his eyes had to be mutedly glowing at this point—something they did whenever he was very aroused or angry—Kian closed them.

The kiss became more carnal, their tongues dueling with each other. The sound of Jorja's rapidly beating heart and harsh breathing filled his ears. He ran his hand down her cheek to stroke the side of her neck to her shoulder. He skimmed across the front of her violet, silky blouse until he reached her full breast. She moaned into his mouth as he stroked the taut nipple with his thumb.

Needing to touch more of her, Kian lifted Jorja and seated her sideways across his lap. His aching cock pressed against her ass. Still kissing her, he ran a hand down from her knee to her foot. He made quick work of pulling off the black pumps she wore.

That done, he stroked back up her leg. Since she didn't wear any pantyhose, there was nothing between her skin and his hand. Higher he caressed until he reached her knee once again.

Kian broke away from her mouth and dropped his head to nuzzle the hollow of Jorja's throat. "Will you let me touch you?" he asked.

Her reply was a breathy, "Yes."

He licked a path to her upper chest and nudged the vee of her blouse open wider with his nose as his hand continued its upward exploration. Reaching the hem of her skirt, Kian ran his fingers along her inner thigh, diving under it. Her skin felt like silk beneath his fingertips. He wanted to take the same path with his lips and tongue.

Encountering the edge of her panties, Kian brushed his hand against her pussy. The material felt damp. A small, whimpered moan escaped Jorja as he stroked her there, causing her to become even wetter.

His wolf howled in his mind, a mournful cry for his mate. With Jorja so willing in his arms, Kian surrendered to his animal side. All the reasons why he shouldn't claim her right then and there no longer meant anything. The only thing that mattered was having her, making her his, so no other could take her from him.

In a show of strength, he gathered her close in his arms and stood. Jorja rested her head on his shoulder as he carried her to the king-sized bed. He placed her on the center of the mattress and crawled up to straddle her thighs. Keeping his gaze averted, he went to work unbuttoning her blouse. Her chest rapidly rose and fell with her breaths.

Once the last button was undone, Kian parted the material and stared at her breasts. They were more than a handful and encased in satin that matched the color of her blouse. He pulled Jorja into a sitting position, deftly removed her top and threw it over the side of the bed. Taking her lips once more, he undid the back clasp of her bra and stripped her of it.

With a gentle push, he got her to lie back down. He bent and supported his upper body on his hands on either side of her head as he left her lips, trailing kisses down to her collarbone. Lower he went, shifting along her body, until he reached her breasts. He flicked a taut nipple with the tip of his tongue. Jorja moaned and arched her back in invitation.

He rubbed his cheek against the tight peak. "So beautiful. I could get lost in your body all night. I want to learn every inch of you with my lips and tongue."

"Yes," she panted. "Touch me, Kian."

As he sucked her nipple into his mouth, his head continued to swim, his mating urge riding him even harder. There was only one way to stop it—claim Jorja as his mate.

Kian paid equal attention to her other breast before continuing his downward path. The sounds of enjoyment Jorja made caused his cock to jerk. The smell of her arousal had him longing for a taste of her pussy. He found the hook and zipper at the side of her skirt and quickly undid both. Kian pushed it down over her hips as Jorja wriggled out of it.

He hooked his fingers into the top of her panties and tugged them down. He nibbled at her hipbone as he pulled her last article of clothing off. To make more room for himself, Kian put his hands on Jorja's hips and slid her up closer to the headboard. He then shifted to kneel between her spread legs. Swirling his tongue into her bellybutton, he stretched out, his shoulders forcing her thighs farther apart.

At his first lick of her pussy, Jorja arched her hips and sucked in a sharp breath. "More," she panted. "I need more."

"I will," he reassured her. "I won't stop until you come."

Kian used his fingers to spread her pussy open and thoroughly licked her. He lapped at her, making sure to pay attention to her clit. Jorja's moans increased in volume when he sucked on the small bundle of nerves and pushed a finger into her wet opening. Her inner walls clamped down around it, squeezing tight. Another wolf's growl left him as he swirled his tongue around her clit and pushed a second finger inside her. In and out he pumped, moving at a pace that would push Jorja ever nearer to her climax.

Jorja buried her hands in his hair and rocked her hips to ride his fingers. "Kian…I'm going…I'm going to come."

"Give it to me, babe," he said against her tender flesh.

Jorja arched her back and cried out as her pussy clamped down on his fingers in a stranglehold, then rhythmically clutched them while her orgasm tore through her. Kian continued to lap at her clit, reveling in the sensation of his mate coming.

Once it ended, he knelt between Jorja's spread legs and pulled her into a sitting position. "Take off my shirt," he said in a strained voice. "I have to have your hands on me."

Her fingers quickly went to the buttons on his black, button-down shirt. He yanked the bottom out of his jeans, so she could reach all of them. After she undid each one, Jorja smoothed her hands across his chest to his shoulders and pushed his shirt off. Impatiently he tore the garment down his arms and threw it to the floor.

"My jeans, Jorja. Undo them."

His cock ached, the front of his pants too tight for his erection. He felt a measure of relief when Jorja undid the button and pulled down the zipper. As she reached inside and wrapped her hand around his shaft, he sucked in a breath through his teeth. It wouldn't take much to have him reach his first orgasm. But he wanted to be inside her when he did that.

Kian took her lips, his tongue stroking hers, as he rid himself of his jeans. He brought Jorja's hand back to his cock. She grasped him and pumped her fist. He rocked his hips, pressing tighter into her hold. The pre-cum that leaked from the tip lubricated his skin as she stroked him.

Needing to be inside her, now, he pushed her down onto the mattress and covered her body with his. Taking his cock in hand, he led it to her wet pussy and rubbed the tip against her, bathing himself in her juices. Jorja panted beneath him. Angling himself, Kian sheathed his cock deep inside her pussy with one stroke. He closed his eyes to better savor the feel of her closing around him, and to keep Jorja from seeing them.

He pulled back, then sank into her once again. She lifted her legs and put them around his waist as he set a steady pace. In and out he rode her, his pleasure mounting with each stroke of his cock. She squeezed her inner walls around him, increasing the sensations he felt along his length.

As he took her harder, faster, Kian felt it—a piece of his soul reaching out. In return, he felt a piece of Jorja's brush up against it. As the two joined and became one, the mating bond snapped into place. He fought to hold back the howl of satisfaction that built inside him. She was his, never to be taken from him.

His balls drew up closer to his body as his climax inched nearer. Setting a faster pace, he angled his hips so his cock rubbed Jorja's clit with each stroke in. A keening cry escaped her as her pussy clutched and released his shaft, milking it in a tight fist. It was enough to send him over the edge. With a low growl, he came deep inside her, filling her with his cum.

Still hard after coming—something all male werewolves could do, keep an erection for hours, even after climaxing several times—Kian didn't give her any time to recover. He pulled out of Jorja and urged her onto her stomach. Placing a hand under her, he lifted her onto her hands and knees so he could take her the way his wolf wanted her.

Kian held onto her hips to keep her in position as he slowly sank back into her pussy. Jorja moaned, her head hanging down. He pistoned his hips, almost pulling out all the way before stroking into her again. Jorja pushed back to match the pace he set.

It didn't take long to have another orgasm build. He rode her faster, his balls slapping against her pussy as he pushed inside her. In this position, she took more of him, making it so he didn't know where he ended and she began. And knowing that he took his mate, the one woman meant for him, made their joining that much more pleasurable.

About ready to explode, Kian said huskily, "Come for me, Jorja. I want to feel your pussy clutching my cock while I do."

"Just a...little bit...more. Oh god, I'm coming," Jorja whimpered.

Kian slammed into her one final time and groaned as he spilled inside her. Still erect, he wrapped an arm around her waist and brought them down onto the bed on their sides after it was over. Keeping her held tightly to him, he opened his eyes to find the room spinning. He rested his head on Jorja's and let sleep claim him.

Chapter Three

Jorja came awake to the sound of deep, even breathing in her ear. She had no idea how long she'd slept, but she didn't think it had been all that long. At first, she didn't remember where she was. But as her gaze landed on the furnishings in the room, it all came rushing back. She'd slept with Kian. And it had been amazing. She also couldn't believe she went that far with him. It so wasn't like her to jump into the sack with a man she was attracted to. But there was something about Kian, and the way she felt pulled toward him, that she'd thrown caution to the wind and went with what her body demanded. Once again she thought of how good it had been. Some men had problems performing while a little drunk, but that didn't seem to be the case with him. He'd been more than able to keep it up, even after coming twice. Just before she'd fallen asleep, she'd realized his cock was still hard, buried deep inside her. She'd never been with a man who could do that.

And just before he'd come the first time, she swore something had passed between them. It was unlike anything she'd ever felt. It hadn't been unpleasant, just different.

Knowing it had to be very late, Jorja slowly slipped out from under Kian's arm. He didn't stir. She sat up and looked at him. She still found it hard to believe she'd actually had sex with him. Running her gaze over his naked form, her pussy clenched. As she'd surmised earlier, he had the body of an underwear model. Only his muscles were a bit too big to actually be one.

Her gaze lingered over his well-defined chest and washboard abs before it landed on his cock. Even though he was soft, it was still big. While fully erect, it was thick and long, filling her up. And boy did he know how to use it. She'd never been so well fucked in her life. Even now she wanted more of him.

Jorja silently sighed in regret and slipped off the bed. She checked Kian once more and found he still slept on. He had to be a heavy sleeper, or the alcohol made him one. Not wanting to wake him in case he tried to get her to stay the rest of the night, which she wasn't comfortable doing, she gathered her clothes. She didn't need some of the people she worked with noticing her leaving the resort in the morning.

After a quick pit stop in the bathroom where Jorja dressed, she went to the conversation area and picked up her coat and purse from the couch. She thought of at least leaving her cell phone number for Kian, but decided against it. He wasn't drunk enough to forget he'd slept with her, but once he sobered up there could be a chance he'd change his mind about wanting anything more to do with her. Especially since she couldn't have a normal conversation with him without stuttering.

With one last look at Kian, she opened the door and silently stepped out into the hall, then quietly pulled it closed behind her. She hurried down the long stretch of hallway to the elevators. She pushed the call button and watched to see which set of doors would open.

Jorja made it all the way down to the lobby and outside to the parking lot before she felt as if she should go back to Kian. With a shake of her head, she brushed the feeling aside. She was not going back. She had to get some much-needed sleep, or she'd be dragging her ass during her next shift that coming evening.

She unlocked the driver's door of her ten-year-old Chevy Cavalier and got inside. After putting the key in the ignition, Jorja sent up a silent prayer it would start before she turned it. Much to her relief it worked. Her car was getting to be a beater, but she couldn't afford to look for another used one at the moment. Nor could she pay for costly repairs on the Cavalier.

On the drive to her apartment, the feeling of wanting to see Kian returned, only this time it was a bit stronger. Great, Jorja thought. She'd gotten laid and now she was going to be obsessed with him.

Reaching her building, a small duplex, Jorja drove around to the back and parked. She got out, walked to the back door and let herself inside. As she went up the stairs to her apartment, she took a deep breath. She felt out of sorts, as if something were missing. It had to be tiredness. Usually she would already be home and in bed.

Once she was inside her apartment, Jorja put her coat away, then headed to her bedroom to change into her pajamas—a pair of light, cotton sleep pants and a loose t-shirt.

Forgoing brushing her teeth for one night, she got into her queen-sized bed, stretching out in the middle of it. She closed her eyes and waited for sleep to come. It didn't. Instead of being relaxed, her body felt tense. Thoughts of Kian filled her head. Was he okay? Had she done the right thing by leaving without waking him? It had only been a little over a half hour since she'd last seen him, but it felt like a day. The need to see him, hear his voice, touch him, bordered on desperate.

Jorja rolled to her side and punched her pillow into the shape she wanted it. She had to stop with these thoughts. She would not allow herself to become obsessed with a man. Just because she'd slept with Kian once did not mean it went beyond the great sex. Christ, she knew nothing about him.

After another half-hour went by, and the desperate feeling became even stronger, Jorja knew she wouldn't be able to sleep if she couldn't settle her mind. She felt about ready to climb the walls. With an exasperated huff, she threw back the covers and got out of bed. She needed to take a warm bath. A good, long soak should do the trick.

In the bathroom, she turned on the taps in the tub to as hot as she could stand it. As she waited for it to fill, she stripped out of her pajamas and clipped up her hair. She wrapped her arms around her middle, hoping they would ease the terrible ache she felt inside for Kian. They didn't.

Jorja turned off the taps and got into the steaming water. She sank all the way down until her head rested on the back of the tub. She closed her eyes and tried to will all the tension out of her body. If anything, it made it worse. The moment she closed her eyes her thoughts centered more on Kian.

She forced herself to stay in the tub until the water cooled. As she toweled dry, she caught her reflection in the mirror over the sink. Her eyes looked wild, and there were strain lines around the corners of her mouth. What the hell was wrong with her? All she knew was she couldn't stand this feeling much longer. It would drive her crazy. As for being able to sleep, there was no way that would happen while she was in this state. The only rest she'd managed so far was the short amount she'd gotten in Kian's arms.

Jorja bit back a whimper at the thought of being held by him. Every fiber in her being called out for him, needed to be with him. Whatever happened to her didn't seem to get any better. If anything, it only worsened as time went on.

Running a shaky hand through her hair after she let it down, Jorja couldn't take it anymore. Whether it made her a crazy stalker, or she'd just plain lost her mind, she had to go back to the resort, and back to Kian.

She returned to her bedroom and dressed in a pair of sweatpants and a long-sleeved t-shirt. A quick glance at her alarm clock showed it was five thirty in the morning. Kian should still be in his hotel room, at least she hoped. If he wasn't, Jorja had no idea what she'd do.

* * * * *

Kian woke himself up as a growl of agitation rumbled out of him. His eyes snapped open and he quickly scanned the room with his gaze. Nothing seemed out of place. The light of dawn streamed through the wall of windows, telling him it was already morning. What the hell was the matter? Inside him, one sensation after another slammed into him—agitation, desperation, the feeling that something, or someone, was missing.

He took a deep breath, scenting the air. That's when it hit him over the head—the scent of his mate, Jorja. His gaze whipped around to the spot on the bed next to him. It was empty. It didn't take him long to realize she wasn't anywhere in the room. Her scent was no longer fresh.

Kian shook his head to see if it would help him get a handle on his jumbled thoughts, and immediately regretted it. A throbbing ache pounded in his temples. He'd had way too much to drink the night before, and now suffered the consequences in more ways than one. Because he hadn't been thinking straight, he'd gone and done something he shouldn't have, at least not yet. He'd slept with Jorja, claiming her as his, making them mates before he explained anything about what he was, or what she was to him. *Fuck!* He'd screwed up.

And because of his stupidity, he suffered because his mate had left sometime while he'd slept without telling her what would happen to them both if she did. Now he knew what the desperate feelings were that roiled inside him, and what Jorja had to be suffering through as well without a clue as to why.

He flipped back the covers and got out of bed, quickly dressing in a clean pair of jeans and t-shirt. If he hadn't basically passed out after he'd made love to Jorja, he wouldn't have let her leave. He would have made sure she'd stayed in his bed, then found some excuse to keep her with him while he figured out how to tell her he was a werewolf.

He had to somehow find her. Considering how bad he felt, she had to have been gone for at least an hour, likely more. That was why it had awakened him. Hoping against hope Jorja had at least left something as a way for him to get in touch with her, he stalked over to the desk and looked at the hotel scratch pad. There was nothing written on it.

Kian ran his hands agitatedly through his hair. Shit, this was not good. Last night he'd been so desperate for her, he hadn't even asked what her last name was. So that ruled out looking her up in the phonebook. He knew for a fact she had to work tonight, but neither one of them would make it that long without feeling as if they had totally lost it. His mind already played tricks on him, making him think something bad had happened to Jorja. His wolf snarled and snapped his teeth, feeling just as strung out as he.

He paced up and down the room, and when that didn't help, he slammed the flat of his fist against one of the adjoining walls. Kian did it a few more times, trying to give his frustration some kind of outlet.

A loud pounding on his door stopped him before he could hit the wall for a third time. He rushed over to it, praying it was Jorja. It wasn't. It was a sleepy-eyed Soren dressed only in a low-slung pair of jeans. Kian cursed and stepped back into the room as his friend joined him.

Soren looked him up and down. "You look like hell. And do you mind telling me why you've decided to beat the shit out of the wall between our rooms?"

Kian paced once more. "I fucked up. Big-time."

"What did you do?" Soren asked. Then quickly added, "Aw shit. You slept with your mate."

"Yeah, I claimed her as mine."

"Did you tell her what you are? What being a mate means?"

Kian stopped and held out his arms. "Do I look as if I did? The fact my mate isn't here should be answer enough."

"You have to find her."

"No shit, Sherlock. I would if I could, but she'd didn't leave a number for me to reach her before she walked out. And I have no idea what her last name is."

Soren shook his head. "I have to tell you, you did an awesome job of wooing your mortal mate. *Not*. I thought you had more finesse than that."

"I didn't exactly plan to sleep with her." At his friend's arched brow, Kian said, "Okay, I did, but I hadn't planned on things getting so out of control that I slept with her without explaining anything. I was drunk, and the mating urge was too hard to ignore."

"I had thought to suggest you give Atticus a call to get his advice on wooing a mortal mate, since his is one, but it's a little too late for that."

Atticus, another good friend, was the next in line to be their pack leader, and had recently found his mortal mate, Rylee. She hadn't taken the news of Atticus being a werewolf very well in the beginning, but his friend had been able to hold off on claiming her until she'd come to terms with it.

"Yeah," Kian said, "it's a little too late for that. What I need right now is to find Jorja."

Soren sighed. "All right. Have you tried contacting someone who works at the resort? They more than likely won't give you her phone number, but they can maybe call her on your behalf. I know it sucks, but that's your only option at this point."

"No, I hadn't thought of that. I guess that's all I can do. I'll call down to the concierge desk."

Kian went to the phone and dialed the number for the concierge. After a man on the other end answered, he said, "I'm a guest here and I'm looking for some information on one of your employees."

"Do you have a problem, sir?"

"No, nothing like that. The opposite in fact. I'd like to get in touch with one of the employees here, but I don't know her last name. I wondered if you could help me get a message to her at home."

"I'm glad to hear you don't have any complaints about the service at the resort. Who is this employee?"

"Her name is Jorja, and she works as a cocktail waitress in the casino. She worked the night shift last night."

"I know exactly who you mean. We only have one Jorja working for us. I'd be happy to call her for you. What is your message?"

"Just tell her I would like for her to contact me as soon as she can." He gave the man his suite number. "Thanks. I appreciate this." Kian hung up the phone and looked at Soren. "He'll do it."

"What are you going to do if she doesn't call back?" Soren asked.

"Then I'm going to have to find another way to find her. I'm not going to be able to sit here all day and suffer."

"It's that bad, huh?"

"You could say that. I knew it would be, but not like this. It's enough to drive someone insane. We've grown up knowing what separation would do to mates, but Jorja hasn't a clue what's going on. She must think she's lost her mind."

Soren opened his mouth to say something when a knock sounded on the door. Kian crossed over to it and flung it open. The sight of Jorja, standing out in the hall, looking as strung out as he, made him feel as if a great weight had been lifted from his shoulders. Then a second later, a surge of lust so intense he couldn't ignore it seared through him. He yanked her to him and kissed her with all the desire that pounded inside him.

Vaguely he heard Soren say, "I'm getting out of here before I see something I'll have to wash my eyeballs out with bleach for." His friend squeezed past him and Jorja and pulled the door closed behind him.

Kian picked Jorja up off her feet and put her back against the nearest wall. Lifting his head, he gazed into her eyes, which were dilated with passion. "I have to have you Jorja. Right now."

Jorja felt as if her entire body had gone up in flames. Arousal like nothing she'd ever experienced before took over her. When Kian had opened the door, just the sight of him had her pussy drenched. All the anxiety, agitation, everything, disappeared to be replaced with the need to have him inside her. She needed, she ached. She was more than desperate for him. And when Kian said he wanted her, she was already ready for him.

"Yes, god, yes."

Kian let her down on her feet only long enough to strip her of her sweatpants, taking her panties with them. He fumbled with the front of his jeans and pushed them down far enough for his erect cock to spring free. Claiming her lips in a desperate kiss, he lifted her once more, pressing her back against the wall. With one thrust, he was buried to the hilt inside her. Jorja cried out in pleasure.

In and out he stroked, his full length filling her to bursting. As if her body were starved for his, her pussy clenched his thrusting shaft, trying to draw more of him inside. She gripped his hair, kissing Kian with wild abandon as her orgasm tore through her. Jorja couldn't hold back her loud moan. He thrust harder, faster, then stiffened as he reached his own release. This joining had been quick and hard, just the way she'd needed it.

Her breath sawed in and out of her lungs as she broke their kiss and rested her forehead against Kian's shoulder. That had been the most intense sex she'd ever had. And just like the first time, he was still hard. She squeezed her inner muscles around his cock and received a moan in response.

Without a word, Kian carried her to the bed, his cock still buried inside her pussy. He turned and sat, scooting back until there was enough room for her knees to rest on the mattress.

Kian leaned back on his hands. His eyes were closed to mere slits. "Ride me, Jorja. Take me however you want me."

She nodded before pulling her shirt over her head and taking off her bra. She placed her hands on top of Kian's shoulders and started a slow ride. Up and down she moved, grinding her clit against his pubic bone with each downward thrust.

He sat up and lifted one of her breasts to swirl his tongue around her taut nipple. "That's it, baby. Make us both come again. You feel so damn good."

Getting swept away with desire, and the sensation of Kian's big cock filling her, Jorja arched her back, wanting him to suck at her breast. He flicked her nipple once with the tip of his tongue before he sucked it into his warm mouth. She felt each pull deep in her pussy, causing her to move on him faster.

Even though she'd come not long ago, another intense orgasm quickly built. Kian's cock grew even harder inside her. Their heavy breathing filled the room. Her body coiled tighter around his. He switched to her other breast, sucking the nipple deep.

Jorja's movements became jerky the closer her climax came. Kian reached between their bodies and rubbed her clit. That was all she needed to send her flying. A whimpered moan escaped her lips as she came, her pussy clutching at his thick shaft.

Kian released her nipple and placed his hand on her hips. He lifted her up and down his cock as he thrust his hips to meet hers, striving for his own release. An animalistic growl tore out of his throat when he climaxed. He pushed inside her one final time, hard enough to lift her knees off the bed. She felt his cock pulse inside her pussy. Feeling completely boneless, she collapsed against his chest. He wrapped an arm around her and fell back on the bed.

Chapter Four

Jorja was quite content to lie on Kian's chest as he stroked her back. She also noticed for the first time that while she was completely naked, he still wore his t-shirt and jeans. He'd only opened his pants and shoved them down his hips enough to pull out his cock. Not that she cared. All that had mattered was getting him inside her.

She shifted and lifted her head to look at Kian. He had his eyes closed. "That...that was intense."

"I know," he said, his voice husky.

He opened his eyes, and Jorja swore they had a muted glow to them for a split second before he blinked and it was gone. "I didn't come here expecting to jump you as soon as I saw you."

Kian chuckled. "I think I did the jumping more than you." He then grew serious. "Why did you leave in the first place?"

"I needed to get some sleep, and I didn't think it would look good for one of the other employees to see me leave the resort in the morning in the same outfit I wore last night."

"You left without saying goodbye, or leaving a number for me to call you."

"Well...I thought...maybe once you sobered up you'd not want to see me again."

Kian cupped her face and looked into her eyes. "Why would you think that?"

Jorja tried to duck her head, but he wouldn't let her. "With your looks, you probably have women falling at your feet all the time. I-I'm not exactly what you would call supermodel material, not like you."

He kissed her slow and hard until he had her clutching at his shoulders. Once he pulled away, he said, "I might have been drunk, but I wasn't so gone I didn't know who I slept with. I kind of rushed things last night, because I *did* have too much to drink, but I don't just want you for a good fuck."

"Are you sure?"

Kian blinked. "Of course I'm sure. Why wouldn't I want something more than that with you?"

"Well... Well, I can't talk half the time around you without stuttering like an idiot. Then there's..." Jorja let her words trail away. She had been about to tell Kian about the obsessive feelings that had swamped her while she'd been at her apartment. Did she really want him to think she was some kind of stalker?

"I think your stuttering is cute. That just means you're a bit on the shy side. There's nothing wrong with that. Once you get to know me better, I'm sure it'll go away. Now finish what you were going to say. Then there is what?"

She shook her head. "Forget it. I-I'll sound like a loon."

"No you won't."

Jorja took a deep breath. "All right. After I left you, I...kind of couldn't stop thinking about you. It's crazy, but I felt as though if I didn't come back something bad would happen to you. I tried to ignore it, I really did, but it only got worse."

"But it's gone now, right?"

She nodded. "Yes. Actually as soon as I saw you standing in the doorway it disappeared. Then all I could think about was...sleeping with you again." Jorja felt her face heat as she blushed.

Kian smiled. "There is nothing to be embarrassed about. I felt the same way."

"You did?" Did he actually mean he'd felt desperate away from her as well?

"Yes. So much so I called the concierge desk and asked him to call you and pass on a message from me. I'd only just gotten off the phone with him when you knocked on the door."

The thought that Kian would have gone to that extent to get in contact with her sent a little thrill through Jorja. He had to be interested in her. "Oh," she said shyly. She shifted on him and his now-softened cock slipped free of her body. Also a wave of tiredness washed over her. "I should go."

As she tried to roll off him, Kian grasped her hips to hold her to him. "Stay."

"I haven't gotten any sleep. And I need some before I work tonight."

"You can sleep here. I want to spend the day with you. We can catch up on our rest, then you can show me the Falls. I've only seen them outside my room's windows. Then when it's closer to the time for you to work, we can go to your apartment so you can change before your shift starts."

Spending the day with Kian would be no hardship. And it wasn't as if she had anything else planned. And to be honest, after going through what had overtaken her when they'd been apart, she didn't know if she had enough energy to get dressed and drive to her apartment to sleep.

Jorja nodded. "Okay, I'll stay."

"Great." Kian lifted her off his body and placed her next to him. He then slipped off the bed and stripped out of his clothes. "The room has a large whirlpool tub. I haven't used it yet. I'm pretty sure there will be enough room for both of us. Does a bit of a soak sound okay to you before we get some sleep?"

She bit her bottom lip and nodded. Jorja ran her gaze over Kian's body. The sight of him standing there in all his naked glory turned her on. If she hadn't felt so tired, she'd be more than willing to have another round of hot, intense sex with him.

As if he'd read her mind, Kian said with a chuckle, "There will be plenty of time for lovemaking after we sleep. So the only thing I'm going to do in the tub is hold you."

Jorja felt herself blush again. She then let out a squeal of surprise as Kian scooped her off the bed and carried her to the bathroom. Once inside, he put her down on her feet and turned on the taps to fill the large whirlpool bathtub.

After the water level rose high enough to cover them, Kian picked her up again and put her inside the tub. He got in behind her and positioned her so she sat between his legs with her back resting against his chest. Once the whirlpool was full, he reached over and turned off the water before turning on the bubbles.

Jorja relaxed against Kian, loving the feel of him along her skin. Add in the jets of the whirlpool and she felt as if she were in heaven. But then he grabbed a bar of soap and lathered his hands. She sucked in a breath when he ran them over her front, paying extra care to her breasts. If Kian thought this would be relaxing, he was mistaken.

He lathered his hands a second time and washed each of her arms, his knuckles brushing against the sides of her breasts. Jorja's heart beat faster as her pussy grew wet with arousal. She squirmed, and his cock, which was trapped between them, hardened. The feel of it only caused desire to heat her blood even more.

As Kian's soapy hand disappeared under the water to stroke along her stomach, Jorja knew the demands of her body wouldn't let her sleep until he gave her the release she needed. Lower his hand went until his fingers brushed against her mound.

Jorja couldn't hold back a small moan. "I thought you said you were only going to hold me."

He nudged her hair away from the side her neck with his chin, then gently nipped her. "You're just too tempting. Having you naked and slippery from the water, in my arms, I can't not touch." He licked her skin. "I don't think I'll ever get enough of you."

Kian's hand drifted lower until he found her clit. Jorja spread her legs, putting them on top of his as she panted from the arousal coursing through her body. "You make me ache. I need more."

"I'll give it to you," he said, his voice strained.

He pushed two fingers inside her pussy, causing her to moan. As he pumped them in and out, she lifted her hips to match his strokes. The water in the tub sloshed around them. Kian worked her faster, his thumb stroking her clit. Jorja felt his hard cock jerk against her back as she squeezed her inner muscles around his fingers.

"That's it, Jorja," he ground out. "Fuck my fingers. Come for me."

He added a third and she felt herself coming. A keening moan escaped her as she held onto the sides of the tub for dear life. Wave after wave of pleasure tore through her. She hadn't thought she'd had enough energy to climax again, but obviously she'd been wrong.

Once it ended, Kian pulled his fingers out of her. His cock was thick and long against her back. She turned in the water to face him. He had his eyes closed as his chest rapidly rose and fell. She more than wanted to give him the same pleasure he'd given her.

Jorja fisted his cock under the water and pumped her hand up and down his length. He rocked his hips, the tip of his shaft breaking the water's surface with each upward thrust. Wanting to taste him, she bent her head and swiped her tongue over the slit when it appeared again.

Kian made a sound between a growl and a moan in the back of his throat. "More," he panted before he shifted and rose to stand.

Jorja knelt on her knees before him, his big cock now eye level with her. She flicked his slit again with the tip of her tongue, swiping at the bead of pre-cum that had appeared. With a firm grip on the base of his shaft, she sucked him inside her mouth. Her head bobbed as she took him in and out.

"Yes," Kian hissed. "Suck me. Harder."

She increased the suction, taking his cock almost to the back of her throat. Kian thrust his hips as he fucked her mouth. His shaft grew even harder. An ache pounded deep inside her pussy.

"I can smell your desire, Jorja," he said hoarsely. "You want to come again?"

She moaned around his cock in answer.

Kian pulled out of her mouth and lifted her onto her feet. He shifted them both until she stood in front of him, facing the back wall. He ran his hand down her thigh, then lifted her leg, placing her foot to rest on the corner of the tub. His cock brushed her pussy just before he thrust home.

He took her from behind in hard, fast strokes. "I can't hold back much longer," Kian moaned. "Come, Jorja. Now."

She pushed back on him, matching his pace, then fell over the edge into an intense release. His hoarse cry told her he'd followed suit. Once her pussy relaxed around his cock, Kian pulled out of her, even though he was still hard. She put her hands on the wall to support herself. Satiated, tiredness beat at her.

Kian turned off the whirlpool's jets and pulled the plug to drain the water. She said nothing as he lifted her out of the tub, dried her and then himself. He carried her to the bed and tucked her under the covers before he joined her. The last thought Jorja had before sleep overcame her was Kian had just ruined her for other men.

* * * * *

Kian awoke before Jorja did. They both lay on their sides, facing each other. He had his arm under her neck while the other was over her waist. He also had one of his legs between hers. He stared at her, still finding it hard to believe he'd finally found his mate. It had only taken him nine hundred years. He snorted to himself. Atticus was nine hundred years old as well, and had just found his. Soren was the same age too, which meant there was a good possibility he'd be finding his mate in the not-too-distant future. Maybe.

He ran his gaze over his mate's face. He'd been shocked as all hell when she'd said she'd thought he wouldn't want her once he'd sobered up. She was everything he could ask for in a mate. She was pretty, had a great personality and had a body he'd never tire of. And making love to her didn't compare to any of his past experiences. Sex with Jorja would always be intense. And each time they shared their bodies the closer the mating bond would become.

Thinking of that bond, Kian knew he'd have to convince her to stay the night. No fucking way was he going through a separation again. The one experience had been more than enough. He'd have to tell Jorja what it all meant, but he was reluctant to do it just yet. She was already nervous around him. He didn't need her fearing him as well.

He breathed a silent sigh. How could he tell a mortal that werewolves actually existed and not have one freak out? He hadn't a clue how to go about it. In all of his nine hundred years, he'd never told a mortal what he was. He'd had mortal acquaintances, but never ones he'd been close with. To this day, Atticus and Soren were his closest friends. And now he'd gone and claimed a mate who was mortal. Damn, he wasn't looking forward to the explanations he'd have to give Jorja.

Maybe it was a little bit selfish on his part, but he wanted at least a day with her where she thought he was just like her. Then tonight, after she finished her shift, he'd bring her up here to his room and tell her the truth. And he'd be dead sober when he did it too.

Kian leaned in and gently kissed Jorja awake. Her eyes fluttered open, and when she focused on him, she smiled. "Hi," she said in a sleep-roughened voice.

"Hi, yourself. I'm hungry, so I'm going to order some room service. Do you want something?"

"Sure."

"What do you want? Since it's pushing noon, we can either have a late breakfast or an early lunch. Which would you prefer?"

"A late breakfast sounds good."

"All right. I'll order a little bit of everything and we can have our own buffet. I'm going to use the bathroom, then I'll order the food."

Kian got out of bed, collected his clothes and went into the bathroom. He used the toilet, brushed his teeth and even managed to do a quick shave. When he came out Jorja was already dressed and sitting on the couch in the conversation area of the room.

He crossed over to her and sat beside her. "I'll order the food in a minute, but I was thinking, do you mind if I ask my friend Soren to come along when we go see the Falls?"

"He's the blond man you were with last night?"

"Yes. He's in the room next door."

"N-No I don't mind. You came to the resort with him, after all."

"He wouldn't care if I abandoned him for you. He's probably expecting it."

"You can ask him."

"I'll call room service, then pop over to his room. I want to catch him before he decides to hit the casino."

Kian phoned in their order before going to Soren's room. His friend opened the door after the first knock. He eyed Kian. "You look better. I take it your mate is still here."

"Yes, so I'll make this short and sweet, though being this far from her won't set off the separation anxiety. I ordered Jorja and me some room service, then we're going to check out the Falls. I want you to come with us."

"Why would you want me around as a third wheel?"

"Because I think it would be better for Jorja to get to know both of us before I tell her the truth. I want her to see werewolves can be just like everyone else."

Soren laughed. "In other words, you're scared shitless to tell her and you're using me as an excuse not to."

Kian frowned. "I'm not scared shitless. I just want one day with her without the whole werewolf and mate thing coming between us. So will you come with us or not?"

"Fine, I'll tag along, though I still want to have some time at the gaming tables. We have to check out tomorrow. And speaking of that, what are you going to do about your mate? It isn't as if you can leave her behind."

"I'll have to convince her to come back to Toronto with us."

"And if she wants to stay in Niagara Falls?"

"Then I guess I'll buy a place here as well. I'm not going to go lone wolf if that's what you're suggesting. With Atticus' mating, the pack is a little more understanding about mortal mates."

The pack's understanding of one of their kind taking a mortal mate had gone through a radical change with the arrival of Rylee, Atticus' mate. Their pack leader, Grant, had had a strong dislike for mortals, and of course, the rest of the pack had taken his lead. That is except for his mate, Krystal. According to Atticus, his mother had accepted Rylee with open arms, and had cowed his father into accepting Atticus' mate as well.

"I guess that will just be another thing you'll have to work out with your mate," Soren said. "Anyway, come and get me once you two have finished eating."

"I will."

Kian left Soren and returned to his room. Jorja still sat on the couch where he'd left her. The room service arrived a few minutes later and they ate until neither one of them could eat anymore. During the meal, he noticed she relaxed around him more and more, and hardly stuttered. Now if only she'd get over the fact he was a werewolf so easily.

Chapter Five

Jorja waited outside in the hallway as Kian knocked on Soren's door. The blond man answered and stepped out to join them. She still found it hard to believe two men as good looking as Soren and Kian could be at the same place at the same time. Both were well over six feet tall and had well-muscled bodies. She couldn't help staring at them as they walked toward her.

"So I hear you're going to act the tour guide and shows us around the Falls," Soren said as soon as they stood in front of her.

"I'll try," she said. "Though it won't be that hard. We just have to walk to Queen Victoria Park and follow the walkway."

"Well, since neither one of us has come to the Falls before," Kian said, "you're the expert. So lead on."

They took the elevator down to the lobby and walked out of the resort. It wasn't all that long of a walk before they reached the park and the walkway. At this end, the Rainbow Bridge, the Canadian and American border, was in easy sight. Jorja spied the long line of cars waiting to cross over into the States. Now with the Canadian dollar being close to, if not equal or better than, the American dollar, she knew more than a few people did a lot of cross-border shopping. She'd done it a few times herself. The outlet stores just over the border in Niagara Falls, New York were a good place for her to spend money she shouldn't.

Also at this end there was a good view of the American Falls. But the real draw was farther along—the Horseshoe Falls, the Canadian falls. And Jorja knew of something that would take them up close.

Reaching that particular spot, Jorja said, "Let's go on the *Maid of the Mist*."

Kian nodded in agreement, but Soren looked a little pale. He said, "Ah, why don't the two of you go? I'll wait for you."

"What's the matter, Soren?" Kian asked. "Are you afraid of water?"

"No, dumbass. I just don't feel like going."

Jorja quickly added, "Anyone who comes to Niagara Falls should at least once take a ride on the *Maid of the Mist*. It's nice. I've been on it a few times. The big thrill is when the boat goes to the foot of the Horseshoe Falls and you get wet."

"See," Kian said. "The expert thinks you should go. Or maybe you're just a wuss and don't like the idea of getting a little sprayed."

Much to Jorja's surprise, Soren made a growling sound very similar to the ones Kian could make. "I'm no wuss."

"Then prove it."

Soren swore. "All right, I'll go. If I don't you'll just harass the shit out of me."

"And you know it."

Jorja smiled at the men's back and forth banter. It was obvious they'd known each other for a long time—considering they could sling insults at one another and neither one took real offense.

"Come on," she said. "The *Maid of the Mist* plaza is just up ahead. There are four *Maids* with one departing every fifteen minutes. There's not too many people around today, so we shouldn't have too big of a crowd on the boat."

She led them to the plaza that was built right into the gorge's wall. All the buildings were below ground level. They paid for their entrance and then entered the brown, stone tower that housed the four high-speed elevators that would take them down to the docks at the Niagara River's edge.

Once they were on one of the *Maid*s, they pulled on their recyclable souvenir raincoats that were given to them for free. And they'd need them. It was a guarantee they'd get wet before the ride was over.

After all the passengers boarded, the Maid pulled away from the dock. It took them past the base of the American Falls before heading for the basin of the Horseshoe Falls. That was where they'd get really soaked.

As the boat came closer to the falls, Jorja looked over at Soren, who stood on Kian's other side. They were lined up along the rail. His face looked a trifle green. She nudged Kian. When he looked at her, she said quietly, "Ah, I think I know why Soren didn't want to go. He's not looking too good right about now."

Kian turned his head toward his friend. "You're not going to hurl, are you?"

Soren took a deep breath in through his nose and let it out through his mouth. "I will if you don't leave me alone. I knew this was going to happen. I once had the marvelous idea of taking the Toronto Island Ferry to Centreville Amusement Park for a date. I hurled during both crossings. So stop talking to me, so I can concentrate on not losing my lunch."

At that moment the boat reached the Horseshoe Falls. Jorja giggled as she pulled up the hood of her raincoat, catching spray directly in the face. Poor Soren looked even greener as the boat rocked a bit in the current. If she'd known he got seasick, she wouldn't have pushed so much for him to come along. What was it about men that they couldn't admit to a weakness? If it had been her, she'd have owned up to it real quick and not have thought it would make her appear any weaker.

Luckily for Soren the boat ride didn't take much longer after that. Once the *Maid* docked, they took one of the elevators up to the walkway. They each had taken off their raincoats and carried them as they walked. Now back on solid ground, Soren lost the green tinge to his face. Kian took her hand, linking their fingers, as he walked at her side.

To start up a conversation, Jorja asked, "Where are you two from?" She glanced at Kian. "You never told me."

He chuckled. "I guess I didn't. We were too busy doing other things."

Jorja felt her cheeks warm as she shot a look over at Soren who chuckled and shook his head.

"Kian," Soren said, "I think you just embarrassed the hell out of Jorja. Just a little bit too much information, if you know what I mean. You're one of my best friends, but really, dude, I don't need to hear about your sex life."

Kian flipped Soren off, then turned his head toward her. "Sorry, I didn't mean to embarrass you. Both Soren and I live in Toronto. We came to the casino for a weekend of gambling."

Jorja nodded. If they were only here for the weekend, that meant Kian would be going back to Toronto the next day. And the check-out time at the hotel was eleven in the morning. So far the topic of what would happen between them when that time arrived hadn't come up.

"I guess you both have jobs you have to get back to," she said, not really knowing how else to respond.

Soren snorted. "No. The best way to describe Kian and me is the idle rich. We play a bit in the stock market, but other than that, we pretty much do whatever we want."

Considering both men were staying in some of the pricier rooms in the resort, and the way they'd tipped the night before, she figured they had some money. She hadn't figured on Kian being that rich, though.

"So you're kind of well to-do, huh? Then I suppose both of you live in mansions somewhere in the wealthy part of downtown Toronto."

Kian smirked. "Soren does, with his parents. I own a penthouse apartment and live on my own."

Soren scowled at Kian. "What my friend over there left out is he lived in a mansion with his parents as well up until six months ago. And his penthouse is only a short drive to his parents' place. And if I remember correctly, Kian also brings his laundry home and eats there at least twice a week."

Jorja chuckled. "Hey, if I could get someone else to do my laundry and cook me some meals, I'd be all for it."

Kian put his arm around her shoulders and pulled her close against his side. He kissed the top of her head. "Thanks for sticking up for me."

The topic of conversation changed to trivial things about the Falls as they stopped from time to time to look at them. Jorja enjoyed both men's company. She decided to push away the thought of Kian leaving the next day and enjoy what time she had left with him. If what they had started here went past the weekend, she was more than willing to give a long-distance relationship a try. And if Kian decided the weekend was enough for him, she'd let him walk out of her life. It would hurt, since she had already started to fall for him, but begging him to give her something more would only belittle her. And that was not the last impression she wanted Kian to have of her.

* * * * *

After their view of the Falls, they returned to the resort. As promised, Kian allowed Soren to drag Jorja and him to the casino. Soren went off to the blackjack table while he and Jorja went to play the slot machines. Instead of alcohol they both drank pop.

At one point the cocktail waitress, who had served them during the day yesterday, stopped to chat with Jorja. The woman, who was named Connie, seemed thrilled to see Jorja with him. Before she left, she leaned in to his mate and whispered in her ear. With his acute werewolf hearing, Kian had no problem picking up what Connie said. The woman told his mate it was about time she'd found a man, and for her to hold onto him tight, not let him slip through her fingers. Kian had to bite the inside of his cheek to stop from smiling like an idiot, especially when Jorja told Connie not to worry, that he would be a permanent fixture in her life from here on out.

As it was, he was already head over heels in love with his mate. Spending the day with her, getting to know her better, just cemented his feelings. For his kind, love at first sight was pretty much the norm. A male's mating urge wouldn't be set off if there weren't a chance of the male and female falling almost instantly in love. He had to believe Jorja felt as strongly for him as he did for her, but her being mortal, there was no guarantee.

Jorja bounced in her chair and let out a little shout of, "I won" as the slot machine she played chimed away and spit out some quarters. It wasn't much, but his mate seemed thrilled with it all the same. He smiled as he watched her scoop up her winnings and put the money in the large plastic cup she held.

He pulled out his cell phone and checked the time. "How about we go get some dinner? Then once we're done I can take you to your apartment, so you can get ready for work."

Jorja nodded. "Sure. But you know I do have my car here. I can drive myself to my place. You don't have to come with me. I don't live all that far from the resort. I'll change and be back before you know it."

"I insist on taking you," he said. Kian leaned in and brushed his lips across hers. "Let's just say I don't want to miss out on spending any time with you." He hoped she'd accept that and not push to go on her own. But to his relief, in the end, she nodded.

"Okay," she said with a chuckle. "If you insist. Where do you want to eat? And we should probably ask Soren if he wants to join us."

"Do you like Chinese? I thought of trying the buffet at the Golden Lotus here in the hotel. And sure we can ask Soren if he wants to eat with us."

"The Golden Lotus is really good. They serve real authentic Chinese food. It's one of my favorite places to eat."

"Then let's go collect Soren."

They managed to pry Soren away from the blackjack table and they had a good meal at the restaurant. Once they finished eating, Kian led Jorja outside to the hotel's parking lot while Soren went back to the gaming tables.

He led her to his red Cadillac CTS sedan and opened the front passenger door for her. He came around the back of the car and got into the driver's side.

"Nice car," Jorja said as she ran her hands over the black leather seating.

"Thanks. You'll have to give me directions to your place."

As Jorja had said, her apartment wasn't that long of a drive from the resort. She directed him to park in her empty space behind the small duplex. Kian turned off the car, expecting her to get out, only to find her making no move to open the door.

"What's the matter, Jorja?"

"I think maybe it would be better if you wait out here."

"Why?"

She swallowed. "My apartment isn't exactly as nice as what you'd be used to."

"So?"

"So maybe you'd be more comfortable waiting out in the car."

He shook his head. In way of an answer, Kian got out and came around to her side. He opened her door and held out his hand. "I'm not waiting out here for you. And I don't care what your apartment is like. As long as you're in it, that's all that matters."

Jorja placed her hand in his and allowed him to help her out. He used the remote to lock the car as they walked toward the back door of the building. He followed her up the stairs and into her apartment. Her place was small, about a third the size of his penthouse, but it was clean. Breathing in, he smelled her scent. As he'd said to Jorja, he didn't care where she lived, that this was hers made it a place he'd be more than happy to spend time in.

"Make yourself at home," she said. "It won't take me long to change."

Before she could walk away, Kian pulled Jorja into his arms and took her lips in a hungry kiss. She clung to him, kissing him back passionately. His cock throbbed, but he did nothing further than take her lips.

He pulled away from her mouth and rested his forehead on hers. "I've been dying to do that for the last couple of hours. And more. But it will have to wait until much later tonight when we're back in my hotel room."

"You want me to spend the night with you?"

"Yes." He dropped his hands to her ass and pulled her closer, so she felt his erection. "You drive me wild, Jorja. All I can think about is making love to you again." He brushed her lips once more with his and lifted his head. "Plus we need to talk."

"About what?"

"About us." She opened her mouth to speak, but he stopped her by placing a finger across her lips. "Not right now. Tonight, after I've made love to you a couple of times."

She smiled. "I'll hold you to that." Jorja stepped out of his embrace. "I'd better hurry, or I'll be late for the start of my shift."

Kian watched her walk into her bedroom. Once she was out of sight, he took a deep breath. So far Jorja hadn't balked at any of his suggestions. She'd promised to spend the night with him. He just hoped it wouldn't end with her running from him in fear.

* * * * *

Jorja returned with her empty tray and ordered more drinks for one of her tables. She placed her hand on the small of her back and groaned while she stretched. The hours on her feet weren't doing her any favors.

"Is your back sore?" Kian asked. He sat at the bar next to her.

"Yeah. It usually is on a Saturday night. This is our busiest night of the week."

He gave her a suggestive look. "Then I'll just have to rub it for you tonight."

Jorja felt a shiver of desire go through her at his words. Ever since Kian had kissed her at her apartment, she kept thinking about the night to come in his hotel room. She was a little worried about this talk he wanted to have, but she'd try to distract him as long as she could.

Soren joined them at the bar. He'd been back at the blackjack table again. From his expression, he didn't look too thrilled about something.

Kian must have seen his friend's expression as well. "What's got your undies in a bunch?"

"You mean if I actually wore some?" Soren asked.

"Now who is giving out too much information?"

"Whatever. Just take a gander over at the craps table."

Kian shifted on the barstool and looked in the direction Soren had indicated. "Fuck. What the hell is he doing here?"

Soren shrugged. "Being a royal pain in the ass? He knew this was where we were going for the weekend." Jorja noticed Soren shot a glance her way before he said, "I'd watch him, Kian. He's nothing but a jerk-off who likes to stir up shit when he can."

Jorja looked over at the craps table, but there were too many people there for her to pinpoint exactly who Kian and Soren talked about. And it was the one place she had to take her next drink orders.

She loaded up her tray with the drinks the bartender had prepared and was about to walk away when Kian stopped her with a hand on her elbow. She gave him a questioning look.

"Try to avoid the craps table, Jorja," he said.

"I can't. It's in my section."

"Then maybe I should go with you."

"Ah," Soren said, "I don't think that would be a good idea, Kian. It will just draw unwanted attention to Jorja. And it could cause questions you aren't ready to answer just yet. Let her do her job."

Kian reluctantly let go of her arm. "Fine, but I'll be watching."

Jorja left the bar, dropping off the first set of drinks before she headed to the craps table. She had no idea why Kian didn't want her near it, but she had a feeling she was missing something. It was almost as if Soren and Kian knew something she didn't. They obviously both knew this man and had a dislike for him. And since neither one of them had thought to point him out, or describe what he looked like, she had no idea which man at the table she should watch out for.

At the table, she passed out the drinks, collecting the money for each one as she went. Handing the last drink off to a man who was surprisingly as good looking as Soren and Kian, she quickly pulled her hand away as his brushed against hers. While he fished out the money to pay for his drink, she took in his short brown hair and large, muscular body. Could he be the one Kian and Soren referred to?

"Here you go," he said. "And you can keep the change."

Jorja reached for the bills he held out. He placed them on her palm and leaned closer as if trying to smell her. She took a step back, not liking how much of her personal space he invaded.

He gave her a leer and a knowing smile. "Now isn't that surprising. I never would have expected it."

"Expected what?"

The man only shook his head and returned his attention to the table. Jorja walked away, thinking he had to be the ass Kian and Soren knew. Even though what he'd said made no sense to her, she decided she wouldn't be repeating it to the other men. All she needed was for them to butt heads with the jerk over something stupid.

After she arrived at the bar, Kian asked, "What did the jackass say to you?"

"Nothing really. I can see why you don't like him. There's just something about him that rubs the wrong way. At least he's a good tipper."

A half hour went by, and Kian finally seemed to relax a bit, even though he kept glancing over at the craps table from time to time. Soren had opted to stay at the bar as well. She'd just returned from serving another table when a deep voice sounded behind her.

"Well, if it isn't Kian and Soren."

The two men turned on the barstools they sat on to face the newcomer, but it was Kian who talked. "Well, if it isn't Brad—ley."

The other man stiffened and snarled his lip before he said, "Brad. Not Bradley. Just Brad."

Obviously, it was a sore spot for Brad when someone called him Bradley. And from Kian's smirk, he had to know that as well.

"All right then, *Brad*. What do you want?"

Brad quickly lost his irritated look. "I saw you two and thought I'd see if you'd want to join me in a poker game. But I see, Kian, you have other things going on." He glanced at her suggestively. "And I must say I'm not surprised you'd follow in Atticus' footsteps."

"Shut the fuck up," Kian almost growled.

"Oh come on, Kian. I guess congratulations are in order. And as I said, I'm not surprised you have a mortal mate just as Atticus does. I bet Soren will find his very soon as well, since the three of you are so close." Brad looked at her. "So how do you like being mated to a werewolf, mortal?"

Jorja blinked at him as Kian growled and snapped his teeth in his direction. "What are you talking about? I'm not mated, as you put it, and I'd have to be an idiot to believe werewolves existed. And mortal?"

Brad threw back his head and laughed, drawing some stares in the casino. "Oh, Kian. You claimed your mate without telling her you have a furry side. And I know you did claim her. Your scent is too deeply ingrained in her skin for that not to be the case."

Kian let loose with a low growl and appeared about ready to launch himself at Brad. Only Soren's hand on his shoulder held him in place. The way Kian reacted, with the animal-like growls and snarling of his lip, Jorja heard the word werewolf repeating inside her head. No way. Brad was just being a jerk. She wasn't so naïve as to believe his nonsense about Kian being a werewolf.

"Get lost, Brad," Soren snapped. "Push Kian any more and I won't stop him from trying to rip your jugular out. Once again you've just proved what an asshole you really are."

With an amused chuckle, Brad backed away. But before he left, he said to her, "Welcome to the pack, little mortal."

Kian let out another animalistic growl. Jorja turned in his direction and saw Soren slip off his barstool to stand in front of his friend. Much to her shock, Kian's eyes were mutedly glowing. This time she couldn't say it was hers playing tricks on her when she blinked and they remained the same way.

"Get a grip on yourself, Kian," Soren said. "Your eyes are giving you away. Rein the wolf back."

Jorja swallowed. Soren really believed Kian was a werewolf?

Chapter Six

Kian closed his eyes and took deep breaths to calm himself. He should have known Brad would do something like this. The prick loved to get digs in with him, Soren and Atticus whenever he possibly could. Kian could kick himself for ever letting Jorja serve the bastard. Of course Brad would have been able to tell from her scent she was a claimed mate, and who had been the male to claim her. But he wouldn't have known Jorja knew nothing about their kind.

"Can somebody tell me what is going on, and what Brad meant?" He heard the strain in Jorja's voice.

Kian opened his eyes to find Soren giving him a look of sympathy before he said quietly, "Sorry, my man, it looks as if you're going to have to have that chat with Jorja sooner than you would have liked."

Soren stepped away and Kian saw his mate looking between the two of them as if they had both lost their minds. He got off the barstool and stood in front of her. "I'll explain everything."

"What was with your eyes?" she whispered.

"Not here," he said. "Up in my room. Right now."

She shook her head. "I can't. My shift isn't over."

"Tell them you suddenly don't feel well. I need to talk to you now before Brad comes back and decides to cause more crap between us."

Jorja searched his gaze, then nodded. "Okay, but I'm going to lose out on a lot of tips. And since money is kind of tight, it'll hurt."

"Forget about the damn money," he said, a little shorter than he'd wanted. "Sorry. I didn't mean to snap. I just want to get you out of here."

She seemed to hesitate before she went off to tell whoever she needed to that she was leaving. Kian spotted her talking to a man at a door that led to an employee-only section of the casino. He rubbed a hand over his face, dreading what was to come next.

"Do you want me to stay with you when you tell Jorja?" Soren asked.

"Actually, yeah, I do. Maybe if the two of us explain it we can get her to accept it easier."

"Hopefully that shithead Brad didn't fuck things up too much."

Jorja returned, carrying her purse. "My supervisor let me go, since I've never left early like this before, so he believed me when I said I wasn't feeling well. If I don't want him to think I lied, I need to get out of sight before he comes back into the casino."

All three of them hurried over to the bank of elevators and were soon on their way up to their floor. At Kian's door, he used his keycard to open it and pushed it open for Jorja to step in first. He followed with Soren bringing up the rear.

Jorja only waited until the door shut behind them before she asked, "Why did your eyes glow like that? And don't tell me it's because you're a werewolf. That's utter bullshit."

Kian looked at Soren before he turned back to Jorja. Yup, this was not going to be easy. "Take a seat, Jorja, then Soren and I will do our best to explain."

She sat on the leather couch in the conversation area and looked up at them, waiting. Kian paced back and forth in front of her as he tried to get the words straight in his mind. He thought it best just to stick with the straight facts.

"Okay," he said. "The reason why my eyes glowed was because I was pissed off at Brad."

"Because of the things he said?"

"Yes."

"So he pissed you off when he said I was your mate and that you were a werewolf? Please tell me it made you mad because he fed me a line of crap."

Kian stared at her, wishing this part was over and done with. "Yes, I was pissed with what he told you. Jorja, what he said was the truth. He made me angry because I hadn't had the chance to tell you those things myself."

"In other words, you believe you're a werewolf and I'm your mate? You can't expect me to accept that as the truth. I don't know what world you live in, but in mine they don't exist."

Kian sighed. "In my world they do. My kind keep what we truly are well hidden from the mortals around us."

"Do you know how crazy you sound? No one in their right mind would believe it."

He squatted in front of Jorja and took her hands in his. They were cold to the touch. "I know this is hard for you to accept. But you have to. You *are* my mate. I claimed you the first time we made love. Now that the mating bond is in place, we need to stay together. If we don't we'll go through separation anxiety. You've already felt what it's like."

"Last night, when I thought I would lose my mind if I didn't come back to you?"

"Yes. It's worse in the beginning of a mating. After a year or so, mates can stand to be apart a lot longer without suffering from it."

Jorja held his gaze and he saw in her eyes that she didn't want to believe what he'd told her.

"I'm trying here, I really am," she said. "I'll admit I felt this separation anxiety, but the rest, I don't know, Kian. It's all so farfetched. And why did Brad keep referring to me as a mortal?"

Kian squeezed her hands. "Because to us, to werewolves, you are. We're not exactly immortal, but are extremely long-lived compared to your kind. We can live to be up to three thousand years old. I've already seen nine hundred years, the same with Soren."

Jorja's gaze shot to Soren. "You're a werewolf too?"

His friend nodded. "Yes, and so was that asshole Brad. We're all from the same pack."

Jorja's gaze landed back on him. "This just seems to get weirder and weirder. Let me get this straight. I'm supposed to believe you're a werewolf who is nine hundred years old, who could live to be three thousand and I'm mated to you, for life?"

Kian nodded. "Yes, it's for life."

"Whose lifetime? Yours or mine? Because if you live as long as you say, I won't be around for even half of it."

"Our friend, Atticus, has a mortal mate as well. He's decided to have the same lifespan as her. Just as I'll choose yours." He gazed into her eyes. "I love you, Jorja. Where you go, I go."

Jorja surged to her feet, almost knocking Kian on his butt as she brushed past him to stand a little way away from him and Soren. "Too much, too much, too much. And here I had been worried about you leaving tomorrow and not wanting anything more to do with me," she said shrilly.

Kian rose to his feet. "I know this is a lot, but there is no going back. We're mates. There is no breaking the mating bond."

"So basically we're married. Is that what you're telling me?"

"That would be the mortal way of describing it, I guess. Only there is no divorce."

"And you said this mating bond formed the first time we made love. You knew it would happen yet you did it anyway, taking my choice away from me."

Kian groaned inside. Now he'd have to tell Jorja he fucked up. "I was drunk. I wasn't thinking straight. I just acted on instinct."

"So in other words, I was a mistake."

"No, never. Jorja, if you weren't the one meant for me, my mating urge wouldn't have been set off the instant I saw you. Being drunk, I sort of lost control of my wolf side and acted on what instinct demanded I do. I'm sorry I took your choice away, but I don't regret doing it." He tried to take a step toward her, but Jorja backed up. He stopped in place.

"Soren referred to your wolf downstairs, now you have. I'm going to be blunt here. You really don't look any different than me. And I haven't seen any evidence of you going 'wolf'. Other than your eyes glowing, that is."

She still didn't really believe he was a werewolf. There was only one way to give her the irrefutable proof she so obviously needed. He shifted. He held out his hand and saw it shimmer and blur as he took on his wolf form. Jorja's eyes widened, her breathing growing ever more rapid. Once he was completely wolf, he looked up at her and held his paw out. Still she didn't move. Hoping he could get her to touch him, to show her he was not a figment of her imagination, Kian took a step toward her.

Jorja's eyes rolled back inside her head and she collapsed.

Able to move much faster than any mortal, Soren was there to catch her before she hit the floor. His friend looked at him and shook his head. "I don't think that was a smart move on your part, shifting without giving Jorja any warning."

Kian shifted back to his human form, willing his clothes on at the same time. He gently took Jorja from Soren and held her close to his chest with her head resting on his shoulder. "I didn't know what else to do to get her to believe."

"I think I've helped out here as much as I can. I'm going to my room. At least you got the hard part over with."

Kian watched Soren leave the room before he went to the bed and placed Jorja on it. She was still out cold. All he could do was wait until she woke up.

* * * * *

Jorja opened her eyes to find herself lying on the bed in Kian's hotel room. Everything he'd said, what she'd seen him do — actually shift into a wolf — all came rushing back. She sat up and scanned the room, finding Kian nowhere in sight. Then she heard the sound of the toilet flush. Her gaze landed on the bathroom door as he opened it and stepped into the room. His steps faltered a bit when he saw she was awake.

He slowly crossed to the bed. "Are you okay with what I am, Jorja?"

"I don't know."

And honestly she didn't. She'd gone from thinking he and Soren were a couple of loons to having the truth practically shoved down her throat when Kian had taken on his wolf form. All he'd told her had to be the truth. He was a werewolf and she was his mate, bonded to him for the rest of her life. She needed to think everything through, order her thoughts. And she couldn't do that very well with Kian nearby.

She slid off the bed, making sure she kept some distance between them. "I have to be alone. Please don't stop me from leaving."

Kian gave her a pained look. "If you leave, we'll both suffer for it."

"I don't care," she snapped. Jorja took a deep breath to calm herself. She felt on the verge of hyperventilating again. One fainting spell was enough for her. "If you don't let me go I'll never come to grips with this all. I need some time away from you to get this all straight in my head."

He sighed and stepped to the side. "Fine. Go. The only thing I ask is that you don't let the separation anxiety get too bad. It will defeat the purpose of you wanting to be alone. It will play tricks on your mind. You'll think something bad has happened to me, making you desperate to return. Remember what it was like when you saw me again the last time. I can guarantee that will be the end result."

Sex. That's what Kian meant. They'd end up having hot, desperate sex like they had in the early hours of the morning. Which meant when she returned, she'd better know exactly how she felt about him, and be willing to accept the new life they would have together.

Jorja gave a short nod and walked past Kian. She didn't look back as she opened the door and stepped into the hallway. With no idea where she'd go, but just knowing she had to get out of the resort, she took the elevator down to the lobby. A minute later, she was outside breathing in the night air.

Fishing her keys out of her purse, she headed for the parking lot. She'd go for a short drive and come back. Surely she could handle that much. She got in her car and drove away from the resort.

Already she felt as if she missed Kian. She pulled everything she'd learned to the forefront of her mind and quickly sorted through it. Kian was a werewolf. Could she accept that? More than likely, yes. Not once had she felt threatened by him. Obviously, his type of werewolf wasn't the snarling, bloodthirsty beast movies portrayed them as. She would just need time to get used to him in his wolf form. By nature, she adapted to change easier than some people.

Then there was the issue of them being mates. Were her feelings for Kian strong enough for her to spend the rest of her life with him, even though they'd just recently met? Only earlier today she'd admitted to herself she'd fallen for him. Now that she knew he loved her, was happy to have her as his mate, her feelings for him were a bit stronger. The only thing holding her back from actually saying she loved him was how fast everything had happened. In a normal relationship, it could take months, if not years, to reach that stage in a long-term commitment. Hers and Kian's had formed the first night they'd met.

She'd been gone fifteen minutes and the need to return to Kian was more than noticeable. As he'd told her, she felt as if something terrible had happened to him. She did her best to ignore it. She wasn't ready to go back just yet.

Jorja pulled up the last thing she needed to make a decision on. If she did love him, could she give up her life in Niagara Falls? There was no question Kian would want to return to Toronto. And to be honest, why would he want to stay here? It wasn't as if she had much in her life to offer him. He was the one with the wealth and family. She was all alone, had been for a long time. After her parents had died in a car crash when she'd been fifteen, and no relatives had surfaced to claim her, she'd been placed in the foster care system. Once she'd reached adulthood, she'd left to strike out on her own, and hadn't looked back since.

The need to be with Kian increased even more. She thought of the way he'd been with her today. She'd felt protected, cared for. And when she'd caught him staring at her, she'd seen the love he'd professed lurking in his eyes. Then she'd thought maybe it had been wishful thinking on her part. Now she knew those emotions had been real. No man had looked at her like that before.

Jorja roughly wiped a tear out of her eye as she thought about all Kian offered her. She had a gorgeous man who would never leave her, would never cheat on her, would always be there for her. She'd have a real family again, something she'd missed. And she'd never have to worry about money again. Did she love him? As sudden as it was, she thought she did.

Having finally sorted out her feelings, and made the decision to not make Kian suffer anymore, Jorja turned the car around and headed back to the resort. And back to her man. She would jump into her new life with both feet and hit the ground running.

By the time she arrived at the resort, she desperately wanted to feel Kian's arms around her, holding her tight. There were going to be some adjustments for both of them, but the main thing was they loved each other. They could work out the rest as they went.

It seemed to take forever for the elevator to arrive, and for it to reach Kian's floor. With no keycard to get in, she knocked on his door. He opened it, his gaze seeming to eat her up where she stood.

She looked into his eyes and said, "I want you. All of you."

With a groan, Kian wrapped his arms around her and pulled her into the room. As his lips took hers, kissing her as if he were a starved man and only she could save him, he let the door close behind them. Jorja kissed him back, the tears that had threatened finally falling.

Kian pulled back and wiped them away with his thumbs. "Don't cry, Jorja."

She gave him a watery smile. "I'm fine. It's just I love you. I haven't had someone in my life who has loved me in return for a very long time. Right now, you're all the family I have."

He kissed her again. "I'm never going to leave you, Jorja. Ever. I've waited a long time for you, my mate. The love I have for you will always be." He picked her up and carried her to the bed. "Now I intend to make love to you until neither one of us can move."

Jorja surrendered herself to her werewolf mate's arms, knowing she couldn't ask for a better start to her new life with him.

The End

WEREWOLF'S TREASURE
ಐ

Chapter One

Soren parked his black luxury sports car in the visitor's parking and got out. He looked way up at the condo high-rise before him. He'd come to see a furnished penthouse apartment that was for sale. He'd already been in contact with the real estate agent who had the listing and booked an appointment to view it. The condo was situated in Toronto's Harbourfront area, close to the Toronto Harbour and Lake Ontario.

At nine hundred years old, Soren figured it was about time he moved out of his parents' mansion. Plus it didn't help that one of his best friends, Kian, took every opportunity he could get to rib him about it. Yes, Kian had left his family's home first, and was now mated to Jorja, but that didn't give him the right to ride Soren's ass just for the fun of it. For werewolf kind, the age of nine hundred was young in their years, since they could live to be three thousand.

Soren strolled toward the front of the building and looked around. So far he liked what he saw. There was some greenery in the way of potted plants running along the walkway. The agent was supposed to meet him just inside the entrance. Her name was Treasure. He'd wondered what it had been like for her growing up with a name like that. She'd sounded young over the phone, but for all he knew she could be someone's grandma.

Reaching the heavy glass doors, he pulled one open and stepped into the vestibule. On the other side of the locked glass door a woman stood with her back toward him. If this was Treasure, she definitely wasn't anybody's grandmother. He ran his gaze down her. She wore a dark-blue, short-sleeved dress that hugged her curved-in waist and rounded bottom to perfection. The hem of it ended just past the middle of her thighs, giving him an excellent view of her long, toned legs. She wore strappy high heels that matched the color of her dress. Lifting his gaze again, Soren followed the waves of copper-blonde hair that fell to the middle of her back.

He stepped closer to the inner door and rapped on the glass to draw the woman's attention. She turned and smiled when she saw him standing there. Soren found the front view just as appealing as the back. Flashing, dark-green eyes were set in a face that was more than pretty for a mortal. His kind all had supermodel good looks, even the males.

She crossed the short distance to the door and opened it, stepping aside for him to walk through. As the air stirred between them, Soren got his first whiff of her scent. It slammed into him, almost causing him to trip over his feet as his body went haywire. His cock was instantly rock hard, straining against the front of his black jeans. He had to fight back a growl of need that threatened to break loose. His mating urge dug its claws deep into him and didn't let go.

Oblivious to what surged through him, she continued to smile and held out her hand in his direction. "Hi, I'm Treasure. You must be Soren."

Oh, she was treasure all right. His treasure, his mate. He breathed in more of her enticing scent and swallowed as he tried to keep himself from pulling her to him and devouring her mouth.

He nodded and took her hand. "Yes, I'm Soren. It's really nice to meet you, Treasure." His voice had a huskiness to it caused by the demanding need pulsing through his body.

"Shall we go look at the penthouse?"

At his nod, Treasure turned and led him to the bank of elevators. Soren's gaze locked on her, unable to look away. She was his. *His. His.* That word seemed to echo inside him with each rapid beat of his heart. He reined those thoughts back. If he wasn't careful, his control would slip and his eyes would mutedly glow, showing just how much she turned him on.

Since she was a mortal, it would more than likely have Treasure running from him. And he definitely didn't want that.

The elevator arrived and they stepped inside. The doors swished closed and Soren wondered how he was going to stand being in such a close space with Treasure and not act on what his mating urge pushed him to do. Her scent intensified, filling his head until it swam and he'd become intoxicated.

Treasure pushed the button for the very top floor and the elevator rose. "I think you'll like the penthouse," she said. "It's fully furnished, so it's move-in ready. The maintenance fees are seven hundred and fifty-one dollars, which includes the HST."

Soren forced himself to focus on what Treasure said, not on the way her kissable lips moved as she spoke. It took him a second to remember what HST meant—harmonized sales tax. It had only been a year since it had replaced the GST—goods and service tax. Now instead of the government getting fifteen percent from the sale of all goods and services, the HST allowed them to get thirteen percent from almost every purchase. He didn't know which one was really better. They both sucked.

He cleared his throat. "Ah, what is the closing date?"

"Thirty days from today, but it's negotiable. The present owners aren't living here and want to sell it as soon as they can. They've already moved into their new home. It was a job transfer to another province."

"I see," Soren said.

He sounded inane, but that was about all his poor brain could manage with all the blood in his body pooling to his cock. The elevator doors slid open and Treasure stepped out into the hallway. Still oblivious to what happened to him, she crossed to a door and unlocked it. If she'd been a werewolf like him, she'd have scented his arousal by now. She'd also know what she meant to him. Female werewolves didn't experience the mating urge, but they had the ability to sense it, especially when the male meant for them was in the throes of it.

Treasure stopped just inside the entranceway. Soren couldn't resist invading her personal space and taking a quick sniff of her hair. It smelled of the flowery shampoo she used. He took a step back when she spun around to face him with a leery look on her face. She shifted away a little, and Soren silently cursed himself. He didn't need her thinking he was some kind of sicko or something.

Hoping to lay her mind to rest, he stepped around her and headed farther into the penthouse. The living room was spacious with a bank of floor-to-ceiling windows at the far end. On the other side of the glass was a balcony. To collect himself a bit better before he faced Treasure again, Soren walked over to the windows and looked out. There was an excellent view of the ships docked at the marina in the harbor. Beyond that was the large expanse of Lake Ontario.

Soren took a deep breath and turned to Treasure. "I like what I'm seeing so far."

"Good." She smiled. "There are eight rooms in total — living room, dining room, kitchen, three bedrooms and two full baths. The square footage is almost twenty-five hundred."

He looked at the black leather couches, armchairs and the rest of the heavy, dark wood furnishings. He also noted the large fifty-five-inch LCD television hanging on a wall across from one of the couches. "And the asking price is five hundred and forty thousand?"

"Correct. Shall we look at the other rooms?"

Soren nodded, then followed Treasure into the dining room, which only had an archway separating it from the living room. It had a nice large oak dining table with six high-backed matching chairs. A china cabinet sat along one of the walls, also matching the design of the rest of the furniture. A modern-looking chandelier hung from the ceiling over the center of the table. Like the living room, there was light-colored hardwood flooring.

Next they went to the kitchen, which was off the dining room. Since Soren really couldn't cook worth a shit, he gave it a cursory glance, noting the granite countertops and stainless-steel fridge, stove and dishwasher.

Treasure kept up a commentary, giving sizes of rooms and whatnot as she took Soren from room to room. One time she stopped short and he ended up almost ramming into the back of her. As it was, her bottom brushed against the erection that had yet to go down. He quickly pulled away before she noticed the condition he was in, even though that slight contact had made his cock jerk and a surge of pleasure shoot through him.

At the large master bedroom, the sight of the king-sized bed had thoughts of what he wanted to do to Treasure on it flitting through Soren's head. He'd slowly peel off the dress she wore while he kissed and licked every inch of her skin. He'd strip her out of her bra and panties, equally slow, making sure to lavish attention on her breasts before he tasted her pussy. Then he'd use his mouth to pleasure her until she came, crying out his name.

Soren's cock throbbed painfully as he let his imagination run away with him. The sound of Treasure saying his name brought him quickly back to the here and now. He focused his gaze on her and found hers locked on the crotch of his jeans. He didn't have to look down to know there would be no missing the large bulge there. He wasn't exactly a small man in that area of his person. It was too late to try to hide it, so he stood there and let Treasure check him out.

He took a deep breath and fisted his hands at his sides when he picked out the sweet scent of Treasure's arousal. It caused his cock to jerk again, which had her gaze snapping up to meet his. A small sound like a gasp slipped past her lips, and Soren knew his eyes had to be glowing mutedly. He hurriedly turned his back on her and headed for the en suite bathroom.

Soren really didn't see anything, but used the time it took for Treasure to join him to wrench himself back under control. A quick look in the mirror above the sink showed his eyes were back to normal.

He faced her once again and found her staring at him with stark interest. Her professional mien had definitely slipped. Treasure licked her lips, and Soren bit back a growl of need that threatened to rumble out of him. He wanted to taste those lips, feel them closing around his cock while she sucked him into her mouth.

Feeling a bit overcome by the mating urge again, Soren stepped closer to Treasure, backing her up against the counter. The sound of her heart beating faster thundered in his ears, and the scent of her arousal growing stronger made him ache even more. He put his hands on the hard surface on either side of her hips as he leaned in slightly and breathed in more of her heady scent.

"I'll take y...it," he said huskily. He'd almost said he'd take her instead of the penthouse.

"You will?" she asked, her voice soft and breathy.

"Yes." Soren shifted even closer. "Are you free for dinner tonight?"

Treasure looked into Soren's light-brown eyes and felt herself drowning in them. He stood so close all it would take to feel his lips on hers was for her to let herself lean in ever so slightly. The urge was almost too much to resist.

She was also horny as hell. First seeing Soren in the vestibule downstairs, she'd found him more than attractive. He had the good looks any male supermodel would possess. With his short, blond hair, chiseled features, well-muscled body and standing at least six-foot-five, he had everything she was drawn to in a man. And being enclosed in the elevator car with him, she'd found it hard to keep her attraction from showing.

As she took Soren on the tour of the penthouse, Treasure had a harder time keeping her professional face, as she liked to call it—the look that put a prospective client at ease and had them believing she knew what she talked about, hopefully leading them to purchase a property through her. With Soren, though, she had to work at it when it usually came so easily. She found herself getting distracted by him time and time again. Not that he seemed to have noticed.

But it wasn't until they'd come to the master bedroom and she'd spotted the large erection he had going on in his jeans did she lose it all together. Her gaze had become frozen to that spot between his legs as she pictured what his cock would look like, and how it would feel sliding deep inside her pussy. Her nipples had grown taut and wetness pooled in her core as an ache pounded there.

Then his cock had noticeably jerked and she'd looked up to find she'd been caught staring. Looking into Soren's eyes, Treasure had swallowed at the hunger and arousal she'd seen in their depths, which turned her on even more. And for a split second before he'd walked into the en suite, she thought she saw his eyes glow, though that had to be her imagination.

Now, caged in by Soren's large, muscular body, Treasure felt the ache between her legs intensify. Her brain seemed to misfire and it took her a few seconds to sort out that he'd said he would take the penthouse, and almost on the same breath, asked her out for dinner.

"Dinner?" she asked stupidly.

A sexy grin formed on his lips, heating her body even more. "Yes, dinner. As in I take you out for a good meal, then we see how things go from there."

Treasure knew how she wanted the rest of the evening to go, but the big question was should she go out with Soren? She was without a doubt attracted to him, and he seemed to be interested in her as well, but he was going to be a client, since he wanted the penthouse. She had a personal rule where she didn't date any client of hers—ever. As a real estate agent, she counted on having the people she sold properties to come back if they decided to sell. If she were to date one and then have the relationship fall through, that was one less commission check for her. Treasure had to decide whether a date with Soren would be worth it to break that longstanding rule.

Looking into his handsome face, seeing his eyes heavy-lidded with desire, she wavered.

"I don't know," she said.

"It's not that hard of a question," Soren responded. "Just a simple yes or no will suffice, though I would strongly urge you to say yes."

He definitely wasn't making this easy on her. He leaned over a bit more, causing her to bend slightly back. His lips came nearer to hers, and her gaze became locked on them. She drew in a shaky breath. Soren smelled of the cologne he wore and a scent that was all male. Her pussy clenched and wetness leaked into her thong. She was on the brink of throwing herself into his arms and begging him to take her right there and then. And wouldn't that be professional?

Needing some space between them, so she'd be able to think straight once again, Treasure pushed Soren away, walked out of the bathroom and into the bedroom. The bed seemed to loom before her, giving her wicked thoughts.

She jumped when Soren trailed a finger down the back of her arm. She hadn't even heard him come up behind her. Treasure turned to face him. She knew he waited for an answer, but she wasn't ready to give him one just yet. There was business to finish first.

"If you really want the penthouse," she said, "then we can go to my office and fill out the paperwork to place an offer."

He shook his head and chuckled. "Shouldn't we settle the first offer before we start on the second?"

"No. Business first, then pleasure."

"You could at least give me a hint as to what your answer will be for dinner."

Soren's gaze swept the entire length of her body, causing goose bumps to break out all over her skin. Looking into his eyes, seeing the tamped-down hunger simmering just below the surface, Treasure knew she wouldn't be strong enough to resist him for very long.

She licked her dry lips and Soren's gaze followed the movement. "The best I can do is tell you maybe," she said.

"Do you always put business before pleasure?" he asked huskily.

"Always. I wouldn't be as good a real estate agent as I am if I didn't."

It was true. Treasure always made sure all her work was done before she took time to enjoy other things. And since she was an agent, the business part tended to take up more time than the pleasure. Her being on call if someone wanted to see a listing, along with having open houses on the weekends, didn't give her a lot of free time. The amount of hours a week she put into her job had pissed off more than a few boyfriends until they eventually wanted out of the relationship. Not that Treasure had minded. She hadn't met a man yet who she'd give up her career for. She worked hard at what she did—and was damn good at it—so she wouldn't just up and leave it.

"I guess I can't fault you for wanting to be a success," Soren said with a smile. "How about this? Since you are such a career-minded woman, what if I were to make an offer on the penthouse, for the full asking price with the condition I get possession by the end of the week. And…" He let his words trail off and shifted to stand toe-to-toe with her. "And you say you'll go out with me."

"What if I say no?"

"Then I might have to rethink the whole offer thing."

Treasure gnawed on her bottom lip. It was as if Soren knew exactly what button to push to get her to agree. She didn't want to lose the offer. With him willing to pay the full asking price, she stood to earn a hefty commission.

She looked at Soren, already knowing what her answer would be. And it wasn't just because of what she stood to lose money-wise. She really didn't want to turn down an evening with the man in front of her. The ones who looked like him didn't come around too often. Plus she hadn't been out on a date in some time. Now that she thought about it, it had to have been at least nine months since she'd been on her last one.

With a nod, she said, "You drive a hard bargain, but it's a deal. We'll go to my office now and start the offer. After I present it to my other client, you can take me to dinner." Treasure stuck out her hand to seal the deal, but Soren didn't take it.

He shook his head. "A handshake isn't going to cut it this time."

Soren captured her lips with his. Treasure didn't do anything to stop him. A surge of arousal shot through her as he slanted his mouth more firmly over hers, sweeping his tongue along the seam of her lips. She opened and he took the unspoken invitation to take the kiss deeper.

Treasure found her hands coming up to rest on Soren's hard chest as he snaked his arms around her waist, holding her against him. She kissed him back, her tongue twining with his, learning the taste of him. His erection pressed along her stomach, making her ache to feel it more intimately.

With a deep groan, Soren ended their kiss. She opened her eyes to find his closed as he breathed heavily. After a few seconds, he lifted his eyelids and looked at her.

"Let's do that offer before I forget where I am and get ahead of myself," he said in a gruff voice.

She nodded, feeling quite breathless. Turning, Treasure didn't wait to see if Soren followed her as she led the way to the penthouse door. If that kiss were any indication of what was in store for her this evening, breaking her rule would be well worth it indeed.

Chapter Two

Soren walked Treasure to her car out in the parking lot at the front of the building. Hers was just about as expensive as his own sports model.

"I'll follow you," he said once she unlocked the driver's door.

"Okay. It's not too far from here. And there is parking nearby."

He hurried over to his own car and got in. He had the engine started by the time Treasure drove past on her way to the parking lot exit. Soren pulled in behind her.

As he followed her out onto the street, he thought about all that Treasure meant to him over and over in his head. A mate, he'd actually found his mate. His friends, Atticus and Kian, had recently found theirs. Soren hadn't expected to find the woman meant for him quite so soon. He'd known it would happen eventually, but it still had taken him by surprise.

Now that he had found Treasure, there was no way he'd let her go. He'd claim her as his mate, but it was just a question of how long he could fight the mating urge. Her being mortal would add extra strain, since he'd have to be careful he didn't give away what he was until he'd told her. And telling her he was a werewolf wasn't something he particularly relished. She'd be the first mortal he told. Even though his pack had lived in Toronto among mortals for years, they'd kept what they were from them.

Soren licked his lips and caught the taste of Treasure that still lingered there. It was just as heady as her scent. Kissing her had left him desperate and wanting. He didn't think he'd ever get enough of her. His cock throbbed painfully in response to his thoughts. He wouldn't be getting much relief any time soon. He couldn't fully make love to her yet. If he were to do so it would have their souls joining, bonding them to the point they wouldn't be able to stand to be apart from each other. They'd go through separation anxiety with their minds playing tricks on them. They'd think something bad had happened to the other, and an hour apart would feel like a month. No, he couldn't bond with Treasure until she knew exactly what she'd gotten herself into. It wouldn't be fair to her.

That only left heavy petting and oral sex, which he hoped to hell he'd get some of before the night was over. It wouldn't do him any favors, since penetration was the only thing that would ease his mating urge, and anything else would just make it worse. But Soren was willing to pay that price. He wanted to make Treasure come with his fingers, his mouth, any way he could, while she called his name in passion.

Noticing they were near Treasure's office, since she'd given him the address before leaving the penthouse, Soren pushed all the carnal thoughts out of his head. It wouldn't do to walk into where she worked with a massive erection. Her coworkers would think he was some kind of pervert. It would be bad enough he'd have to walk around semi-aroused most of the time until he claimed Treasure as his, anyway.

He followed behind Treasure's car as she pulled into the Green P municipal parking. They managed to find two parking spots side by side. Soren turned off his car and got out. He waited as Treasure collected the briefcase on her passenger seat before she joined him.

After pushing the remote to lock her car, she walked with him toward the stairs that would take them to street level. "It's not too far of a walk from here," she said with a smile.

It could have been a ten-mile hike that he had to make barefoot in blistering sun and Soren still would have gone with her. "Lead on."

Once out on the sidewalk, Treasure turned left. Soren kept pace with her by shortening his strides. She had long legs, but being a foot shorter than him, his were longer. He would have taken her hand until they reached her office building, except for the fact she carried her briefcase with it. He could have shifted to her other side to hold her free one, but he didn't want to come across as too needy. She really didn't know him yet, after all.

Inside the corporate building, it was another agonizing ride in an elevator up a couple of floors to where the offices for the real estate company were located. Soren didn't know how many more of those rides he'd be able to take with her before he lost all his senses and took her against the elevator's wall.

Soren followed Treasure past the front desk and down a long stretch of carpet that had offices lining either side of it. There weren't many, since this real estate company wasn't one of the larger, well-known ones. It only had high-end listings that the average middle-class person couldn't afford. He'd gotten that much from their website once he'd found the listing for the penthouse on the MLS website.

After stopping halfway down the row, Treasure unlocked her office door and pushed it open. She walked around the desk and placed her briefcase on top of it. She pulled out the chair and motioned for him to take one of the ones on the other side. Once he sat, she took out some papers from a desk drawer.

"So you still want to offer the full asking price and have a closing date for the end of this week?" she asked, all professional-like.

The woman who had passionately kissed him back at the penthouse was no longer there. In her place was one totally focused on the business at hand. Soren had no idea how Treasure did it. Just being near her had his blood heating.

"Yes," he said. "My lawyer who will handle the closing can get it done by that time. I haven't changed my mind.

Unless you've changed yours about going out to dinner with me?"

Treasure looked up from the papers in front of her, and for a split second, Soren saw a flash of desire in her dark-green eyes. Maybe she hadn't been able to completely shut off the desire she felt. He must have gotten to her. Bad. Her scent had said so.

Her gaze flicked to his mouth before she met his. "No, I haven't. I'll finish filling out the offer, you can sign it and then I'll call the owners about faxing it to them."

Soren nodded, then watched as Treasure bent her head and concentrated on the papers on the desk. He couldn't help tracing her features with his gaze as she worked. At her lips, he remembered the feel of them moving under his. He wanted, no needed, to taste them again. Preferably in a place where he could explore the rest of her body.

Treasure took another pen from her desk drawer, then placed it in front of him as she turned the papers his way. He forced his gaze off her mouth and looked down at them. He gave it a cursory look before he signed and initialed where she indicated. That done, she took them back and added her own signature.

"Now to call the owners," she said.

Soren sat back in the chair and watched her make the phone call. He listened as she spoke to the person on the other end. The conversation wasn't very long.

She hung up and stood, taking the papers with her. "I'll just be a few minutes while I go fax these."

He nodded and she left the office. Alone, Soren looked around. With Treasure in the room, he hadn't done much of that earlier. He'd been more interested in looking at her. The desk was a heavy piece of furniture found in any corporate office. She had a small file cabinet in the back corner. A desktop computer sat on one side of the desk. On the other, Soren noticed a framed picture. He leaned forward and picked it up to turn it his way. It was a picture of Treasure with an older couple, probably her parents. They stood on a dock on a lake. The picture could have been taken up north in Muskoka. He wondered if her family had a cottage up there.

Personally, he loved going to Muskoka to spend some weekends out of the summer at his parents' lake house. He'd go wolf and take a run through the bush without having to worry about any mortals seeing him, since the nearest neighbor was over a mile away. Soren put the picture back.

A minute or so later, Treasure returned. She sat behind her desk before she spoke. "We shouldn't have too long of a wait to get an answer on your offer."

Soren sat on the edge of the chair and reached across the desk to take Treasure's hand. "Good. While we wait, we can decide where we're going to eat."

"I thought maybe we could go to a place on the Harbourfront, since it's close by. Maybe seafood or steak."

"Or both," Soren said. "Why don't we go to that steak house restaurant? They serve seafood as well."

"Okay."

Silence fell between them. Soren stared at Treasure, wanting nothing more than to pull her on top of her desk and pick up where their earlier kiss had left off. The way she looked back at him, he didn't think she'd refuse. He stroked the top of her hand with his thumb, caressing back and forth. Treasure breathed a little faster. Using their joined hands, he pulled her toward him as he slowly leaned farther over the desk.

Just before their lips had a chance to meet, the phone sitting next to the computer rang, causing them both to sit back in their chairs. Treasure let go of his hand and answered it.

Once she hung up, she said, "The owners have faxed the offer back. I'll just go get it."

Treasure left and Soren took a deep breath. His mating urge rode him hard, and it would only get worse the longer he held off claiming her as his mate. She returned and sat once more. The smile she gave him had to mean the fax was good news.

"They accepted my offer?" he asked.

She nodded. "Yes. The penthouse is yours. I just need you to pay the down payment and you'll be well on your way to owning it."

Soren fished his wallet out of his jeans back pocket and took out the blank check he'd put there before going to see the property. Treasure told him who to make it out to and then he passed it over once he signed it.

After giving it a final look, Treasure slipped the check into the file folder where she'd put the accepted offer. She held out her hand. "Congratulations, Soren. You're now the almost proud owner of a penthouse."

He wrapped his hand around hers and shook it. Before he released it, he brought her fingers to his mouth and kissed each one. Treasure's breath quickened. "Thanks. Now we can go celebrate."

Gaining his feet, he gathered his copy of the offer together and picked up the sheets of paper. He then waited for Treasure to come around her desk and join him with briefcase in hand. He let her lead as they walked out of her office and past the reception area, through the double doors and to the bank of elevators.

They stepped into the car when it arrived, and Soren prepared for another assault of Treasure's scent to his senses that would mess with his control. To try to distract himself, he asked, "Shall we take your car or mine?"

Treasure turned her head to look at him. "Actually, I'd prefer to drive my own. I already pay enough for parking as is. Plus it would be less of a hassle for me if I don't have to come and get it later."

"I wasn't thinking about the parking," he said.

Outside the building, they walked to the Green P parking. He ended up being in the lead as they drove to the restaurant. Since it was still on the early side for dinner, they were quickly seated. Their waitress came to take their drink order, and Soren would have had a beer, except Treasure ordered a tonic water, so he settled for an iced tea instead.

As if she'd sensed his reluctance in not ordering something alcoholic, Treasure said, "You could have had something else to drink. I don't drink and drive."

Being a werewolf, it took a shitload of alcohol to get him drunk. He actually had to really work at it. The last time he'd done that was almost a month ago when he'd gone to Niagara Falls with Kian for their gambling weekend at the Fallsview Casino Resort. That was also the weekend Kian met his mate, Jorja.

"It's okay," he said. "I can have a drink anytime. It's probably better if I don't."

Not that one drink would ever make him go over the limit. But he should keep a clear head, so he wouldn't do something stupid like claim his mate without explaining anything about what it meant to be one to a werewolf. Kian had been pissed to the gills when he'd claimed Jorja, and he'd ended up suffering through the separation anxiety when she'd left once he'd fallen asleep.

After ordering their food and having it arrive, Soren ate his steak with relish as Treasure and he talked. He found out she'd been a real estate agent for the last five years, and had done well for herself from the start. He also learned she was an only child and was very close to her parents who also lived in the city. By the end of the meal, the professional woman was gone and he felt as if he knew Treasure a bit better. He also enjoyed being with her. She could carry on a witty conversation as well as set him to laughing. She was comfortable to be around, and he was attracted not only to her physically, but to the whole package.

Soren didn't want their evening to end after they left the restaurant. He walked with her to their cars. Reaching the driver's side of hers, he did what he'd been dying to do almost the entire time they ate. He pulled her into his arms and held her tightly against him as he took her mouth in a heated kiss. Standing this close, he knew she'd be able to feel how hard his cock was, but he didn't care. He swept the inside of her mouth with his tongue, stroking it along hers. He moaned low in his throat when Treasure put her arms around his waist and kissed him back.

With reluctance, Soren broke their kiss first. The parking lot of a restaurant in the middle of downtown wasn't exactly a romantic place to heat things up between them. He met her gaze with his. Treasure's eyes had dilated, telling him she wasn't unaffected by his nearness.

"I'd ask you back to my place," he said, "but I don't have it yet."

Treasure bit her bottom lip. "There is always mine."

He'd hoped she'd say that, but hadn't wanted to ask. Soren knew Treasure was the one for him and she didn't. He didn't want to rush things and push her away. He'd hoped what time they had spent together so far would have had her trusting him.

Soren gently brushed her lips with his. "I thought you'd never ask," he said with a smile.

She grinned. "I'm glad I didn't disappoint then. You can follow me this time."

He dropped his arms from around her waist and Treasure unlocked her car. Soren quickly got into his. He drove behind her, at first not knowing where exactly she led him. But when she pulled into the parking lot of the nearby marina, he had a sinking feeling.

His fears were confirmed when Treasure waited for him to join her, then led the way down to where different-sized boats and yachts were docked. *Oh god, please don't make it so*

Treasure's place is one of these boats. Soren's fears turned into a waking nightmare a few seconds later when she stopped at a docked yacht.

She turned to face him and smiled. "I hope you don't mind being on a yacht. I'm in between apartments myself and a friend of mine, who also happens to be a client, has let me stay here until I find a new place."

Soren swallowed. Fuck, what was he going to do? He didn't want to tell Treasure he got seasick, and that he avoided anything that floated on water. That would end the evening right there and then. He looked at the yacht. It had to be at least fifty-six feet, so it wasn't exactly a small one. And it was also securely docked, which he could only hope would help cut down on any seasickness he experienced.

Mustering a smile, Soren looked at Treasure. "No, I don't mind." He swallowed again. "Lead on."

She gave him a quizzical look. "Are you sure? You don't look so certain."

To reassure her, Soren leaned in and kissed her, letting out some of the hunger the mating urge caused. He pulled away once they were both breathing hard. "I'm sure."

Treasure nodded and turned toward the yacht. Soren followed her, hoping like hell this didn't turn out with him embarrassing himself by puking his guts up. Wouldn't that be romantic if he threw up all over his mate?

Taking a quick look behind her to make sure Soren followed, Treasure stepped on board the yacht. He might have said he was okay with being on it, but his expression had said otherwise. His face had gone pale, and the way he'd looked at the boat, she could tell he really didn't want to go anywhere near it.

But since he'd said he was okay with it, she wasn't going to suggest they go somewhere else. She wanted to be alone with Soren. During dinner, she'd really enjoyed his company.

They'd gotten on so well, she felt as if she'd known him a lot longer than half a day. Then there was the desire that seemed to sizzle between them, always hovering near the surface. Treasure definitely wanted to explore that further.

Holding onto the rail, she led Soren to the main cabin below deck. There was a sitting area complete with a wet bar. She crossed over to it, then turned to face him. "Would you like something to drink? There's a fully stocked bar here."

Soren swallowed audibly. "No, I'm good."

"Okay," she said slowly. "Then is there anything else I can offer you?"

Treasure licked her lips and pointedly looked Soren up and down. She wasn't one to pussyfoot around when she wanted something. And she wanted Soren. It only took a few steps for her to stand in front of him. She went up on tiptoe and lightly kissed him. He hauled her up against his chest and deepened the kiss.

She opened her mouth to allow his tongue entrance when he licked the seam of her lips. Treasure sucked on it, causing Soren to let out a deep moan. She shoved her fingers into the sides of his hair and increased the pressure of her lips. Liquid heat pooled in her pussy. Her breasts rubbed against his hard chest, and her nipples drew into tight buds.

Soren ground his hips into her. His cock felt thick and long, pressing into her belly. The feel of it made the ache between her legs grow even stronger. She wanted him. Wanted his cock buried deep inside her pussy, wanted the length of it moving in and out of her as he rode her to climax. He aroused her with the simplest of touches.

Treasure released his hair and placed her hands on his broad shoulders. She then ran them down his chest to his stomach. She lifted the bottom of his t-shirt and shoved her hands up inside it. Her fingers glided across well-defined abs. Remaining on her tiptoes, she stretched to kiss a trail to his square jaw and down the side of Soren's neck. He stiffened, a large hand cupping the back of her head, when she reached where his shoulder and neck met. He pressed her mouth closer as she dragged her tongue across his skin. A low, almost animalistic growl punched out of him.

"God, Treasure," he said huskily. "You're driving me crazy. I have to touch you."

In answer, she took Soren by the hand and led him to the bedroom. Once they reached it, Treasure undid the hidden zipper at her side and then pulled her dress off over her head. Standing only in her high heels, bra and thong, she let the garment fall from her hand onto the floor. Soren's gaze seemed to eat her up as it trailed over every inch of her.

Pushing her hair over her shoulder, she said, "Touch me, Soren. Make me come."

Chapter Three

For a split second, Treasure thought Soren's eyes mutedly glowed again. But it disappeared before she could convince herself it wasn't a trick of her mind. She soon forgot about it when he shifted closer and touched her. His big hand stroked along her shoulder and down across the top of her breasts. She sucked in a breath as one of his fingers circled her nipple through her bra.

Wanting to see more of Soren, she took hold of the bottom of his t-shirt and lifted it. Once she reached his chin he took over, roughly yanking it off over his head. She ran an appreciative gaze over his bare chest. He was beautiful with his well-defined pecs and cut abs. She couldn't wait to touch all that naked skin. Soren put all her past boyfriends to shame.

"I have to see more of you, Treasure," he said, his voice gruff.

"And I want to see more of you," she said softly in return.

Soren took her lips again, kissing her passionately. His hands came around her back and undid the clasp on her bra. He brushed the straps down her arms and Treasure let it fall to their feet. She gave it a little kick out of the way.

While he plucked at one nipple, Soren flicked the other with his tongue. Treasure pushed her chest closer, a silent plea for him to suck on her breast. He laved the taut peak, then gently blew on it before he sucked it into his mouth.

Treasure held onto his shoulders to keep her balance as Soren drew on her nipple. Her pussy clenched and wetness leaked into her thong. He switched to her other breast, giving it the same attention. He didn't seem to be in a hurry, taking her nipple in slow, hard sucks.

She ran a hand through his short, blond hair, holding him to her. Waves of pleasure shot through her, her arousal becoming more intense. Soren released her breast and worked his way down to her stomach, going on his knees before her. His large hands circled her waist as his tongue dipped into her bellybutton.

Treasure's legs shook as Soren went lower. His firm grip on her waist kept her steady. His tongue followed the top of her thong, making her stomach quiver. Dropping a hand to the inside of her thighs, he gently pushed them farther apart and rubbed his cheek against her mound. Her breathing became harsh as she tightened with anticipation.

She clutched his shoulders hard when his tongue dragged along her pussy through the lacy material of her thong. What sounded like a rumbling growl pushed out of Soren, vibrating against her clit. Treasure couldn't hold back a low moan.

"More, Soren," she gasped. "Touch me."

"I will, but first let's get rid of these."

His hands trailed down the outside of her legs until he reached her ankles. Grasping the back of her high heels, he took each one off and tossed them aside. That done, he focused on her pussy. His tongue lapped at her, wetting her thong even more. Just when she thought she couldn't take any more of his teasing, Soren used a finger to pull aside the material over her sex. He then feasted on her, licking her from bottom to top and stiffening his tongue to push inside her slick opening.

Feeling a climax build, Treasure couldn't stop herself from grinding against Soren's mouth. What he did just felt too good. She panted, her body coiling tighter. Her fingers dug into the tops of his shoulders as he alternated between licking and sucking on her clit. But it wasn't until he pushed a finger, and then another, inside her pussy while he continued to stimulate her clit did she feel her climax racing up to meet her.

With a strangled cry, she continued to rock against his mouth, her inner walls clutching at the finger inside her as she found her release. Soren didn't stop pumping until the last wave of pleasure receded.

They were both breathing hard as Soren wrapped his arms around her waist and pressed his face to her stomach. Treasure pulled at his shoulders. "Now I get to do to you what you did to me."

Not sure her legs would keep holding her up, she quickly undid Soren's jeans and yanked them down past his hips before she nudged him toward the bed. He kicked off his pants and climbed onto the mattress. She shimmied out of her thong, then joined him.

Settling at his side, she stroked her fingers across his hairless chest and down his sculptured abs. She saw he had his eyes closed when she looked at him to gauge his reaction to her touch. His fully engorged cock stuck out straight from his body. He was thick and long. As she watched, a bead of pre-cum appeared on the very tip. Treasure gathered it on her fingertip and brought it to her mouth before she licked it off.

Fisting her hand around his shaft, Treasure pumped it up and down. Soren moaned and clutched at the comforter beneath him as he lifted his hips, matching her strokes. More pre-cum welled from the slit. This time she bent and licked it off. He made another animal-like growl.

"You're going to kill me, Treasure," he said in a strained voice.

"I'm not done yet," she said. "I plan to do a lot more than this."

Straddling Soren's lower legs, she kept hold of his cock and swirled her tongue around the thick head. She took it inside her mouth. Sucking, Treasure slid him in and out. What she couldn't handle, she stroked with her fist.

Soren moaned, his hips lifting off the bed as he matched her rhythm. She took his cock as far back as she could, the tip almost touching the back of her throat. He hardened even more.

"Christ," he groaned. "Almost... I'm going to...ahh...come."

Treasure didn't stop pleasuring him. She wanted him to, wanted everything he had to give her. She sucked harder, squeezing the base of his shaft. Soren's loud moans of release filled the room as he arched his back and came. She didn't let go until he had nothing left to give. Much to her pleased surprise, his cock didn't soften.

Still straddling his body, Treasure crawled up the bed. She stopped when her mouth hovered over his. Even though Soren had made her come earlier, that had just been a small taste. She now wanted the whole thing.

She settled on top of his body, trapping his cock between them. "I'm glad to feel you're still ready to go," she said, her voice dropped to a husky timbre. "Because I definitely want more."

Treasure would have lowered her mouth to his, but she noticed his face had suddenly gone pale with almost a greenish tinge to it. He took some quick breaths through his nose, then shook his head.

He roughly shoved her off and bolted out of bed, heading for the en suite bathroom. The door slammed behind him, and the next thing Treasure heard was the sound of Soren getting sick.

* * * * *

With a shaky hand, Soren collected some of the water that ran out of the tap. He brought it to his mouth and swished it around before he spat in the sink. Next he splashed water on his face. He used one of the hand towels on the rack to dry it.

Another wave of queasiness hit him and he braced his hands on the counter, concentrating on breathing through his nose. He'd been so sure he'd be okay. While holding Treasure in his arms, touching her, tasting her, he hadn't felt bad. It wasn't until after he'd come that what he'd always suffered while on any kind of water vessel slammed into him.

He felt his stomach roll. He was *not* going to puke again. It was bad enough he'd already done it once. There was one thing he could say about seasickness—it sure as hell blocked out the mating urge. Male werewolves could keep an erection for hours, even after coming several times. Well, Soren was no longer hard, and didn't think he'd be able to get it up again until after his stomach settled, which he felt pretty sure wasn't going to happen as long as he stayed on the yacht.

He heard a soft tap on the door just before Treasure stepped inside the small bathroom. Any other time, Soren would have been hungrily staring at her, since she was still as naked as he, but he had to concentrate on not throwing up.

"Soren, are you okay?" she asked, stepping beside him.

He met her gaze in the mirror above the sink and gave her a short nod.

She gnawed on her bottom lip. "I don't think you are. You're looking awfully pale. You were sick, weren't you?"

At the reminder, his stomach did another roll, and this time he couldn't stop it. He pushed Treasure out of his way and bent over as he heaved into the toilet. He didn't stop until he'd lost the last of his dinner.

A cool, wet washcloth was pressed to the back of his neck. He flushed the toilet and straightened. Treasure wiped his forehead and mouth. She ran the water in the sink and rinsed the cloth before she used it on the rest of his face.

"You get seasick, huh?" she asked softly. "That's why you seemed reluctant to come on the yacht. You should have said something."

"Yeah, I do," he croaked. Soren cleared his throat. "I hoped it wouldn't be too bad since we're docked. I guess I was wrong."

"Are you feeling any better?"

He shook his head. "Not really." His stomach was more than a bit queasy.

"Well, you know the cure for that. You're going to have to get back on dry land."

"Sorry for wrecking your night."

She smiled. "There is nothing to apologize for. It's not as if you planned to get sick. We just know for next time we'll have to go somewhere else."

"So I haven't turned you off by puking my guts up?"

Treasure chuckled. "Lucky for you I'm not one of those people who get sick when they see someone else doing it. And I don't suffer from seasickness. No, I definitely want to see you again. But right now, I think we need to get you dressed and off the yacht before you feel much worse."

He gave her a sheepish look. "I hate to say it, but I think you're right. This wasn't exactly how I wanted to see our date end."

"We'll do better next time."

"When?" Soren felt his stomach working up for another bout over the toilet. He had to get out of there before that happened.

Treasure gave his forehead one last wipe before she put the damp washcloth on the side of the sink. She looked back at him. "Well, for the next few days I'm busy with appointments and viewings, so closer to the end of the week. I'll wait until you have possession of your penthouse and I'll come over with a housewarming present."

Soren swallowed, still fighting his traitorous stomach. Even though it would only give his family's lawyer four days, he would have no problem closing on the penthouse by then. His family paid him very well, and they were his top clients. With the mating urge riding him it would seem like forever. The longer he waited to claim her, and the more time he spent away from her, the worse it would be. He expected he'd be able to at least see Treasure every day until he felt comfortable telling her about him being a werewolf. And he'd thought it would be a lot sooner than four days. But he was stuck. He didn't want Treasure to think he was some kind of stalker, needing to be with her every day. By the end of the four days, his control would be holding on by a thread. He hoped he'd be able to hold back long enough to tell her everything before he couldn't stop himself from claiming her.

He nodded. "All right. Come to my penthouse on Friday, any time you want. I'll be there."

Treasure smiled. "It's a date. Now let's get you out of here. You're definitely not looking any better."

Soren followed her out of the bathroom and into the bedroom. He collected his clothes as Treasure went to the dresser and pulled out a pair of capri pants and a t-shirt. After he put on his jeans, he had to sit down on the end of the bed as he fought the urge to get sick again. Now dressed, she must have noticed his distress, because she picked up his shirt where it lay next to him and helped him put it on. Next she took hold of his hands and helped him stand.

With his fingers linked with Treasure's, Soren allowed her to lead him back to the main cabin and then up the small flight of stairs to the deck above. He made sure he kept his gaze off the water and horizon, concentrating on his feet instead. Once on the dock, he breathed a little easier.

At the marina's parking lot, Treasure stopped under one of the tall lights and looked at him closely. "You're already looking a bit better, but I think a walk is in order before you get into your car."

He took a deep breath, feeling some of the queasiness recede a little. "I think you're right."

They held hands as they walked out of the parking lot. Even though it was dark, they headed for one of the small parks next to the marina. Not that the darkness bothered him. Being a werewolf, he was able to see as if it were daylight. They only saw a few other people who seemed to be enjoying the summer air. At least it still wasn't humid. The heat wave they'd had for the last few days had abated with the rain they'd gotten the day before.

By the time Treasure and he had done a short circuit around the park, Soren felt like himself again. And the mating urge once more rode him hard. Even though Treasure had brought him to release with her mouth, it really hadn't done anything to relieve him. If anything, oral sex made it worse, and would be even more so if he came that way again. Since he wouldn't be seeing Treasure for four days, it definitely meant he couldn't become intimate with her like that again. It would only push the limits of his control.

Back at the parking lot, Soren pulled Treasure into a hug and kissed the top of her head. She fit nicely in his arms. After a few seconds, he released her with a sigh. "I guess I'll see you on Friday then."

She nodded. "Yes, but you can call me before that if you want. I might be too busy to see you, but I can still fit in a phone call. My cell phone number is on the business card I stapled to your copy of the offer."

"I'll do that." He kissed her forehead. "Talk to you later."

Hating having to leave his soon-to-be mate behind, Soren got into his car and drove away. Friday would seem a long time in coming.

* * * * *

After Soren's car disappeared down the street, Treasure turned and headed back to the yacht. She hated to see him go, but it wouldn't have been fair to let him suffer any more than he had. She winced inwardly when she thought about how sick Soren had been. Maybe she should have told him where she was staying while they were still at the restaurant once she'd invited him over. It might have saved him a bout of seasickness. But the thought that he would suffer from it had never crossed her mind. The few friends and family she had over didn't get seasick.

Treasure stepped onto the yacht and went below deck. She headed straight for the wet bar, put some ice in a glass and poured a shot of rum into it before she added some cola. With drink in hand, she went and sat on the couch and switched on the large LCD TV. It wasn't all that late, and she wasn't tired.

Thoughts of what she'd shared with Soren, before he'd gotten sick, kept flashing through her head. She really liked him. A lot. And the way he touched her, kissed her, she would have had no problem asking him to stay the night with her. Not only was he a nice guy who she wanted to get to know better, but he also rocked in bed.

Treasure took a sip of her drink and sighed. She could see herself easily falling for Soren. So far she couldn't find anything wrong with him. And that he didn't mind waiting until Friday to see her, because of her busy schedule, it just put him in better standing. Maybe he would be the one who stuck around for a while. She knew she wanted him to.

* * * * *

Soren closed his bedroom door behind him and blew out a breath. After he'd arrived at his parents' mansion he'd told them the good news about having bought his very own penthouse. Much to his surprise, they hadn't seemed all that thrilled with the idea of him moving out, especially his mother. It had been hard seeing the tears she'd held back, making her eyes glassy, as he'd told them about his new place. Shit, he was nine hundred years old. His mom had to expect he'd eventually move out. But he had a feeling he knew why she'd been so emotional. He was her youngest—his two older sisters were already mated and lived in their own homes—and only son. His mother was going to have a hard time letting him go. He couldn't imagine how she'd take the news that he'd found his mate.

As he walked toward his bed, his cell phone rang. Soren pulled it out of his pocket and looked at the display. It wasn't Treasure calling, it was his friend, Kian.

He flipped open his cell, and said, "Hello, Kian. I thought you'd be too busy spending time with your mate to call me."

Kian chuckled. "Hey, I had to, to see how your appointment to view that penthouse went."

"It went well."

"And?"

"And you can stop teasing the shit out of me about living at home."

"You bought it?"

"Yeah, I did."

"I guess that means you're finally growing up, since you won't be living with Mommy and Daddy anymore," Kian said with a laugh.

"If this is how the conversation is going to go, I'm hanging up." Soren let a little growl seep into his voice.

"Relax already. I had to take one last pot shot at you. Why I'm calling is Jorja and I are going to Niagara Falls for the weekend. Her lease on her apartment is up on Sunday, so we're going to clear out the rest of her stuff. While we're there we thought we'd hit the casino as well. And I figured you might like to tag along."

"Ah, I can't. I get possession of the penthouse on Friday." Soren hoped Kian wouldn't push it. But of course that didn't happen.

"So what…" his friend said. "You told me the place was fully furnished. It's not as if you will have a lot of work to get the place set up. Since you have to be around for the closing on Friday, we'll leave for Niagara Falls on Saturday instead."

"No, I think I'll pass."

"Soren, I'm going to be blunt here, but since when do you turn down a weekend at a casino? The last time we went you spent the majority of the time at the blackjack table. There would have to be something better than moving into your own place to get you to pass."

This was what Soren had hoped to avoid. But knowing Kian, he wouldn't let this go until he was satisfied with the answer, which meant Soren would have to tell him the truth just to get Kian to leave him in peace.

"It's something better. Like, life-changing better," Soren said.

"Well, I'll be damned. You found your mate. Where did you meet her?"

"She was the real estate agent who had the penthouse listed. So that's why I won't be going to Niagara Falls with you and Jorja."

"Understandable," Kian said. He paused for a few seconds, then continued. "Hey, it's not that late. Why aren't you with your mate? I know you aren't, because we wouldn't be having this conversation right now, since she's a mortal. She is one, isn't she? Right?"

Soren groaned to himself. "Yes, she's mortal. And before you can ask, she doesn't know I'm a werewolf yet. And I'm not with her."

"Why?"

"What do you mean why?"

"There has to be a reason why you're not with her. I know what it's like to be in the throes of the mating urge, remember? It would have taken wild horses to drag me away from Jorja."

Soren snorted. "That's because like a drunken ass you claimed her the night you met her. You didn't exactly give the girl a chance, now did you?"

"Hey, no turning it on me. We're discussing why you aren't with your mate. So what happened? Did she take one look at your ugly mug and tell you to hit the road?"

"Hardly. I did buy the penthouse through her."

"Okay. Maybe she tolerated you being around only long enough to make the sale, then told you to get lost."

"That didn't happen either. I took Treasure out for dinner after we finished the paperwork."

"Treasure?" Kian asked. "Her name is Treasure?"

Soren growled. "Yes. What of it?"

"Nothing. It's just not a common one. No need to be so touchy. So if she did all that with you, then why are you not with her?"

"Kian," Soren said, "can't you keep your nose out of my business just this once? I swear you're as bad as an old woman looking for gossip."

His friend laughed. "Why would I do that? How else would I come up with things to ride you about? So you might as well tell me."

Soren growled again. "Fine," he said through clenched teeth. "You want to know why I'm not with Treasure? She's living on a friend's yacht at one of the Harbourfront marinas. After dinner we went back to her place." He waited for Kian to put two and two together. It didn't take him very long.

"A yacht? Let me get this straight. You went to the yacht with your soon-to-be mate?"

"Yes."

"You got seasick, didn't you? And you probably got sick on her."

"Well, not exactly on her. I managed to make it to the toilet before it was too late, though it wasn't perfect timing, since we'd been fooling around in bed."

Kian's howling laughter loudly filled Soren's ear. Once he got himself back under control, he said, "I'm sure that will be one date she never forgets."

"Shut the fuck up. I knew I shouldn't have told you."

"So when are you going to see her again, on dry land?"

"Umm…not until the penthouse closes."

There was a short stretch of silence. "Ah, Soren, you do realize what kind of shape you're going to be in by then, right? The mating urge is going to ride your ass harder as each day passes and you don't claim her."

"I know that. But what can I do? She's busy with appointments and such. She doesn't know what I'm going through. I would hate for her to think I'm too clingy and dump my ass."

"You do have a point there. Just don't let it get too bad. Go to her with some kind of excuse if you have to before Friday rolls around."

"I'll manage," Soren said. "Now talking about Friday, since you won't be going to Niagara Falls until Saturday, you can help me move. I'm going to hit up Atticus as well."

"Fine, I'll tell Jorja we'll go a day later. I should get you to return the favor by helping us move my mate's things, but I doubt you'll be in any condition to be of much use."

"Whatever. I'll call you closer to the day."

After saying goodbye, Soren snapped his phone closed. He glanced at his bed. He doubted he'd get much sleep tonight, or any of the following ones, if he could fall asleep at all. Thanks to the mating urge, if he did manage it, he'd have one erotic dream after another about Treasure. He had a feeling he'd have blue balls before the end of the week.

Chapter Four

Treasure's cell phone beeped, and she smiled when she saw she had one unheard message. She figured Soren had left it. He'd made a point of calling her every day for the last two days. He mostly called around now, later in the afternoon and close to the evening, but this time she'd had a viewing that had turned into an offer. She'd just finished placing a counteroffer that had been accepted in the end.

Listening to the message from Soren, she felt a thrill go through her at the sound of his voice. She could listen to his deep baritone all day and never get sick of it.

About ready to finally leave her office for the day, Treasure quickly texted Soren to tell him she'd call him back as soon as she got home. Since their phone calls tended to run on the long side, there was no point in calling him now.

On board the yacht, she hurried below deck and went to her bedroom to change. It didn't take her long to replace her skirt and short-sleeved blouse with a pair of shorts and a tank top. Back in the main cabin, she debated whether or not she should get something to eat first before she called Soren, since the last time she'd eaten had been at lunch. Deciding she could wait a little longer, she sat on the couch with her cell phone in hand.

Soren picked up after the second ring. "So how did your day go?" he asked after saying hello.

"Busy," she replied. "But I sold one of my properties."

"Then you had a good day."

"Yes."

Treasure settled more comfortably on the couch. Soren didn't mind when she talked about her work. He was usually quick to praise and ask questions none of her previous boyfriends would have. Soren seemed completely interested in all aspects of her life. Their phone calls lasted an hour or more. They'd talked so much about each other, she felt as if she'd known him for a very long time. She found it hard to believe she'd only seen him in person that one day, and the rest had just been phone conversations.

She did miss seeing him, and counted the days until Friday arrived. Soren didn't know it yet, but she planned to spend the night with him. With no seasickness to interrupt them, there would be nothing stopping them from taking things to the very end.

"I've been thinking about you all day," Soren said.

Treasure smiled. "And I've thought of you. Is it Friday yet?"

He chuckled. "I feel the same way. Talking to you on the phone is nice and all, but it doesn't beat holding you in my arms. I'd invite you over to the mansion, but then I'd have to put you through the whole 'meet my parents' kind of thing. I don't think either of us is ready for that yet."

"No," she said. "It's a little early for that."

Treasure had been a bit surprised to hear Soren had never before moved out of his parents' house. But hearing how well-to-do they were, it made a bit of sense. Families with money tended to stay together, some having their children remain in the family home even after they'd gotten married. Personally, she couldn't have done it. She loved her parents and all, but she liked being on her own.

"So what do you have on?" Soren asked in a husky voice.

She laughed. "Is this your attempt at starting some phone sex?"

"What if I were to say yes?"

"I don't know. I've never done it before," she said, grinning, even though Soren couldn't see her. She really didn't know if he was joking with her or not.

"Then I guess that would make us a couple of phone sex virgins."

Getting into the game, Treasure said, "Okay. If we were to do this, how would you start?"

"I'd probably tell you how I would picture myself kissing you, tasting you, letting you know how much I thought of doing it. I'd kiss you until I had you moaning and pressing yourself as close to me as you could get."

Treasure licked her lips, easily able to imagine the kind of kiss Soren talked about. She could almost feel his mouth moving on hers. "And after that?"

"I'd slowly strip you out of your clothes, making sure I learned every inch of skin with my lips and tongue before I focused on your breasts. Those, I'd suck on until you begged me for more." Soren's voice sounded strained.

She squirmed on the couch, squeezing her legs together to try to alleviate the ache that built deep inside her pussy. She felt herself grow wet. "And what would I do to you? Would I undo the button and zipper on your jeans? If I did, I'd reach in and pull out your cock, which would already be hard for me. I'd stroke you, making you even harder until you begged to be put inside me."

"Oh god, enough. This is just making it harder," Soren said in a tight voice.

"What is harder? Your cock?"

"We have to stop, Treasure." A loud animalistic growl sounded on the other end.

This time, not swept away on a wave of passion, it registered as strange. "Soren? Did you just growl like some kind of animal?"

"No. It was something on my television. I have on a documentary about wolves."

"It sounded a lot closer than coming from a TV."

Treasure could tell the difference between background noise and something that was done directly into the phone. The growl had sounded too clear.

"It really was the TV. I've turned it off now."

"I could go for a documentary, and I do like wolves. What channel is it on?"

"Ah, I don't remember."

"Well, turn the TV back on. It'll still be set to the same channel." Why was she getting the impression Soren fibbed to her?

"It won't be," he said. "While we talked I channel-surfed, so I'd have to flip through them all to find it again."

Feeling the tension that suddenly built between them, Treasure tried to lighten the mood. "What? You were sex-talking me and you channel-surfed at the same time? I don't know if I should be insulted," she said with a small laugh. It ended up working.

"Hey, I had to do something to distract myself, or I would have made a mess in my pants," he replied, the strain in his voice not as pronounced.

She was about to say something else when her stomach growled—loudly. "Now I'm doing some growling of my own."

"What?" Soren asked, unease in his tone.

"My stomach growled. I haven't had dinner yet."

"Oh," he said with a chuckle. "Then I'd better let you go so you can eat something. It's getting late."

"All right. Will you call me tomorrow? I shouldn't be as late getting home."

"I will. Have a good night. I'll be thinking of you."

"And I'll be thinking of you. Bye."

Treasure hung up and smiled, hugging her arms around her middle. She really hoped Soren would be the one man who'd want something lasting with her. At thirty, she was ready to settle down when she found the right guy. And more and more she thought Soren was that man. Time would only tell, but she'd do her best to get him to think she could be his one.

* * * * *

Soren tossed his cell phone on the bed next to him. That had been a close one. And could he have thought up a more stupid excuse than saying he watched a wolf documentary? And then when she called him on it, he'd said he had channel-surfed while he'd phone-sexed her. He wouldn't blame Treasure if she thought he was an idiot.

But he hadn't been able to come up with anything better that quickly. He'd thought he'd have some fun with Treasure with the sexy talk over the phone. Only it had backfired on him. He'd become so turned-on it had the mating urge riding him as if there were no tomorrow. If he'd come, which he had been pretty damn close to doing, it would have made it almost unbearable.

The last two days it had reached the point where he couldn't think about anything else except for Treasure. The erotic dreams he had each time he fell asleep left him aching with arousal. He didn't even want to think about what shape he'd be in when Friday rolled around. It was going to be pure torture to hold off making love to Treasure to tell her what he was. He could just imagine himself falling on her as soon as she walked through the penthouse door. That was something he couldn't allow to happen.

Letting out a long breath, Soren picked up the remote to the TV that sat in a wall unit at the end of his bed. He hadn't had the damn thing on when he talked to Treasure, but he now needed the distraction it would give him. He just hoped there was a documentary about wolves on somewhere, or his soon-to-be mate would think he'd lied to her.

He flipped the channels and breathed a sigh of relief when he did find one. Soren looked over the pack of wild wolves that were on the screen and decided his fur while in wolf form looked a lot better than theirs.

* * * * *

Soren opened the door to the mansion and then stepped back to allow the two men who stood on the other side to come in. It was finally Friday and Atticus and Kian had come to help him move out. A fourteen-foot rental truck sat already parked out front just waiting to be loaded. Once that was done, he had to wait for the final word from his lawyer that the penthouse had closed, then he could go get the keys.

Kian gave Soren a close look as he walked past. "I have to say you appear a bit strung out. Don't you think he does, Atticus?"

The other man stepped inside and nodded. "I'd say more than a little," Atticus said with a chuckle.

Soren narrowed his eyes at them and snarled his lip. "Ha ha. You both can laugh at my expense. Where are your mates? You wouldn't have left them behind, since you'd be suffering from the separation."

"They're outside," Kian replied. "They thought they'd wait until we saw what condition you were in, whether you were in any mood to have females around."

He rolled his eyes. "More like you two were worried the sight of anything female would have me jumping your mates or something. As if that would happen. Being mated, you both should know I only want to jump one woman, and she isn't either of your mates."

"We weren't so much worried about that," Atticus said. "More to the point of you being in such a foul mood you'd snap at them."

Soren shook his head. "My mood might not be great, but I won't snap at Rylee and Jorja." Seeing his friends' doubtful looks, he said, "Forget it. Tell your mates they can come in, so we can get started on putting things on the truck. I'm expecting the lawyer to call in an hour to let me know I can pick up the keys from his office."

Atticus stepped through the still-open door and waved the two women in. Rylee and Jorja greeted him with a kiss on the cheek. They then stood beside their mates.

"See," Jorja said to Kian. "Soren didn't try to bite my head off or anything. I knew you two made Rylee and me wait outside for nothing." She looked at Soren. "How are you holding up?"

"As well as can be expected," he replied. "I'll just be glad to have the mating urge stop riding my ass. Hopefully by the end of tonight."

"You plan to tell Treasure everything then?"

"Yeah. Tonight is the night."

"What will you do if she rejects you?" Rylee asked. "I know I had a hard time accepting Atticus for what he was right after I found out."

Soren grimaced. "I don't even want to think about it. I'm hoping since we've gotten to know each other a lot better with all our phone conversations, Treasure will take the news better than if I hadn't waited."

"Well, I didn't wait with Jorja and in the end she was fine with me being a werewolf." Kian grunted when his mate elbowed him in the ribs. "What did I do now?"

Jorja frowned. "Don't be comparing how I was. The only reason why you didn't give me a choice was because you were shitfaced drunk. I never stood a chance." She gave Kian a kiss on the lips. "Not that I'm complaining now, but it was not fun having to go through separation anxiety with no clue as to what the hell was wrong with me."

"Right," Soren said. "Enough mate talk. It's not exactly helping me any. It's just making me think of Treasure. Let's get to work. My parents went to the lake house for the weekend, so we don't have to worry about disturbing them."

He led them upstairs to his bedroom where there was a collection of boxes already packed and ready to go. Soren really didn't have that many things he would take with him. Since he'd bought the bedroom furniture himself, he wasn't leaving it behind, which meant once they were in the penthouse he'd have to get Kian and Atticus to help him move the things already in what would be his bedroom to one of the spare rooms. He'd then deal with getting rid of it at a later date.

The physical labor helped distract Soren from the ever-present mating urge, though it was hard seeing Atticus and Kian with their mates. Each couple couldn't seem to stop touching their other halves in some small way every few minutes.

Once the truck was loaded, Soren passed out bottled water to everyone as he waited for his lawyer to call. A bit earlier than expected, it came through. He left his friends at the mansion as he drove to the lawyer's office and picked up the keys for the penthouse.

After he returned to his parents' house, it was decided the three men would ride in the truck together while the women took the car the couples had arrived in. Soren's car was already parked at the penthouse. He'd dropped it off there on the way back from the lawyer's office and had taken a taxi back to the mansion.

Making sure he didn't lose the women, Soren drove in front. He stuck his hand out the truck's window when they arrived at the building and directed them toward the visitors' parking while he continued on to the back where there was access to the moving elevator.

They waited for the women to join them before Soren opened the back of the truck and they got to work putting his things in the elevator. Once they were down to the last few boxes, he set Kian and Atticus to work dismantling the bed already in the master bedroom while he and the women went for the remaining items on the truck.

Soren had just set down the box he carried in the living room when a scent hit him like a ton of bricks. He whirled around and saw Treasure standing in the entranceway talking to Rylee, who obviously had let her into the penthouse.

Jorja snapped her fingers in front of his face and broke his gaze. "You'd better get a grip on yourself," she said quietly. "Your eyes are glowing. You don't want to let the cat, or should I say wolf, out of the bag just yet."

He reined himself back. It was a struggle, but he just managed. Drawn to Treasure like a magnet to metal, Soren walked past Jorja and went to greet his soon-to-be mate.

She looked at him and smiled, and his cock went rock hard. Soren tugged at the bottom of his t-shirt to hide his erection, thankful it was a little on the long side. With Treasure near, he knew he'd be in a constant state of arousal.

"Hi," she said as her gaze met his.

"Hi back. I see you met Rylee."

"Yes. She told me she's married to one of your best friends."

"And I'm Jorja, the wife of his other," Jorja said as she joined them.

His would-be mate smiled, and said, "Hi, Jorja. I'm Treasure."

Rylee cleared her throat. "I think Jorja and I should go see how the guys are managing with that bedroom furniture." She gave Jorja a pointed look.

Kian's mate nodded. "Good idea."

Once the two women were gone, Treasure chuckled. "I guess that was Rylee's subtle way of giving us a chance to be alone together."

"It would appear so. We might as well not waste it."

Soren had to keep tight control over himself as he pulled Treasure into his arms and kissed her. The feel and taste of her had him wanting to take her to the floor and claim her as his mate. The mating urge demanded he do it, not caring there were other people just in the other room. He deepened the kiss as Treasure clung to him, her throaty moan filling his ears while she rubbed up against him.

"Hey, enough of that," Kian said loudly. "We still have to get the bed set up before we leave."

He silently thanked his friend as he broke contact with Treasure's lips and turned to see Kian and Atticus carrying out a headboard. If not for the interruption, Soren knew he would have let things get out of hand.

"You also didn't tell us which room you want us to put the furniture you don't want in," Atticus said.

Taking Treasure by the hand, Soren led her through the living room and to the hallway where Atticus and Kian stood. "This is Treasure. Treasure, this is Atticus and Kian." Each man nodded in her direction when he said their name. "You can put this in the bedroom closest to the master."

Now that Treasure was here, he wanted the others to leave. Between Kian, Atticus and himself, it didn't take very long to finish moving the rest of the furniture out and have his bed set up. A few minutes after that, Soren ushered his friends and their mates out the door with Atticus agreeing to return the rental truck for him.

Alone with Treasure, Soren knew he rode too close to the edge, his mating urge pushing him to make her his. He had to put them in a situation where he couldn't act on his impulses. Turning away from the door to face her, he asked, "How about we go get something to eat?"

She nodded. "I could go for some food. Where do you want to go?"

"How about we go to the CN Tower's 360 restaurant?"

"All right. I haven't been there in ages."

They decided he'd drive. The elevator ride down to the parking garage just about killed him, but Soren somehow managed. Being inside his car with her so close didn't do him any favors, either. After they arrived at the base of the CN Tower, he drew in big gulps of air, diluting Treasure's enticing scent.

The trip up to the restaurant—which was three hundred and fifty-one meters straight up—didn't take very long in the fast-moving elevator. But it was still long enough to mess with Soren's control. At least this time they didn't ride alone.

Having not thought of calling ahead to see if there would be a table open, they were lucky one was. They were seated at a table for two that flanked the glass windows. Soren turned his head to look outside. The restaurant slowly revolved around the top of the tower, giving a spectacular view of Toronto, hence the name 360.

Unlike the first time they'd gone out for dinner, Soren had a hard time concentrating on what Treasure said. His mating urge rode him harder than it had the last few days, all because he was in the presence of his unclaimed mate.

Even though the food was known to be excellent, Soren had no idea what he ordered, or how it tasted. His gaze kept locking on Treasure's mouth as he pictured what it would feel like to have her lush lips wrapped around his cock. He must have been able to say the appropriate things, because not once did she question him.

The meal finished, they stood at the elevator doors, waiting for the car to arrive. Treasure nudged him, the contact causing him to bite back a growl of need.

"Do you want to stop at the level that has the glass floor?" she asked. "I like the thrill of being able look straight down from so high up."

He turned his gaze on her and let some of what he felt show in his eyes. "Maybe another time. How about we go back to my penthouse and finish getting my bed together?"

She swallowed, the scent of her arousal permeating the air. "I think I'd enjoy that more."

"I know I would," Soren replied huskily.

The elevator ride passed in a blur, as did the drive back to his penthouse. He let Treasure inside and told her to go ahead to his room, that he would join her in a minute. Soren went to the kitchen and took out a bottle of water. His control was slowly slipping by degrees. After drinking half the bottle, he felt somewhat better that he could behave around his would-be mate without jumping her the instant he saw her.

Treasure had only managed to slip the fitted sheet on the mattress by the time he reached the bedroom. He walked up behind her and wrapped his arms around her waist. He pulled her back hard enough against him so she'd feel just how aroused he was. She pushed into him, causing Soren to bite back a growl.

Her arm snaked up and her hand wrapped around the back of his neck as he bent his head to nibble on her ear. "Mmm," she said. "I've been waiting all week to see you again. I'd thought I'd help you unpack a bit before we got to the making up for lost time, but I don't want to wait any longer."

Treasure withdrew her hand and turned in his arms. Her hands fisted in the front of his t-shirt as she pulled him closer and went on tiptoe to kiss him. Soren knew he should slow things down, but he was too hungry for her. He needed to have a taste of her now. He wouldn't go all the way, he'd satisfy her with his mouth first, then he'd tell her everything. He could control himself that much.

Desperate to get her naked, he wasted no time stripping Treasure out of her clothes in between kisses. She did the same for him. They were both undressed in no time flat. Picking her up, Soren turned toward the bed and laid her on the middle of the mattress. He climbed up beside her, partially covering her body with his.

Leaving her mouth, he worked his way down to her breasts. He circled a taut nipple with the tip of his tongue before he sucked it past his lips. Treasure arched her back, pushing it deeper. Her breath came in pants, and the scent of her arousal had his dick even harder.

As he switched to her other breast, Soren trailed his fingers down her flat stomach to the apex of her legs. She spread her thighs to give him better access. He stroked her with a fingertip and found her wet. He released her nipple and kissed a path down her body until he'd wedged his shoulders between Treasure's legs. He focused on her pussy, loving the sight of her all wet and swollen for him. His tongue flicked out and stroked her clit. She moaned, lifting her hips off the bed.

"Yes, Soren," she panted. "More."

He licked her again. "I could taste you all night."

Spreading her pussy, he delved inside with his stiffened tongue. Treasure rocked against his mouth, her throaty moans filling his ears. Wanting to make her come, Soren sucked on her clit as he pushed two fingers inside her slick opening. He pumped them in and out. He felt her inner walls clutching the digits as he worked her.

Soren rubbed his aching cock against the mattress. He stroked her faster, then she was there. Whimpering his name, Treasure climaxed, her inner muscles clutching his fingers as he continued to move them in and out of her.

Once she settled, he rolled over onto his back and put his arm over his eyes. His chest rapidly rose and fell as he fought to catch his breath and resist claiming Treasure. He heard and felt her shift on the bed beside him. Soren kept his eyes closed and from her sight. They had to be mutedly glowing.

"Soren?" she asked tentatively.

"I'm okay," he said. "I'm just trying to calm down a bit. I'd hate to finish too soon, if you know what I mean." Not that that was the real problem. Being able to keep hard after coming meant ejaculating early wouldn't ruin lovemaking.

She shifted closer. "Maybe I can help with that."

Soren groaned as Treasure took his cock in hand and stroked him. It probably wasn't a good idea to let her pleasure him in any way before they had their talk, but he couldn't bring himself to stop her. It felt too good. Instead, he focused on his control.

At first he was so focused on Treasure stroking him and maintaining the tight rein on his mating urge, Soren didn't know what she was up to. It wasn't until he felt the warm wetness of her pussy closing around his cock that he realized Treasure had straddled him to take him inside her. Feeling her taking every inch of him, Soren knew it was too late for both of them. There would be no stopping what would happen next. His control shattered like a rock thrown at a window.

Chapter Five

With a wolf's growl he had no chance of holding back, he dropped his arm from his eyes but kept them closed, and put his hands on Treasure's hips, urging her on as she rode him. He lifted his hips to meet each of her thrusts, impaling her on the full length of his cock. After waiting to claim her, the sensation of her inner walls squeezing around his shaft had him feeling as if he'd died and gone to heaven.

Surging up into a sitting position, Soren sucked one of Treasure's nipples into his mouth as she rode him faster. Their moans and heavy breathing were the only sounds in the room. Her fingers sank into his hair, slightly pulling on the strands.

He continued to thrust into Treasure and felt his balls tighten against his body as he came closer and closer to his climax. She rode him faster, harder, grinding down on his pubic bone with each stroke. Just before he reached the point of no return, Soren felt it happen. A piece of his soul reached out for a piece of Treasure's. As hers joined with his, becoming one, he let out a strangled moan. He came the same time her inner walls milked his shaft with her orgasm. He held her tight against him and filled her with his cum.

Soren pressed the side of his face against Treasure's chest and stroked her back. He was still hard, buried deep inside her pussy. She kissed the top of his head and wrapped her arms around his shoulders.

"That was amazing," Treasure said, a bit breathless. "And you're still hard."

He nuzzled the top of her breasts. "That's because I'm not done with you yet." His wolf wanted to claim her as his mate as well.

Lifting her off his lap, he placed her on her knees on the bed beside him. Soren shifted behind her and pushed his cock between her legs. He didn't enter her just yet. He covered her breasts with his hands and squeezed them as he shoved her hair away from her neck with his chin and sucked on the delicate skin there. Thrusting his hips, he teased Treasure with his cock, the head of it stroking against her clit. He dropped his hands to her hips to hold her still as he rocked against her.

Treasure reached around and held onto his ass, digging her nails into it as she pushed back. "Mmm, Soren, I want you deep inside me again. Give it to me."

"I'll give it to you, babe."

Situating his teeth where her shoulder and neck met, he gently bit down. Bending over her, he forced her to let go of his ass, so she could support her weight on her hands. He positioned himself and surged into her to the hilt with one stroke. Treasure hung her head forward and moaned.

He pumped in and out of her as she pushed back to meet his thrusts. She felt tighter in this position, her inner walls clutching at his shaft as he pumped inside her. Knowing they were now truly mates, it increased his arousal. His cock grew even harder. He was already so close to the edge, but he wanted Treasure to come first. He wanted to hear her moaning his name.

Soren pumped faster, reached around and found her clit. He stroked the small bundle of nerves with his finger. Treasure panted and moaned, matching the pace he set. With a whimpered cry, she came, moaning his name as he'd wanted. Her pussy squeezed his cock in a tight fist, milking him into a climax of his own. He growled and groaned as he emptied deep inside her.

Even though he was still hard—and would remain so for a while—Soren pulled out of Treasure and took them both to their sides. He pulled her tight against him with her back pressed to his chest. Treasure was his. His mate. Having lost control of the situation, he now had the dreaded task of telling her what he was, and what she meant to him after he bound them together.

Treasure nestled closer. His still-hard cock nestled along her bottom. He wanted her again, but he'd give her a breather. And with that thought, Soren decided he'd wait until the morning to confess everything. There was no point spoiling the rest of what would be a very pleasurable night for both of them.

* * * * *

Treasure came awake and shifted slightly. She felt a bit of soreness between her legs. A smile tugged at her lips when she remembered how she had ended up that way. Soren had been practically insatiable during the night. They'd made love so many times she'd lost count. In between bouts, they'd managed to finish putting the sheets on the bed and order some food for delivery. Soren had slipped on his jeans to answer the door and shucked them soon after.

She'd never been with so demanding a lover. He seemed never to get enough of her, and made sure she found her pleasure first before his. And his ability to retain an erection after coming, not once but several times, had her climaxing again and again.

Rolling over in bed, she found the side Soren had slept on empty. She buried her nose in his pillow and sniffed, drawing his scent deep into her lungs. Smelling it made her pussy clench. She wouldn't be able to smell it and not think of their first night together in Soren's penthouse. Nor the first time they had made love. She had no idea if he'd experienced it as well, but Treasure had felt something pass between them, as if it connected them. Afterward, she'd never come so hard or so long in her life.

Whatever it had been, Treasure now felt very close to Soren. It was silly, but after a marathon of great sex, she thought she might be falling for him to the point she didn't want to let him go—ever. The more times they made love the more that feeling intensified. Could she have really fallen in love with Soren that fast?

Deciding to get up to see where Soren had gone, Treasure quickly used the en suite bathroom. After she finished, she returned to the bedroom. She looked at her scattered clothes on the floor. She didn't feel like putting them on just yet. Instead, she picked up Soren's discarded t-shirt and slipped it on. It was so long the bottom hit the middle of her thighs, and the short sleeves covered her elbows.

Satisfied she was covered enough, Treasure crossed the room to the closed door. She opened it and stepped into the hallway. As she walked down it, she smelled fresh-brewed coffee in the air. Obviously, Soren had taken the time to unpack his coffeemaker.

She walked into the kitchen and saw he stood at the counter. She closed the distance between them, stepped behind him and wrapped her arms around his waist. "You could have woken me up, you know."

Soren looked over his shoulder at her and smiled. "I think I wore you out last night. I figured you needed the extra sleep. And I bet you're hungry."

"Starved, actually."

"Well, it's not much, since I don't have a whole lot of food stocked in the fridge right now, but I hope you like toasted bagels with cream cheese."

"That with a cup of coffee sounds wonderful."

"Then go take a seat at the table and I'll bring it to you. How do you like your coffee?"

"Cream, no sugar."

Treasure sat at the table and watched Soren move around the kitchen as he finished preparing their breakfast. He brought over their coffees first before the bagels. She took a sip and breathed a contented sigh. It was good. At least her man knew how to make great-tasting coffee. As she lifted the cup to her lips, she smiled. She already thought of Soren as her man.

He placed a plate with a bagel slathered in cream cheese in front of her. "What's causing that smile?" he asked as he sat in the chair next to her.

She put the cup down. "Nothing really. You make good coffee."

"Thanks. It's one of the things I can do in a kitchen without the chance of ruining it."

"Not much of a cook, are you?"

He laughed. "You could say that. I have a feeling I'll be getting a lot of takeout until I learn to do better. Unless someone would like to teach me?"

Treasure chuckled. "You're lucky I don't mind cooking, and can show you a few simple things to start off with." She tried to put an innocent look on her face. "As long as I get more of what I got last night."

Soren gazed at her almost as if he physically touched her. "Oh, I don't think that would be a problem at all. Now eat up before your bagel gets cold."

She picked up one half of her bagel and took a bite at the same time Soren took one of his. They sat in companionable silence. While they ate, from time to time, he would stare at her, looking as if he would say something, only to fill his mouth with more food.

After he'd done it for the fourth time, Treasure finally asked, "What? You keep looking as if you want to start a conversation, then don't."

Soren swallowed his bite of bagel before he took a sip of his coffee. "There's something I want to say to you, but I'm really not sure how to go about it. Mostly I'm not sure what your reaction will be."

"I'm not that hard to talk to. Just spit it out."

"Let's finish our breakfast first, then I'll tell you."

"All right."

"On second thought, I want to do some shopping, then we'll have a talk."

Treasure had the feeling Soren used the shopping idea as a stall tactic. "Shopping where?"

"The St. Lawrence Market. It's Saturday, so there should be a ton of fresh produce there."

She chuckled. "I thought you said you couldn't cook."

Soren nudged her arm with his elbow. "Well, someone did offer to teach me how. I need to stock the fridge, anyway."

Treasure pushed aside thoughts of what Soren wanted to discuss with her and smiled. "Okay, you don't have to twist my arm. I love going to the market." She stood. "We'd better hurry and get dressed. It opened at five this morning, and we don't want to end up with nothing good."

Soren stood as well. "I do have to say you look better in my shirt than I do."

She helped Soren load the dishes into the dishwasher before returning to the bedroom to get dressed. Once they were ready, Treasure followed him onto the elevator, then to his car in the parking garage.

The St. Lawrence Market wasn't too far from where Soren lived. There were actually two parts to it—the north and south markets. On the way down to the car, they decided to go to the south. It was inside the historic building that had served as Toronto's first City Hall from 1845 to 1899. It became a market in 1901. With two levels, it had more than fresh produce available for sale. Treasure had a feeling she'd be doing some shopping herself.

It was a bit on the crowded side, but she didn't mind. With a simple meal of steak, potatoes and veggies, which she decided she'd teach Soren how to cook, they soon had what he needed. He bought other items he figured would be fresher than what the grocery store would have.

All the while they shopped, Treasure thought of what Soren might have to say to her. She didn't think it was anything too serious or bad, since he seemed more relaxed than he had been the night before. And from time to time, she caught him staring at her as if she were the most precious thing in the world. Not that she would complain about that.

After they returned to Soren's penthouse and put his purchases away, he led her to the bedroom. Treasure climbed onto the bed and sat in the middle of it as she waited for him to join her. He just stood at the end and stared at her.

"I have to tell you, Soren, you're making me a bit nervous standing there like that. I now wonder what it is you want to say, and if it's a bad thing."

Soren's gaze became more intense, not straying from her face. "How good are you at accepting change, sudden or otherwise?"

"Pretty good. I'm not one of those people who have a set schedule in their lives and stick to it no matter what. Considering what I do for a living that wouldn't exactly work."

"Okay. How about accepting something you would think is totally bizarre and not the standard?"

Treasure furrowed her brow. Just where exactly was Soren going with this line of questioning? The part about accepting sudden change, she thought he referred to maybe them forming a committed relationship, or even him asking her to move in with him. But the second question blew that theory out of the water. She didn't know how the bizarre part figured into what they had together.

"Ah, I guess I'd be okay with it," she said. "Though it would have to depend on what exactly you mean by bizarre."

"All right, let me simplify it a bit more then. What if it were something to do with me?"

"With you?"

"Yes. Do you have strong enough feelings for me that you would be able to accept it if I were…different?"

She narrowed her eyes. "You're starting to lose me here, Soren. I haven't a clue what you mean by you being 'different'. And as for my feelings for you…" She paused and met his gaze squarely. "I do have them. Stronger than I've ever felt for another man."

Soren smiled, one that made her long to pull him onto the bed and have her way with him again. But she remained where she was, sensing he wouldn't go for it until he'd said what he wanted to.

"I've fallen for you, Treasure," he said. "And I want you to move in with me, but I'm jumping ahead of myself." He stopped speaking and took a deep breath before he continued. "Now I know this will be hard for you to believe, but I'm telling you the absolute truth." He paused a second time. "I'm a werewolf, Treasure."

She blinked a few times. She couldn't have heard Soren right. "A werewolf? Did you just tell me you're a werewolf?"

"Yes."

Treasure looked him up and down. He didn't look any different from the Soren she'd come to know and had started to fall in love with. There were no signs she could see of him all of a sudden becoming delusional. He appeared to be the same good-looking guy who had her craving his touch like chocolate.

"And how did you become a werewolf?" she asked. "Were you bitten by one on a night of the full moon?"

"No. That's just superstitious crap made up by mortals who didn't understand my kind. And is one of the main reasons why we keep hidden what we are. The only way for someone to be a werewolf is if they are born one."

Shit, he had the whole theory of him being a shapeshifter already all worked out in his head. "So you were born a werewolf from werewolf parents?"

"Correct." Soren ran a hand through his short, blond hair. "You're not believing me, are you?"

Treasure climbed off the bed to stand in front of Soren. "You have to admit it sounds more than just bizarre. It makes you sound as if you have a problem telling reality from make-believe."

He reached up and stroked her cheek with the backs of his fingers. "I know it does, but I'm not losing it." Soren took her face in his hands and held it in place. "If I were lying, or had lost touch with reality, would I be able to do this with my eyes?"

She tried to jerk free of his hold when they glowed mutedly, but he held on. There was no mistaking it this time. He didn't look away, but steadily held her gaze. "How..." She let the rest of what she was going to say trail off.

Soren gave her a slight smile. "All I have to do is think of you and how much you turn me on. My eyes glow when I'm aroused or angry, or just before I shift."

Treasure's heart tried to beat out of her chest, and not because desire coursed through her, heating her blood. She couldn't pull her gaze off Soren's eyes. "What do you mean by shift?"

"I'm a werewolf. What do you think it means?"

She swallowed, her pulse racing as a shiver ran down her spine. "That you can shape-shift into something half wolf and half human."

"Another tale told by superstitious mortals. The only thing I can shift into is a wolf. Like the ones in the wild, except I retain my ability to think as a human."

This time she jerked away hard enough to force Soren to let her go. She wrapped her arms around her stomach as she trembled. "The other night on the phone, that growl I heard wasn't from your TV, was it? You made that sound."

"Yeah, it was me," he said. "When I get too aroused, I have a hard time keeping the wolf growls back."

"I see," she said and took a little step back.

Soren must have noticed. "Treasure, you don't have to be afraid."

"I'm not," she quickly replied.

"You are. I can smell your fear. My kind smell emotions. Each one has its own unique scent. And right now you're giving off fear."

Even though she really didn't want to see it, Treasure knew she had to. Soren had already shown how his eyes glowed, but she needed to see the rest for herself.

"I want to see you as a wolf," she said quietly, her voice almost breaking.

Chapter Six

He looked at her, not really knowing if she was ready to see him in his wolf form. Soren wanted to shift, because he wanted to prove he wasn't an animal filled with bloodlust. So far Treasure was only marginally taking the fact he was a werewolf well. The scent of her fear still perfumed the air around her. And he still hadn't told her anything about her being his mate, and that after last night, they were irrevocably bonded. Nor how old he actually was.

"Are you sure you want me to shift?" he asked.

Her arms seemed to wrap tighter around her middle. "Yes."

Soren still wasn't sure, but he figured it might be better for Treasure if he got this all out in the open at once. With a nod, he stepped back to put some space between them. He watched her as he willed on the change, calling on the magic deep inside him. She gasped and her eyes widened. He knew what she saw. As he shifted his eyes would glow, his body would shimmer, then blur as he took on his wolf form.

The change complete, he sat on his haunches and looked up at Treasure. Her face had turned white. She stared at him with a look of shock clearly written on her features. The scent of her fear increased.

He knew he had to convince her he wasn't some kind of killer she had to be afraid of. If he could only get her to touch him in this form, run her hands through his fur that was just a shade darker blond than his hair, then maybe they would be okay.

Soren got up and tried to take a step closer. She jerked back hard enough to lose her balance and she fell sideways onto the bed. He jumped up beside her and she scrambled away toward the head of the mattress and leapt onto the floor. For a mortal, she could move pretty fast.

"Stay away," she said, her voice shaking as she spoke. "Just stay the hell away from me."

Sensing her fear was about to take her over, Soren quickly shifted back to human form, willing his clothes on. "Treasure, calm down. I'm still the same man. I was a werewolf on the day we met, and I'll always be one."

"I have to get out of here."

She tried to walk past him, but he stopped her with a hand on her arm. Treasure shot out of reach as if he'd burned her with fire. "You can't leave. I haven't told you the rest."

The laugh that bubbled out of her had a tinge of hysteria in it. "Don't bother. I don't want to hear any more. And I *am* leaving."

He stood in front of her, blocking her way out of the room. "You have to stay with me."

"What are you going to do? Hold me prisoner?"

"No, of course not." This was going from not too bad to a hot mess in no time at all.

"Then get out of my way."

Treasure walked around him, and Soren blurted out everything else. "You can't leave, because you're my mate. Last night the mate bond formed between us, which means we're considered married. And with the bond, we won't be able to stand to be away from each other. The separation will play with our minds, make us think something bad happened, and that it has been months instead of hours that we've been together. And once we are reunited, if it's been a long period of time, all we'll be able to think about is reaffirming what is between us in the most intimate of ways."

As he spoke Treasure had come to a standstill. "Bullshit."

"It isn't. You had to have felt it during the first time we made love. I know I did. It was a part of my soul reaching out for yours, then the two combined to become one. You *are* my mate, Treasure. If you weren't I wouldn't love you as I do now."

She shook her head. "I can't do this right now. I really can't. This is too much to accept all at once. You'll let me leave, because if you don't, I'll be on my cell phone so fast, calling 9-1-1, you won't know what hit you."

Soren let out a deep growl as she turned and walked out of the room. He followed her and watched her snatch up her purse from the couch on her way to the penthouse door. Shit, he was going to have to let her leave. She was in no condition to think things through.

Treasure undid the deadbolt and opened the door. It slammed behind her. Soren hurried back to his room, donned a clean t-shirt and put on his shoes. He raced to the kitchen at werewolf speed and collected his keys. He might have to let her go, but that didn't mean he couldn't follow. After seeing how Kian had gone through the separation anxiety in Niagara Falls, there was no way Soren wanted to experience it. It almost drove his friend nuts.

Out in the hallway, Treasure was nowhere to be seen. Not wanting to take the time to wait for another elevator, Soren headed for the door to the stairs. Werewolves could move faster than any mortal. He took the steps two at a time, moving at a speed that would have him quickly on the ground floor.

Once in the parking garage, he got inside his car and revved the engine before slamming it into reverse. He reached street level just as Treasure's car turned out of the parking lot.

Soren followed behind her at a discreet distance, making sure her car remained in sight at all times. As long as he could keep her from getting too far ahead of him they'd both be fine. He groaned to himself when she reached her destination. He'd figured she would go back to the yacht. And it didn't bode well for him.

He hung back a bit as Treasure parked in the marina's lot, then headed for the docks where the boats were moored. He pulled into a slot a little away from her car. With his excellent eyesight, it wasn't too hard for him to watch his mate walk down the dock before stepping onto the yacht's deck.

He waited until Treasure disappeared below, then Soren got out of his car and walked toward what would soon be the object of his misery. He had no idea if she knew how to captain the yacht, or if she could call someone to do it for her, but Soren didn't want to take the risk of his mate taking it out on the lake with the hopes of keeping him away. He didn't think she would do it, but there was a slim, very slim, chance it could happen.

Walking on silent feet, Soren reached the yacht and lightly stepped on board. He looked for a place to duck out of sight. The only place was at the very back of the boat where there was a platform close to the water that could be used by swimmers. This was not going to end well for him.

With a burst of werewolf speed and stealth, he raced past the windows of the main cabin below and onto the platform. He sat with his back against the yacht, facing the water, wanting something solid behind him. He brought his knees to his chest and rested his forehead on them. Soren shut his eyes and concentrated on not getting seasick.

He listened to the seagulls flying around, and the sound of some of the other vessels leaving the marina. Actually the latter part he had to force himself to ignore, since it made him think of what he sat on. He was forced to swallow a few times.

Soren guessed an hour had gone by before he felt his stomach roil with the familiar queasiness. He kept his eyes closed and leaned his head back against the yacht, breathing in and out through his nose. The upside of this was he wasn't suffering from separation anxiety, which meant neither was Treasure. So what if he upchucked? It was better than being away from her. Without their minds playing tricks on them, he hoped his mate would be able to sort things out and realize he was the one she wanted.

If she couldn't, it meant he had more hours of seasickness to look forward to, because he planned to go wherever Treasure went to save them both.

Eventually his stomach couldn't take any more. Soren crawled to the edge of the platform and barfed up his guts. He used some of the lake water to wipe his mouth, and risked taking a quick look around to see if anybody saw him. That would just be the icing on the cake, to have an audience while he was sick.

Fighting his stomach again, Soren stretched out on the platform. Treasure was worth it. He just had to keep reminding himself of that.

* * * * *

The sound of her cell phone ringing caused Treasure to jump. She'd been sitting on the couch for who knows how long, lost in her thoughts. Of course they all centered on Soren and what he'd revealed to her.

Thinking it could be him calling, she fished her cell out of her purse and looked at the call display. She breathed a silent sigh of relief when she saw it wasn't Soren, but she did recognize the number.

"Hi, Rach." Rachel owned one of the other yachts nearby. They'd struck up a friendship shortly after Treasure had moved to the marina, even though Rachel only came during the weekends.

"Hi, Treasure. Are you on the yacht?"

"Yeah. Why?"

"Bill and I are just leaving the marina to take a cruise on the lake. We just went past you. Did you know you have a man on the very back of the yacht who is sick as a dog?"

Treasure stiffened. "You mean he's there right now?"

"Yes, we just cruised by. Do you know him? Because if you don't, I'd call the cops to get rid of him."

"That won't be necessary. I know him. Thanks for calling."

"No problem. Since he's a friend of yours, I suggest you get him back on dry land. Obviously, the yacht doesn't agree with him."

"I will."

She ended the call. The man had to be Soren. He must have followed her back here. Did she really want to go out and confront him? Now that she'd had time away from him to sort things out, her initial fear had subsided. She could look at things from a proper perspective. Had Soren ever tried to harm her in any way since she'd met him? No, he hadn't. If anything, he made her feel protected, safe. As if nothing would get through him to her. Maybe that had to be his being a werewolf, she didn't know. In hindsight, in his wolf form, he really hadn't been all that scary. He could almost pass for a dog, if you didn't look too closely at him.

Treasure blew out a breath. She thought of what Soren had said about them becoming bonded the first time they'd made love. She'd felt it, and the thought of never seeing him again actually didn't sit well with her. If she were honest with herself, she'd admit she had fallen in love with a werewolf. And he'd already told her he loved her.

Knowing perfectly well she couldn't leave things how they were, Treasure pushed to her feet. She couldn't have Soren getting sick outside for everyone to see. But before she took him off the yacht, she wanted to get some answers to her questions.

She climbed the stairs to the deck above and headed straight for the back. She looked down at the platform and saw Soren stretched out on his belly, his head over the edge as he threw up. A wave of pity washed over her. So much for the big, bad werewolf. Right now he was probably as weak as a kitten.

Once she stood beside him, Treasure squatted and rubbed his back. "Let's get you below deck. You can wash up there."

Soren lifted his head and looked up at her. "Treasure? How did you know I was here?"

She smiled. "A friend of mine who has a yacht here as well cruised by and saw you. She called to let me know I had a strange man on mine getting sick."

He groaned. "Great."

With a hand around his arm, she helped him to stand. "Come on. We're going to have a talk before we get you off the yacht."

"You're going to put me through the third degree while I'm down?"

"It won't be that bad."

Soren managed to get himself to the main cabin without her help, but the paleness of his face told her he still wasn't feeling well. She led him to the bedroom and waited while he went inside the bathroom and rinsed his mouth. Treasure sat on the bed and patted the spot next to her when he came back out.

"Sit," she said. Once Soren sat beside her, she continued, "I overreacted when you first told me about you being a werewolf, but it's not something I ever expected to have to handle."

"I know. It's a big shock to learn a creature out of myth and legend is actually real. I tried to break it to you the easiest way I knew how. I've never told a mortal before."

"Mortal? You must mean everyone else who isn't a werewolf, right?"

"Yes. To set the record straight, my kind really isn't immortal. We're just really long-lived. The oldest we get is around three thousand years old."

Treasure swallowed. "Then how old are you, Soren?"

"Nine hundred."

She tried to not let on how shocking she found that. Soren might be that old, but he definitely didn't look it. He appeared to be her age.

"Okay. I can handle that, I think. Now you said I'm your mate and that we're bonded. Is it because of this separation anxiety you spoke of that you followed me home?"

Soren swallowed a few times, as if he fought not to get sick. "Yes. Mates can't stand to be apart from each other, or it plays nasty tricks on their minds. It's not something either one of us should go through if it can be prevented. I'd rather suffer through a bout of seasickness than be apart from you for any length of time. Though after a couple of years it does get better, allowing us more time to be away from each other."

This separation anxiety had to be pretty bad if Soren was willing to purposely suffer through seasickness. Right now, he looked like death warmed over. And being with him again, all the reasons why she'd fallen for him in the first place came to the forefront of her mind.

Soren groaned, then shot to his feet, making a hasty retreat to the bathroom. She followed more slowly. She grimaced when she saw he had nothing left in his stomach to get rid of and only had the dry heaves.

"All right," she said once he finished. "Time to get you out of here. I think you've suffered enough. We'll continue our chat at the penthouse."

He took a step toward her and tentatively took her in his arms. "Does that mean you're willing to stay with me? Be my Treasure?" He grinned. "Pun intended."

She couldn't help but smile back. "As if I haven't heard that one before." Treasure grew serious. "I do love you, Soren. Just take things slow with me, okay?"

Soren kissed her forehead. "I will. I'm sorry we became mated before I had a chance to tell you about this. That had been my intention. Until somebody decided she couldn't wait to have me."

Treasure smiled. "Yeah, I guess you can blame me for that one." She hugged him before she pulled back to look him in the face. "It's going to take some work, but I think we'll make it."

"We'll get it figured out. Now can we go, because if I stay here much longer I'll be praying to the porcelain god again."

"We can't have that."

With an arm around Soren's waist, Treasure helped her mate off the yacht. She also decided she liked being the werewolf's treasure.

The End

WEREWOLF CLAIMED
ೞ

Chapter One

Draven lifted his lupine head and sniffed the air. He couldn't get enough of it. Compared to downtown Toronto, the scents up north in Muskoka were clean and fresh. Maybe that was why he felt drawn to come to the lake house on Buck Lake more often than not lately. It was good to get away from the smog, to run through the bush as a wolf.

Then there was the whole Rick fiasco. God, Draven couldn't believe he had called that scumbag a friend. Rick was the lowest of the low, and deserved being kicked out of their pack. The other man's last words to Draven had been a threat to find him and make him pay for turning Rick in. His ex pack mate knew Draven had a lake house here, but Draven doubted Rick would be so stupid as to follow him. If it came down to a fight, Draven was the stronger of the two. And Rick knew it.

Draven loped through the trees, enjoying the fact there was no one else around for miles. No mortals he'd have to hide from while in this form. He'd made sure when he bought the lakefront property twenty years before that he could purchase the lots on either side of it. He liked his privacy and didn't want mortal neighbors intruding upon it.

Lowering his nose to the ground he smelled the scent of a rabbit that had recently been in the area. Draven didn't bother to try to pick up its trail. He wasn't in the mood to chase one for the fun of it. He'd arrived late that morning and hadn't been able to ignore the call of the great outdoors. He'd already been out running for a few hours and it was now early afternoon.

He continued on his way, making the wide loop he'd set for himself back toward the house. The sun that managed to shine through the thick foliage high above him was hot. It was a perfect day for a swim. He intended to jump into the lake and do just that very soon.

Reaching the back of the place he considered his second home, Draven reached for the magic deep inside him and shifted to his human form, willing his athletic shorts and muscle shirt on at the same time. He'd go inside, change into his bathing suit and head for his dock.

Draven had only taken a step in the direction of the sliding glass door when he heard a male voice swearing up a storm. Sound traveled better over the water, but with his sensitive werewolf hearing, he knew the man wasn't far from the waterside of his property. Deciding he'd better investigate, he changed direction and headed toward the front of the house.

He spotted a small boat on the lake about twenty feet away from the end of his dock. A solitary man stood at the back of it, smacking the hell out of the top of the outboard motor.

Draven quickly walked down the well-worn path to the dock. He smiled as the man swore again.

"You goddamn mother fucker, start already."

"You sound as if you could use a little help," Draven said loud enough for the man to hear.

The other man's head whipped around, causing the boat to rock. He used his hand to shade his eyes as he looked at Draven. "Maybe a little. This piece-of-crap motor won't start. It seemed fine when I left the cottage."

As if to show the truth of his words, he took hold of the manual pull start and roughly yanked on it. After the third time, the boat rocked so violently the man lost his balance and fell over the side into the water. Draven roughly pulled off his shirt, prepared to dive in after him, but the other man surfaced a few seconds later.

He smacked the water. "Just fucking perfect." He swam closer to the boat and hauled himself into it.

"Why don't you use one of the oars to paddle over to my dock," Draven called. "I'm pretty handy when it comes to motors."

The man snorted. "I would if I could. Dumb-ass that I am, I didn't think to look to see if there were any in the boat before I left. And wouldn't you know it, there aren't. I've drifted, allowing the current to take me wherever it wants for the last twenty minutes."

"Hold on. I have some rope that should be long enough to reach you."

Draven took off at a run and went to his boathouse situated close to the dock. Inside, he grabbed the length of coiled rope out of the bottom of his power boat before heading back outside. At the end of the dock, he tied it to one of the attached metal rings.

"Are you ready to catch?" he asked the man.

"Yeah, but I don't know if you're going to be able throw it this far."

Without answering, Draven flung the coil of rope out over the water, putting all of his werewolf strength behind it. It came up a little short, but the other man was able to fish the end out of the lake. Seeing he had a good hold of it, Draven pulled, towing the boat toward the dock. Once it was parallel with it, he held the side of the small water craft while the man used another rope to tie it to the dock.

Draven backed away as his visitor stepped up beside him. The breeze changed direction, blowing in his face. Drawing in a deep breath of the man's scent, realization hit him like a ton of bricks. He stiffened, fighting not to pounce on him as his mating urge roared to life. His cock instantly became hard. It was all he could do to stop the growl of need that built inside him from pushing past his lips.

Completely unaware of Draven's state, his would-be mate said, "Thanks, man. I don't know what I would have done if you hadn't happened to come along. I'm Wyatt, by the way." He stuck out his hand.

"Draven," he said, gritting his teeth against the shot of arousal the simple touch of shaking hands caused.

"Do you think you can fix the motor enough for me to get back to the cottage, Draven?"

"I'll give it a shot. I just need to get some tools first. You must be new around here. I haven't seen you before."

"You could say that. I've rented a cottage on the other end of the lake for a couple of weeks. I thought I'd try a little fishing." Wyatt motioned to the rod and tackle box that sat on the bottom of the boat.

While Wyatt spoke, Draven ran his gaze over him, taking all of him in. His would-be mate was about four inches shorter than him, standing around six feet. His body was muscular, though not as big as Draven. And from the way Wyatt's wet t-shirt and shorts clung to him, there didn't appear to be an inch of fat on him anywhere. His short, dark-blond hair just brushed the top of his collar. Wyatt also had rugged good looks.

Wyatt came across as straight, but that didn't mean he was. And just because he set Draven's mating urge off, it wasn't a foregone conclusion that Wyatt was into men. It just meant he was the one for Draven, who happened to be. At fifteen hundred years old, he'd known for a long time that a woman would never be his mate. He'd slept with one once, but had found it totally unsatisfying and unappealing.

Pulling himself back to the present, Draven found Wyatt's hazel-eyed gaze directed on him. He realized he'd been silent for a bit too long. Draven cleared his throat, trying to pull it together. It was hard to concentrate on anything else with the mating urge riding his ass, making him so horny for the man in front of him he wanted to go down on his knees and suck Wyatt's cock.

He didn't. Instead, he said, "The fishing usually isn't good this time of day. It's better to go out in the early evening. That's when they start biting. I think I know which cottage you're staying at. It's the only one on the lake that is a rental, as far as I know."

"I'll have to try later then," Wyatt said in return. "If the boat is up and running again, that is."

"Let me get some tools and see if I can get the motor to start."

Drawing one more lungful of his would-be mate's scent, Draven felt it fill him as he burned it to his brain to never be forgotten. He turned and walked down the dock toward the boathouse where he kept his toolbox.

Wyatt watched Draven walk away and felt the tension in his body slowly leave him. It had been a strain to act as if nothing was really out of the ordinary when it had been far from it. Getting his first look of Draven up close, Wyatt had been instantly attracted to him. The man was his walking wet dream with model good looks, longish brown hair and light-green eyes. The man also had a body of a bodybuilder, all cut and well padded with muscle. Plus, Wyatt liked the fact Draven was taller than him. He was always attracted to a man who was bigger than himself.

He shook his head at his musings. The odds were very good that Draven was as straight as they came. Most men who looked like him were. And given Draven's size, there was no way Wyatt would test the waters. He didn't feel like finding out how much strength Draven could put behind a punch.

It only took a few minutes for Draven to return, carrying a small toolbox. Wyatt couldn't help running his gaze over him as he watched him walk down the dock. God, he wished he could explore that hard body with his lips and tongue. Men who looked like Draven were few and far between, and were usually way out of Wyatt's league, if they happened to be gay in the first place.

Drawing even with Wyatt, Draven said, "You can stay on the dock, since there isn't a whole lot of room on the boat."

"Sounds good to me. One dunking is enough."

Draven stepped into the boat, and with ease walked to the back to the outboard motor. Wyatt followed his movements with his gaze, marveling at how easily the other man was able to keep his balance without rocking the small craft. Christ, if Wyatt tried that he'd end up in the drink for sure.

Once Draven had the cover off the engine he bent over, giving it a closer look. Wyatt stared at his wide, tanned back, watching the muscles move as he poked at a few of the parts of the motor. Wyatt bit back a moan, resisting the urge to adjust his hardening cock in his shorts. He was torturing himself, but he couldn't stop looking at Draven.

"I think I see the problem," Draven said after a few minutes. "This is a newer engine, so it's a four-stroke, which means oil needs to be added separately instead of using an oil-and-gas mixture that older two-stroke engines require." He straightened and looked at Wyatt. "From the looks of it, oil hasn't been added for a long time and there wasn't enough, so the motor is seized. I doubt an oil change has ever been done on it."

Wyatt blew out a breath. "So in other words, it's completely fucked."

"Basically. Sorry, but I can't fix that kind of damage."

"Well, shit. There goes some of the fishing I'd planned to do. I was hoping to troll for perch. You can't catch those from the shore."

Draven replaced the cover on the engine before stepping onto the dock. He met Wyatt's gaze. "There's not many of them left. What I've been mostly catching is sunfish, rock bass, catfish and a few smallmouth bass. The first two you can't eat—one being full of bones and the other, worms."

"Good to know." Wyatt did his best to keep his gaze on Draven's, but it was a losing battle. It skimmed down the man in front of him, taking in his well-defined chest and abs. He forced his gaze to rise back to his face just before he reached the crotch of Draven's shorts.

Draven picked up his toolbox. "It looks as if I'll have to give you a tow with my boat back to the cottage where you're staying."

"Thanks, I appreciate that." Wyatt took a deep breath before he said, "For all your help, would you like to have a beer with me? It doesn't have to be right now if you're busy. You can stop by later."

He held himself still, waiting for Draven's answer. He hoped the other man would say yes. Wyatt might not be able to touch Draven the way he wanted, but he wouldn't mind getting to know him better as a friend.

Draven smiled, one that made Wyatt's cock twitch. "A beer sounds good. I'm also in the mood to do some fishing later today. Why don't I take you out on my boat? That way your holiday won't be completely ruined."

Wyatt nodded like an idiot. "I'd like that. If we do go fishing, I can cook some burgers for us to go along with the beer, then we can go out in your boat." The words came out in a rush, making him sound completely desperate, at least to his ears.

"You know what? I'll take you up on that offer," Draven said with another devastating smile. "I only arrived this morning and I haven't had a chance to go into Gravenhurst to buy some groceries. There isn't a whole lot in the fridge."

For the first time Wyatt glanced at the house behind Draven. It was larger than all the other cottages in the area. From what he could see of it, it was gorgeous and the type of place he wished he could have afforded to rent for his holiday.

"You renting as well?" Wyatt asked.

Draven shook his head. "No. It's mine. I've had it for a number of years. I had the house totally rebuilt not too long ago, since I seem to spend more time up here than I have in the past."

If Draven could afford to do that, he had to have a hell of a lot more money than Wyatt did. "It's really nice. Now I'm not so sure if you'll be comfortable in my dinky little cottage."

"As long as there are food and beer, it's all good."

It was Wyatt's turn to smile. "There's plenty of beer, you don't have to worry about that."

"Then I'm definitely in. Let's get your boat towed to your cottage, then I'll come back whenever you think those burgers will be ready."

"I'll shoot for around five. That way we can eat early before we go out fishing."

"Good plan. I'll put my toolbox away then get my boat out of the boathouse."

Once Draven turned and walked away, Wyatt couldn't stop grinning like a dork. He reminded himself it wasn't a date, but he still had that excited feeling in the pit of his stomach he got when he met a new guy and they went out for the first time. He still had no reason to assume Draven was anything but straight, though that didn't mean Wyatt couldn't dream.

The sound of a powerful engine being started drew Wyatt's attention to the nearby boathouse. A few seconds later the door on the end lifted and a sleek powerboat slowly backed out. It looked as if Draven had the fancy toy to go with his fancy lake house.

The larger boat pulled up to the dock and Draven cut the engine. He secured it before he hopped out and rejoined Wyatt. "Tying your boat to the back of mine is the best way to do this. I just won't be able to go too fast."

With a little jockeying about, they managed to get his boat tied up behind Draven's and then they were leaving the dock. Wyatt sat in the seat at the back just to make sure nothing went wrong during the towing. His gaze kept straying over to Draven as the other man drove the powerful boat. One time he thought for sure Draven turned his head to stare at him with something like desire showing in his light-green eyes, but Draven quickly looked away.

Once they reached the other side of the lake, Wyatt directed Draven to his rental's dock. It didn't take them long to secure the smaller boat. He made a mental note to contact the owner of the cottage about the motor no longer working.

Straightening from tying the rope he worked on, Wyatt turned to face Draven. "Thanks for the tow. I guess I'll see you in a little while then."

Draven nodded. "I'll be here right at five."

They stood silently staring at each other. Wyatt held his breath when he saw what he thought was hunger lingering in Draven's eyes. He swallowed, not sure if he was reading the other man wrong or not. Afraid to move in case he was mistaken and acted on the desire Draven roused in him, he waited to see what Draven would do next.

The air left Wyatt's lungs in a whoosh as Draven turned without a word and got back into his boat. The engine roared to life and the powerful watercraft sped away.

Wyatt walked toward the end of the dock, now completely confused. If Draven was in fact straight, he wouldn't have looked at him like that, would he? Just thinking about it made his cock throb. He'd have to wait and see what happened later. And Wyatt hoped to god he read the signs Draven gave him correctly.

Chapter Two

Draven pushed the power boat to a faster speed as he fought the surging desire that threatened to take him over. Damn, the mating urge rode him hard. Every time he'd looked at Wyatt, he'd wanted to pull the smaller man into his arms and kiss him until neither one of them could think straight. But he just barely managed to restrain himself. He didn't want to make a mistake with Wyatt. As they'd interacted, Draven had been able to smell his would-be mate's arousal, but Wyatt had held himself back. As a werewolf, Draven could pick up the scent of mortals' emotions. Wyatt's had been that of being unsure.

He drew in a deep breath, trying to tamp down some of the arousal that still heated his blood. Draven had to wonder if some of what Wyatt could have felt had to do with being straight and finding himself attracted to another man. It wouldn't be the first time Draven had that happen to him. Werewolves were known for their supermodel good looks, which a lot of mortals were attracted to.

After arriving back at his property, Draven parked in the boathouse. He jogged up to the house, wishing he could go for another run in his wolf from to expend some of the pent-up longing the mating urge caused. He couldn't, though. Going wolf would only make things worse for him. The instinct to claim and take what was his would be harder to resist. Until he figured out how things would go between him and Wyatt, he had to keep himself under tight control.

Having over an hour before he had to return to Wyatt's cottage, Draven decided a swim in the lake would have to do for now. Since it was the middle of the summer, the water wouldn't be too cold, but there were spots where the water was cooler than others. He'd find as many of them as he could and see if that would help with his racing libido. He doubted it would, but he'd find it more palatable than a cold shower.

* * * * *

After a forty-five minute swim that did nothing but tire him out a bit, Draven took a quick shower before he dressed in a pair of blue jeans and a black t-shirt. As he walked to the boathouse, the thought of seeing Wyatt again had his erection pressing against the front of his pants. In the throes of the mating urge, he knew he'd be walking around with a hard-on, or at least be semi-hard, all the time until he claimed his mate. *If* he could claim him, that is. It was already complicated enough that Wyatt was mortal, more than likely not knowing werewolves even existed, but Draven not being sure of his sexual orientation just made it even tougher.

Draven threw his fishing rod and tackle box into his boat before he started it and backed out of the boathouse. His heart beat a little faster the closer he came to Wyatt's cottage. Thoughts of all the things he wanted to do to him while he explored every inch of Wyatt's body flashed through his mind.

After securely tying his boat to the dock, Draven headed for the small cottage close by. The building was in need of a paint job. It looked as if the outboard motor wasn't the only thing the owners had neglected. He didn't like the thought of his would-be mating staying in a place like this. He had a feeling the inside wouldn't be much better.

Draven knocked on the door and Wyatt opened it. A smile spread across the other man's face. "Draven. Come in. You're right on time."

He stepped into the cottage as Wyatt backed up to give him room. "I do try to be punctual." Draven sniffed the air. "Something smells good."

"Thanks. I have the burgers cooking outside on the portable charcoal grill I brought with me, which I'm glad I did, since there isn't one here. Would you like a beer?"

"Sure. I could go for one right about now."

"Then make yourself at home and I'll get you one."

Draven walked farther into the large room, which was the combined living room and kitchen. He sat on the couch that had seen better days. He looked around, noting less than stellar furnishings and flooring. There wasn't even a television. Since cable wasn't available at the lake, it wasn't too surprising. At his place, he had satellite TV.

Wyatt returned, carrying two bottles of beer. After he passed one to Draven, he sat next to him. "Just a few more minutes, then the burgers will be ready. Dinner is nothing fancy, since I'm not that great of a cook. But it's eatable."

"I'm sure it'll be fine." Draven took a sip of his cold beer. "So are you ready to do some fishing after we eat?"

Wyatt nodded. "Definitely. I ended up calling the owner of this place and told him what happened to the outboard motor. He apologized, but he won't be able to get it repaired until after I leave. He's an older man, and I don't think he has much interest in this place. It's probably the reason why he rents it out."

Draven had never met the owner, and to be honest, he really hadn't met any of the other people who owned cottages on the lake. He liked to keep to himself. Plus, there was the fact that if he got too friendly with them they'd soon question why he wasn't aging at all over the years. Werewolves being very long-lived, the oldest his kind reached was three thousand. It was just easier for him to keep his distance.

Wyatt and he drank their beer in silence before his would-be mate spoke. "So you said you just arrived this morning. Was it a long drive for you?"

"Not really. Only a couple of hours. I live in Toronto."

Wyatt sat up straighter. "I'm in Mississauga, so we're almost neighbors."

Draven chuckled. "Yeah, you could say that." He paused, then asked, "What do you do back in Mississauga?"

"I'm the manager of a small electronics store."

"I bet that's an interesting job."

Wyatt laughed and shook his head. "No, not really. To be honest, it's damn boring at times. Then there is the whole having-to-deal-with-customers thing. The majority of them are easy to be around, but there are others who have me biting my tongue over their insults. As you can probably tell, this isn't my dream job, by any means."

"Yeah, I can see that," he said with a smile. "It wouldn't be my choice, since I'm not much of a people person." Draven sniffed the air. "It smells as if those burgers are done."

"Crap. I forgot all about them."

Wyatt shot to his feet and went out the back door at the kitchen area. Draven stood and walked over to where Wyatt had disappeared. Standing at the screen door, he watched his would-be mate take the burgers off the grill and put them on the plate he held.

"Do you need some help, Wyatt?"

The other man looked up from what he was doing and shook his head. "No, I'm good. You can get the door for me, though."

Draven pushed it open and held it as Wyatt walked by him. It wasn't long before the small kitchen table was set and they were sitting to eat. He took a bite of his burger, enjoying the taste of it, but would have liked it better if it had been more on the undercooked side. As a werewolf, he liked his beef rare to the point it was basically raw.

After they finished their meal, Draven and Wyatt got ready to go fishing. Draven had left his windbreaker in the boat, so he told Wyatt to meet him at the dock when he was ready.

He'd just finished checking over his rod when a god-awful stench filled his nose. It felt as if it were burning his nostrils. Turning to face the dock, he saw Wyatt walking down toward him. Whatever it was, it came from the other man.

Once Wyatt drew even with the boat, Draven asked, "All ready to go?" He took another deep breath, which caused him to sneeze, repeatedly, his body's way of clearing out the offending smell from his nostrils.

"Yeah, I am. Are you okay? You're not coming down with a cold, are you?"

Draven shook his head. "No...ah, I think it's something you must have put on. Your scent is a bit...different. Stronger."

Wyatt gave him a confused look. "Really? It's mosquito repellent. I didn't think it smelled that bad. It's supposed to be the kind that doesn't have an unpleasant odor."

Draven scrunched his nose. The repellent was not only repelling the insects, it was doing it to him as well. He didn't want to get anywhere near Wyatt because of it, which didn't sit well with him. He'd hoped to put some feelers out while they fished, to see if his would-be mate was into men or not. But as it stood now, that wouldn't be happening. With his heightened senses, if he smelled the repellent long enough, it would feel as if the inside of his nose was burning. Draven would have to somehow get Wyatt to wash the crap off before he did any of that.

"Why would you use that?" Draven asked. "I thought the DEET inside the spray wasn't supposed to be good for you."

Wyatt stepped into the boat, carrying his fishing pole and tackle box. "I figure it's better to use repellent, rather than risk the chance of a mosquito biting me that has West Nile virus. You should probably use some as well." He pulled out a spray bottle from his jacket pocket and held it out.

Draven backed up as the smell of the repellent grew stronger. "Ah, thanks, but no thanks. I don't need it, anyway.

The mosquitoes leave me alone. I never get bitten." Which was the truth. Being what he was, there had to be something in his blood the insects didn't like.

"Lucky you. I wish I could say the same. When I get bitten, I break out in huge welts and they itch like crazy."

"Why don't you get seated, then I'll take us out." Wyatt drew near and Draven sneezed repeatedly again.

Wyatt gave him a worried look. "If you aren't coming down with a cold, I have a feeling you're allergic to the repellent." He backed up a little. "I think it would be better if I don't get too close to you while we're fishing."

"You don't have to do that." Draven sneezed again.

"Oh yes, I do. I don't mind."

Draven sighed, then said, "Once we're finished, you can wash it off and get as close to me as you want."

At Wyatt's sharp, indrawn breath, Draven realized what he'd just implied. His gaze met his would-be mate's and he found uncertainty lurking in his hazel eyes. Had he said too much? Draven was about to do some backtracking, but Wyatt spoke before he could.

"So you still want to hang out after we're done fishing?"

Draven nodded. "Sure, but back at my place. I have satellite television. We can look for a movie to watch or something while we have a few beers."

Wyatt gave him a crooked smile. "Yeah, the cottage doesn't have that. Watching some TV later sounds good."

"Let's go see what kind of fish are biting this evening."

"I'm ready. I even have the worms. I bought some on the way here." Wyatt held up his tackle box.

Draven gave a short nod, then started the boat's motor. He focused on what he was doing as Wyatt settled himself on the seat next to him. If not for that stench masking most of his would-be mate's scent, Draven would have enjoyed his closeness. He made a mental note not to take Wyatt out fishing in the evening again.

* * * * *

Wyatt watched as Draven put a worm on his hook before he cast his line into the water. His was already out, and he sat almost at the very end of the boat while Draven was closer to the front. He still didn't think the repellent was *that* bad. Draven must have a really sensitive nose, or allergies like Wyatt had thought if it affected him that much.

If it weren't for the fact he'd be eaten alive without it, he would have used some of the lake water to rinse it off his skin, though he'd sprayed it on his clothes as well. Wyatt looked over at his line, seeing the float was still above the surface. No takers yet.

He glanced at Draven again. Thinking of Draven's reaction to the smell of the repellent, Wyatt recalled what Draven had said about him being able to get as close to him as he wanted once he washed it off. Right after Draven had said it, a shot of intense arousal had surged through Wyatt. Then he'd questioned if Draven actually meant what Wyatt thought he implied. That one statement did give him some hope that Draven was attracted to men the same as he was.

But being able to see one way or the other wasn't a possibility at the moment, not with them practically sitting at opposite ends of the boat. The notion that Draven could be interested in him in that way had his cock hard.

Wyatt's attention soon focused back on his fishing pole when he felt a jerk on the line. The float attached to it bobbed in the water, then sank beneath. He gave a hard tug on his rod, able to feel that he'd managed to keep the fish on the hook.

"I've got one," he shouted.

Draven looked over. "Reel it in."

Wyatt did exactly that, quickly working the reel to bring the fish to the surface. Once he brought it out of the water, it appeared to be a good-sized bass, but not the smallmouth variety he was familiar with. This fish was darker in coloring and the scales were bigger.

"Rock bass," Draven said. "Full of worms. With some of the fish, you can see white lumps on their sides from them."

At closer inspection, Wyatt saw what Draven had described. "They're there. It's going back in the water." Making sure to push the dorsal fin flat along the fish's back, he took out the hook before throwing it into the lake.

Draven and he spent the next hour catching nothing but rock bass. A little disappointed, Wyatt agreed there was no point in staying out much longer after Draven suggested they pack it in for the night. Wyatt remained at the back of the boat as Draven started it and headed to his lake house.

Wyatt hopped out of the boat when Draven pulled up to the dock and grabbed one of the ropes to secure it there. That done, they both walked toward the large house. Wyatt kept some distance between them.

Draven opened the door and stepped aside for Wyatt to enter. As Wyatt walked past, Draven sneezed again. He met Wyatt's gaze. "Sorry."

"I'll take my jacket off, then go wash up in the bathroom."

Draven pointed to the left. "It's just down the hallway over there."

Wyatt shrugged out of said garment before he went where Draven indicated. He found the bathroom no problem and used the soap in the dish on the corner of the counter to wash off the repellent.

Wyatt headed out of the bathroom and back to the main part of the house, admiring Draven's place. It looked as if it had been professionally decorated with dark, hardwood floors and modern furniture. Reaching the spacious, cathedral-ceilinged entrance, he didn't see Draven anywhere.

"Draven?" he called.

"I'm in the living room."

Wyatt followed where the sound of Draven's voice had come from and found him sitting on a black leather couch across from a large HD LCD television. Two bottles of beer sat on the dark wood coffee table in front of him.

"I hope you don't mind," Draven said as Wyatt crossed the room. "I hung your jacket outside on the porch."

"That's fine," he replied with a chuckle. "It's your place."

Draven stood and stopped Wyatt before he could sit on the couch next to him. "Wait." Draven leaned in and took an audible deep breath. He then quickly turned his head away and sneezed. "I thought you washed off the repellent."

"Yeah, off my skin, but I can't do much about it being on my clothes." Wyatt's heart beat faster at Draven's closeness. The other man hadn't moved away.

"I guess there isn't much you can do about that then."

Draven's gaze seemed to heat with desire, making Wyatt hope like hell he was reading him right and not seeing what he wanted to. The more time he spent with Draven the more Wyatt wanted him.

Wyatt reached for the bottom of his t-shirt and yanked it over his head. He didn't mind taking that off, but his jeans, which had been sprayed as well, were another story. The problem wasn't that he didn't have any underwear on, because he did; it was the state of his cock. Being so close to Draven had turned him on. If he were to remove his pants, there was no way in hell he'd be able to hide the fact he was attracted to Draven.

Holding his t-shirt in front of his crotch to help hide the state he was in, Wyatt said with humor in his voice, "Will this help?"

He looked at Draven and found the other man's gaze hungrily roaming over his bared upper body. There was no mistaking the desire that lurked in Draven's eyes this time. Wyatt's heart beat even faster, forcing more blood into his already hard cock.

Draven lifted his gaze and met Wyatt's. "Yes. What would you say if I told you I wished that wasn't the only thing you'd take off?"

The husky timbre of Draven's voice seemed to wrap around his erection, stroking it. Wyatt swallowed. "My answer would be I'd want the same from you."

Wyatt swore Draven's eyes glowed mutedly for a split second before the other man closed the short distance between them and cupped his face. Draven's lips descended on his, hungrily taking them in a heated kiss. Wyatt dropped his shirt and put his hands on Draven's waist.

The feel of Draven swiping his tongue over the seam of his lips had Wyatt opening to allow him entrance. What sounded like an animal-like growl rumbled out of Draven. The sound had Wyatt pulling the man who kissed him so thoroughly against his body so their cocks met. He moaned when he felt Draven's hard length pressed against his own.

The kiss seemed to go on forever, but Draven pulled away first. He had his eyes closed while he breathed rapidly. Wyatt had thought Draven couldn't look any sexier, but seeing the other man's face flushed with desire and his lips swollen from his kisses, proved him wrong.

After a few seconds passed, Draven opened his eyes. "I guess I don't have to worry about you being straight anymore."

"I'm most definitely not. And now I can say the same thing about you."

Draven dropped his hands and took a small step back. "If you're in the mood to take off your clothes, I might as well put them in the washer."

A thrill shot through Wyatt's body at Draven's words. He dropped his hands to the top of his jeans. "You want them, you can have them."

He quickly undid the button and pulled down the zipper. He pushed off the jeans and stepped out of them before he held the pants out to Draven. The other man took them and bent to pick up the discarded t-shirt before he straightened.

"Don't go anywhere," Draven said. "I won't be long."

"Even if you didn't have my clothes, I wouldn't leave."

Wyatt turned to follow Draven with his gaze as the other man walked out of the living room. Alone, he let out a shaky breath. Arousal pounded through him. That one kiss hadn't been enough. Now that he knew Draven wasn't off-limits, he wanted to act on every hot, sexy thought he'd had about him. With his clothes in the wash, Wyatt was sure Draven and he could come up with something to help pass the time.

Chapter Three

೧೦

Draven fought to keep control of his mating urge as he took Wyatt's clothes to the main floor laundry room. Kissing his would-be mate had his hold over himself slipping a tiny bit. Now that he knew for sure Wyatt was gay, the instinct to claim him as his mate rode him harder. There was no longer any need to pussyfoot around.

He checked Wyatt's jeans pockets before he threw them in the front-load washer. The t-shirt followed. As he put liquid laundry detergent in the machine, he ran through his head how he wanted this night to go with Wyatt. Fully making love was out of the question. For if he did, he'd claim the other man as his, forming the mating bond between them. Once that happened, neither one of them would be able to stand to be apart from the other. The separation anxiety that would cause would be a bitch. Over his very long life, Draven had seen mated couples go through it, seen how they practically climbed the walls, worried something bad had happened to their mates.

And it wasn't just the separation anxiety Draven was concerned about, either. Wyatt didn't know what Draven truly was. They'd gotten over the hurdle of knowing what each other's sexual orientation was, but Draven had the bigger one of telling his would-be mate all about werewolves. It wasn't something he could just blurt out and have Wyatt accept. Having him run from him was the last thing Draven wanted. It was hard enough with the mating urge riding his ass, but having to chase Wyatt down would cause it to be even more torturous. And that wouldn't go away until he'd made Wyatt his. As the days went by and he didn't claim him, it would only get worse.

Draven started the washer, then headed back to the living room. With the terrible chemical stench finally undetectable, he dragged in a deep breath. He could now smell Wyatt's scent unhindered. It smelled of man and arousal. Though he couldn't make love to Wyatt the way he wanted, Draven still intended to do other things that would make them both come. The entire time they'd been on his boat he'd ached to touch Wyatt, to learn what would turn him on, make him moan.

He walked into the living room to find Wyatt still standing where he'd left him. As he approached, Draven ran his gaze over the other man's hard body. He was all sleek muscles with a defined chest and abs. Draven found the sight of Wyatt only in his black boxer-briefs with his erection tenting the front of them a beautiful sight.

Lifting his gaze so it locked on Wyatt's, Draven closed the distance between them and took up where they had left off. He wrapped his arms around Wyatt's waist, holding him close. The other man sank his fingers into his hair and held his head exactly where he wanted as he deepened their kiss, pushing his tongue past Draven's lips.

Draven closed his eyes, knowing they had to be mutedly glowing with his arousal. It wasn't something he could control when he was this turned-on, or angry. He dropped his hands to Wyatt's ass and held him tighter against him as he rubbed his hard cock against his would-be mate's. They both gasped at the contact.

"God, you make me ache," Wyatt said between kisses.

Draven pulled slightly away, making sure to keep his eyes open to mere slits. "I have to touch you, Wyatt. Now."

"Do it," Wyatt said on a moan.

Inching Wyatt backward until his legs hit the couch, Draven then pushed him onto it. Before he joined him, he dragged off his own t-shirt, needing to feel his skin against his would-be mate's with nothing between. Climbing onto the couch, Draven positioned Wyatt so he lay stretched out on it.

He then followed him down, blanketing the other man with his body.

He kissed Wyatt, letting the pent-up desire coursing through him come to the surface. He sucked Wyatt's tongue into his mouth, enjoying the taste of his soon-to-be mate. It went straight to his head just as Wyatt's scent did. Draven would never get enough of the man in his arms.

Draven released Wyatt's mouth and made a wet trail along the side of his jaw, the other man's whiskers rough against his lips. Continuing downward, he sucked and licked until he reached where Wyatt's neck and shoulder met. He bit him hard enough to leave a mark. If Wyatt had been a werewolf, the feel of Draven's teeth marking him would have shattered any control he had over himself. Wyatt only groaned and bucked beneath him.

After releasing his hold on Wyatt's neck, Draven worked his way lower. He laved his tongue over each flat nipple before he gently took them one at a time between his teeth and tugged. Wyatt's fingers threaded in Draven's hair as he continued his downward trail.

At Wyatt's stomach, Draven said in a gruff voice against his skin, "I'm going to suck your cock, Wyatt. I've been dying to do it since I saw you this afternoon."

The other man bucked once again, pushing his hips against Draven's chest. "Oh god, Draven, you're making me so hard. Yes, suck me."

Not wasting any more time, Draven took hold of the waistband of Wyatt's underwear and pulled it down past his hips. Wyatt's cock sprang free. It was long and thick, not nearly as big as Draven's, but close enough. It was fully engorged with a bead of pre-cum sitting on the very tip. Draven growled deep in his chest at the sight of Wyatt's excitement.

Draven took hold of Wyatt's shaft and pumped his hand up and down. More pre-cum appeared on the slit. He flicked out his tongue and licked it off, reveling in the salty taste of his would-be mate. Wyatt sucked a breath through his teeth and groaned.

Needing to taste more of him, Draven rose and straddled Wyatt's legs, keeping a tight hold on the other man's cock. Bending, he opened his mouth and took the head inside. The feel of Wyatt on his tongue made his shaft jerk, demanding attention. Draven ignored his own need, wanting to give Wyatt pleasure first.

As Draven sucked, he reached between Wyatt's legs and fondled his balls, rolling them ever so gently in his hand. In and out he took his would-be mate's big cock. It grew even harder as Wyatt's breath came in pants.

"Fuck," Wyatt groaned. "That feels so damn good. Christ, you know how to suck cock."

Draven increased the suction, making sure he paid extra attention to the spot under the flared head. Wyatt rocked his hips, fucking Draven's mouth. He could tell Wyatt was close to release, especially when the other man gripped his hair at the back of his head to hold him where he wanted while he pumped his shaft past his lips.

"Shit...fuck...Draven...I'm coming," Wyatt panted before he moaned loudly.

Draven continued pleasuring Wyatt with his mouth. He kept sucking, taking everything he had to give him. He didn't stop until Wyatt's cock ceased jerking and he relaxed on the couch.

With desperate need pulsing through him, Draven sat up straight and undid his jeans. Unlike Wyatt, he'd gone commando, so his cock sprang free as soon as he parted the material of his pants. With eyes only open to mere slits, Draven watched Wyatt and took hold of his own cock, pumping his hand along his full length.

Wyatt sat up and brushed his hand away. "Let me do that." He stroked Draven's shaft. "I'm going to enjoy going down on you. There's nothing I like better than a big cock in my mouth."

Draven growled low. "Then take it," he said as he nudged forward, the tip of his shaft brushing against Wyatt's lips.

It seemed that was all the invitation Wyatt needed, because he sucked the head of Draven's cock into the warm, wet cavern of his mouth. Draven's head fell back in ecstasy at finally having his would-be mate touching him in one of the most intimate way. He rolled his hips, pushing more of his length past Wyatt's lips, wanting him to take more of him.

Wyatt moaned, sending vibrations along Draven's entire shaft. A howl of pleasure threatened to break free, but Draven tenaciously held it back. Instead, he pumped his hips faster, his cock growing harder as his balls rose closer to his body. It wasn't going to take much to send him into his own climax. Bringing Wyatt to his had increased Draven's arousal to the point of pain.

"Harder. Suck harder," Draven ground out through gritted teeth.

Wyatt did just that while he reached around Draven and shoved a hand down the back of his jeans. He squeezed his ass before he stroked a finger between the crack, caressing Draven's hole. Draven moaned, not knowing whether he wanted to push more into Wyatt's mouth, or back onto the finger that played with his anus.

It soon didn't matter when Wyatt held Draven's cock in a tighter hold and pushed his finger inside his hole at the same time, hitting his prostate. Draven yelled Wyatt's name as he came, emptying himself inside his would-be mate's mouth.

Once it was over, Draven cupped Wyatt's face and titled it up for his kiss. As blowjobs went, that one had been pretty explosive, mostly due to what Wyatt meant to him. No other man would turn him on as his mate did.

"You're still hard," Wyatt said with a moan. "How the hell did you manage that?"

"It's just something I can do," Draven replied. Wrapping his arms around Wyatt, he rolled, going down on the couch, taking the other man with him so Wyatt ended up sprawled along him. "That was amazing."

"I have to agree with that," Wyatt said as he snuggled closer. "Unlike you, I need a few minutes to recover, then we can indulge in something that will be even better than oral sex."

Draven had known this would come up, and had an excuse at the ready. He ran his hand up and down Wyatt's back. "Ah, actually, we can't."

Wyatt lifted his head to look at him. "Why not? Please don't tell me you have a boyfriend back in Toronto."

He cupped Wyatt's cheek. "Relax, babe. It's nothing like that. I haven't had a relationship for a very long time. And since I really wasn't expecting to meet someone here, I'm not prepared for this. Unless you have condoms and lube with you."

Wyatt gave him a sheepish smile. "Oh. I totally took that the wrong way. And no I don't, not even back at the cottage. Like you, I thought I'd be spending my holiday alone at the lake."

"So you can see why this is as far as we can go for now." He gave Wyatt a lingering kiss. "It doesn't mean I don't want to, because I do. Badly. But I don't mind waiting."

Wyatt sighed. "I guess I don't, either."

"Stay with me," Draven blurted.

"You mean overnight?"

"No, I mean stay here at the lake house with me for the rest of your holiday. Forget the cottage. If you aren't comfortable sharing my bed, I do have a couple of spare bedrooms."

Now that Draven had put Wyatt and him on the path to becoming mates, he wanted the other man close. Plus, he didn't like the idea of Wyatt staying at the neglected cottage.

"Really?" Wyatt asked. "You want me to spend the next two weeks here at your lake house?"

"Yeah." He stroked Wyatt's stubble-roughened cheek. "I do. I'd much rather have you here with me instead of way over on the other side of the lake."

"But how long are you going to be up here? Don't you have to work?"

Draven chuckled. "No. I don't have a job. To be honest, I'm rich enough that I'll never have to work."

Wyatt shook his head. "I should have known."

"So will you stay or not?"

"Let me think here. You have a huge lake house with satellite TV and a flashy power boat. The cottage has no television, no radio and looks as if it has seen better days. Um, I think my answer is yes."

"Does all that mean you're using me for what my money can buy?" Draven asked with a smile.

"Hell no. I'm using you for your hot body and that big cock of yours."

Draven laughed. "I guess I can live with that."

Wyatt rolled off Draven and stood. He jerked his boxer-briefs up. "Good. Now let's have the beers that are sitting on the table getting warm and watch some TV." His gaze landed on Draven's still hard cock. "I need the distraction, unless you want to go another round of what we just did."

Draven stood and shoved his erection back into his jeans before he zipped them up, leaving the button undone. One bout of oral sex was enough. Even though he got to come, it only made his mating urge increase. Hand-jobs and blowjobs wouldn't give him any kind of relief until he'd made Wyatt his.

"TV and beer it is," he said. "I'm not pushing my luck."

Wyatt nodded. "All right, but tomorrow one of us will have to make the trip to Gravenhurst and pick up condoms and lube." He leaned in and brushed his lips across Draven's. "Then I want to put them to use."

Draven nodded, even though he knew he'd have to think of another excuse to not fully make love to Wyatt. But right now he wanted to enjoy the rest of the night just holding his would-be mate. He picked up the beers and handed one to Wyatt before he put his arm around the other man's shoulders and maneuvered him so he sat on the couch beside him. Holding Wyatt while he sat with his back against his chest, Draven grabbed the TV remote and turned it on. He hoped to have many more nights like this with Wyatt.

* * * * *

Wyatt followed Draven up the stairs to the next level. It was late. His clothes had long since come out of the dryer, but he still was only in his underwear. Mostly because he liked snuggling skin to skin with Draven. The other man hadn't donned his t-shirt again, and hadn't said a word about Wyatt getting dressed either.

Once they reached the top of the steps, Draven brought them to a stop and turned to face Wyatt. "So what will it be? Are you going to sleep in my bed, or do you want one of the guestrooms?"

Wyatt didn't like his answer any more than he guessed Draven would. But if he wanted to spend the rest of his holiday with him, Wyatt knew it was best to be upfront with Draven.

He cleared his throat. "Ah, I think it would be better if I took the guestroom. For both of us, actually."

"And why is that?"

"I tend to do…things…in my sleep."

"What things?"

"It's sort of along the lines of sleep walking, but I'm not walking. My last boyfriend called it sleep fucking."

Draven's lips twitched as if he held back a laugh. "So what you're telling me is you fuck while you're off in dreamland?"

Wyatt ran a hand through his hair. "I know you think I'm feeding you a line of bullshit, but I'm not. I don't do it all the time, just once in a while. I've been told I mostly do a lot of groping, but there have been a few instances where I've come awake while in the middle of sex. Supposedly I had initiated and have no recollection of it."

This time Draven's lips didn't just twitch. A wide smile broke across his face before he bellowed with laughter. It took some seconds until he managed to calm himself enough to speak. "Oh, Wyatt, that's hilarious. Sleep fucking."

"It's not that funny. Hey, you were the one who wanted us to stop at oral sex. I figured if we sleep apart I can avoid doing something you aren't prepared for."

Draven caught Wyatt by the back of the neck and pulled him closer before he claimed his lips. They were both noticeably breathing harder when Draven released his mouth and placed his forehead against his. "I didn't mean to make you feel uncomfortable, but you have to admit it is kind of funny." Draven let go of Wyatt's neck and took a step back. "You can have your pick of the guestrooms. But don't expect to sleep there for the rest of your holidays. I want you in my bed."

Wyatt nodded, still having a hard time getting his brain to function properly after the searing kiss he'd just shared with Draven. "I won't."

The other man turned and led Wyatt farther down the short hallway. He stopped at an open door and turned on the light. "This is the first guestroom. The other one is just across from it, and my bedroom is at the very end of the hall."

Wyatt looked inside the room before he said, "This one is fine."

"Then I'll say good night." Draven gave him another quick, hard kiss, then slowly backed down the hall. "And Wyatt, no sleep masturbating."

Wyatt flipped the other man off. "Smart ass."

Draven's laughter followed him as he turned and walked toward his bedroom. Wyatt strode into the guestroom. He didn't bother shutting the door. He crossed the room, his feet seeming to sink into the plush dark-blue carpet under them. The king-sized bed was already made up with sheets and a comforter that matched the color of the walls, which were a lighter shade than the carpeting.

Wyatt changed direction and headed toward the en suite bathroom. After he used the toilet and washed his hands, he went back to the main room and switched off the light. The high bed was calling. He pulled down the covers and climbed in. He wished Draven lay next to him, but as he told the other man, Wyatt didn't trust himself not to do something in his sleep if he wasn't alone.

He rolled onto his side and punched the pillow into the shape he wanted. Wyatt couldn't believe his good luck in meeting Draven. The other man was everything he looked for in a boyfriend, not that he thought Draven was that quite yet. Although there was a possibility of it after his holidays were over, if they hit it off. Some guys weren't into the relationship thing and liked to just have their fun, but Wyatt had a feeling Draven wasn't like that. For one thing, Draven was up here alone. With his looks, he assuredly had no problem picking up men.

Feeling sleep slowly overtaking him, Wyatt smiled in the darkness as he remembered what it was like to be held in Draven's arms, and making him come. His two-week vacation up north in Muskoka had definitely taken a turn for the better.

Chapter Four

&

Draven rolled over in bed and groaned as the sunlight that filtered into the room through the slight gap in the curtains hit his eyes. He wanted nothing more than to bury his head under one of his pillows and get some more sleep. But there really was no point in that. As a byproduct of the mating urge, his rest had been filled with erotic dreams of Wyatt, bringing him awake aching and hard. And they would continue to plague him every time he slept deep enough until he claimed the other man. So it was pointless trying to make up what he'd lost through the night.

At the thought of Wyatt, Draven turned his head and looked at his closed bedroom door. He couldn't hear the other man moving around. Having his would-be mate sleeping just down the hall had been torture. Each time he'd woken up after one of those erotic dreams, he'd been so tempted to climb into bed with Wyatt. Only thoughts of what would happen if he did had kept him in his own.

Draven quietly chuckled as he recalled how Wyatt had told him about his penchant for fucking while asleep. That would make the nights they did sleep in the same bed very interesting. If it weren't for the mating urge riding his ass, Draven would have actually told Wyatt it didn't matter. Even if they didn't have any condoms. As a werewolf, Draven couldn't "catch" anything or pass it on to his partners.

He stretched, sat up and readjusted his erection in his sleep pants. He didn't normally wear anything to bed, but since Wyatt was here, Draven had figured being naked was only asking for trouble if Wyatt came to his door for some reason during the night.

Draven threw back the covers and swung his legs over the side of the mattress. He'd take a shower, then go see if Wyatt was awake. He really didn't have anything to make for breakfast, but they could get something in Gravenhurst before they hit the grocery store to pick up food and the other items he'd used as an excuse last night.

After pushing to his feet, Draven took off the sleep pants and walked naked to the en suite. He only took the time to brush his teeth, then used the toilet before he got into the shower.

He was rinsing his hair when he heard the sound of the shower curtain being opened. With his eyes closed to prevent shampoo from getting in them, he said, "You do realize coming in here with me is playing with fire." Draven felt Wyatt's presence at his back.

"You in the shower is just too hard to resist," Wyatt said as he wrapped his arms around Draven's waist. He reached lower and grasped Draven's cock. "And especially when I had a feeling you'd be in this condition."

Draven groaned as Wyatt pumped his shaft. He couldn't stop himself from pushing himself tighter into the other man's hand. After all the erotic dreams he'd had of his would-be mate, he was horny as hell. Letting Wyatt make him come would only increase the mating urge even more, but Draven was past caring. He wanted it. He needed it.

He pulled Wyatt's hand off him and turned in his direction. "I guess both of us want to play with fire this morning."

Draven brought their mouths together in an intense kiss. The warm spray of the shower beat on his back as he pressed his front against Wyatt. The scent and feel of his would-be mate in his arms increased his libido. And it showed how much Draven had missed being with Wyatt, even though he had only been the short distance down the hall the entire night.

He backed Wyatt to the end of the tub until the other man's back hit the tiles. Draven angled his head to get a tighter fit of their lips as he stroked Wyatt's tongue with his, savoring the taste of him. Wyatt must have made use of the spare toothbrush and paste in the guestroom's en suite, since he tasted like mint.

Draven left Wyatt's mouth and placed kisses along his jaw. He pushed his hips forward until his cock pressed up against his would-be mate's. They both moaned in response. Draven ground along him, loving the friction it caused.

"Fuck, Draven," Wyatt said with a low groan. "You make me want to come so bad."

"Then I shouldn't make you wait."

Draven took hold of Wyatt and spun him around so he faced the wall that had been at his back. He then got the other man to place his hands flat against it. He ran his own down Wyatt's body, tracing and learning every inch as he went. Draven stopped his downward progress when he reached Wyatt's ass. It was muscled and taut. He cupped each globe in his hands, squeezing. Wyatt moaned and pushed back.

"You're driving me crazy, Draven."

"But in a good way, right?"

"God, yes."

He reached around for Wyatt's hard cock at the same time he stroked a finger down his crack. Draven pumped his fist up and down the other man's entire length, catching the pre-cum that leaked from the tip, using it as lubricant. He delved deeper between Wyatt's ass cheeks and ran a fingertip around his hole. His would-be mate pushed back as he panted. Draven sank a digit inside Wyatt's anus, slowly working his way deeper. He slid it in and out, matching his strokes on Wyatt's cock, before he inserted a second finger to join the first.

As he finger-fucked the other man's ass, Draven said huskily, "This is where I want my cock, deep inside you. Only when I do, you'll be on your hands and knees and I'll take you from behind." He hit Wyatt's prostate. "I'll make it so you'll want no other cock but mine."

Wyatt cried out as his climaxed, his cum shooting out of his shaft, hitting the tiled wall as his ass spasmed around Draven's fingers. Once the tremors subsided, he pulled out and ground his aching shaft against Wyatt's butt, pumping his hips until he bellowed with his own release. His seed shot out along Wyatt's lower back and Draven's stomach when he leaned into the other man, wrapping his arms around his would-be mate's waist.

Once he'd caught his breath and he was sure his eyes no longer glowed, Draven turned Wyatt and gave him a languid kiss. After he lifted his head, he said, "We both need a shower now."

Wyatt smiled. "Not that I'll complain about why I need one." He glanced down at Draven's still hard cock. "Are you sure you're finished, though?"

"Don't worry about it. It will eventually go down. Maybe. Being around you just makes me horny all the time."

Wyatt nipped Draven's chin. "You do realize I'll want to see how many times you can come before you finally lose your erection?"

"I don't think I'll mind that. But I have a feeling I'll tire you out first before that happens."

"Hmm, a challenge. I do love those. Once we get the condoms and lube, you better watch out. I might not let you out of the bed for the rest of the day."

Draven spun them around so Wyatt ended up under the spray of water. "In that case, we'd better hurry up and hit the store. And since I really don't have anything much to eat around here, we can go out for breakfast first."

Wyatt tipped back his head and wet his hair. "Now that I can go for. I'm starved. Too bad we didn't catch any fish we could eat last evening. Oh, and on the return trip, we should stop by the cottage so I can pack my things and get my car."

"Good idea." Draven grabbed the shampoo bottle and squeezed some into his hand. He then washed Wyatt's hair. "I'm glad you said you'll stay here with me, Wyatt."

The other man leaned in and kissed Draven. "I'm glad you invited me. I like the idea of having you all to myself."

"I feel the same way." He motioned for Wyatt to rinse his hair as he reached for the bottle of conditioner. "It will also give us a chance to get to know each other better. And once your holidays are over, we can work something so we can be together afterward."

"You want to see me once I go back to Mississauga?"

Draven bent his head so he looked directly into Wyatt's eyes. "Of course I do. You don't think I invite just any man to stay here with me, do you?"

Wyatt gave him a sheepish smile and shrugged. "Well, to be honest, the thought did cross my mind. I'm sure you have men lining up at your door."

He shook his head and put his hands on the top of Wyatt's shoulders. "No, I don't. Not that I would want it, anyway. I'm a private person and generally keep to myself. That's part of the reason I like coming up here so much. I have no neighbors on either side of my property and I have the bush to explore."

"So I guess it means something, since you did invite me to stay here?" Wyatt asked.

"Definitely. And I want to continue seeing you after you go home. I think you're exactly what I've wanted in a partner." When Wyatt didn't say anything right away, Draven asked, "Did I say something wrong?"

"No, not at all. I'm hoping I don't do anything to fuck this up."

Draven chuckled. "You won't have to worry about that. You'll soon realize it." He grabbed the bar of soap. "Let's get the shower over with so we can get something to eat."

"And get back here so we can indulge in our other cravings."

Draven had a feeling he'd be telling Wyatt about his being a werewolf sooner, rather than later. He didn't think he'd be able to hold off his would-be mate much longer. He'd just have to make sure they took their time in town and returned later in the day to the lake house.

* * * * *

Wyatt let out a low whistle when he got his first look at Draven's luxury sedan. The shiny, dark-gray paint job sparkled in the bright sun. A quick glance inside showed it had black leather seats.

"Now this is what I call a ride," Wyatt said as he looked over his shoulder at Draven. "You're going to laugh at my piece-of-shit car when you see it."

"No, I won't," Draven said. "I might be rich, but I'm not a snob." He cupped the back of Wyatt's head and gave him a quick, hard kiss. "I want you for who you are." He smiled. "And your hard body as well."

Wyatt grinned back. "I think I can live with that."

Draven aimed the remote on his keychain at the car and pushed the button to unlock it. "Get in before I think of other things I'd much rather be doing with, and to, you."

He laughed as he got in the passenger side, then watched Draven walk around to the driver's. Once the car's engine roared to life, the other man turned onto the gravel trail that would take them to the main road.

"I never asked," Draven said. "Have you stayed at Buck Lake before?"

"No, this is my first time here, but not to the Muskoka area. Growing up, my parents liked to rent a cottage in Bracebridge for a week during the summer every year. It was situated on Wood Lake."

"You said you went there as a kid. Does that mean you visited Santa's Village as well?"

Wyatt chuckled. "I have to admit we did. I remember I especially liked the swan paddle boats. And seeing the deer and Santa. Of course that was when I was much younger. At twenty-six, I'm way too old for it, and it's not as if I have kids to take there."

Draven glanced over with a smile. "Are you sure you aren't too big to go see Santa? Maybe you'd like to sit on his knee."

"Ha ha. The only Santa's lap I'd be willing to sit on would be yours, if you were dressed up in his red-and-white suit."

"I'll have to remember that when Christmas comes around. Then you'll have to show me just how much of a good boy you are."

Wyatt burst out laughing. "I bet you would want me to. Picturing you in a Santa suit is going to make me get a hard-on every time I hear his name."

"Kinky," Draven said with a wink.

Wyatt shook his head. "You're bad." He then looked out the windshield and saw they were entering the town. "So this is Gravenhurst."

"Yeah. It's a little smaller than Bracebridge, with a population of around eleven thousand. One of its claims to fame is having the oldest operating steamship in North America. Apparently, the R.M.S. Segwen was built in 1887. Its homeport is the Muskoka Wharf."

"Interesting. You know, I'm surprised you chose this part of Muskoka."

"Really? Why?"

"Well, for one thing you're rich. I would have thought Port Carling would have been more your style. They have those really big cottages there on Lake Muskoka."

"I told you already that I like my privacy. Port Carling wouldn't have given me that."

"That's true. That area does tend to get a fair amount of tourists."

Draven pulled into the parking lot of a family-type restaurant. He drove into an empty space, then turned off the engine. Once they both got out of the car, Draven said, "You should like this place. I know I do. They have the best omelets around, and the servings are on the large size, so I've never walked away without a full stomach."

"My kind of place," Wyatt said as they headed for the entrance. "If I go out to eat, I at least want to feel as if I got my money's worth."

It didn't take long after they were seated and ordered for their food to arrive. As Draven had said, the omelet Wyatt ordered was one of the best he'd ever eaten. And with the mound of home-fried potatoes that came with it, he doubted he'd need to eat anything more until dinner.

After their meal, it was only a short trip to the local IGA grocery store. As Draven grabbed one of the shopping carts, Wyatt said, "You're probably not going to want to buy a whole lot of food. I bought enough to last me at least the week before I left Mississauga. I figured the last week I'd come into town to purchase what I'd need for the rest of my holidays."

Draven nodded. "All right, but I think I'll pick up a few extra items that you might not have brought with you. I'm going to get us some thick steaks and ribs to do on the barbeque."

"If I weren't so full, that would sound good right about now. I take it you're a meat eater."

Draven seemed to stiffen at his question. "What do you mean?"

"All the meat you want to buy. I assume you aren't one of those people who think it's bad for you, especially the red variety."

He chuckled. "Oh. No, I'd never be able to give up meat. If it were all I had to eat, I'd have no problem having it every day. And I like my steaks really rare."

"I like mine cooked a little bit more than that, but it has to be pink on the inside."

They arrived at the meat department and Draven picked up the most expensive steaks he could find and put them in the shopping cart. Wyatt couldn't afford cuts like that on his budget.

"Well, well. If it isn't the queer."

Wyatt turned toward the male voice the same time Draven did. Draven's upper lip curled into a snarl as he stared at the other man. "What the hell are you doing here, Rick?"

Rick walked closer. "Maybe I've been looking for you."

Wyatt shot his gaze from Draven to Rick and back again. It was more than obvious there was bad blood between the two of them. They way Draven held his body, he looked just about ready to pounce on Rick, and not in a good way.

"And why would you be doing that?" Draven asked with an almost growl.

"You know why. It's because of you I had to go lone wolf. If you'd just kept your nose out of my damn business everything would have been fine."

"Maybe some of the other assholes you surround yourself with would have let it slide, but I'm not like that. You know what drugs do to us. I can't believe I ever considered you a friend."

"Do you think I care? The money was good. I'm not as old as you, Draven. I haven't had all those years to amass the fortune you have. And I don't want to wait that long to enjoy the better things in life."

Looking at Rick, Wyatt didn't think he was that much younger than Draven. If anything they appeared to be around the same age.

"Which goes to show how much of a pup you still are," Draven shot back.

Rick got right up into Draven's face. "Don't ever call me that again."

Draven shoved the other man away. "Back off, Rick. Think of where we are."

Rick rolled his shoulders. His gaze landed on Wyatt and he sniffed the air. "I don't think you're worried about that so much as the fact this one probably doesn't know the truth about you." He laughed. "You were always a sucker for his kind. Are you going to properly introduce me to your boyfriend, Draven? You don't have to be afraid about me trying to steal him away from you, since I don't like shoving my cock up some guy's ass."

There was no mistaking the growl that rumbled out of Draven for anything but what it was. Wyatt thought Draven's eyes might have glowed mutedly for a split second before Rick laughed again, drawing his attention.

"At least I don't have to force my bed partners to sleep with me. Unlike you," Draven said between clenched teeth.

At first glance, Rick was just as good-looking as Draven. It wasn't until Wyatt stared into the other man's eyes did he see the cruelness that seemed to cling to him, making him appear less attractive. To be honest, Rick gave Wyatt a bit of the creeps. Just as big and tall as Draven, Rick was one person he'd never want to meet in a dark alley.

Rick's face turned hard. "I'd watch what you say to me."

"I'm not scared of you," Draven said. "You want a piece of me? Name the place and time and I'll gladly show you who the better man is."

Rick slowly backed away as he pointed at Draven. "That day will come, old man." With that said, he turned and walked away.

Wyatt gazed at Draven and found him still staring in the direction Rick had gone. His fists were clenched at his sides, the muscles in his arms standing out. This was a side of Draven he hadn't seen before. A wilder, fiercer one.

"Why the hell would he call you an old man?" Wyatt asked. "He can't be that much younger than you."

Draven took a deep breath and slowly unclenched his hands. He turned to the shopping cart and walked away. "He was just being an asshole. Forget about him."

Wyatt hurried to catch up with Draven. "It looked as if the two of you were ready to tear into each other, literally."

Draven came to a sudden stop. "Rick is no concern of yours. Like I said, forget about him."

"But he said he'd been looking for you."

"So?"

"Aren't you a little worried he might try and confront you again?"

Draven turned a hard look on Wyatt. "He can try, but I guarantee he won't come out of it unscathed. The bastard knows better than to challenge me."

"What did he mean about his being a lone wolf? And what was the crack about me probably not knowing the truth about you?"

Chapter Five

Draven started them walking again. He pushed the cart down the next aisle he came to. He felt Wyatt's gaze following him as he walked. That fucking Rick. He'd said a bunch of shit Draven wasn't ready to tell Wyatt about. Now Wyatt had questions he wanted answered.

"Draven? Are you just going to ignore me?"

Yup, Wyatt definitely wanted answers. "Let it go. The bastard was talking crap just to see if he could get a rise out of me."

"Well, he must have, because I don't think it would have taken much to have you swinging a punch at him."

"Oh, it would have been a lot more than me using my fists on him, believe me." He turned his head toward Wyatt. "Look, let's get what we came for, all right? I really don't want Rick to mess up the day we had planned for ourselves."

"Fine, but if he comes around again, I might be the one throwing the first punch."

Draven came to an abrupt stop once again, causing Wyatt to almost run into him. "No, you won't. Do I make myself clear?"

Wyatt scowled. "Why? I might not be much of a fighter, but if threatened I don't back down."

"That's not what I'm worried about. You don't know what he's capable of. I'll put it to you this way, if you fought him, you wouldn't come out of it in one piece."

Wyatt gave him a cool look. "Whatever you say. I obviously don't know him as well as you do." He then maneuvered around the shopping cart and walked farther down the aisle.

Shit. Now Wyatt was pissed off at him. Just another reason why he should go wolf all over Rick's ass. The asshole had deserved to be kicked out of their pack, forced to go lone wolf. Rick had sold drugs to some of the younger members. Alone, that crap was bad enough, but how it reacted to the magic all werewolves carried inside them was even worse. It messed with their ability to shift. Certain drugs, if taken long-term, took it away completely. Forever, with no way to get it back. Unable to ever take on their wolf forms again, it wasn't unheard of for the affected person to end their life. Draven shuddered at the thought of never being able to shift.

He silently followed behind Wyatt as the other man turned down the next aisle. This one was where all the personal hygiene products were, along with condoms and lube. He watched Wyatt go to the shelves where those items were and pick up one of each. Without another word, he turned toward Draven and walked over to him before he threw the things he carried into the cart.

"That's everything I needed to buy," Wyatt said.

"Should we make a trip to The Beer Store before we hit the rental?"

"I brought a twelve pack up with me. We only had one each out of it."

"I brought one as well. So I guess we don't need to go there. Let me get some snack things, then I'll pay for all of this."

That accomplished, Wyatt remained silent as they stood in line, and even after they carried the bags out to Draven's car. With them stored in the trunk, Draven got into the driver's side, but he didn't turn the key in the ignition.

He looked at the man sitting in the passenger seat. "Are you pissed off at me, Wyatt?"

"Not really."

"Then why the silent treatment?"

Wyatt turned to look at him. "I'm trying to figure out this other side of you. Before Rick came along, I felt you were more open with me. Now it feels as if you're keeping something back like the prick said. I'll tell you this right now—I don't like being lied to."

"I'm not lying to you about anything. There're just some things I'm not comfortable talking about. The subject of Rick is one of them. I didn't mean to be sharp with you. I was only angry at him."

"All right. I can accept that. He pissed me off too."

"He's gone now. Let's move on."

"Fine with me."

Draven started the car and pulled out of the grocery store parking lot. With Wyatt's directions, he drove to the rented cottage. The narrow gravel trail that led to it was in as much of a neglected state as everything else on the property. Draven was sure no car would be able to drive down to it come winter time. Not with the amount of snow Muskoka got.

He parked next to Wyatt's older-model car. Following his would-be mate to the cottage door, Draven noticed the rust mixed in with the faded red paint job. He made a mental note to buy Wyatt a brand new vehicle. As his mate, Draven had the right to ensure all of Wyatt's needs were taken care of. That included making sure he didn't have an old beater to drive. The other man didn't know it yet, but once Draven claimed him, Wyatt's life was about to change. He wouldn't want for anything ever again.

Wyatt unlocked the cottage and Draven walked in behind him. "Why don't you go grab your things while I pack up the food to take with us?"

"Sounds like a plan," Wyatt said in return. "You'll find the boxes I used in the kitchen on the floor near the back door."

Draven nodded and walked to where Wyatt indicated. He picked up one of said boxes and went to the fridge. It didn't take him very long to pack the food for the trip to his lake house. He carried them one at a time out to his car and put them in the trunk with the other groceries.

He'd just come back inside to grab the beer when Wyatt came out of the single bedroom carrying a large duffle bag. "I have everything."

"I already put the food in my car."

"Then we're all set. I'll follow you to your lake house."

Draven nodded and led the way outside. He waited as Wyatt locked the cottage, then got into his car. Once Wyatt was behind the wheel, Draven headed for the trail to the main road with the other man following behind.

It wasn't too long of a drive, since they were just looping around the lake. At his place, Draven brought the groceries he purchased inside, then helped Wyatt with his things.

As Wyatt put away the last of the food, Draven took the other man's duffel bag up to his bedroom. There was no question why Wyatt wouldn't be sharing his bed. Starting today.

After his run-in with Rick, Draven had to bite the bullet and tell Wyatt about werewolves and what it meant to be a mate to one. Even though he hadn't said as much to his would-be mate, he had a feeling they hadn't seen the last of Rick. And Draven knew it was going to come down to the other werewolf challenging him, which meant a fight in wolf form.

Draven set Wyatt's duffel on the floor at the end of the bed. Before he turned to leave the room, a package of condoms and lube flew past him and landed on the mattress. Draven spun around to find Wyatt standing behind him.

"I was just going to—"

Draven never got a chance to finish his sentence. Wyatt closed the small space between them and took his mouth. He sank his hands in Draven's hair and held him in place as he increased the pressure on his lips, pushing his tongue past them.

With a loud groan, Draven wrapped his arms around Wyatt's waist and held him tight, grinding their cocks together. The control over his mating urge was tenuous at best. After what they'd done in the shower earlier, the need to claim his mate rode him almost to the breaking point. It was also part of the reason why he'd let Rick get to him so much.

The sound of their harsh breathing filled the room before Wyatt let him up for air. "You no longer have any excuse to not make love to me, Draven. I want you — bad. I want your big cock buried in my ass. And I'm not going to take no for an answer, because I know you want me as much as I want you."

Draven felt his control slip even more. The scent of Wyatt's arousal had him weakening. He wanted him, wanted to take his mate in every way he could. The longer he spent with his would-be mate, the harder it was to deny him, especially when he was denying himself as well.

Seeing the hunger in Wyatt's eyes, the longing deep inside them, Draven felt he was losing the battle. Lust and desire caused his control to seep away until he felt as if he would never feel whole again without claiming Wyatt as his. The mating urge dug its claws deeper into him, his wolf pushing for what was his.

Wyatt's gaze became even more heated. He moaned low in his throat as he took Draven's lips again. He nipped and sucked, his hands clutching Draven's ass while he rubbed their cocks together. The friction made Draven harder. The rest of his resolve to wait faded away, leaving nothing but pure longing behind.

He let Wyatt have control for a bit longer before he took it from him. *His* control was going up in smoke. To resist his mate was a fight he was losing, fast. Only the certainty that Wyatt would want him forever too had him admitting defeat. He kissed him hungrily and turned the other man toward the bed. With a flick of his wrist, he tore back the covers and urged Wyatt onto the mattress. Draven followed him down, stretching onto his side along Wyatt.

Putting all the pent-up hunger the mating urge stirred inside him into his kiss, Draven took hold of Wyatt's t-shirt and lifted it to his chin. He broke contact with his mate's mouth only long enough to yank the shirt off. Draven trailed his hand across Wyatt's defined pecs, stroking a fingertip across his flat nipples.

Wyatt yanked on the bottom of Draven's shirt, pulling it up his back. Draven took hold of it by the collar, released the other man's lips and drew it over his head. With eyes mere slits, he watched Wyatt stroke his hands along his chest, then down to the button on Draven's jeans. Wyatt made short work of undoing them before he pushed the parted material open wider, springing Draven's cock.

"Do you always walk around like this?" Wyatt asked huskily. "Wearing no underwear?"

"Actually, yes. I never got used to them."

Wyatt chuckled. "Well, I'm not going to complain about that." He wrapped his fingers around Draven's shaft and stroked him. "I like being able to just open your pants and have nothing else come between me and your cock."

Draven moaned and pushed himself tighter into Wyatt's hand. "It does make it easier." He rocked his hips. "I want you naked. Now."

In short order, Draven had Wyatt out of his pants and underwear before tossing them onto the floor. His own jeans soon followed suit. Now pressed skin to skin with his mate, he turned his attention to Wyatt's dick. It was fully engorged and pre-cum leaked from the tip.

Unable to resist, he went down on Wyatt, sucking the other man's cock into his mouth. Wyatt moaned, his hands landing on Draven's head as he thrust his hips, pushing his shaft deeper. Draven growled low, loving how turned-on

Wyatt was. He continued to suck Wyatt's dick as he reached between his mate's legs and fondled his balls. Wyatt's moans grew louder, his breath rasped in and out of his lungs.

After a few minutes, Wyatt yanked at Draven's hair. "Enough," he panted. "You're going to make me lose it."

Draven released him and rose farther up his body. "Not yet. I want to be deep inside you when you do that."

Reaching around in the covers, Draven found the two items he'd bought at the store. With hands that shook with his arousal, he tore open the lube's packaging and unscrewed the cap on the tube. He urged Wyatt onto his stomach, then squeezed some of the lubricant onto his fingers.

He nipped the back of Wyatt's neck as he delved between the other man's cheek's. Wyatt groaned and spread his legs wider. Draven circled the puckered hole, lubing it up before he pushed a finger inside. Wyatt's anus gripped the digit as Draven sank past the ring of tight muscle.

"Yes," Wyatt moaned. "Give me more."

Draven added a second finger, scissoring them as he pumped in and out to ready Wyatt for his cock. "It's going to feel so good being inside you. So damn tight."

"Fuck me, Draven."

He made sure Wyatt's ass was lubed up enough to ease his way before he reached for the box of condoms. After taking one out, Draven opened the foil package. He rolled the latex down his shaft, then thoroughly lubricated himself.

"Get on your hands and knees, Wyatt."

His mate did as he asked, his head hanging down as he panted. Wyatt's erection stuck out straight from his body, leaking with his need. Draven shifted into position behind him. He rubbed his cock in Wyatt's crack, teasing them both.

No longer able to hold back from being inside the other man, Draven took hold of Wyatt's hips and pressed the head of his shaft slowly into his mate's body. He took shallow thrusts, each one taking him deeper until he passed the ring of muscle that wanted to keep him out.

Once he was buried to the hilt, Draven gritted his teeth to stop himself from coming. Wyatt's ass gripped his cock in a tight fist. He pulled back then pushed forward. Wyatt moaned, rocking backward to meet each of his strokes. Draven increased the pace he set, his thrusts faster, harder.

"Fuck, take me, Draven," Wyatt ground out. "You feel so damn good."

A wolf's growl rumbled out of Draven before he could stop it. The pleasure of taking his mate, claiming him, was beyond compare. Right at that moment, Draven felt it. Felt the mating bond begin to form between them. A piece of his soul reached for Wyatt's. Draven pumped harder, growling and moaning, as Wyatt's soul met and became one with his.

With a loud howl, Draven felt the point of no return hit him. He rammed into Wyatt one last time, then emptied his cock into the other man's ass. Wyatt groaned and came all over the sheets. Draven held him in place until his shaft stopped pulsing. Pulling free of Wyatt's body, he got out of bed and disposed of the used condom in the small wastebasket next to the nightstand.

Before climbing back up next to Wyatt, he collected the discarded box of protection and lube. Draven handed them to his mate and stretched out next to him. "Take me. Make me yours."

Wyatt chuckled as he reached down and stroked Draven's still hard cock. "Unlike you, I'm still not raring to go."

"I think I can help with that."

Draven took hold of Wyatt's softened shaft and stroked him. He'd get Wyatt hard again. Draven's wolf wanted to be claimed, wanted his mate to mount him. With the mating bond in place, every time he made love to Wyatt, it would only bring them closer, making their feelings for each other stronger. Draven loved Wyatt, had known it the instant his mating urge went off, which wouldn't have happened if Wyatt hadn't been meant to be his. Love at first sight was the norm for werewolves because of that fact. Wyatt had to be capable of loving him as well, or he wouldn't have been his mate.

Wyatt's dick twitched, showing definite promise. Draven inched down the mattress and took Wyatt into his mouth to speed things up. His mate groaned, stroking his cock between Draven's lips. He didn't have to work very hard to have Wyatt standing at full attention.

Draven released Wyatt's shaft and in one smooth move, rolled to his back and pulled his bent legs to his chest, exposing his hole. "Now, Wyatt. Fuck me hard and fast."

The other man made short work of lubing up Draven's ass, preparing him for what was to come. He then rolled on a condom. Wyatt settled on top of him, kissing Draven hungrily as he pushed his cock into Draven's ass.

Draven bore down on Wyatt's shaft, loving the burn and pleasure of being stretched and filled. He closed his eyes and fisted his hands in the sheets as Wyatt rode him hard, hitting Draven's prostate with each thrust in.

The sound of their heavy breathing and bodies slapping together filled the room. Draven's dick ached with the need for release. He wrapped his hand around his cock and pumped, matching Wyatt's thrusts in his ass.

Wyatt groaned. "I'm going to come again."

"I'm right there with you."

Draven pumped his cock faster, increasing the pressure of his hand. Just as Wyatt stiffened above him, his shaft pulsing with his orgasm, Draven let out a shout as he found his own. His cum shot in thick streams over his and Wyatt's stomach.

His mate slowly pulled his softening cock out of Draven's hole. He then flopped onto the bed next to him. "That was pretty intense," Wyatt said as he fought to catch his breath.

Draven turned on his side and put an arm across his mate's chest and kissed his shoulder. "I have a feeling it'll always be like this between us."

Wyatt chuckled. "If that's the case, I doubt either one of us will live very long." He got up and disposed of the condom before he returned to the bed and took Draven into his arms.

Draven snuggled closer, his ear pressed to Wyatt's chest, listening to the other man's heart beat. "I think we'll survive. Tough men like us."

This time Wyatt laughed. "I don't know how tough I am right now. My legs feel like rubber."

"Then I suggest we take a little rest, because I'm far from done with you."

Wyatt looked down at Draven's still erect cock. "You're going to have to teach me how you do that, so I can keep up with you."

"Sorry, it's not something you can learn. I'm just gifted."

"I have to agree with that. I just hope I'm the only lucky man who gets to use that special ability of yours."

Draven cupped Wyatt's cheek and brushed his lips over his. "You're the one and only. Now try to get some sleep. We still have most of the day, and I don't intend to leave this bed for the majority of it."

Chapter Six

Draven hadn't kidded when he'd told Wyatt he wanted to spend the rest of the day in bed. Actually, it turned out to be the entire night as well. Wyatt had been taken, and took Draven, so many times he thought he had to be all fucked out. But being woken up to the sensation of Draven sucking his cock until he had almost come, had told another story. The other man was almost insatiable. And his ability to keep an erection after climaxing countless times, and for hours, just prolonged their lovemaking.

Now that morning had dawned, Wyatt stood in the en suite and looked at himself in the mirror above the sink. He definitely looked like a man who had been well and truly fucked, repeatedly. He had whisker burn on his chest from where Draven had kissed and licked every inch of it.

Reaching for his toothbrush, Wyatt sighed deeply. Sometime during their marathon of sex, he'd fallen hard for Draven. He didn't want to ever let the other man go. It was as if they were meant to be. Soul mates. The first time they'd fully made love, Wyatt had felt something pass between them. Something that brought them closer together, bonded them. It was hard for him to even describe. And it wasn't because the sex was explosive, either. Though it was the best he'd ever had. It went deeper than that.

Finished brushing his teeth, Wyatt rinsed his mouth and turned to the shower. After Draven's and his romp in bed, he needed it. Draven had gotten up earlier, after they'd made love, and had taken one already. Right now he was downstairs whipping up some breakfast. Wyatt patted his stomach as it growled. The only real meal he'd had yesterday had been what he'd eaten in the morning at the restaurant in Gravenhurst.

The beer and chips Draven and he had consumed at some point in the evening hadn't exactly cut it.

Wyatt didn't take any longer than he needed in the shower. After toweling off, he returned to the bedroom and pulled on some athletic shorts and a tank top. It was supposed be another hot summer day in Muskoka. Draven had also mentioned after he'd woken Wyatt up for the second time that he wanted to go for a walk in the bush with him. Wyatt had been quick to say he'd tag along.

Dressed, Wyatt headed downstairs. The smell of bacon made his stomach growl again. He probably could eat a whole pound of it himself, he was that hungry. Entering the kitchen, he saw Draven set two heaping plates of bacon and fluffy-looking scrambled eggs on the table. Seeing Wyatt, he crossed the room and took him in his arms. The kiss he laid on him had Wyatt's cock twitching with interest. Mentally telling it to forget, Wyatt released Draven's lips.

"Mmm, that was nice," he said. "But right now food is taking precedence over sex. My stomach is about to eat itself."

Draven laughed. "Then I'd better feed you. Go sit down. The food is ready."

Wyatt took a seat and pulled the plate closer. He picked up his fork and scooped a large amount of the eggs into his mouth. After that, he practically inhaled the rest of the food in front of him. He was up getting himself seconds before Draven had even finished his first helping.

"Don't worry, I left you some," he said as Draven glanced at his full plate.

"I'm not. I made extra, thinking we'd both eat lots." Draven dished up the last of the eggs and bacon for himself and sat once again. "So you're still willing to go for a walk in the bush with me?"

"Of course. Just as long as we don't get lost in it for days."

Draven chuckled. "It's just on my property, and I've walked it so many times, there is no way we'd lose our way. I know it like the back of my hand." He paused, then said, "I also thought it would be a good time to talk more. Get to know each other better." Draven met his gaze. "Talk about our future together."

Wyatt swallowed his mouthful and nodded. "I'd like that. Plus, it has the added advantage of getting us away from any nearby beds. If we stay inside, I think we'd be fucking more than talking."

Draven shook his head and smiled. "Probably, but what's to stop us from getting naked and doing it against a tree? There will be no one around to see us."

"Don't tempt me."

"You're the one who brought up the subject of sex," Draven said with a laugh.

"Okay, you got me on that one. So when do you want to go on this walk?"

"In a few minutes." Draven glanced at Wyatt's plate. "Since you've just about inhaled all your food again, why don't you go wait for me outside? It will only take me a few minutes."

Popping the last piece of bacon into his mouth, Wyatt nodded and stood. "I'll do that. If you don't see me at the back of the house, I'll be at the dock."

Wyatt headed outside. He walked around the side of the house and down toward the dock. The sun reflected off the water, making it seem even brighter. There wasn't a cloud in the sky. He hoped the weather would stay this nice for the rest of his holiday, not that he wouldn't mind being stuck in the lake house with Draven. They would find something to do to entertain themselves.

He walked to the end of the dock, turning into the slight breeze that blew in his face. He smiled and searched the lake when he heard the tremolo call of the common loon. Shading his eyes with his hand, Wyatt spotted the bird way out in the water. It made the call again. Some people thought it sounded like insane laughter. It was actually a series of notes voiced rapidly in different degrees of frequency and intensity. The one Wyatt loved hearing the most was the wail of the loon. The bird only did it in the evenings and at night, and it could be heard for miles. Wyatt thought it sounded haunting.

While he watched, the loon suddenly dove under the water. It wouldn't come back up for some time, and not in the same spot. They could hold their breath for eight and a half to sixty seconds, even longer if they were scared of something. Wyatt once watched one go under for three whole minutes before he saw it resurface.

"See anything interesting?" Draven asked as he came to stand beside him.

"There was a loon out there, but it just went for a dive."

"I love listening to their calls. I've sat out here in the evenings doing just that."

"To me, the call of the loon will always remind me of Muskoka."

"I feel the same way. Come on, let's go for that walk."

Draven held out his hand. Wyatt slipped his into it, linking their fingers together. Hand in hand, they walked up the length of the dock and around the house until they reached the back. At the edge of the bush, Draven let go and went ahead, leading the way.

The other man set an easy pace that Wyatt had no trouble keeping up with. After a full minute had gone by in silence, he asked, "So what do you want to talk about, Draven?"

"Anything, everything. Why don't we start off with you? You said you used to come up here with your parents when growing up. Do you have any brothers or sisters?"

"Nope. It's just me. My parents only wanted the one child. I don't think my mom would have been able to handle any more than that. She's what I would call a bit of a worrywart. Any time I hurt myself, skinned knees, you name it, she'd just about freak out, think it was a life-and-death situation. If she had to go through that with two kids, I think it would have made her a basket case."

Draven laughed. "That must have been tough on you growing up, having a clingy mother."

"It wasn't so bad, really. It was harder on Mom to cut the cord, if you know what I mean. She didn't want to accept the fact I grew into a man and didn't need her to watch over me all the time. She's a lot better now, though sometimes she can still hover, especially if I end up getting sick. What about you? Your parents still around? Do you have any siblings?"

"No to both of those. I lost my parents some years ago, and I had an older brother, but he died when I was a teenager."

"That has to be rough, being all alone in the world."

"Like I said, I lost them a long time ago. I'm not completely alone, though. There are others I can go to if I need to."

"I'm glad to hear that." He paused, then added, "And you have me now."

Draven stopped walking and turned to face Wyatt. He pulled him into his arms and brushed a kiss across his lips before he rested his forehead against Wyatt's. "Yeah, I do have you." He lifted his head and looked into Wyatt's eyes. "I want you to know I have very strong feelings for you. I don't want to freak you out, but I love you, Wyatt. I know it's rushed, but you're the one for me. And will always be. I want us to live together."

Wyatt nodded as a thrill shot through his body at Draven's words. "I love you too," he said in a rush. "I was just waiting for the right time to tell you. I thought if I told you too soon, you'd want to run."

Draven kissed him again before he dropped his arms and took a step back. "Speaking of running, there's something else about me I have to tell you. And I'm not sure how well you're going to take it."

"You can tell me anything, Draven. I don't think there is anything you can say that will cause me to leave you."

Draven gave him a slight smile. "I hope that remains the case." He took a couple of steps back again, putting more space between them.

Wyatt's gaze jerked in the direction of something over Draven's shoulder. At the same time, he yelled, "Holy shit, there's a wolf." Draven turned and growled, sounding like the animal that slowly stalked toward them.

He then felt the air become trapped in his lungs when Draven's body blurred and shimmered, taking on the form of a wolf right before his eyes. The animal had brown fur that matched the color of Draven's hair.

"Draven?" Wyatt finally managed to ask while his heart tried to pound out of his chest. Was what he'd seen actually real?

The wolf didn't look his way, only curled its upper lip, hackles rising, as he watched the black one who continued toward them. Just as Draven looked as if he were about ready to go on the attack, a man who moved so fast Wyatt had a hard time tracking him, came out of nowhere and threw a rope net over the brown wolf. He jumped onto Draven's back, pinning him to the ground.

Wyatt gave a shout and was about to go to his rescue when he was hit from behind and fell forward. Rough hands grabbed him, pulling his arms behind his back as a heavy weight sat on his legs. He struggled, but it didn't stop his assailant from binding his wrists together.

"I've got him," the man who'd taken down Wyatt yelled.

Wyatt was yanked to his feet and force marched over to the others. The black wolf's body blurred and shimmered, and Rick took its place. He walked over to the man who pinned Draven down and held up a rope that had something inside it that reflected the sun. Wyatt's heart was still trying to beat out of his chest, and he was more than a little freaked by what he'd just witnessed. But on the outside, he acted as if seeing men turn into wolves and vice versa was an everyday occurrence for him.

"Tie him up with this," Rick said. "Make sure it's tight enough."

"What the fuck are you?" Wyatt yelled. Some of the stress he felt leaked into his voice.

Rick walked over to stand in front of him. "You don't know, mortal? I would have thought your butt buddy over there would have told you."

Wyatt barely stopped himself from flinching, not wanting the other man anywhere near him. "Told me what?"

"That he's a werewolf. Just like we are." Rick waved his hand to encompass the other men. He then leaned forward and took a deep breath. He smiled, one that didn't reach his eyes. "From how ingrained Draven's scent is in your skin, it leads me to only one thing—you're his mate. I guess the queer finally found one. It only took him fifteen hundred years. That's what happens when you want to fuck someone of the same sex."

"Fifteen hundred years?" Wyatt asked, thinking Rick was talking shit again. Okay, the werewolf thing he couldn't deny, since he'd seen Draven shift, but that many years? It couldn't be possible. His gut clenched at the thought that it could be true.

"Why do you think I called you mortal, mortal? Werewolves can live to the age of three thousand. Your lover boy over there has been knocking around for fifteen hundred years. That's also the reason why he has such antiquated standards of what is right and wrong. He believes in the whole his word is his bond sort of thing. It dates back to when he swung a sword, defending the honor of one and all. The stupid shit."

"Then how old are you?"

"Me?" Rick asked with a laugh. "I'm nowhere near as old as that relic of the past over there. I'm three hundred."

"So compared to Draven, you really are a pup," Wyatt spat.

He's head whipped to the side as Rick's fist connected with his jaw. "Don't ever call me that again. I'm no child. I'm more than capable of going wolf and using my teeth to rip your throat out."

"Not unless Draven stops you first."

"Sorry, but your mate won't be able to do a damn thing. You see that rope we've trussed him up with, and the net? It has silver threads mixed in it. That metal, when in contact with us in any way, hampers our ability to shift and hold whatever form we try to take on. Since Draven is in his wolf one, he's stuck like that until we take the ropes off, which won't be anytime soon. I'm going to make him pay for getting me kicked out of our pack. He could have turned a blind eye to my drug-dealing ways, but he had to play the hero."

"What are you going to do to him?"

"First, take him far away from you."

"What do you expect that will do?"

Rick shook his head. "You haven't a clue about anything, do you? Draven has claimed you as his, which means you two won't be able to stand to be apart from each other. We call it separation anxiety. It won't take long before you feel as if you're going to lose your mind, same with Draven. All the two of you will be able to think about is returning to each other. The longer apart, the worse it'll get. I couldn't have asked for a better means to torture Draven." Rick turned his head and said to the man who held Draven, "Get him out of here."

Draven howled, struggling against his captor. Having a good feeling that everything Rick had said would happen, Wyatt threw his head back, knocking the man who held him in the nose. A loud wolflike growl sounded before a thick arm caught him around his throat and applied enough pressure so Wyatt could barely get enough air to fill his lungs.

"Nice try," Rick snarled. "One other thing you should know about werewolves—we're faster and stronger than mortals."

Wyatt found himself dragged away in the opposite direction with Rick in tow as the other man hefted Draven onto his shoulders and took off, moving faster than a normal person could. Right about now, Wyatt figured Draven and he were fucked.

* * * * *

Draven had no idea how much time had passed since he'd been carted away trussed up like a Christmas turkey. All he knew was it was long enough and far enough for him to already feel the separation anxiety. He had to somehow escape his bonds and get back to save Wyatt from Rick. How he was going to accomplish getting out of ropes threaded with silver, he had no idea. Being basically stuck in his wolf form had its disadvantages, like not having opposable thumbs.

The werewolf who carried him, and the one who had jumped Wyatt, were lone wolves like Rick. They had at one time been in his pack as well. If he remembered correctly, they had been kicked out for the same reason and around the same time Rick had been.

Finally his captor emerged from the trees at the edge of the water. A small boat had been pulled halfway out of the water and secured to one of the nearby trees. There was no dock, but Draven recognized the area as being on the opposite end of the lake, close to where Wyatt's rental was. And it was far enough away to have him really feeling the separation anxiety.

The other werewolf none too gently put Draven down at his feet. He pulled the rope net off Draven and threw it into the boat, leaving only his four legs bound. His captor gave him a kick in the ribs. "Don't go anywhere. I have to take a leak."

The other man walked a little ways into the trees and turned his back to him. Draven moved, hoping there was something he could use to cut the ropes. As he did this, he felt one of his bonds loosen. Looking at it, Draven would have smiled if he were in human form. The dumb bastard didn't know how to tie a proper knot. He rolled around, dragging the ropes along the ground, feeling them becoming looser until he had enough space to pull his legs out.

Gaining his paws, Draven silently snuck up behind the other werewolf, who was too busy pissing into the trees to notice he was being stalked. Once he was close enough, with his scent carried downwind by the breeze, Draven bunched his back legs under him and pounced. After bringing the man down, he quickly shifted to his human form and beat him with his fists until he knocked him out.

Hefting the other werewolf over his shoulder, Draven carried him over to the boat and threw him into the bottom of it. He then proceeded to tie his wrists and ankles with the silver-threaded ropes. The knots he used wouldn't slip loose.

Draven took off at a run into the bush, shifting on the fly. He could move faster through the trees in his wolf form. He didn't stop running until he'd reached his lake house. Stealthily, he worked his way around to the front and inside the open door. On silent paws, he followed the scent of his mate to the living room. Wanting to get the jump on Rick, he launched himself into the room, hitting the other werewolf before he knew what happened.

Rick shifted to his wolf form, using his sharp teeth and claws to fight Draven off. Draven didn't even try to look for Wyatt to see how he was. He had to stay focused on defeating Rick. As he'd expected, the fight didn't last long. Draven had superior fighting skills and was stronger than his opponent. He brought Rick down on his back and took hold of his throat in his jaws. Draven bit down hard enough until he tasted blood in his mouth.

"Let Rick go, or else your mate is going to have a new hole to breathe from," the other man in the room yelled.

Draven didn't release his jaws. He lifted his gaze to meet the other lone wolf's and growled loudly. He bit down harder, causing more blood to fill his mouth as Rick whimpered, his tail coming between his legs in surrender.

"Fuck this," the other werewolf said. "It's not worth it." He then shoved Wyatt to the floor and ran out of the room. The sound of his footsteps could be heard outside the house shortly after.

Draven shifted to human form and held onto Rick's throat as he shifted as well. "Now we know who the better wolf is. If you ever come back here again, or come near me or my mate, I'll be contacting my pack leader. I'm sure Grant would love to hear about a bunch of lone wolves attacking members of his pack."

Draven released the other man and stood. Rick held his throat as he slowly gained his feet. He ducked his head and stumbled out of the room. Draven followed him to make sure he left the house and closed and locked the door behind him. He then returned to the living room.

Wyatt had propped himself into a sitting position with his back against the front of the couch. He turned and lifted his hands as Draven undid the ropes that bound them. Once he had him free, Draven pulled him into his arms and held him tight.

"Are you okay? The bastard didn't hurt you, did he?"

Wyatt shook his head. "Not really. I can handle a slug to the jaw. It was what I felt after that other werewolf took you away that I had a hard time handling."

Draven kissed Wyatt, needing the taste of him in his mouth to reassure him he was still his. He pulled back after a few seconds. "I'm sorry you had to find out about werewolves this way. We're not all like Rick and those lone wolves."

Wyatt cupped Draven's cheek in his hand. "I figured that out for myself. Rick wasn't kicked out of your pack for being a nice guy. So what he said about us being mates is true?"

"Yes. I claimed you the first time we fully made love yesterday. Our souls joined. There's no undoing it. I should have let you have a choice, but I was afraid you'd want to leave me. The instant I smelled your scent, I knew you were mine."

Wyatt shook his head. "I have to say werewolves have an easier time of finding their mates than mortals do." He breathed a sigh. "Right now, this is all a bit confusing and new to me. I'm not going to lie—I'm feeling a little freaked out right now, but I would never run from you. You've never given me a reason to fear you. Rick and werewolves like him, I can't say the same thing."

Draven chuckled. "Does that mean you can accept me for what I am?"

Wyatt launched himself at Draven and took him to the floor, flat on his back, and came down on top of him. "Yes, it does, my ancient warrior werewolf."

"I might be old, but I'm far from ancient." He thrust his hips up into Wyatt, pressing his hard cock against his.

Wyatt groaned. "I think you'd better remind me of that again."

Draven rolled, switching positions with Wyatt. "And I think I have a demanding mate."

He then proceeded to see how many times he could make Wyatt moan and shout his name.

The End

LOVED BY A WEREWOLF
◊

Chapter One

Sierra sat on the bride's side of the room as she watched her cousin, Yvonne, exchange vows with her groom. The wedding was at Hatley Castle, which was situated in Hatley Park National Historic Site in Victoria, British Columbia. The Edwardian castle had been built in 1908 and was a beautiful setting for the ceremony. And it was totally Yvonne's style with the exquisite gardens surrounding it. Even seeing the glacier-capped Olympic Mountains in the distance on the way in just added to the location.

After the ceremony ended, the new husband and wife departed with the rest of the bridal party to have pictures taken. That left the hundred guests they'd invited to find their way into the large room where the reception would be held.

As Sierra followed the crowd, her mother, who walked beside her, asked, "Wasn't Yvonne stunning?"

"Yes, she was."

"And she looked so happy."

"She did." Sierra steeled herself for what was surely to come next.

Her mother sighed dramatically. "I doubt I'll live long enough to see you walk down the aisle, let alone see grandchildren from you."

Sierra barely restrained herself from rolling her eyes. "Mom, I'm only twenty-nine. I'm not over the hill yet. Nowadays, not everyone gets married at twenty-three and pops out two kids by their second anniversary like you did. And at fifty-five, that hardly makes you that old. Why aren't you bugging Trevor about his not being married? He's a year older than me."

Her mother waved away what she said with a flick of her hand. "Leave Trevor out of this. It's different with men. He doesn't have a biological clock ticking like you."

"Mother," Sierra said sharply when she noticed a few heads had turned their way. Her mom hadn't been all that quiet while she'd talked. Finally reaching the room for the reception, Sierra said, "I'm going to pretend you didn't say that. And speaking of Trevor, where the hell is he?"

As they worked their way around the large, open-concept room to the table they were to sit at, her mom did a quick search with her gaze. "Oh, there he is. He's at the bar."

Of course he was. Where else would he be? With an open bar for the entire reception, Trevor wouldn't be able to stay away. It also meant Sierra would have to watch his dumb ass to make sure he didn't do anything embarrassing. Trevor and alcohol did not mix. When her brother drank, he always ended up shitfaced drunk and did the most idiotic things.

With her father gone—he'd passed away two years before from cancer—that left Sierra to take her brother in hand when he got out of control. Her mother wouldn't do it. For some screwed-up reason, her mom turned a blind eye on his antics. It was almost as if she never saw his faults, or if she did, she didn't want to accept them. But when it came to Sierra, her mom nitpicked everything she thought her daughter was lacking in. Double standards much?

After the wedding party arrived, the meal was served. That also meant the bar was closed until it was over. Trevor finally came to their table and sat on their mother's other side. He put down the mixed drink he carried before he snatched the open bottle of wine and filled his glass.

Sierra leaned forward to look around her mother at her brother. "Take it easy on the alcohol, Trevor."

He gave her a scowl. "Lighten up, would you? I'm fine. Unlike you, I'm going to enjoy myself."

She settled back in her chair and didn't even bother responding. She'd just be wasting her breath anyway. But he was right about her not being able to enjoy herself. Because of him, Sierra would feel as if she were babysitting his ass the entire night. Kind of hard to have a good time when she was on idiot watch.

While they ate, every once in a while one of the guests would tap a wineglass with a piece of cutlery to start everyone else in the room doing it to get the bride and groom to kiss. And of course Trevor had to whistle and make catcalls each time, which became louder the more wine he drank. It reached the point where Sierra wanted to duck under the table and not come out.

Once the meal was finished, the speeches and toasts began. It took some time to get through them all, but at least her brother kept his mouth shut during them. After that part of the reception came to an end, the newly married couple moved to the middle of the room and danced the first dance.

As the night progressed, Sierra kept an eye on her brother. True to form, the drunker he got the more his IQ seemed to drop. And seeing him leave the reception with a woman who didn't appear any steadier on her feet set warning bells off in Sierra's head. Mostly because she knew said woman was married to a friend of Yvonne's brother. And the husband was supposedly known for being the jealous type who went after any man who came on to his wife.

So far the husband hadn't noticed his other half had left with Trevor. Sierra spotted him standing on the opposite side of the room with a few other men, talking. Not bothering to tell her mother where she was going, Sierra stood and went in search of her brother.

She walked through the room's entrance and came to a stop as she looked for any sign of Trevor and the woman with him. She spotted him down the opposite end of the long hallway at the door to the castle. Without looking back, he opened it and went outside with his companion.

Cursing under her breath, Sierra went in pursuit. She didn't hurry, not wanting to make a scene. By the time she'd made it through the front door, Trevor was nowhere in sight.

She grumbled to herself as she headed around to the back of the castle and the gardens. Sierra still didn't catch sight of Trevor. Not that she expected him to be out in the open with the woman. Since it was early evening and still light out, Trevor would have gone somewhere less conspicuous.

Sierra had no idea how long she walked, wishing her brother to hell every time she stumbled or almost twisted her ankle. Her high heels weren't exactly the right type of footwear to be traipsing outside in for any length of time.

When she reached one of the many hiking trails in the forest, she figured Trevor wouldn't have come this far. *Shit*. She was going to string him up by his balls, if the woman's husband didn't get to him first. Sierra wished she didn't give a crap what her dumbass brother got up to, but that wasn't going to happen. When he was alive, their father had been the one to keep Trevor in line. After his passing, she'd figured her dad would have wanted her to step in and take his place. So she really did it for him, not her brother.

Deciding she'd have to backtrack, Sierra went to turn around. She stopped partway after spotting something on the trail. She automatically froze in place while her heart beat at a faster rate. A wolf stood not too far away, eyeing her up, and she had no idea how she was going to get out of this one.

* * * * *

On vacation in Victoria from Toronto, Cale had made it a point to come to Hatley Park, especially the forest, to do some running in his wolf form. With all the large trees around him — the park had some of the biggest and oldest in the province — he didn't think he'd have to worry about mortals seeing him, even during the day.

Taking advantage of the good weather, he'd come to the forest that evening to do just that. After making sure no one was around, Cale had gone wolf and taken off into the dense trees. He gloried in the stretch of muscles as he jumped, dodged and worked his way through the bush. He wished there was a park like this close to downtown Toronto, but the closest was a couple of hours drive up north in Muskoka.

Coming near to where there was a hiking trail, and to Hatley Castle, he slowed his run to a walk as the wind blew in his face, bringing the nearby scents with it. One, that came from somewhere up ahead, slammed into him like a freight train. He lifted his head and breathed deeper as his mating urge threatened to take him over. Being in wolf form only heightened it until all he could think about was finding the owner of the scent and mating—claiming the woman as his own.

Cale took off in a fast run, following the delicious scent of his would-be mate. It didn't take long before he found himself out of the trees and on a hiking trail. His nose unerringly led him straight to the one he sought.

A woman stood in the middle of the trail, turned away from him. She wore a pale-pink, silky dress that fell to just above her knees and hugged her curves in all the right places. On her feet were high-heeled shoes that matched the color of her outfit. They also showcased her toned legs. Long, dark-brown hair hung to the middle of her back. He itched to take on his human form and run his fingers through it to see if it was as soft as it looked.

She turned and spotted him. He held back a growl of need as intense arousal shot through his body. She was gorgeous, not supermodel beautiful like his kind was known for, but she was far from ugly. Cale clenched all his muscles to stop himself from going to her. From her scent, he knew she was mortal. And that being the case, he'd have to tread carefully. No matter how badly he wanted to do it, shifting to his human form in the middle of the trail in front of her would not be the way to go. It would more than likely scare the bejesus out of her.

His would-be mate waved a hand in his direction. "Shoo," she said a bit shakily. "Go on. Get out of here."

She was already more than a little afraid of him. He could smell it in her scent. That left Cale with two choices. He could either approach her as a wolf, and hope she didn't run from him, or he could go back into the trees, deep enough for her not to see him shift, then come back and hope she was still there. She soon made his decision for him.

She bent down, picked up a rock and hurled it at him. "Don't come any closer."

The projectile didn't hit him, but it came close enough for Cale to realize she felt as if she had to defend herself. He dove into the bush on the opposite side of the trail he'd exited from. As he searched for a tree big enough to hide behind and shift, he heard her yell, "Not that way. That's the direction I have to go."

Well, at least she should stay where she is for a little while. Cale doubted she'd want to take the chance of meeting up with the wolf again. At last finding a suitable tree, he ducked behind it and drew on the spark of magic deep inside him to bring on the change to his human form.

The shift complete—dressed in dark-blue jeans and a black t-shirt—Cale circled around to the trail so he wouldn't come out of the trees in the same place he'd gone into them as a wolf. Even though he wasn't as agile in human form, he still could run faster than any mortal.

Cale broke out onto the hiking path a little farther down from where he'd first spotted his would-be mate. The sight of her made his cock harden while his mating urge rode his ass, demanding he take her. He reined it back as much as he could.

Walking closer, he saw her following him with her gaze. "Are you okay?" he asked. "I heard yelling."

She slowly nodded. "Yeah, I'm fine. I just saw a wolf on the trail." She looked from Cale to the trees, then back to him again. "It took off though."

He came to a stop once he was a few feet away from her. Her scent seemed to wrap around him, filling his head until he found it hard to think. His cock jerked inside his jeans when he looked into her blue eyes.

"Really? I didn't see it," he said.

"Maybe it heard you coming and ran from you. But thanks for coming to see if I was all right."

Cale smiled. "It was no hardship, especially if it means I get to meet a pretty woman like you. I'm Cale."

Her cheeks turned a becoming shade of pink. "Thanks. I'm Sierra."

"Nice to meet you, Sierra." He pointed toward her dress. "I take it you aren't out here hiking."

Sierra shook her head and chuckled. "How could you tell? No, I came from Hatley Castle where my cousin is having her wedding."

"If you don't mind me asking, what are you doing out here? I'm not from around Victoria, but I do know it's a bit of a walk from the castle to the hiking trails."

She blew out a breath. "I was looking for my idiot brother. He left the reception with a woman. I'm trying to find them before her husband does, but I think I've gone too far."

"Why don't I help you find him? Or at least walk you back to the castle? It's going to be dark pretty soon."

Dusk was just starting to settle in. It gave Cale the perfect excuse to stay with Sierra a little longer. Being what she was to him, there was no way he could just let her walk away without arranging to see her again. At nine hundred years old, he'd waited a very long time to find her. Letting her slip between his fingers at this early stage was out of the question.

Sierra's gaze drifted to his mouth and stayed there as her tongue came out to wet her lips. "Actually, I think I'll take you up on both those offers. As you said, I'm not exactly dressed to be trudging around in the bush."

Cale closed more of the distance between them, then followed Sierra as she left the trail and headed into the trees. While they walked, from time to time, he'd reach out to catch her elbow if she stumbled.

After the last time, she said, "Thanks. It was hard enough the first time, but now that it's getting dark, I can't see where to step."

"How about we switch places?" he asked. "I have good night vision. You can follow in my footsteps and I can hold your hand to keep you steady. Just point me in the right direction. I've never been to the castle before."

Sierra came to a standstill. "All right. If you keep going straight, we should end up in one of the gardens." She shifted to the side for him to get in front of her, then placed her hand in his when he held it out. Once he got them walking again, she said, "So where are you from?"

Cale found it hard to focus on what she said as pounding arousal shot through his body all because he only held her hand. "Ah, I'm from Toronto."

"Are you in Victoria for business or pleasure?"

He looked over his shoulder and gave her a smile. "Definitely for pleasure, especially now that I've met you."

"That's the second time you've given me a line. I don't think I've had a man butter me up that fast, unless I was at a bar, that is."

Cale turned his head to look forward and smiled, even though Sierra wouldn't see it. "Well? Is it working?"

"I don't know. I usually don't fall for the one-liners."

Right after Sierra finished saying that, she stumbled and would have fallen if Cale hadn't held her hand. Deciding to make the most of the opportunity, he turned, scooped her up in his arms and continued walking. Her arms looped around his neck as she let out a cry of surprise. With her cradled against him, he had to resist the urge to hold her tighter. To bury his face in the crook of her neck and just breathe her scent.

"Maybe this will help my cause," Cale said in a voice a little on the husky side.

The light scent of her arousal perfumed the air around them and he felt his mating urge ride his ass harder. One taste, that's all he needed. His steps slowed as he met her gaze, letting some of the desire he felt for her show in his eyes. But not so much that they would glow, something he had no control over when he became very aroused or angry.

Her tongue came out and licked her lips again. It was more than he could bear. He brushed his mouth across hers, then pulled back to see what Sierra's reaction was. Cale let out a grunt of surprise when she sank her hands into his hair on either side of his head and kissed him as if there were no tomorrow. With all the blood definitely now rushing to his aching cock, Cale halted his forward movement. If he kept going he was liable to walk right smack into a tree.

As she devoured his mouth, he pushed his tongue inside hers. The taste of his would-be mate caused him to moan in pleasure. Pounding need coursed through him. The scent of Sierra's arousal became stronger, making him long to strip her naked right there and then and go down on her, taste her pussy as he now tasted her lips.

Sierra's grip on his hair tightened, pulling his face even closer. She sucked on his tongue as one of her breasts rubbed against his chest. Their kiss became more carnal, the sounds of their moans and groans filling the air around them. Things were heating up so quickly between them Cale was surprised they hadn't set any of the trees in the vicinity on fire.

The idea to put Sierra down, let her slide along the length his body until she stood on her feet, popped into his head when the sound of raised voices reached his ears. They weren't very close, but with his sensitive werewolf hearing, he could just make out what was being said.

With a reluctant groan, Cale broke contact with Sierra's mouth. They were both breathing heavily, as if they'd just finished a marathon. "I think I hear your brother, and from the sound of it, the husband found him first."

Chapter Two

It took Sierra a few seconds to unscramble her brain and figure out what Cale had said. "My brother? I can't hear anything."

Cale put her on her feet, and said, "I can. Come on."

He took her hand and led her out of the trees and into one of the castle's gardens. Sierra had to quicken her steps to keep up with Cale's long strides as they followed the path that took them to the Japanese Garden, which was a tortoise-shaped island. As they neared the arched bridge, Sierra finally heard two male voices raised in anger. One she recognized as Trevor's.

Arriving on the scene, Sierra saw it didn't bode well for her brother. The husband was practically up in his face, yelling. Demanding to know what the hell Trevor thought he was doing out here alone in the dark with another man's wife. The woman stood near her husband with a guilty expression on her face.

Sierra pulled her hand out of Cale's and rushed toward the men, not wanting things to go any further than they already had. "Trevor, enough," she said loudly enough to be heard over their raised voices. The two of them stepped away from each other and turned in her direction.

Her brother scowled at her. "Sierra? What are you doing out here?"

She gave Trevor a hard stare. "Looking for you. Get your ass back in the reception."

"Just wait a minute," the husband said. "He's not going anywhere until he tells me what the fuck he was doing with my wife."

Sierra turned her attention on him. "Maybe you should be asking your wife why she came out here with my brother. She might be drunk, but I don't think she's that far gone that she didn't know what she was doing."

"Leave my wife out of this for now," he snarled. "I want an answer from your brother first."

From behind Sierra, Cale cleared his throat. "Why don't you just let this go? There's no reason to make a big scene out of it."

"And why don't you keep your opinions to yourself, asshole? I don't know who the fuck you are, but you're getting on my nerves. After I teach this other jerk a lesson or two, maybe I should do the same for you."

In a blink of an eye, Cale had shifted around Sierra until he stood between the husband and her. She'd thought the other man was big, but seeing Cale in front of him, she realized he was bigger. Cale had to stand at least six-foot-five, so he towered over the husband by about three inches. He was also broader of shoulder and had a bigger muscle mass. If it came down to a fight, Sierra had a feeling Cale would wipe the floor with the other man.

"I'd like to see you try," Cale said in a hard voice. "I've dealt with idiots like you before. You're all talk and no bite." He then got up into the other man's face.

The husband must have seen something in Cale's expression, because he quickly backed down. He grabbed hold of his wife's hand and towed her away. Sierra watched until they disappeared from sight. Then she focused on her brother.

"When are you going to stop doing crap like this, Trevor?" she snapped. "One day I'm not going to make it in time to smooth things over."

"I never asked you to save me, Sierra. Do you have any idea how embarrassing it is to have my little sis constantly watching everything I do?"

"Then grow the hell up and act like a thirty-year-old man is supposed to and I won't have to do this."

"Like you're so perfect. At least I can attract a member of the opposite sex, unlike you who sits alone in her apartment every weekend."

Sierra opened her mouth to lay into her brother, but ended up not having to. Cale did it for her.

"Watch what you say about your sister," he said, an almost audible growl lacing each word. "And she had no problem attracting me. Now apologize to Sierra and return to the reception like she told you."

Trevor snorted. "Go to hell."

In a move that was almost too fast for Sierra to track, Cale had Trevor by the back of the neck and gave him a little shake. "Not going to happen, pup. Now do as I said. Unless you think you're man enough to take on the likes of me. And believe me, you aren't."

Cale gave Trevor another hard shake, then shoved him away. Sierra easily saw the anger her brother must be feeling on his face. Trevor liked to think he was the top dog, and hated when someone showed him he wasn't. He scowled one last time at Cale before he crossed the bridge in the direction of the castle.

Sierra turned to Cale. "Sorry," she said. "He isn't usually this much of a jerk. He had a lot to drink at the wedding. And knowing Trevor, he'll be right back into the alcohol as soon as he gets to the reception."

"Maybe I should go inside with you to make sure he doesn't do anything else that'll have you chasing after him."

She ran her gaze over Cale, taking in his longish black hair, dark-green eyes and the jeans and t-shirt he wore. He was so good-looking she didn't think she'd have any problem staring at him for an entire day. He had a face she expected to see in fashion magazines. And she'd actually kissed him.

Just thinking about how she'd practically devoured his mouth, taking over the control, made her cheeks heat. She'd be lucky if Cale didn't think she was desperate, especially after Trevor's comment about her being alone. The awful thing, though, was it wasn't a lie. It'd been almost a year since she'd last slept with a man, and that relationship had lasted only a couple of months. Sierra never thought she'd attract a man like Cale. He looked way out of her league.

"Are you sure?" she asked. "If you do go with me, not only will you be subjected to my brother again, you'll have to deal with my mother. She always turns a blind eye on whatever Trevor does."

He smiled, making him look even more devastatingly handsome. "I think I can handle them. Just so long as you don't think your cousin will mind me crashing her wedding, I'll come with you."

"I doubt she will."

"Good." Cale closed the space between them. "What are the chances of me being able to slow dance with you?"

She stared into his eyes, feeling her heart race. An ache deep inside her pussy made itself known. Sierra fought the urge to squeeze her legs together to try to alleviate it. Her sex-starved body wanted Cale, all of him. While he'd carried her in his arms, it had turned her on more than it should have. Then he'd brushed her lips with his and she'd been lost.

"I think that can be arranged," she said softly.

"I'll have something to look forward to then."

"We should really get to the reception."

"First, I have to do this."

Cale placed his hands on her hips and drew her closer until their chests touched. He bent his head and took her lips in a kiss that had her aching for a whole lot more. His tongue pushed inside her mouth, stroking hers, tasting. Sierra reached up and held onto his shoulders as he deepened the meeting of their mouths. Once again she found herself lost on a tide of arousal. Her nipples pebbled beneath her dress, making her wish there were no clothes separating them. Wetness pooled between her legs, intensifying the ache inside her pussy. Just a kiss and she was ready to strip naked and jump on Cale.

With a reluctant-sounding groan, he lifted his head. "We better go inside before I completely forget where we are."

Sierra blinked open her eyes, still feeling lost in the spell that had come over her. "Or I do the same thing and let you have whatever you want."

Cale groaned again. "You're not helping." He threaded his fingers with hers and turned them in the direction Trevor had gone. "Time to go."

It wasn't long before she guided Cale to the room where her cousin's reception was being held. Loud music played and the lights had been dimmed. Quite a few guests were out on the dance floor. It seemed as if most of them were having a good time. Still holding onto Cale's hand, Sierra led him over to the table where her mother and brother sat. As she'd predicted, Trevor held a drink. Her mom, of course, wouldn't cut him off.

Trevor glared at Cale as Sierra and he took a seat in a couple of empty chairs. "What the hell is he doing here?" her brother slurred.

Yup, Trevor was still pissed off. Sierra really didn't give a crap. "I invited him, and it's none of your damn business."

"Sierra, don't be rude to your brother," her mother said. "Introduce us." Her gaze settled on Cale.

Of course her mom didn't reprimand Trevor for his rudeness to Sierra. Sierra clenched her jaw to hold back the caustic remark she oh so wanted to make. What held her back was the fact it wouldn't make a bit of difference. "Mom, this is Cale. Cale, this is my mother, Nancy."

Her mom smiled at Cale. "When did you meet my daughter? I had no idea she was seeing someone. If I'd known, I would have told her to invite you to the wedding when she received the invitation, instead of bringing you on the spur of the moment. At least then you would have had a chance to dress appropriately."

Sierra felt like crawling under the table again. If it wasn't her brother, it was her mom saying something to embarrass her. She really couldn't win when it came to her family.

Cale seemed to overlook what her mother said and replied, "Actually, Sierra and I just met outside while she was looking for Trevor. So she really couldn't have asked me to come with her to the wedding any earlier."

"Oh," her mom said. "Did you ask her out on a date? Sierra desperately needs a man in her life. Her last boyfriend was a year ago. And with her track record, I'm not sure I'll ever get to see her walk down the aisle or give me grandchildren."

"Mother!" Sierra said in a shocked voice. She really wanted to disappear now. She couldn't even look at Cale, afraid to see his reaction to what her mom had said.

As if he knew how embarrassed Sierra felt, Cale shifted his chair closer to hers and put his arm around her shoulders. "If I were to ask Sierra out, would I meet with your approval, Nancy?"

Cale smiled, and Sierra watched her mother return it with a coy one of her own, practically batting her eyelashes. She didn't know what she thought was worse—her mom's embarrassing statements, or her flirting with a man Sierra was more than interested in.

"Of course I approve," her mother said. "I don't think my daughter has dated a man quite as good-looking as you. If she's smart, she'll hold on to you before someone else snaps you up."

Cale turned his head toward Sierra and gave her a look so heated she almost melted in her chair. Her pussy clenched in longing to be filled by a big cock. Having checked out the bulge in the front of Cale's jeans, she had a feeling he'd be large enough to do the job.

The heat in Cale's gaze seemed to increase as he took a deep breath through his nose. Without looking away from Sierra, he answered her mother. "I don't think Sierra has to worry about another woman taking me away from her. We've gotten off to a great start, as far as I'm concerned."

As she stared back, she really felt as if Cale thought she was the only woman he'd ever want. She had no idea if he did it on purpose to put on a show for her mother or not, but that didn't stop her body from reacting to him. Arousal flooded through her, making her wish Cale and she were alone. Hell, she'd even risk running into the wolf again by going back out to the hiking trail with him.

Cale took another big inhalation through his nose, and in between blinks, Sierra thought she saw his eyes glow mutedly. She really couldn't have seen that, though.

Trevor snorted, ending whatever moment had come over her and Cale. "I need another drink," her brother said as he rose unsteadily to his feet.

It was her turn to snort. "Good luck with that. I'm sure you'll be cut off soon, if they haven't done so already. You've had more than enough."

Sierra watched Trevor walk away, but soon found her attention on Cale when he stood and held his hand out to her.

"It's a slow song," he said with a smile. "And you promised you'd dance with me."

She put her hand in his and allowed him to pull her to her feet. He then led her out to the center of the room where other couples danced to the music. Sierra put her arms around Cale's neck as he took her in his arms, holding her around the waist.

They drew a few stares. Sierra figured it was because Cale was dressed casually while everyone else around them wore dressier clothes. She ignored the others as Cale started them dancing.

The heat from Cale's body seeped right into hers as they swayed to the music together. His arms around her held her tighter, pulling her flush against him. Sierra sucked in a breath when the hardness of his erection brushed her lower stomach. He felt thick and long. Wetness pooled deep inside her pussy and her nipples grew taut, begging to be sucked on.

She lifted her gaze to look at his face. His eyes were heavy lidded and totally focused on her. She seemed to fall into them, where no one else mattered but the man who held her close. Sierra no longer heard the music or saw the people around them. Cale had become the center of her universe. Her body ached for his, the need to get closer to him was almost too hard to resist. Never before had she been drawn to a man quite like she was to Cale. And from the way his gaze seemed to eat her up, she had the feeling he felt the same way about her, which blew her mind.

Even though her mother had embarrassed her by saying Sierra hadn't dated a man as good-looking as Cale, it was true. She didn't consider herself ugly, but she usually attracted men she didn't consider out of her reach, ones who were nothing really special. And she had to admit she felt safer going after men like that, which wasn't what she needed when it came right down to it. Finding herself bored after a few months was the first stage of her wanting out of the relationship.

But with Cale, it was different. She had a feeling the boredom wouldn't set in as it had with the others. And it wasn't because he turned her on until she couldn't think straight. The little time she'd spent with him, she knew she wanted to see him again, hopefully the next day.

"Sierra," Cale said in a husky voice. "The way you're looking at me, soon I'm not going to be responsible for my actions. And I doubt you'll want to give your mom and brother any more ammo to use against you later."

She licked her suddenly dry lips. "Are you saying you'd make a move on me in front of my family and the other wedding guests?" Cale rocked his hips into her and she bit back a moan when she felt his cock jerk inside his jeans.

"That's exactly what I'm saying. As is, I'm going to have a hard time walking off the dance floor without everyone knowing what condition I'm in."

"Then maybe we should stop dancing."

His hold tightened. "Don't you dare. I like you exactly where you are."

To distract herself from the arousal Cale's words caused, Sierra asked, "How long are you here in Victoria? You never said when you were going back to Toronto."

He gave her a crooked grin. "I guess that depends on you."

"On me? Why?"

"Because you've put a new spin on my holiday. You might have thought I shot you a line when I said meeting you has made it more interesting, but I meant it. You are a pleasant surprise I hadn't expected."

The need to giggle like a silly teenager built inside Sierra. She squashed it before it could rise to the surface. She was too old to be acting like a ninny because a man showed interest in her.

She cleared her throat before she spoke. "Don't you have to worry about your work? I'm sure your employer won't take too kindly to the idea of you having even more time off than you already booked. I took next week off and I know my work wouldn't be too thrilled if I took more."

Cale grinned. "I don't have to worry about that. I'm my own boss. I own a gym, and my employees are quite capable of looking after it while I'm away."

And that would explain why Cale was so muscular. He had the build of a man who spent many hours in a gym lifting weights. "You're lucky. I wish I could say my job was that interesting, because it's not. I work at the call center for the local cable company. I get to take phone calls from customers all day, the majority of which are complaints."

"I suppose that could be a stressful place to work."

"You have no idea. I love having customers yell at me, calling me stupid, or worse, when I won't give them what they want and aren't entitled to, and all the while I have to remain courteous. Sometimes I wish I could reach through the phone and smack some of these people."

Cale bent his head and kissed her softly. "You could always move to Toronto and come work for me. I could use another person to work the front desk."

Sierra studied Cale's face. He appeared to be serious. There was no playfulness showing in his dark-green eyes. "Are you really offering me a job?"

He nodded. "Yes."

She shook her head. "Don't you think that's a bit premature? You only just met me. For all you know, I could be a crappy worker and try to rob you blind."

A smile spread across Cale's face as he laughed. "Some people might think I'm getting ahead of myself, but I'm a pretty good judge of character. You don't come across as a person who would do any of those things. And think of it this way, it has the added bonus of you getting away from your mother and brother."

"Now you're really not playing fair," she said with a chuckle. "After tonight, I'm more than ready to put as much distance as I can between them and me."

"Well, Toronto will give you that." Cale kissed her again. This time he lingered, his lips taking hers until he had her clutching him. He pulled away with a groan. "I had better watch myself. You're just too tempting to resist."

"I could say the same thing about you," Sierra said, a bit breathless.

"Do you need a ride home? I left my rental in the parking lot in the park. I'm finding myself reluctant to see tonight come to an end."

"Sorry. I'm the one who drove my mom and Trevor to the wedding. I have to take them to their places." She met Cale's gaze. "There's always tomorrow." Sierra gave him a hopeful look, even though she had a feeling he wouldn't turn her down.

"Tomorrow won't come soon enough." The song ended, but Cale kept them slow dancing, though the music had a faster tempo. "We can even make it a real date. I planned on going whale watching while I was here. I think we can still do that even on a Sunday."

"I've been a couple of times, but I'd love to go with you. Just don't ask me to go on a kayak tour to see them. The idea of being out on the water in a small boat with a huge animal swimming under it gives me the willies. I'd much rather be on a ship and watch whales that way. There isn't any chance of them capsizing it."

Cale laughed. "It's a deal. I'll call around tomorrow morning and set something up for the afternoon. And I promise no kayaks." He paused and looked at something behind her. "I think we'd better go back to the table. Your mother is doing her best to get your attention."

Sierra stepped out of Cale's arms and turned around. Sure enough, her mom was frantically waving at her. She also noticed Trevor was sitting at the table looking none too happy. Seeing no drink in his hand, she had a feeling she knew the reason why—he'd been cut off as she'd predicted.

"I'd better go," she said to Cale. "Come back to the table with me and I'll give you my phone number."

"Sure. I'll call you in the latter part of the morning tomorrow."

With Cale's hand on her lower back, she was guided through the dancing couples and over to her mother. Sierra had been right about her brother being pissed about not being served any more alcohol. He was the reason why their mother wanted to leave all of a sudden.

After writing her telephone number on one of the paper napkins on the table, she handed it to Cale. He gave her a kiss along with a promise to call her, then left the reception. Sierra sighed to herself as she followed him with her gaze, lingering on his tight ass. As Cale had said, tomorrow couldn't get here soon enough.

Chapter Three

Cale went wolf as soon as he reached the trees at the end of the garden. His mating urge rode him harder in this form, but he needed to experience the freedom it gave him. He felt as if his body were all tied up in knots. And he knew it would only get worse until he claimed Sierra as his own.

He sniffed the night air, smelling all the scents around him. The numerous insects that came out once it was dark echoed in his sensitive ears. None of those things distracted his thoughts from Sierra. Spending time with her made him want her even more. He enjoyed being in her company, wanted to make love to her so badly he found it hard to concentrate on anything else. But he couldn't take her yet. She was mortal and didn't know a thing about his kind. The first time they slept together, and he took her fully, their souls would join and they wouldn't be able to stand to be apart for any length of time. He couldn't do that to her until she understood what it all meant.

Just before he reached the parking lot where he'd left his rental, Cale shifted back to his human form, willing his clothes on at the same time. The greater the distance he put between him and Sierra the more he longed to turn around and go back to her. He also didn't look forward to the erotic dreams he'd have of her when he slept tonight. They would only ramp up his arousal even more. It was bad enough he was still semi-hard.

After he unlocked the four-door sedan, he got inside and started the engine. It didn't take him long to reach his hotel, The Fairmont Empress, which was situated at Victoria's Inner Harbour, and was around eight kilometers from the castle. Once he parked the rental, Cale went up to his floor and into his room.

He walked over to the desk, which held some brochures, and picked up the one he'd looked at earlier on whale watching. Cale took it over to the bed and sat down to read. The touring company ended up being the one he wanted. It offered the choice of going out in either a Zodiac or a luxury yacht. The latter seemed like the best one, and there was a tour at two in the afternoon the next day.

That decided, he toed off his shoes and shifted on the mattress until he sat with his back against the headboard. He grabbed the remote off the small table next to the bed and turned on the LCD TV. Cale switched the channel to a movie, but he couldn't stay focused on it. Sierra just occupied too much of his mind.

At least he had the next day all planned. And that was when he'd really start to take steps to make Sierra his mate, something he planned on doing before he left Victoria. That way he could bring her home with him. She didn't know it yet, but he was going to be the best thing that ever happened to her. He'd make sure of it.

* * * * *

After taking her mom and brother home to their respective residences, Sierra had then gone to her apartment, glad to be free of them. She hated to think it, but Cale had planted the idea of working for him in Toronto inside her head and it was taking root. She really wasn't that close to her mother or Trevor, and never had been. She didn't have a relationship with them as she'd had with her father. They'd been two of a kind, right down to sharing similar looks and personality. And she missed him every day since his passing. It sounded cruel, but in some ways, Sierra wished it had been her mother instead of her father who had died. At least that way she would have still felt as if she had close family.

Now the day after the wedding, her nerves felt as if someone had taken a grater to them. Something she always felt after spending any length of time with Trevor and her mother.

As people said, you couldn't pick your family. At times she wished she could.

But she could pick her boyfriend. Just thinking about the kisses she'd shared with Cale the night before brought a smile to her face. She couldn't wait to see him again today. That was why she sat in her living room with the phone in her lap, waiting for him to call.

Ever since she last saw him, she really hadn't been able to stop thinking about Cale. Hell, she'd even dreamed about him, and it hadn't been the tame variety either. It had been as erotic as dreams went. She had it bad. Sierra didn't know how far this romance would go, but she intended to spend at least one night screwing his brains out before he went home. And maybe, just maybe, if his holiday came to a close and they were still going strong, she'd seriously think about taking him up on his job offer. She was ready for a change in her life. She felt as if she were stuck in a rut and couldn't get out of it. Moving to a new city and province—far away from her immediate family—could be just what she needed.

The phone rang and Sierra almost jumped out of her skin. Placing a hand over her rapidly beating heart, she picked up the cordless and pushed the button to answer. "Hello?"

"Hi, Sierra, it's Cale. How are you doing today?"

"Hi. Not bad. I was just sitting here waiting for you to call."

"Well, I managed to book the whale-watching tour. We'll go out at two. I found it in one of the brochures in my room. Since it's not quite eleven thirty, how about you come to the hotel and we can order room service for lunch? Or if you don't want to do that, we could go to one of the restaurants here. There are a couple of them to choose from."

The thought of being alone with Cale in his room appealed to Sierra more. "Room service is fine."

"Great. Then why don't you come over now, if you don't have anything else you need to do first, that is."

"No, I don't. Where are you staying?"

"I have a room at The Fairmont Empress. Why don't I meet you downstairs in the lobby?"

"Sure. It'll only take me about ten minutes to get there."

"I'll see you then."

"All right."

Sierra ended the call and let out a low whistle. Cale had to be doing well in the gym business. The Fairmont Empress was one of Victoria's five-star hotels. She knew the rooms started at over two hundred dollars a night. If he planned on staying for at least a week, that was a lot of money. She'd never be able to stay there for that length of time. Maybe for one night, but that would be it.

Before leaving her apartment, Sierra gave herself one quick look over. She wore a pair of dark-gray jeans and a light-pink, long-sleeve t-shirt. She also planned to take a windbreaker with her. The day was sunny, but the breeze was a bit on the cool side, and being out on the water would make it feel even cooler. She wore the tiniest amount of makeup. She'd pulled her hair back into a high ponytail to keep it from getting tangled in the wind. Satisfied that she didn't look terrible, she gathered up her jacket and purse and left.

The entire drive to the hotel, Sierra thought about Cale and what their day together would be like. She had to admit she did too much thinking about him. They hadn't officially been out on a first date and already she'd begun to obsess over him. She'd have to watch it. If it didn't work out between Cale and her, she could end up getting hurt in the end.

At the hotel, Sierra parked her car before she walked to the front entrance. She looked up at the stone edifice in front of her. The Fairmont Empress was known for its afternoon tea, which was only served during the summer, and had been since 1908 when it first opened. It was also a hotel where royalty and celebrities alike stayed. There were also reportedly two ghosts in residence—a little girl and an early twentieth-century maid who showed up on the sixth floor sometimes to help clean the rooms.

Sierra entered the spacious lobby and looked around. It didn't take long to spot Cale. He was so tall he stood out in any crowd. She headed for him and smiled when he met her halfway. Once again she was struck by how handsome he was.

"You made it," he said.

"Yeah. My apartment isn't too far from here."

"Let's go upstairs." Cale brushed her lips with his. "Are you hungry?"

She nodded. "Actually, I am."

"Good. You can order whatever you want from the room service menu. We still have plenty of time before we go whale watching."

He twined his fingers with hers and guided her over to the elevator. After he pushed the call button a car came within seconds. They got on and the doors silently slid shut. Sierra watched as Cale jabbed the button for his floor. Her heart beat a little faster just from being around him. And the simple brush of his lips had her body craving his. Even now her nipples remained taut beneath her shirt and her lace bra rubbed against them, making them ache.

Once the elevator stopped and the doors opened, they stepped out into the hallway. Cale guided her down to his room. As he used the keycard to unlock it, he said, "I booked one of the junior suites, so it's quite spacious." He stepped to the side to let her go in ahead of him.

Sierra saw what Cale meant. The room was open-concept with a studio design. There was a sitting area with an armchair and couch, and a thick glass table in the center. Behind the couch was the bedroom area with a king-sized bed. Since the curtains were open on the two windows, she saw the view was of the city.

"It's a great room," she said.

Cale came in behind her and shut the door. Her gaze followed him as he closed the distance between them. He took her in his arms. "I know I asked you if you were hungry for food, but right now I find I'm craving a taste of you more."

His deep, husky voice seemed to go right through her, causing her pussy to clench. "I won't stop you," Sierra whispered.

He bent his head and his lips took hers in a heated kiss. Cale's arms tightened around her, bringing their lower bodies into contact. He already sported an erection, which had her sex growing wet, needing to be filled. Sierra kissed him back, opening her mouth when his tongue pushed inside. He licked and sucked, increasing her arousal.

The thought of food went right out of her head as she clutched at Cale. Her blood heated, the sound of her heart pounding loudly in her ears. Wetness pooled in her pussy. God, he made her horny. She was more than ready to break her dry spell with the man who kissed her so expertly. She knew sex with Cale would more than likely be just as good.

Cale's hand came up and covered one of her breasts. His thumb brushed back and forth across her nipple. It tightened even more, begging for attention. She let out a low moan as she pressed herself firmly into his grasp. He seemed to know what she needed and rolled the taut peak between his thumb and forefinger.

He left her mouth and trailed kisses down to her jaw and along the side of her neck. She tilted her head to the side to give him better access. Goose bumps broke out on her body as Cale gently nipped her.

"We should probably stop," he said huskily against her skin. "Before we get too carried away and I forget about our plans for the day."

"Hmm, not yet." Sierra reached up and threaded her fingers through his hair. "I need more."

A sound rumbled out of Cale's chest, close to an animalistic growl. "You're too tempting to refuse."

Picking her up off her feet, he carried her to the sitting area, then let her slowly slide down his body. His hands dropped to her bottom and yanked her closer as he ground his hard cock against her. Sierra pulled his head down and claimed his mouth. Cale groaned and sucked her tongue past his lips.

Cale shifted his hands to the bottom of her shirt and thrust them under it. His fingers skimmed across the small of her back, causing a shiver to go through her. He worked his way to her sides, then to her stomach. He pushed higher, lifting her top as he went, until he reached her breasts.

Sierra raised her arms above her head when Cale pulled her shirt off. He dropped his hands to the top of her jeans and slid a finger under the waistband, teasing her as he stroked the skin of her belly. His lips trailed down the side of her neck.

"Cale," she moaned. "More."

In answer, he undid the button and zipper on her pants. One hand pushed inside and covered the front of her panties. He ran a finger along the material that was damp with her juices. Sierra sucked in a sharp breath, pressing her hips forward.

Cale stroked her once more before he released her altogether and took a step back. With his eyes closed to mere slits, he yanked his shirt up and over his head. Sierra ran her gaze over his well-defined chest and abs. He was a work of art she wanted to learn with her tongue. Her gaze dropped lower to the large bulge in the front of his jeans. She licked her lips at the thought of seeing what was hidden beneath the material.

"Take your pants off for me," Cale said, his voice deep and husky.

With no hesitation, Sierra pushed the top of her jeans down past her hips until they dropped onto the floor, pooling around her ankles. She stepped out of them and kicked them out of the way. She breathed heavier as Cale's heated gaze looked her up and down, then back up again.

Becoming more aroused, she said, "Your turn. Lose the jeans."

He chuckled. "Not yet, babe." He scooped her up and carried her over to the large armchair before he sat her on the thick seat cushion.

Sierra looked up at Cale as he stood in front of her. For a brief moment, she thought it looked as if his eyes were mutedly glowing, but with them closed to mere slits, it could have been a trick of the light.

Then she thought nothing more of it when Cale dropped to his knees before her and placed his hands on either side of her hips. Leaning forward, he kissed her until she squirmed in the chair. He had her so worked up she wanted to tear off her panties, open the front of his jeans and take his cock deep inside her. Let him plunge into her until they both came.

Cale left her mouth and tasted the skin along her collarbone as he undid the front clasp on her bra. He pushed both cups aside and pulled back to look at her breasts. She took her bottom lip between her teeth. Anticipation had her body coiling tight. Her breath left her lungs in a *whoosh* when Cale bent his head and flicked one of her nipples with the tip of his tongue.

He opened his mouth and took the taut peak inside. A low, needy moan pushed out of Sierra. As Cale sucked, she felt a corresponding pull deep inside her pussy. Her panties became wetter, her juices leaking from her slick opening.

Cale shifted to her other nipple and paid it the same attention. Sierra's excitement grew. The sound of their heavy breathing filled her ears. She buried her fingers in his hair and held him to her.

Her belly quivered as he trailed his hands down it to the top of her panties. With two quick tugs, Cale had them yanked down her legs and off. Once he tossed them aside, he left her breast and continued downward, pushing her legs farther apart as he went.

The first swipe of his tongue along her pussy had Sierra's hips arching off the chair. She gripped the armrests, digging her nails into the material, as Cale licked her again and circled her clit. "Yes," she moaned.

"I'm just getting started," Cale said against her skin.

He licked and sucked on her pussy. Her whimpered cries filled the room. They increased in volume when he pushed one finger and then another inside her. She clamped her inner walls around the digits and rode them as they stroked in and out. Cale used his tongue to stimulate her clit at the same time, driving her closer and closer to her release.

As if he sensed how near she actually was, Cale changed the position of his fingers so they caressed her G-spot. A few strokes and he had her tumbling over the edge into orgasm. Sierra let out a strangled cry, her pussy clutching the digits that still moved inside her.

After the last wave of pleasure hit her, Sierra opened her eyes and looked down at Cale. He had his head resting on her thigh as his broad shoulders lifted with each rapid breath he took.

She stroked a hand through his soft hair. "I want to touch you like you touched me. Stand up."

Cale did as she'd asked and rose to his feet. Sierra inched to the edge of the seat and stroked her hands from his hard chest down his six-pack abs. She looked up at him and saw he had his eyes closed. His face was strained, as if he were holding himself back.

Looking at what she had at eye level, Sierra undid Cale's jeans. She parted the material and tugged it down a bit until she'd sprung his cock. Since he wasn't wearing any underwear, there was nothing holding her back from running a finger along his shaft. It jerked in response to her delicate touch.

Wanting to give him as much pleasure as he'd given her, she wrapped her fingers around his thick length and pumped up and down. Cale rocked his hips in time with her movements, pushing his cock tighter into her hand. As she watched, a bead of pre-cum appeared on the very tip. Sierra leaned in and licked it off. Cale groaned deep in his throat.

Sierra took that as encouragement. She stroked down his shaft and grasped him firmly around the base. Inching her bottom even closer to the edge of the seat, she circled the broad head of his cock with the tip of her tongue before she opened her mouth and sucked it inside. She took more of him until she reached the maximum she could handle. The rest she stroked with her hand while she slid him in and out.

"Christ," Cale panted. "Don't stop. That feels so good."

She didn't answer him. Instead, she sucked on him harder and used the flat of her tongue to stroke the sensitive spot just under the head. Cale's hips jerked, pumping, as he fucked her mouth. His cock grew thicker and longer.

She didn't stop pleasuring him this way. She wanted him to come, to give her everything he had. It wasn't long before Cale made a noise between a moan and what sounded like an animalistic growl. His shaft pulsed inside her mouth as he came.

Once it was over, Sierra released him. Amazingly, Cale was still hard, even though he'd reached release. She looked up and found him struggling to regain his breath. She stood, stripped off her bra and wrapped her arms around his neck as she pressed her body against his, trapping his cock between them.

Sierra brushed Cale's lips with hers. "That was nice, but I could go for more." She rubbed against him, eliciting a deep groan. "And from the looks of it so could you."

Cale leaned his forehead against hers and held on to her hips to hold her still. "I think we'd better stop right here for now. We still have to eat before we go on the whale-watching tour."

"We could always do that another day." Sierra dragged her tongue across his lips.

He groaned again. "I've already booked the tour, so we're going. Besides, if we did any more, I'd never let you out of bed for the rest of the day and night."

"Are you sure you don't want to reschedule?"

Cale slapped her ass and lifted his head. "I'm sure. Stop tempting me. I've already strayed from some of my plans I'd laid out for the day."

"Think of what we just did as getting a head start on the most enjoyable part of it. Which I intend to indulge in more of once the tour is over."

"What would you say if I were an old-fashioned type of guy and wanted to wait until we know each other a bit better before we hopped into the sack?"

Sierra giggled. "I'd say forget it. You've already given me a taste of you and I find I'm craving more. A lot more. There's no going back now."

"Well, I tried." Cale stepped back and stuffed his still hard cock into his jeans and did them up. "Even though you make a delectable sight naked, I need you to get dressed. Then we can look at the room service menu."

She sighed dramatically. "All right, if you insist. I just can't promise you that I'll behave later."

He gave her a crooked grin. "Then I've been forewarned. I'll get the menu."

Figuring there would be no changing Cale's mind, Sierra gathered up her clothes then got dressed. It was still early in the day. She'd make sure they took up where they left off sometime before she said goodnight to Cale.

Chapter Four

Cale glanced up from the plate of pan-seared salmon he had in front of him and at Sierra. She'd ordered the same dish as he had. He ran his gaze over her pretty face as he put another bite of the fish in his mouth. He couldn't get enough of looking at her.

What they'd done earlier had only made his mating urge ride his ass harder, but it was totally worth it. And he would do it again. The only thing he had to worry about was his ability to stop himself from making love to Sierra fully. Every time he touched her, kissed her, he wanted her more. He wanted to claim her as his mate and bind her to him.

"I can feel you watching me, you know," Sierra said with a laugh. She looked up and met his gaze. "And if you keep it up, my promise to behave will go out the window."

"I'm just looking and enjoying the view while I eat."

"Well, if you enjoy it too much I won't be responsible for what I do."

Cale speared the last of his salmon with his fork and popped it into his mouth. He chewed and swallowed, then said, "I'm finished eating. What about you? We should get ready to go soon."

Sierra eyed him. "Why do I have the impression that you're trying to get us out of this room as soon as you can?"

"It's not so much getting us out of here as I think we need to slow things down a little. Like I said before, get to know each other better." He grew serious. "I don't want this to end when my vacation is over."

She put down her fork and straightened in her chair. "I'd like that." Sierra cleared her throat. "If we're going to be open about how we want things to go, I have a question to ask."

"Go for it."

"Were you serious about offering me a job at your gym in Toronto?"

"Of course I was."

Sierra bit her lower lip. "Last night got me thinking. I'm due for a change in my life. I have to stop being my brother's keeper, or he'll never smarten up. Now that my dad has passed, and I'm not very close to Trevor or my mother, there really isn't anything holding me here."

Cale reached across the table and picked up her hand, stroking his thumb across the back of it. "If that is what you want to do, the position is yours."

Sierra deciding to move to Toronto couldn't have worked out any more perfect. Once they became mates, she'd have to do that anyway. He couldn't live away from that city. It was where his pack was located. If he were to live in Victoria he'd have to go lone wolf, since there wasn't a werewolf pack here. That wasn't something he wanted to do, not with a mate.

"Then I have some serious thinking to do over the next few days," she said. "I'll also have to look into apartments to rent. I don't want to spend a lot of time staying at a hotel. That could get expensive."

"Don't worry about your living arrangements. You'll be staying with me."

She eyed him. "You want me to move in with you?"

"Yes. By the end of my holidays, I have a feeling we're going to be very close."

"You sound pretty sure of yourself."

"I am. You just wait and see." He turned in his chair and glanced at the clock on the small table next to the bed. "We should probably start getting ready to go. The yacht will be leaving the harbor soon."

"You booked us on a yacht tour?"

He smiled. "Of course. Since kayaks were out, I figured we might as well go in style."

"I can't argue with that."

After he put the tray with their empty plates on it outside in the hallway for room service to pick up, Cale pulled on a windbreaker as Sierra donned hers. Once they were ready, he took her by the hand and brought her down to the lobby.

It was only a short walk from the hotel to the harbor. He guided Sierra over to the yacht used for the tour, and they boarded once their reservation had been verified. There were a few other people standing at the rails. The tour would take up to eighty-four passengers, but Cale doubted that many people would be on this trip, since their two o'clock departure time was nearing.

Once they were underway, the university-degreed marine biologist who was supposed to run the tour came up on deck and told the passengers they could expect to see killer whales, along with humpback, gray and minke whales. There were also supposed to be porpoises around as well.

"I hope we get to hear the humpback's song," Sierra said after the biologist told everyone about the underwater microphones.

"Yeah, me too."

When a pod of killer whales was spotted, Cale guided Sierra over to the rail closest. The large mammals broke the surface of the water, their dorsal fins sticking straight up as they blew mists of water into the air. They were a sight to behold.

"Look," he pointed to the whales, "there are a couple of babies."

"They're beautiful," Sierra said.

They spent the next three hours enjoying being out on the water and watching the whales. Even a few of the humpbacks put on a show by breaching. Cale figured it was well worth the money he'd spent. With no oceans near Toronto, this was something he could never do at home. And seeing the look of awe on Sierra's face when one of the large mammals did something made it even more enjoyable.

Once they were back in the harbor, Cale put his arms around Sierra's shoulders and walked her down the dock. "Would you like to go get something to eat?"

She turned her head to look at him. "Actually, I'm not hungry. I sort of filled up on the snacks and refreshments they put out on the tour. I have a weakness for free food," she said with a laugh. "But if you want something, don't let me stop you."

"No, I'm fine."

Sierra put her arm around his waist. "Then let's go back to your hotel room and watch some TV, maybe have a few drinks."

Cale knew he'd be playing with fire, but he didn't want to tell her no. Spending the afternoon with her had been beyond his expectations. He'd never been this relaxed, or more like himself, around other women. The more Sierra and he talked, the more he found himself falling for her. She was to be his mate, it was expected that he'd have deep feelings for Sierra quite quickly. If that hadn't been possible his mating urge wouldn't have been set off.

Back at The Fairmont Empress, Cale bought a bottle of white wine from the bar inside the restaurant to bring up to his room. Once he and Sierra were closed behind the locked door, he hung their jackets up and went to the bathroom to grab two glasses from the counter.

He held them up as he joined Sierra in the sitting area. "I know these aren't meant for wine, but that's all we have."

"A glass is a glass," she replied with a smile.

Cale sat and opened the bottle of wine and poured some into each small tumbler. He then handed one to Sierra and clinked his against hers. "Here's to getting to know each other better."

She giggled. "I'll drink to that," Sierra said before she took a sip.

As they sat watching TV, Cale found himself not really paying attention. All his senses were more trained on Sierra than anything else. Now that they were alone in his room again, he found himself longing to touch and taste her as he'd done earlier. The mating urge always present, it was hard to ignore. His would-be mate's scent seemed to fill his head with each breath he took, enticing him.

Cale refilled their glasses once they'd drained them. Sierra had settled under his arm with her back pressed to his chest and her head on his shoulder. She stared at the TV as she ran her hand up and down his thigh, each stroke coming ever nearer to his cock. He grew from semi-hard to fully engorged in a matter of seconds. His erection throbbed in time with his rapid heartbeat. The need to have Sierra increased, making it harder for him to resist.

To distract himself from giving free rein to the impulses that battered him, Cale downed his wine in two gulps and poured himself more. It wasn't as if the alcohol would cool his libido. Being a werewolf, he had to drink a shit-ton of booze to even get a good buzz going. He quickly drank the next glass and refilled it again.

Sierra made no comment about how much he was drinking. She continued to keep her gaze on the television and trailed her hand up and down his leg at the same time. When she brushed the tip of his cock, it jerked inside his jeans. The next pass, she closed her fingers over his shaft and stroked his full length. Cale gripped his glass so tightly he was surprised it didn't shatter. He looked down and watched her play with him, breathing as if he'd just run a marathon.

She was working him up to a fever pitch. He ached to feel Sierra's fingers touching his bare cock, pumping and squeezing. He fought a battle with himself. He needed to stay in control, not let things get out of hand, which was hard, considering his body was on fire for Sierra. All he wanted to do was strip her naked, pull her under him and sink his dick between her legs.

As if she'd known what he'd thought, Sierra released him and lifted her hand to the fasteners on his jeans. With a few tugs, she opened them and shoved her hand inside, her fingers wrapping around his shaft as he'd wanted. Cale couldn't hold back the low, quiet growl of need that punched out of him when she pumped up and down.

Out of the corner of his eye, he saw Sierra turn her head to look at him. He turned his in her direction and noted the high color on her cheeks. The pulse in her neck throbbed in a rapid tempo. Her arousal perfumed the air around them.

Without a word, Sierra placed her glass on the table in front of them and shifted so she straddled his lap. Her jean-clad pussy came down on top of his erection as she fisted his hair on both sides of his head and clamped her mouth over his. That was one thing he noticed about his would-be mate, she had no problem taking from him what she wanted when she wanted it. That excited him even more.

She took his mouth in a heady kiss, tasting him as she ground against him. Once they were both moaning, Sierra broke contact with his lips and quickly shed her top and bra. She then took off his shirt before she rubbed her taut nipples against his chest while she reclaimed his mouth once more.

One of her hands reached between them and pushed inside his jeans to latch around his cock. She stroked him in a tight fist. Cale couldn't hold still any longer and lifted his hips in time with her movements. The kiss they shared became more carnal, desperate. Their teeth bumped together in their excitement.

Rising on her knees, Sierra used her free hand to push his jeans farther down until they were past his hips and his cock was free of them. Cale kept his eyes closed as he lost himself in Sierra's touch. Intense arousal pounded through him. The world seemed to fade away until all he felt were her lips on his and her hand wrapped around his dick.

Cale went stiff as a board as slick, warm walls closed around the head of his cock. Sierra had taken another inch of him inside her pussy before he gathered his wits about him. He clamped his hands on her hips and stopped her downward movement.

His whole body shook as he fought the urge to sink home. "Sierra. Stop," he said through gritted teeth. She felt so damn good.

She pushed down again, taking a little bit more of him before he tightened his grip on her hips to halt her. "Yes, Cale. We both want this."

He tried to buck her off, but that only drove his cock deeper inside her pussy. Sierra used that to her advantage and forced him the rest of the way in until he was sheathed to the hilt.

Cale's harsh breathing filled the room. It still wasn't too late, though he barely held on by the skin of his teeth. He was inside her, but the mating process hadn't started yet. As long as he kept her from moving on him maybe he'd be able to pull out. But that was easier said than done. He couldn't make himself lift her off him. He reminded himself that Sierra had no idea what the ramifications would be if they finished what she'd started. She deserved to have the choice. He had to do the honorable thing, even though he'd be in pain for a little while. Having blue balls would only be a minor thing.

But then she leaned forward, clamped her teeth on the spot where his neck and shoulder met, biting, and squeezed his cock with her inner muscles. With a loud growl he did nothing to mask, Cale lifted her on and off him as he thrust into her. Where she'd bitten him was the biggest turn-on for a male werewolf, making him lose all control.

Sierra's cries of passion filled his head as growl after growl rumbled out of him. Feeling more wolf than man, he took her in pounding thrusts that lifted her knees off the couch with each inward movement. The sensation of her pussy closing around his cock, squeezing him tight, felt like heaven.

"Yes, yes, yes," Sierra chanted, matching the pace he'd set. "I'm going to come soon. More."

The ability to form words had left him. All that mattered was making her his. Just as his balls drew up close to his body, Cale felt it happen. A piece of his soul reached out for Sierra's. And hers reached for his. They wrapped around each other, becoming one. As the mating bond snapped into place, Sierra cried out as her pussy rhythmically clamped around his shaft in the throes of climaxing. With a howl, he thrust one final time inside her and came, his cock pulsing as he filled her with his cum.

As Cale fought for breath, he wrapped his arms around Sierra and pulled her close, so her head rested on his shoulder. He was still hard, and would remain so for hours even after coming several times. Something all male werewolves could do.

Sierra was now his mate, there was no breaking the bond that had formed between them. No going back. He should have had better control, but he'd been weak. With his mating urge riding him hard, being inside Sierra had been too much for him. Now he had to figure out how he was going to make sure this didn't turn into a fucking mess.

She sat up and smiled, brushing his lips with hers. "I have to say that was pretty intense." She shifted, then moaned. "And you're still hard." She lifted onto her knees before slowly sinking back down on him. "Time for round two."

Since the damage was already done, Cale no longer felt the need to hold back. "Most definitely."

He held Sierra tighter, and in a show of strength, stood with her in his arms. His cock was still inside her pussy and sank deeper with each step he took toward the bed. Just before he placed her on the mattress, he shed his jeans one-handed and kicked them away.

Now as naked as Sierra, Cale lay her down, following her, keeping their bodies joined. His wolf rose closer to the surface, wanting to claim her as his mate as well. He kissed her thoroughly before he pulled out of her welcoming, wet heat and shifted until he was on his knees. With a hand on her waist, he urged Sierra onto her stomach. Cale stroked his hand down the indent of her spine, reveling in the feel of her soft skin under his fingertips. She was his, truly claimed as his mate. His feelings had intensified for her, had become full-blown love. And that would only increase each time they made love and the mating bond between them grew stronger.

He stroked down her back and stopped at her hips. Gently, he urged her up onto her hands and knees. He then positioned himself behind her and led his cock to her pussy. Keeping a hold on himself, Cale rubbed the very tip along her slick opening. He waited until his shaft was coated with her juices before he sheathed himself deep inside her with one thrust. They both moaned together.

In and out he stroked, pulling almost all the way out before he sank deep again. He slowly increased his pace, taking her in hard, fast thrusts. His balls slapped against her clit. Sierra rocked back to meet him as he held on to her hips. His cock grew harder as she took him deeper than she had while she'd been on top.

Cale felt the point of no return quickly rushing up to meet him. He reached around Sierra and found her clit. He stroked it with his fingers as he pounded into her faster. "Come for me," he half growled.

She moaned and panted. "Don't stop. Just like that. A tiny bit more."

Sierra then let out a keening cry as her pussy milked his entire length, squeezing him in a tight fist. It was enough to send Cale into his own climax. As he emptied himself deep inside her, he howled in pleasure.

Once the last tremor shook him, he didn't pull out of Sierra's body as he put his arm around her waist and took them both to their sides. He tucked her against him and kissed the top of her head.

When he felt her relax along him and her breathing evened out, Cale whispered softly, "I love you, my mate."

Tired from spending the night before having erotic dreams about Sierra and not getting much sleep, Cale closed his eyes and fell into slumber.

Chapter Five

Sierra had started to drift off when she heard Cale's whispered words. *I love you, my mate.* That simple statement kept her awake, even though he'd fallen asleep shortly after. What had he meant by them? And had she heard him correctly? He'd spoken so quietly and low there was a chance she could have misheard him.

The mate part had been strange enough, but that wasn't what bothered her. It was "I love you" she had a hard time dealing with. Cale and she had just met the night before. They were still in the getting-to-know-each-other stage. Sierra thought she was pushing things by seriously considering his offer to move in with him, if and when she decided to go to Toronto.

It wasn't as if she didn't think there was the potential for them to find the big "L-word" in each other. She already felt something for Cale, more than just sexual attraction. And surprisingly, it seemed even deeper now that they'd had sex. Making love to Cale was amazing, but that very first time, something had happened deep inside her. Something she'd never experienced before in a man's arms. It sounded ludicrous to her, but it had felt as if they'd become connected in a way she found hard to describe. As if he'd become a part of her permanently.

And it didn't have to do with the fact his cock was still hard and buried inside her pussy. That Cale was still fully erect after coming twice, Sierra found amazing. She'd never been with a man who could do that. Not that she was complaining. It made her wonder just how long he could keep it up. She squeezed his shaft with her inner muscles, and Cale mumbled something unintelligible in his sleep as his hand came up and covered her breast. She smiled, but decided to let him be.

Sierra snuggled deeper in Cale's embrace. She could get used to lying in bed like this with him surrounding her. She closed her eyes, but didn't think sleep would come to her now. Her brain was working too much for her to shut it down.

She stroked her fingers along Cale's arm. Did she want to move to Toronto and live with him? Now that she thought about it again, Sierra liked the idea more and more. She turned her head and looked over her shoulder at the man who held her so close. Usually not much of a risk taker, she figured she'd be kind of crazy to let Cale just walk out of her life. Spending the afternoon with him on the yacht had shown he had a lot of qualities she liked in the opposite sex. Then there were his good looks and hot body.

A smile stretched along her lips and she pushed her weighty thoughts aside. She didn't have to make any major decisions just yet. Cale's vacation wasn't near to being over. She had plenty of time to enjoy their time together and to get to know him even better. As for what he'd whispered to her, she'd let that slide.

* * * * *

Sierra stood in the shower in Cale's hotel room, working shampoo into her hair the next morning. He hadn't had to work very hard to convince her to stay the night with him. After his nap — she still hadn't been able to sleep — he'd made love to her again. That joining he'd made her come so many times she'd lost count, and she'd gotten to see just how long he lasted. He'd had the same number of orgasms as she, remaining hard until the last one. At that point, Sierra had been almost ready to beg for mercy. Cale seemed to be insatiable.

Once they'd slept again — that time she had — Cale had ordered something to eat through room service, which they then ate naked on the bed. They'd also talked more. And before they'd gone to sleep for the night, he'd even managed to wrangle a promise out of her to leave Victoria with him, at his expense. Whether she'd made the right decision or not, it really didn't matter. She'd done it and she wouldn't be reneging on it.

Sierra turned to look at the end of the bathtub as the shower curtain was pulled back and Cale stepped in. He smiled and yanked it shut.

"I thought you might like some company," he said.

She returned his smile. "Did you think I was lonely in here?"

"Maybe."

Sierra swept her gaze down his body, landing on his cock, which was hard and long. "Or maybe it was you who needs some attention." She looked him in the face. "And I know just what kind you want."

Cale angled her under the spray of water and rinsed the shampoo out of her hair before he answered. "Okay, I won't lie. The thought of you naked and wet in the shower was just too tempting to resist."

She licked her lips. "I have to say the same thing about you." Sierra ran her hands up his muscled biceps to his shoulders and put her arms around his neck. Her pussy grew wet as she stepped closer and rubbed against Cale's erection.

"Mmm," he groaned. "You're making me want you again."

"And that would be a bad thing?" she asked coyly.

"Not necessarily. It's just I think we should leave the hotel at some point today. I'd like to go to your apartment and see how comfortable your bed is."

"Really now? And why would you want to do that?"

Cale reached down and squeezed her bottom as he pulled her closer. "Well, to decide whether yours or the hotel's is better. That way it'll help with the decision to stay at your place or here before we go to Toronto."

"You want to stay at my apartment?" she asked, a bit surprised. "I have to say, it's not as nice as your room here. Actually, it's on the dumpy side."

"It doesn't matter. It could be a real hole in the wall, for all I care. As long as you're there, and the bed is comfortable, that's good enough for me."

Sierra went on tiptoe and lightly kissed Cale. "And what would you say if I didn't want to have you sleeping over?" she asked with a teasing note in her voice.

Cale lifted her slightly and thrust his cock between her legs, stroking its length against her pussy. "I have ways that I'm sure you'll find very convincing. When I'm done, you won't be able to tell me no."

She gasped as the base of his shaft rubbed her clit. "Will it involve me aching in a good way? Have me longing for the one thing that'll make it all better?"

He pushed her wet hair aside and nibbled on the side of her neck. "Hmm, that would be a yes to both those questions. And I can promise you that you'll enjoy every minute of it too."

Sierra's juices leaked out of her pussy, wetting Cale's cock, which still stroked her. "I think I need a sample of your work. Right now."

"That most definitely can be arranged."

Cale bent his head and took one of her nipples into his mouth. He sucked on it and pulled his erection from between her legs. A hand took its place and a finger pushed inside her wet opening. It stroked in and out a few times before a second joined it.

Even though they'd made love for hours the night before, Sierra's libido shot through the roof. Cale knew just how to touch her, make her burn for him. She didn't think there would be a time when her body wouldn't respond to his caresses.

After he gave her other nipple the same attention, Cale buried his face in the crook of her neck. "God, you turn me on, Sierra. I need to feel your pussy wrapped around my cock."

The playfulness had left his voice. It was deep and gruff with desire. The sound of it made her blood heat even more. A throbbing ache pounded deep inside her core. Her body wept for his, readying itself to take the hard length of him.

"Yes," she said huskily.

Cale made that animalistic growl he did. He'd done it so often last night, Sierra no longer found it strange. If anything, it turned her on. He seemed to do it when he was aroused. He lifted one of her legs and wrapped it around his hip. She held on to his broad shoulders and leaned into him to keep her balance. He bent his knees slightly, then slowly entered her.

He worked his cock in and out, sinking deeper with each stroke. Sierra tightened her inner walls around his shaft, loving how big he felt. Her body stretched to accommodate his size as he filled her completely. Once he was seated to the hilt, she moaned.

Keeping hold of her leg around him while his other hand grasped her bottom, Cale set a slow and steady pace that was guaranteed to drive her wild. He speared into her, hitting her cervix with each pass. It didn't take long before Sierra needed him to move faster, take her harder.

"Make me come," she panted.

He thrust at an increased tempo, but it wasn't fast enough. Remembering how he'd reacted the first time she'd done it, Sierra went on tiptoe and bit him where his shoulder and neck met. Between one breath and the next, she found her other leg wrapped around Cale, her back pressed to the cool tile wall as he pounded into her, giving her what she wanted.

"Don't let go," he said on a groan. "Keep biting me. Leave your mark behind." One of his hands cupped the back of her head to hold her in place. "Oh god, that feels so damn good."

Sierra felt his cock harden even more as he surged in and out. An orgasm quickly built, then she was crying out against his skin, lost in wave after wave of pleasure when it tore through her. Cale kept ramming into her, his moans filling her ears. Amazingly, she reached a second climax as he thrust into her one final time, howling like an animal, his cock pulsing with release.

Once it was over, Cale let go of her head and Sierra pulled her mouth away from his shoulder. She saw teeth marks where she'd bitten him and a trickle of blood mixed with the water running down his chest.

She lifted her gaze to his, horrified by what she'd done. "I didn't mean to bite you so hard."

He grinned. "Don't worry about it."

"You're bleeding. You need that cleaned up."

Cale bent his head and took her lips in a slow, deep kiss before he cupped her face and looked her right in the eyes. "Sierra, it's all right. I like it, if you haven't already guessed. You just marked me as yours. You can sink your teeth into me like that any time you want."

"If someone sees it they're going to think you're dating a vampire."

He laughed. "I doubt that. Maybe they'll think I'm seeing a werewolf instead."

She slapped him on the arm. "Ha ha, very funny. I'm serious. It doesn't look good."

Cale wrapped his arms around her and turned her into the warm spray. "No one will see it. My shirts will hide it. Now let's finish with our shower so we can go to your apartment. I'm sure you want to change your clothes, then we can decide what we want to do for the rest of the day."

She shook her head. "Fine. It's a good thing I have the week off of work. You seem to want to monopolize all my time."

"What can I say? I've become addicted to you. If I let you get too far away I'll go into withdrawal."

"I guess we can't have that."

"I'm afraid you're stuck with me now." Cale's face grew serious. "And I wouldn't want it any other way."

Sierra sucked in a breath at the raw emotion in his features. What she saw in his eyes—what she could only describe as love—had her weak in the knees. The whole time they'd talked, not once had the subject of how they truly felt about each other come up.

"I think I'd miss you if you were gone." She stroked a hand down his chest. "I do have strong feelings for you, Cale. This is all happening so fast, though. I can't tell you that I—"

He cut her off with a finger across her lips. "Shh. You're not ready. I know that. I can wait until you are. Just know that how I feel for you won't ever change." Cale gave her a crooked grin. "Like I said, you're stuck with me. Let's get finished in here before we use up all the hotel's hot water."

She chuckled. "I highly doubt that's possible, but I'll hurry."

Sierra tipped her head back to wet her hair and continue washing it. Who knew that seeing a wolf on the hiking trails at Hatley Castle would result in her finding the man who could be the one?

Chapter Six

Cale sat in the passenger side of Sierra's late-model sedan, shifting his gaze from the scenery outside the window to her. They were on their way to her apartment.

Now that they were mated, he had to keep Sierra near him at all times, or they'd both suffer separation anxiety. A few hours apart would feel like a few years. The need to be reunited would be great. They wouldn't be able to think about anything else. And when they did see each other again, they'd come together in the most elemental of ways by having hot and desperate sex.

Cale didn't want either one of them having to go through that, especially when Sierra had no idea he was a werewolf. That was part of the reason he suggested they go to her apartment. He planned to tell her the truth of what he was later in the day. He figured she'd feel more comfortable at her place than his hotel room. He was already worried she'd react badly to the news. She was mortal, and it wasn't common knowledge among her kind that his even existed.

Sierra pulled her car into the parking lot of a small triplex. She turned into an empty spot, then shut off the engine. "Well, here it is," she said as she turned to look at him. "Like I said, it's kind of dumpy compared to The Fairmont Empress."

He reached across and stroked the backs of his fingers along her cheek. "Stop worrying so much about what I'll think of your place. I'm not a snob."

She laughed. "I never thought you were. But you have to be doing pretty well for yourself, considering the hotel you're staying at. I bet your house back in Toronto is one of those large, ritzy types that rich people live in."

There was no point in lying about it. Sierra would find out when she went back home with him. "All right, you've got me there. I do have a big house, and I have more money than I know what to do with. But that doesn't mean I always lived in a place like it."

Being nine hundred years old, he'd lived in dwellings that modern people today would think were nothing more than hovels. He hadn't always had the money he did now.

"I knew it," she said with a smile. "Rich and so very good-looking. I have yet been able to find anything wrong with you."

"Let's hope it stays that way. And I lucked out by finding a beautiful woman who makes me happy."

Sierra swallowed audibly before she leaned in and gave him a soft kiss. "Keep talking like that and you'll turn me into a sap."

Cale kissed her, then opened his car door. He got out and came around the vehicle to walk beside his mate as she headed for the building. They went inside and took a small flight of stairs to the next level. Sierra unlocked the door there and held it open for him to go in ahead of her.

Her apartment was indeed small, but it wasn't dumpy as she described it. She kept it clean and ordered. The walls were white and there was a brightly colored throw rug in the center of the living room. The single couch sat along one wall, facing the TV that was against the opposite one. Cale took a deep breath. The apartment smelled like his mate.

Sierra closed the door behind her. "It's not much, but I call it home."

"It's a nice little place." He waggled his brows at her. "Why don't you show me your bedroom?"

"You're bad," she said with a laugh. "But I guess I am as well, since I was about ready to suggest that very thing."

Forever hungry for her, Cale closed the distance between them and scooped her up in his arms. He took her lips in a heated kiss as he walked to the short hallway where he assumed the bathroom and Sierra's bedroom were located.

"The one on the right," she mumbled against his mouth.

Not breaking stride, he turned to the correct doorway and crossed the threshold. Cale had just put her down on her feet to strip her clothes off when there was a loud pounding on the apartment door.

Sierra pulled back with a scowl. "Shit. I know that knock. It's Trevor," she said quietly.

"Just ignore him and maybe he'll go away," he replied in the same tone.

"Come on, Sierra," Trevor shouted loudly through the door. "I know you're in there. I saw your car out in the parking lot. Open up."

Sierra blew out a breath. "That's not going to happen. He won't go away until I do answer the door. You stay here and I'll try to get rid of him."

Before he could reply, she stepped out of his arms and walked out of the bedroom. Able to hear everything in the other room as if he were there, Cale listened to Sierra open the apartment door.

"What do you want, Trevor?" she asked in an exasperated tone.

Her brother's voice came from somewhere inside the living room. "I'm a little short this week and I wondered if you could front me some cash until I get paid."

"Shouldn't you be at work right now?"

"I called in sick."

"Which you aren't. You have to stop doing that, or you're going to lose your job."

"Would you stop with the lecture? Are you going to lend me the money or not?"

There was a small stretch of silence before Sierra answered Trevor. "Actually, no, I'm not."

"Why?" Trevor almost whined. "I said you'd get it back."

"That's what you promised me the last time. I still have yet to see a looney of it. So my answer remains no."

"Don't be such a bitch, Sierra."

Hearing her brother disrespect her was enough to have Cale walking into the living room and going to Sierra's side. "I'd watch your mouth if I were you," he told the other man. "Since your sister isn't going to lend you any money, I think it's time for you to go."

"Butt out of it, asshole," Trevor said as he glared at Cale. "I thought you would have been gone by now."

"Sorry to say, you'll be seeing a lot more of me, at least until Sierra and I go to Toronto."

Trevor's gaze jerked to Sierra. "You can't be serious about this guy. He's a fucking jerk. Look how he treated me at the wedding. He thinks he's hot shit when he isn't."

Sierra sighed. "Trevor, who I see is none of your business. Now go already. I'm not going to give you any money."

Trevor looked from Sierra to Cale. "I know what this is all about. This asshole has turned you against me. He's filled your head full of shit."

Sierra's brother tried to get up in his face, but she came between them and placed a hand on Trevor's chest. "Back off. Cale has nothing to do with my decision. It's something that has been a long time coming."

"Yeah, right. Get out of my way, Sierra." Trevor roughly shoved her, hard enough to cause her to almost stumble.

Something inside Cale snapped. Sierra was his mate, his to protect and cherish. He wouldn't allow anyone to treat her in such a way. He fisted the front of Trevor's shirt and slammed him against the wall. He then lifted the other man off his feet one-handed. It betrayed that he wasn't mortal, but Cale was beyond caring. He knew his eyes had to be mutedly glowing with anger as he glared at Trevor. He growled, letting his wolf rise to the surface, curling his upper lip before he snapped his teeth at Sierra's brother.

"You ever touch my mate like that again I'll break every bone in your hand. Got it?"

Trevor let out a small whimper. "What the hell are you?"

Cale opened his fist and let the other man drop. "Get out of here before I show you."

Trevor righted himself, and without another word, shot out of the apartment. Cale did nothing to hide his eyes as he turned toward Sierra. She'd seen and heard everything her brother had.

She ran her wide-eyed gaze over his face. "Not to sound like Trevor, but what the hell are you? Your eyes are glowing."

Cale knew no other way than to be straight and to the point. "I'm a nine-hundred-year-old werewolf and I've claimed you as my mate."

"A what?"

"A werewolf." Drawing on the spark of magic deep inside him, Cale shifted into his wolf form.

Sierra shrieked and scrambled away. "That's the wolf I saw on the hiking trail. That was you?" She let out another shriek as he took on his human form once more. He took a step toward her, but she ran to the end of the couch to put it between them. "Don't come any closer," she said fearfully.

"Calm down, Sierra. Knowing what I am doesn't change me. I'm still the same man. You have to let me expl—"

"Get out," she yelled.

"Let me explain. And I can't leave. You are my mate. We have to stay together or we'll suffer."

"Get out, get out, get out," she shouted over him, obviously not hearing a word he said.

As her shouts verged on the side of being hysterical, Cale worried one of Sierra's neighbors would hear her and call the cops. Getting her to listen to him looked to be out of the question. She was too upset, too scared, to think straight at the moment. Even though he hadn't wanted it to happen, he knew leaving was all he could do.

He held up his hands in surrender. "I'm going," he said. "But I will be back."

Sierra just jerkily shook her head in denial. With a long, drawn-out sigh, Cale turned on his heel and walked out of the apartment. As he clomped down the stairs to reach the outside, he steeled himself for what was to come. He was going to leave and put as much distance between him and Sierra as was needed to set off the separation anxiety. In a couple of hours, she'd be in no condition to turn him away.

* * * * *

Sierra was losing her mind, and she didn't know how much more she could stand. Cale had been gone for almost an hour, and it was the longest one of her life. She couldn't stop thinking about him, the need to be with him making her feel like climbing the walls. She should still be afraid of him—he was a freaking werewolf, for chrissake—but she couldn't get past the feeling that something bad had happened to him. That he needed her. And god how she missed him. She felt on the verge of tears.

She paced back and forth in her living room. Seeing Cale shift into a wolf had had her heart trying to beat out of her chest. All the feelings she had for him seemed to disappear as her fear took over. But now they had returned full force, if not stronger than before. She loved him, needed him, found it agonizing that he wasn't with her.

She wanted him to come back, but she had no idea where he was. She'd tried calling his hotel, but he wasn't in his room. And with no cell phone number to contact him, Sierra had just about lost it then.

This had to end. That's all she knew. If it didn't, it would drive her crazy. Right now she didn't give a crap that Cale was a werewolf. This longing for him was too much to bear.

Sierra spun around and came to a standstill at the sound of the doorknob on her apartment door being turned, the tumblers breaking inside. It slammed open and there was Cale. Everything she'd felt disappeared the instant she laid eyes on him, only to be replaced with the most intense arousal she'd ever experienced.

He kicked the door shut behind him, then stalked toward her. "I couldn't stay away any longer. I can't be without you, Sierra. Don't make me go through this again."

Once he reached her, she threw herself into his arms, their mouths meeting hungrily. Being held by him made her feel whole, as if her world had finally righted itself. They tore at each other's clothes as Cale growled like a wolf and she whimpered with need.

With her pussy already wet for him, he lifted her off her feet, then sheathed his cock inside her with one thrust. Sierra locked her ankles at his waist and held on as he pounded into her. Within seconds her climax swept over her. She cried out in ecstasy as her body milked Cale's. Two more thrusts and he came, his cock filling her with his cum.

Breathing hard, he walked to the couch and sat, still sheathed inside her, still hard. He pushed back her hair and cupped her face. "I'm sorry I had to put you through the separation anxiety, but I didn't know any other way to get through to you."

"If you do that again I'll string you up by your balls. Got it?"

He chuckled. "I promise I won't." Cale's expression grew serious. "Are you okay now? About me being a werewolf?"

"Well, there's a lot I don't understand, but obviously being without you isn't an option. Is it really because we're mates?"

He nodded. "The first time we made love our souls joined." He kissed her. "I promise I'll do everything in my power to keep you happy, Sierra. I love you, and have waited a long time for you to come into my life. I don't ever want to lose you."

She bit her bottom lip. "I love you too. I didn't realize it until you put me through hell." Sierra squeezed her pussy around Cale's still-hard cock. "Enough talking. Right now I think you have to make it up to me for scaring the crap out of me, then making me feel as if I were losing my mind."

Cale surged to his feet with her in his arms. "To do a proper job of it, I'll need the bed."

Sierra bent her head and bit him where his shoulder and neck met. After letting loose a very wolflike howl, Cale made it up to her over and over again until neither one of them could move.

The End

Also by Marisa Chenery

eBooks:

Big City Pack 1: The Canuck Werewolf
Big City Pack 2: A Werewolf at the Falls
Big City Pack 3: Werewolf's Treasure
Big City Pack 4; Werewolf Claimed
Big City Pack 5: Loved by a Werewolf
Goddess Revealed 1: Bast's Perfume
Goddess Revealed 2: Love's Fiery Arrow
Goddess Revealed 3: The Goddess' Girdle
Goddess Revealed 4: His Sea Goddess
Ra's Chosen 1: Soul Hunger
Ra's Chosen 2: Mate Hunger
Ra's Chosen 3: Longed-For Hunger
Ra's Chosen 4: Embrace the Hunger
Ra's Chosen 5: Reincarnated Hunger
Ra's Chosen 6: Foreseen Hunger
Ra's Chosen 7: Ra's Hunger
Touched by a Gladiator
Warrior Hunger 1: Embraced by a Warrior
Warrior Hunger 2: Her Eternal Warrior

About the Author

଼ଠ

Marisa Chenery was always a lover of books, but after reading her first historical romance novel she found herself hooked. Having inherited a love for the written word, she soon started writing her own novels.

After trying her hand at writing historicals, she now writes paranormals.

Marisa lives in Ontario, Canada with her husband and four children. She would love to hear from you, so drop her an email while you're there.

଼ଠ

The author welcomes comments from readers. You can find her website and email address on her author bio page at www.ellorascave.com.

Tell Us What You Think

We appreciate hearing reader opinions about our books. You can email us at Comments@EllorasCave.com.

Why an electronic book?

We live in the Information Age—an exciting time in the history of human civilization, in which technology rules supreme and continues to progress in leaps and bounds every minute of every day. For a multitude of reasons, more and more avid literary fans are opting to purchase e-books instead of paper books. The question from those not yet initiated into the world of electronic reading is simply: *Why?*

1. *Price.* An electronic title at Ellora's Cave Publishing runs anywhere from 40% to 75% less than the cover price of the exact same title in paperback format. Why? Basic mathematics and cost. It is less expensive to publish an e-book (no paper and printing, no warehousing and shipping) than it is to publish a paperback, so the savings are passed along to the consumer.
2. *Space.* Running out of room in your house for your books? That is one worry you will never have with electronic books. For a low one-time cost, you can purchase a handheld device specifically designed for e-reading. Many e-readers have large, convenient screens for viewing. Better yet, hundreds of titles can be stored within your new library—on a single microchip. There are a variety of e-readers from different manufacturers. You can also read e-books on your PC or laptop computer. (Please note that Ellora's Cave does not endorse any specific brands.

You can check our website at www.ellorascave.com for information we make available to new consumers.)
3. ***Mobility.*** Because your new e-library consists of only a microchip within a small, easily transportable e-reader, your entire cache of books can be taken with you wherever you go.
4. ***Personal Viewing Preferences.*** Are the words you are currently reading too small? Too large? Too… ANNOYING? Paperback books cannot be modified according to personal preferences, but e-books can.
5. ***Instant Gratification.*** Is it the middle of the night and all the bookstores near you are closed? Are you tired of waiting days, sometimes weeks, for bookstores to ship the novels you bought? Ellora's Cave Publishing sells instantaneous downloads twenty-four hours a day, seven days a week, every day of the year. Our webstore is never closed. Our e-book delivery system is 100% automated, meaning your order is filled as soon as you pay for it.

Those are a few of the top reasons why electronic books are replacing paperbacks for many avid readers.

As always, Ellora's Cave welcomes your questions and comments. We invite you to email us at Comments@ellorascave.com or write to us directly at Ellora's Cave Publishing Inc., 1056 Home Avenue, Akron, OH 44310-3502.

Discover for yourself why readers can't get enough of the multiple award-winning publisher Ellora's Cave.

Whether you prefer e-books or paperbacks, be sure to visit EC on the web at www.ellorascave.com

for an erotic reading experience that will leave you breathless.

CPSIA information can be obtained at www.ICGtesting.com
Printed in the USA
LVOW052041200712

290923LV00002B/62/P